VASSA ^{IN} _{THE} NIGHT

VASSA IN THE NIGHT

SARAH PORTER

TOR TEEN

A TOM DOHERTY ASSOCIATES BOOK
NEW YORK

VASSA IN THE NIGHT

Copyright © 2016 by Sarah Porter

Reading and Activity Guide copyright © 2016 by Tor Books

Illustrations copyright © 2016 by Sarah Porter

All rights reserved.

A Tor Teen Book
Published by Tom Doherty Associates, LLC
175 Fifth Avenue
New York, NY 10010

www.tor-forge.com

Tor® is a registered trademark of Tom Doherty Associates, LLC.

The Library of Congress Cataloging-in-Publication Data is available upon request.

ISBN 978-0-7653-8054-8 (hardcover)
ISBN 978-0-7653-8622-9 (e-book)

Our books may be purchased in bulk for promotional, educational, or business use. Please contact your local bookseller or the Macmillan Corporate and Premium Sales Department at 1-800-221-7945, extension 5442, or by e-mail at MacmillanSpecialMarkets@macmillan.com.

First Edition: September 2016

Printed in the United States of America

0 9 8 7 6 5 4 3 2

For Todd,
who proves that there truly is magic in Brooklyn

Night, you bring home all things
That the shining dawn scatters:
You bring home a lamb,
Bring home a kid,
Bring home a child to its mother.

—Sappho, as translated by
my grandmother, Anne Porter

Then the eyes of the little doll began to shine like two candles. It ate a little of the bread and drank a little of the soup and said: " Don't be afraid, Wassilissa the Beautiful. Be comforted. Say thy prayers, and go to sleep. The morning is wiser than the evening."

—Post Wheeler, "Wassilissa the Beautiful"

to sing, "Turn around. Turn around and run the other way! Chop me, chop me!"

We don't bother. Maybe it means we're getting old. Maybe the nights are so long now that we're only superficially kids, and we've lost years to the darkness.

Steph suddenly puts a hand to her throat and lets out a gasp.

"What?" Chelsea asks her. "You lost your locket?" She shoots me a significant look. The slight squirming in my pocket stops dead.

"I was wearing it! I hope—maybe I just knocked the clasp open?" Steph starts ransacking her pillows.

"It will show up soon, I'm quite sure," Chelsea says, taking time to enunciate each word, and arches her eyebrows my way.

I excuse myself to the bathroom and perch on the toilet lid. The bathroom is bright pink, with this cheesy mermaid wallpaper Steph picked out when she was five; the shower curtain is stained with garish purple streaks from my hair dye. I can feel the lump in the pocket of my hoodie but it's as still as a wad of used tissues. Erg is pretending to be asleep. I get her by one tiny wooden foot and drag her out anyway. She dangles upside down, her eyes closed, her painted black hair gleaming in its flat spit curls. She doesn't react when I drop her in the sink, which is enough to prove that she's faking.

I turn the water on full blast. I'm not a kleptomaniac, really. I just harbor one. Erg leaps up sputtering, water sheeting off her spherical head. Her feet clop on the pink porcelain as she leaps around but the sink is too slippery for her to climb out; she's lacquered so she doesn't have much traction. She lands on her carved blue rear, legs clacking. "You turn that off! Vassa! You'd better stop!"

"Are you going to give the locket back?" I'm not going to yield quite so easily. I'm sick of getting blamed for Erg's lousy behavior.

"Probably. Eventually. If you don't do anything to provoke me in the meantime."

PRELUDE IN NIGHT

EARLY LAST AUTUMN

When Night looked down, it saw its own eyes staring back at it. Two big black eyes, both full of stars. At first Night ignored them. Probably that strange gaze was its own reflection in a puddle, or maybe in a mirror left shattered in the street. Then it noticed something that made it curious: those eyes were full of stars, but the constellations inside them were unfamiliar. It was like gazing into the sky above another world.

Night decided to investigate. It reached out tendrils of darkness to examine this odd phenomenon. The eyes nestled, as eyes often will, inside a human face, at the top of a strong man's body. But how could night—another, different, unimaginable Night—live inside a human being?

The man waited, unmoving, on a dark field ringed by houses. Between his widened lids stars flurried through expanding black. Planets circulated like blood. Night had never seen anything so much like itself before, and a terrible longing surged through it. Maybe, finally, it had found a companion; maybe it was saved from being forever alone!

Night drew closer to him, and then closer still. The man waited, as rigid as death. He did not react in the slightest when Night came and perched on his cheekbones to get a better look. It breathed across his lashes and set them trembling. The man did not answer, not even with a blink. When Night shyly kissed him he felt very cold.

All of that should have been enough to make Night wary. It should have drawn back in alarm, floated safely above the streetlamps. But Night had been lonely for too long, and it forgot all about caution. It did not even notice that the man's face had peculiar coloring: pearly grayish white from the bottom of the nose down and coal black above. All that interested Night was what it saw *inside* his eyes. A meteor shot through their depths trailing brilliance after it. Night yearned, more than anything, to follow that streaking light.

If only it had been honest with itself, it would have admitted that the situation was suspicious. But Night, which hides everything in folds of shadow, is not in the habit of honesty. Since the man did not react to its caresses, it decided to touch him more deeply. A bit nervously, it stroked between his eyelids. His skull seemed to be hollow. He wasn't breathing. Night prodded again, curling a dark tendril through one empty socket. But the man still didn't move or even smile. Didn't he notice that Night was there? Didn't he realize Night loved him? Having gone already so far, too far, Night lost all restraint and licked and coiled its way into those eyes. It tried to speak. To beg for some reply.

And then the eyelids snapped shut, slicing right though Night's soft body.

It took Night a moment to understand. A part of itself was now trapped inside the man and couldn't get out.

It could hear that lost piece of itself crying, crashing frantically around the inside of the hollow man as it searched for an exit. He wasn't a man at all, but a trap, and Night understood what a fool it had been to fall for those glittering stars. They were only an illusion meant to draw it in. They were bait. Night battered at the eyelids, trying to set the stolen part of itself free. They stayed stubbornly closed.

Night raged like a bear that sees its cub caged and wounded.

It grew even more furious when the old woman came and pinned the eyelids securely shut with a pair of needle-sharp golden stars. This must be her doing! If dark could kill, the old woman would have crumpled to the ground in an instant.

But she didn't. She stood there grinning with satisfaction while Night silently shrieked.

"That's right," she told Night. It realized she was no ordinary woman by the fact that she spoke to it in its own language. What human ever talks to Night? "Part of you will be staying with me, you see? Snug as a tapeworm in a rat's gut."

The captured piece of Night's darkness rattled and cried to return to its parent. It seemed like a distinct being now that they were separated. A shadow-baby. It wept and howled and Night couldn't even comfort it.

"Oh, don't fuss," the old woman crooned into the empty man's ear, addressing her captive night-child. "I made a mockery of man. You see? I made him just for you. He's your new home. Isn't he handsome?"

Night hunched over the old woman, wondering desperately how it could hurt her. It managed to yank her hair with a breeze, but that was hardly enough. She only leered at it in response.

"You, too. There's no point in complaining. You won't be getting your little bitty back, you see? Not ever. But don't you worry, I'll treat him humanely. And yes, he's *him*. He's a man now, in a manner of speaking. I'll keep him asleep and he won't need to feel the pain of separation. Not quite so much, at least."

With that she lowered a helmet onto the black-and-white head. The helmet was huge, domed like a planetarium, and though it looked much bigger than the head it still seemed to fit perfectly. She slipped a visor of opaque black glass over the star-stabbed eyes.

The lost fragment of Night quieted, falling into a deep sleep inside what looked like a large, muscular man.

The man was sitting astride what appeared to be a black motor-cycle, and the old woman reached to start something that was not actually an engine, though it sounded like one. Night watched the blind, man-shaped prison begin to drive in a circle. Around and around.

Night's consciousness is one infinite starry moment, timeless and drifting. It was no surprise, then, that it was so easily confused. With-out understanding what was happening, Night was falling for the same trick in a dozen different locations, all at the same moment. A dozen old women sank golden stars into the eyelids of a dozen hol-low men. Night's pieces became like lost children, riding forever on identical motorcycles in identical parking lots in scattered cities. Night lingered wherever it saw them. Hoping someday to bring them home.

Hoping they could all be one again. Join back together, and share the same stars.

CHAPTER 1

People live here on purpose; that's what I've heard. They even cross the country deliberately and move in to the neighborhoods near the river, and suddenly their shoes are cuter than they are, and very possibly smarter and more articulate as well, and their lives are covered in sequins and they tell themselves they've *arrived*. They put on tiny feathered hats and go to parties in warehouses; they drink on rooftops at sunset. It's a destination and everyone piles up and congratulates themselves on having made it all the way here from some wherever or other. To them this is practically an enchanted kingdom. A whole lot of Brooklyn is like that now, but not the part where I live.

Not that there *isn't* any magic around here. If you're dumb enough to look in the wrong places, you'll stumble right into it. It's the stumbling out again that might become an issue. The best thing you can do is ignore it. Cross the street. Don't make eye contact—if by some remote chance you encounter something with eyes.

This isn't even a slum. It's a scrappy neither-nor where no one *arrives*. You just find yourself here for no real reason, the same way the streets and buildings did, squashed against a cemetery that sprawls out for miles. It has to be that big, because the dead of New York keep falling like snow but never melt. There's an elevated train station where a few subway lines rattle overhead in their anxiety to get somewhere else. We have boarded-up appliance stores and nail salons, the Atlantis Wash and Lube, and a mortuary on almost every block. There are houses, the kind that bundle four families close together and roll them around in one another's noise as if the ruckus was bread crumbs and somebody was going to come along soon and deep-fry us. Really, it's such a nothing of a place that I have to dye my hair purple just to have something to look at. If it weren't for those little zigs of color jumping in the corners of my eyes, I might start to think that I was going blind.

It seemed that way even before the nights started lasting such a very, very long time.

We can't prove it. By the clock everything's fine. The sun goes down around seven p.m. these days, right on schedule for your standard New York April, and comes up at six the next morning. The effect was so sneaky at first that it was months before anybody worked up the nerve to say anything. Then, maybe around November, I started hearing discreet wisecracks, muttered like they were something embarrassing, like, "Hey, Vassa! Long time no see!" when I walked into school in the morning. But winter was coming on then, anyway, so you could tell yourself that, hey, the nights are *supposed* to feel long now.

By January, though, it was getting harder to ignore. It gets to the point, when your whole family is waking up around two a.m., and eating cereal, and shuffling around, and watching a lot of old movies, and then it's still only three thirty so you all go back to bed, where you might kind of mention that it seems a little unusual. And when it gets to be February, then March, and the nights are officially getting shorter but everyone can feel how they drag on and on, the hours like legless horses struggling to make it to the end of the darkness, then you might even start to complain. You might say that the nights feel like they're swallowing your drab nowhere neighborhood and refusing to cough it back up again the way they ought to. And the more the nights gobble up, the bigger and fatter and stronger they get, and the more they need to eat, until nobody can fight their way through to the next dawn.

I'm exaggerating. Morning does always come around eventually. At least, it does for now.

See, to whatever degree we have magic around here, it's strictly the kind that's a pain in the ass.

So it's the middle of the night—unprecedented, I know—and the kid upstairs is practicing skateboarding on some kind of janky homemade half pipe and wiping out at ten-second intervals and I'm watching a random black-and-white movie with the girls people call my sisters, though they're sisters step and fractional. I forget, but I think Chelsea is step-half and Stephanie is third-step once removed, or something like that, or possibly it's the other way around. Whatever they are exactly, they've been assigned to me by the twitching of fate, and they're usually at least plausibly sister-esque. We even share a bedroom. The woman who it's fair to assume must have given birth to at least one of us, but by no means to me, is off at the night shift at the pharmacy where she works in Manhattan. Seems awful to be stuck with the night shift now, but she says it's not as bad there. She says people barely notice the difference yet in Manhattan. She says they can afford all the day they want. Maybe they've found some slot where you can stick a credit card and order up a new morning.

Steph whirls in with a bowl of microwave popcorn and sets it on the bed between her and Chels. She scowls a bit when I come crawling across their pink-fleeced legs to snag some, piling it on the back of my chemistry textbook and then carrying it to my own bed. However carefully I balance, there's a fair amount of drift over the book's sides. Popcorn is hardly ideal, too noisy, but it'll have to do.

It's a rotten movie for my purposes. Ingrid Bergman is kissing somebody. Personally I prefer guys who are less gray, though I guess she's in no position to be picky. "Let's watch something else."

"Shut *up*, Vass. It's almost the end!"

"Then you won't be missing much, right?" But there's no hurry. They'll put on something nice and loud eventually. There's a lot of squirming in the pocket of my sweatshirt and I cover it with my hand. Tiny teeth nip at my thumb, though the thick fabric keeps it from hurting much. So *impatient*.

Static abruptly drowns out Ingrid, forcing the issue. That happens a lot these days and then there's nothing to do but change the channel, which Stephanie does after casting a scowl my way. Just because it's convenient for me doesn't make it my fault.

The next movie is tenderly devoted to chasing and shooting and blasting. When the first car goes up in a fireball I slip a puff of corn into my pocket and then start crunching loudly myself for good measure. Chels and Steph don't seem to notice. They're mesmerized by the flashing lights. I can hear it, though, the shrill styrofoamy nibble-squeak from my pocket. I can feel the slight vibrations against my waist as she chews. A tiny fist prodding my guts. Erg wants more. Such a little thing, but she never stops eating, and why should she? When you're carved out of wood you never gain weight. I've seen her gnaw through a candy bar bigger than she is in two hours flat. I've seen her actually burrow under the crispy batter on a chicken leg and then pop out near the bone, leaving the skin sagging into the tunnel left by her mauling.

Erg and I have gone on this long without Chels or Steph or anyone getting wise to her. My sisters think I'm the greedy one, always stashing cookies in my pockets for later. They think I suffer from strange compulsions. All my clothes have grease stains on the right hip. Sometimes I get sick of how demanding she is. Sometimes I've even toyed with the idea of letting her go hungry for a few days, or even not feeding her again. She'd complain at first but eventually, I'm pretty sure, she'd just go back to being inanimate.

Instead I stuff a whole handful of popcorn in. No matter what I pretend, I'll never actually starve her, and she knows it. She's the only thing I have from my mother so there's nostalgia working in her favor, and then I made a promise.

Little crunching noises squeak from my pocket. I'm way ahead on my reading for school, we all are—Chels has already moved on to college math and science textbooks, just to have something to do—but I get out *Great Expectations* anyway and try to concentrate.

In the window it's night, with cottony puffs of light clinging to the streetlamps. In the window there's no hint of dawn. It's been 4:02 a.m. for an astoundingly long time. Then 4:03. Progress!

I look up at the TV for a moment to see a girl with big curls and a plaid cap walking past shuttered stores. The street is dark and she jumps as a rat skitters over her boot. She looks lost and lonely, hunching her shoulders to hold off the night. Then a tide of light washes her face and she looks up in rapture to see a BY's. Wow, you can see her thinking, it's *still open*! The store dances and spins and as the girl pirouettes ecstatically more BY's stores appear around her, and more, all dancing on spindly legs of their own, until the whole dark night gets crowded out by the flash of their windows. "Turn around," the girl sings. "Turn around and stand like Momma placed you! Face me, face me!"

We've all seen this ad a million times, of course. None of us can be bothered to make snide remarks anymore, or to mention that they left out the all-important ring of stakes skewering rotting human heads. All the mockery we could possibly mock is too done and too obvious and wasn't really all that funny in the first place. We used

I reach toward the knob that lowers the stopper into place. "How about you do it tonight? You can put it in her bed. So there's at least some plausible deniability in regard to my being a thieving psycho?"

Erg squeals and snaps her legs closed, wedging her feet below the metal disk that stoppers the sink. I could just pull her out of the way, though. Being fierce doesn't get you too far when you're an imposing four and a half inches tall. "You wouldn't dare!"

"Oh, Erg," I say. She reminds me of my mother more than I like to admit. "Just quit the damn stealing and we won't have these problems. Okay? Say you'll put it back tonight and I'll dry you off."

"And oil me?"

I turn off the tap. No matter how mad she makes me, Erg is still my doll. Her painted lashes flick up and down, batting droplets out of her flat blue eyes. "Sure. Just put it back."

"You're going to ruin my finish if you keep doing this," Erg complains. "I might even split." She waits for me to pick her up, buff her in a warm towel. Instead I stare at her. I know her ways. "I'll slide it in her bed *tonight,* and she won't have any reason to accuse sweet *Vassa* of doing anything untoward, okay? Okay?"

I pick her up between my thumb and forefinger and wrap her in a hand towel. She's a pretty thing with her swooping violet eyelids and tiny ruby mouth, her thin arched black brows and perfect curls. She has a carved wooden dress, sky blue with white painted loops standing in for lace at the collar and cuffs. Her exposed skin is just varnished pale wood, then her legs end in white socks with more of that curly trim and black Mary Janes, all painted. Her knees, elbows, and waist are jointed and she can pivot her head. Nice workmanship. Too bad they didn't spend more time on her personality.

In spite of myself, I kiss the top of her shiny head. She tries to bite my lip, but I yank her back in time and her little wooden jaws snap on empty air.

When I said that magical things in Brooklyn should be shunned like the plague? I'm sorry to say that's not always an option. I was leaving Erg out of the equation although, with her being a talking doll and everything, she'd be magic by anyone's standards. I don't have much chance of avoiding her, since we're bound to each other for life. And no, I didn't name her that. It's what she calls herself. When I was younger I tried to get her to accept names like Jasmine or Clarissa but she wasn't having it.

I plonk Erg down on my lap and get out the bottle of lemon oil from under the sink. It's her favorite and I always try to keep some around. Dab the oil on some toilet paper and give her a nice rub-down, working it up and down her limbs while she makes little purring sounds. Getting oiled makes her sleepy and she rolls on my black flannel pajamas and rubs her face against me like a kitten. She can be cute sometimes. She'd *better* be cute, really, considering all the trouble she causes.

"You don't like Stephanie anyway," Erg murmurs. "She's kind of a bitch."

"I like her fine," I say. "You need to quit projecting." Erg snuggles into the folds of my pajama leg, yawning and wrapping her tiny arms around the loose fabric. By the time I slip her back into my pocket she's fast asleep.

When I get back to the bedroom Chels and Steph are both glowering at me like they have synchronized brain waves. "You were gone a while," Chels observes coolly.

"What?" I say. I'm still standing against the door. "Like two minutes?" We all know how meaningless minutes are now, at night anyway. "Did you find your locket, Steph?"

"Yeah," she says, then pauses. "I did."

"So where was it?" I try to sound uninterested.

"In your shoe. One of the ones with the spikes."

My guts tighten up just a bit. "Weird."

"Under your bed."

"Double weird." Erg will be lucky if she eats again this week.

"You think that just because you can get away with murder with boys, you can mess with me, too? My *mom* gave me that locket, Vassa!" Maybe that's why Erg was attracted to it. Another mom-present, like she and the locket could be comrades and start an insurrection.

"I didn't touch it," I say. But this is one of those times when truth is utterly worthless. They won't stop scowling.

"Vassa," Chelsea hazards, "if you won't admit you have a problem then there's no way we can even *try* to help. You're basically our sister, and we both really want to be able to trust you. Right? And you're a great person, but you have this serious issue which is making everyone feel like you're bad news to be around. I am saying this," she adds carefully, "out of love."

"I appreciate the love part," I tell her. "But I didn't do it."

"Then who did?"

I can't answer that, is the problem. Everything would be so much simpler if I could just tell them the truth, and I *want* to. I could pull Erg out of my pocket and let her take some responsibility for once. But, well, I promised my mom, an hour before she died, that I would keep Erg completely secret forever, and feed her and take care of her, and—like three more times—that I would really, truly never tell *anyone*. I don't want to lie to Chelsea, though. "Not me. That's all I can tell you, Chels. Okay?"

"*Very* not okay." Chelsea is nobody's fool. She has huge dark eyes that could make anyone feel ashamed. "Very, extremely not. When you decide you're ready to try some honesty, V., you let me know."

Since there's nothing else to say I go to my bed and curl up with my book. They both keep watching me to see if I'm embarrassed yet, which I am, so I turn my back. In a way it's my fault that this keeps happening. If Erg can't control herself, then it's my job to keep her in line. I start thinking about those metal key chains that snap shut. Maybe Erg is going to get one installed around her neck, though I'm not sure if there's a way I can attach the other end inside my pocket that she won't be able to undo. Her hands are shaped like mittens with nothing but thin lines to show the separations between her fingers, but she does have opposable thumbs and she can work them like a fiend. You've never seen a human being with hands that quick and sly.

Maybe Stephanie dozes off at some point, because a while later I feel my bed sinking behind me. I roll onto my back and Chelsea is there, looking down at me with concern. "Hey," she whispers, "I can understand if you don't want to talk about it in front of Stephanie, V." I just look at her. She's trying to be sweet but there's nothing much I can say. "Look, okay, I have a theory, Vassa? That you're compensating for your parents being gone by stealing things that represent the love you deserve? Symbolically? And you're right, you do deserve that love, but I'm just trying to tell you that this isn't the way to get it. Nothing you take can make up for your mom dying or your dad being . . . away."

None of us ever say directly what happened to him. The facts of the case just howl for euphemism.

"I know that," I tell her. "Chelsea, look, I really do appreciate what you're trying to do, or what you think you're doing, but I'm not going to confess when I didn't take the damn locket!"

"A present from our mother? When you lost your mom? Really?" She does a fantastic job of loading every syllable with significance. "Anyway he's Steph's dad, too. It's not like you've got some special relationship with tragedy. Do you ever think about how all of this affects her?"

Maybe not. I maybe tend to repress the reality that Steph and I share a father.

"Not when I'm trying to read," I tell her.

Chelsea sighs. "I'm here whenever you want to talk. Just think about what I'm telling you. Please?"

She gets up again, but she's only going back to her own bed a few feet away.

I'll try to break it down for you. Chelsea and Stephanie have the same mother but different fathers; Steph and I have the same father but different mothers; Chelsea is oldest, Steph is second, and I'm the youngest, but only by a week; and yes, that means my dad got both our moms pregnant at almost the same time, maybe on the same night for all I know. He spent the next ten years going back and forth between them, depending on who made him feel guiltiest, I guess, and then my mom considerately died and simplified his decision-making process. So he married Iliana, making her actually my stepmother for all of five months, and then bailed on all of us in dramatic style.

In consequence of our scrambled parentage we're all different colors: Chelsea is chestnut brown, Stephanie is kind of beige, and I'm almost disturbingly pale. If I didn't dye my hair I'd look a lot like a human version of Erg, all blue eyes and raven tresses. Chelsea is the smartest, due to get the hell out of here in September on a full scholarship, assuming September ever comes that is, Stephanie doesn't have two brain cells to bang together, and I get by. So Chelsea and I aren't actually blood but she more or less considers me a sister, and we might even love each other most of the time, but Steph, who is related by blood, definitely thinks of me as an interloper, and we maybe hate each other just a microscopic bit, though sometimes we have fun anyway.

If all of that sounds messy, well, it surely is, but to put it in perspective there are plenty of things that are messier. My own emotions, for example, which could make a city dump look like a library. And the big blue world outside of our apartment is messier and grubbier and more chaotic than anything we've ever personally come up with.

I say that with complete confidence.

CHAPTER 2

Something incredible happens. I fall asleep, and when I wake up—with the lamp still on and my face plopped in my open book—I see actual sunshine beaming through the window. It appears to be made of genuine, organic photons. I see the leaves on the tree outside shaking, throwing little scraps of light around, and a plane of sunlight crumpling as it hits the heaped clothes on the floor. I jump up squealing and throw a pillow at Stephanie before I remember that she hates me. "It's morning! You've got to see this! It's real live morning!"

The look she gives me is triple-distilled venom. Then she turns her head away without saying anything. Chelsea's bed is already empty and I can hear her knocking around in the kitchen. She usually makes breakfast for everyone if there's been some kind of fight, hoping to restore harmony to our home. My alleged psychological disorders might even rate pancakes today.

The purely awesome fact of bright morning sun is too exciting for me to let Steph ruin it and I'm singing as I get dressed: the BY's jingle, which is stuck in my head for some reason. "Face me, face me!"

It is a great melody. A classic, even. Iliana says that her parents knew that jingle from way back in the 1950s, when the very first BY's opened out on Coney Island. It caused a sensation then, since nobody'd ever seen a dancing store before. People lined up around the block to shop there. Iliana says it wasn't as dangerous in those days. She even went there with her mom when she was little, and loved it. You could get amazing candy at BY's, things she'd never seen anywhere else.

But going in got riskier over time, and now most people have the sense to stay away. *If you don't bother it, it won't bother you.*

Steph doesn't tell me to shut up, but she manages to project an impressive amount of loathing through her turned back. I put the same hoodie I slept in back on over my shirt; Erg's already in the right-hand pocket so I won't have to palm her and sneak her into a new hiding place.

Except that she isn't. The pocket is empty. And Erg's field trips are never good.

In the kitchen Chelsea smiles at me even though she thinks I'm a lying, scheming thief and gives me a kiss on the cheek as she hands me my pancakes. They're full of blueberries. Her sweetness this morning might be a ploy based on that theory she told me last night: she's probably demonstrating that I'm loved unconditionally so I'll stop swiping stuff, already. But it's still really nice of her. Nice enough to make me feel kind of shy. "Thanks, Chels."

"Sure thing, li'l sis." I can guarantee she's never called me that before. Ploy for real, then. She's trying to instill a sense of belonging in me. The sick part is that Erg might be rooting through Chelsea's stuff as we speak.

"The crazy thing about these nights," I say, hearing how tense and guilty my voice sounds, "is that they make me so incredibly happy to get up and go to school. Even the most boring class imaginable seems like this huge relief."

She's gone back to the stove, but she shoots me a funny look over her shoulder. "No school today, dumpling. Saturday. Sorry to disappoint you."

"There is absolutely no need for weekends anymore," I tell her. "It's ridiculous. You could stuff like two weekends into a single night now."

"Two very, very dark weekends, though. Get out and enjoy the sunshine. We're probably all getting mad vitamin D deficiencies."

"I'll do that," I say, loudly. Erg has absolutely zero tolerance for my leaving the apartment without her, so the threat of it is a sure way to bring her scampering back. "As soon as I finish eating, I'm taking off for parts unknown. *Williamsburg*, or *SoHo . . .*"

"You'll get some model scout on your ass if you go into SoHo, I bet," Chelsea says. In my explanation of our various attributes I neglected to mention that I'm generally regarded as beautiful. People can think that if they want to, but if they'd ever seen my mother they'd know how I pale by comparison. "At first you'll be seduced by the glamour of it all. Then they'll tell you the purple hair has got to go, and you'll start shouting obscenities and storm out in tears, and maybe come back with a tray of cupcakes and fling them savagely into everyone's faces. And then . . ."

"Not one thing you said will ever happen," I tell her. I keep my tone completely deadpan. "You know my sole ambition is to become a stockbroker."

Chelsea does a double take. Very few people can tell when I'm kidding, but she usually can. "Ah," she says. "I see. That would be a joke. A funny joke."

My sole ambition is to be anyone but me, and anywhere but here. But it would just upset Chelsea if I said that, especially in the middle of this attempt at a stealth therapy session. I finish wolfing my pancakes. "You are the best big *sister* ever," I tell Chelsea, in that pathetic way I have of saying ironically things I'm too much of a wuss to say like I actually mean them, even though I do. *Coward*, I tell myself, and I hug her.

As I'm heading for the door I feel something small and wooden crawling up the leg of my cargo pants. Erg keeps on climbing as I walk down the street, bypassing my pocket completely. She winds up sprawling on my shoulder under my clothes, clutching on to my bra strap. "I can't *believe* you didn't save me a pancake," she says. Her voice is uncomfortably shrill this close to my ear.

"I'm never saving you food again," I tell her. "If you want to eat, you'll stay where you're supposed to stay."

"And where is that?" Erg snips. Impudent little thing. "I had *important work* to do, and I don't think it's too much to expect that you'll think of me when you're pigging out. Pancakes are my *favorite*."

"Important work? Erg, you've done enough *work* already that I can barely face being at home anymore! If I can figure out some way to keep you chained up . . ." A man comes walking down the sidewalk, so I take out my cell phone and hold it to my head. It's my usual stratagem for talking to Erg in public.

"Gosh," she says. "So many negative assumptions. What if I was doing something nice? For someone you like? Maybe I was doing somebody a big favor, but no, you just jump to your nasty little conclusions."

"I dread to think," I tell her. "So what was it this time? Did you poison someone?"

Erg squeaks indignantly and feigns an offended silence for maybe two heartbeats, but then she can't hold out anymore. "You know that guy Miguel? The poetry geek who's on Chelsea's chess team?"

"Not really," I tell her. "Barely. I've seen him making a big deal about how he's going to get back at her after she kicked his ass at their last practice."

"I called him," Erg says. "From her phone."

"You did *what*?"

"And then I hung up. On the third ring."

"At least you didn't try to pretend you were her. But Erg, he's still going to see her number! He'll think . . ."

"He'll think she wanted to call him and then panicked." She sounds gleeful. "He'll think, oh my God, she *likes* me!"

"Great."

"She does like him, though. And he's in *love* with her. But neither of them was ever going to say anything! Until now! And now he'll ask her out! I win!"

It could be worse, I guess. "She'll see the call, too, though. On her phone's history. And she'll think . . ."

"At first she'll think it was you and get mad," Erg says. "But then she'll realize the call went out right when you were eating pancakes with her. See? You have an alibi. Airtight!"

"But then . . . what *will* she think? I guess there's still Steph, but that really doesn't seem like something she'd do."

"Well, I'd think that Chelsea will be very confused," Erg says. "Wouldn't you be?"

"And you should not be messing with people's personal lives this way, Erg. It's none of your business who Chelsea likes."

"Ooh, but it is. I think it's all my business!"

Sometimes I have a hard time knowing what to say to her—not that anything I can say ever makes any difference.

"Leaving him is going to break her heart, though, when she goes off to Stanford," Erg observes after a moment. "Oh, well! Too bad! *C'est la*, and better to have loved and lost, and such."

I should have known there was a catch. "Do you ever do anything that isn't partway mean?"

"And now my exertions on your dear *sister's* behalf have left me quite famished and moreover deprived me of my rightful pancake. The sacrifices I make! At least get me a granola bar or *something*, Vassa!"

She won't stop griping until I do; I know that from experience.

I stop in a bodega and buy one. Erg likes cinnamon almond. Once we're back on the street I say, "You have to get back in my pocket first. I don't want crumbs in my bra!"

"Are we going to SoHo?" Erg asks, clambering down. I'm pretty used to the cold slithery feeling of her grappling inside my clothes, but it still tickles.

"No," I tell her. "I don't feel like getting on the subway. We're just walking wherever. The cemetery, maybe? I really don't care."

"I wanted to go to SoHo!" Erg squeaks, so I unwrap the granola bar and stuff it in my pocket. That'll shut her up. For a little while.

The sweet musky stench of rotting flesh on the breeze lets me know, as if I didn't already, that we're getting near the local BY's. I turn the corner so I won't have to see it all tangerine bright and glossy in the morning sun.

BY's does all kinds of public relations campaigns saying that they only behead shoplifters. They say law-abiding consumers don't have a thing to worry about, and deterring theft is what lets them keep their low, low prices. Somehow everyone seems to accept that, more or less, even though you'd think the police or the mayor or *somebody* should really shut the whole chain down. I mean, beheading must at least count as a violation of the health code, right?

But there's a kind of atmosphere around BY's that makes it hard to stick with the idea that they're doing anything wrong. I've seen cops walking toward BY's, and the closer they get the hazier they look, and their eyes start to go out of focus, and they get these quirky little smiles on their faces like they're thinking, *Boy, those darn thieves sure had it coming!* I even used to think that sometimes, though it felt like the words were creeping into my brain through my ears.

But Joel Diallo was about the straightest arrow in my grade and the last time I passed by his head was still up there, though it wasn't all that fresh anymore. His mom was sitting balled up in the middle

of the parking lot with tears dripping off her chin. At school everyone said his family couldn't even get his body back. He'll never
have a grave. Someone had tied a few pink daisies to his stake,
because what else could they do?

It's probably easier for the police to ignore since the people who
get offed are mostly on the margins: immigrants who don't know
better, tough local teenagers, older women on heavy medication who
go shopping in their nightgowns. Chelsea says that BY's would never
open a branch in Manhattan, for example, because the potential
customers there would be too well-connected to kill. The wrong
people would get upset.

Some kids picked on Joel. He was kind of introverted and
awkward, an easy target for the jerks. People barely had to look at
him to think they knew exactly who he was: that kid who always
wore the school uniform, which most of us blow off; who spoke
even less than I do; who held doors for teachers. I pretty much went
on the default assumption that that stuff summed him up, too. For
years. I mean, when I'm all withdrawn and distant, I know it's
because I have too many secrets to risk getting close to anyone. But
I saw Joel acting basically the same way I do, and for some reason
I thought it meant that there wasn't much to him.

So how did I start to understand I was wrong? It was maybe
January when we were all squeezing down the hallway between
classes, and this guy Andre started harassing him: not pushing him
physically, but just pressing sideways to drive him toward the tile
wall. In the crowd Joel couldn't get away, and when he stumbled
into the tiles Andre laughed. "See, that's the difference between
us," Andre said, like he was picking up some conversation they'd
had earlier. "You have to take shit, and I don't."

I was three rows back, jostling along in the flow of arms and legs
and book bags, half-wondering if I should say something. But as it
turned out I didn't have to, because Joel actually talked back, though

his voice was so soft I could barely make it out. "No. The difference is that you'll always be exactly what you are now. And I won't." There was something in his tone, self-conscious but also *knowing,* like he could see Andre's entire future right there. It was enough of a surprise that I started straining to hear them over the clamor, because who just comes out and says something like that? "And you'll always belong in the same place, but I'll be far away." It had a weirdly authoritative sound, like Joel was sentencing him to be boring for the rest of his life. Andre's jaw was hanging, like a bubble of shocked silence was inflating in his mouth and he couldn't speak.

They'd stopped dead against the wall so that everyone eddied out around them, and I was shoved against Andre's arm. He saw me there and twitched, then started scrambling to save face. "Yeah, you *don't* belong here. You should try a different planet."

It would have been a pretty weak comeback even if Joel hadn't smiled, obviously not insulted at all. He smiled like his spaceship was parked right outside and Andre was just too dumb to realize it. And then the moment was over and we all slipped into our classrooms, but after that I didn't look at Joel the same way; I knew now that he wasn't quiet because he didn't have anything to say. It was because in a way he was already somewhere else, reaching for some beyond, and he'd left the everyday crap at our school behind him. When I heard he'd died at BY's it made a queasy kind of sense that he would have wanted to try going in there: it's the closest thing to *beyond* that we have in the neighborhood, even if it's horrible.

But is it possible he tried to rip off BY's on a dare, striving to seem cool? Maybe, though it feels really out of character. Barely.

Or, more like, not really. Or even, I'd say, not at all.

I should have tried to know him better. We should be wandering together now, saying that we truly will get out of here someday. Reminding each other that it's a big planet and if we can just hang in there we'll both see a lot more of it.

We should have been friends.

Our nights drag on endlessly, but our days are just as perishable as ever. My street, like all the streets around here, runs smack into the stone wall that outlines the Evergreen Cemetery. Block after block, if you try to get through that way you bash against a yellow sign that just says END. Then on top of the stone wall there's a chain-link fence, letting us look in on the elaborate marble tombs with their columns and swags of stone drapery and their perfectly carved climbing roses: these gorgeous miniature mansions. Around here it's the dead who are living large. On the living side of the fence we have plastic kids' bikes wedged into the balconies of burned-out apartment buildings. Mosaics of garbage and broken glass in the mud. So it's not too surprising that I tend to wind up wandering around the graves. It reminds me that there are always options.

I spend hours walking up and down the cemetery's hills with their ranks of spiky white angels. One tomb has a crack-faced statue of a girl, leaning sideways and sunk in the turf up to her knees; I almost feel like I should try to help her climb out. Below me the train station perches on its mess of tracks, and this tinny synthetic voice keeps echoing up and telling the dead how long they have to wait for the next train. There's a bench where I sit reading, then I walk down to a donut shop in the late afternoon—chocolate glazed and a cup of coffee for me, a heinous pink-sprinkled custard-filled blob for Erg—lingering at my outside table until the twilight starts rolling in and I get too hungry and chilled to ignore it anymore. Going home means facing Chelsea's kindhearted efforts to patch up my leaking psyche and Steph's conviction, I bet, that I'm beyond repair, and Iliana too tired and worried to deal with any of it. "Erg? I don't know if I can go home."

She jumps in my pocket. "Sure you can! It's dinnertime!"

"Maybe it's time for us to get out of here. Just get on a bus and go."

I hesitate. "I guess you'd have to swipe our bus fare, though. I only have like ten bucks." I've never asked Erg to steal for me before, but since she started the trouble at home she might as well help get me out of it.

"Oh, no. Nonono, Vassa. Go home. It'll be fine." Her voice wheedles from my right hip. A few times people have heard her and thought that I had a phone with a really weird ringtone.

"You don't understand what this is *doing* to me, Erg. Every time they look at me I feel sick because I know what they're thinking. I just want to get out and start over, and maybe next time you won't—"

"Vassa," Erg says firmly, "it's going to be fine. As long as we're together, you'll be fine. And we'll be together forever! So stop worrying!"

"I think you're missing the point here, dollface. Us being together is what's making things totally *not* fine."

"Vaaaasssaaa." She practically sings it. "Go home. Trust me. Anyway nobody's home but your stepmom, and she's asleep. Okay?"

The surprising thing is that when Erg says something like this she's always right. Anyway, if I do decide to run away, it wouldn't be a bad idea to pack a bag first. "Okay for *now*. I'm not promising anything for later, though."

"I can take care of later," Erg squeaks primly. "I've got everything under perfect control."

It's true, the apartment is totally dark and there's no sound apart from faint snores coming from Iliana's room. I heat up some leftover pasta in the microwave—Erg leans so far into the bowl while she's eating that I'm amazed she doesn't fall in—then watch some TV in our bedroom. I'm chilled and damp from being out for so long and the warmth starts oozing through me, beginning at my stomach and then bobbing up into my head.

The lights were on when I fell asleep, but when I wake up the only light is a dim staticky flicker. Someone is knocking around the bed-room, yanking drawers and dropping things; I know it has to be Stephanie. Chelsea would at least make an effort to be quiet. "Oh my God," she almost shouts, "I can't find anything!"

"You can turn on the light if you want," I tell her. "I'm awake."

"No, I can't, smartass. You try it!"

I'm confused. "You can't? Which one?"

"Any of them!"

My first thought is that there must be a power outage, but the TV still glows and chatters in front of me, its colors ambling from red to blue. I reach for the bedside lamp and twist the knob, once and then again to be sure. She's right, nothing happens. "What's going on?" Through the window I can see the building across the street, its panes a shining yellow grid against the darkness. Stephanie shuf-fles back and forth, blotting out the distant glow. One curve of her cheek is outlined in faint gray, but that's all I can see of her face.

"The bulbs have burned out," Stephanie says with ornate exas-peration. "Duh, Vass."

Maybe I'm still dreaming a little bit because it takes me five heartbeats to realize that there's a problem with this. "All of them? Um, Steph, that doesn't make a lot of sense, does it? Why would they all burn out at the same time?"

"Why is the sky blue? They obviously did! And we don't have a single spare bulb anywhere!"

It's true, I guess, that we've been using all our lights an awful lot, though this still seems like quite a coincidence. "In all the rooms? Did you check Iliana's room? Because we could borrow a lightbulb from her and buy new ones in the morning."

"You think I didn't think of that? Oh, gosh, I just stumbled around the apartment in the dark for an hour, and it never even occurred to me to check my mom's room! Thanks, Vassa!"

Could this be one of Erg's pranks? Not really; she'd never make it to the overhead fixtures. "Go to bed, then. We'll deal with this tomorrow."

"So you expect me to just sit here in the dark for ages? It's only midnight."

"What do you want me to do about it?"

She's closer to me now, enough that her face shows up like an unstable map in the TV light. Terra incognita, an ocean at the edge of the world. Blues and whites squirm across her features; she won't look at me.

"Why don't you go out and buy some? You're dressed." She's wearing pajamas, and she's right, I fell asleep in my clothes. But if it's midnight . . .

"All the stores will be closed, Steph."

"They won't *all* be closed." Her lips pucker as if she's fighting a smile. "BY's is still open. It's like five blocks away."

At first I think she's kidding. At first I think she has to be. Her eyes are flickering toward the shadows behind her dresser and waves of gray light go crashing across her cheeks. *There be monsters.* "You aren't serious."

"Why wouldn't I be? Make yourself useful for once." Her gaze is shifty, darting, and her mouth twists with what looks like embarrassment.

Where is Chelsea? She wouldn't stand for this.

I still can't quite believe it; I'm still trying to give her the benefit of the doubt. "Stephanie? They kill people at BY's. Remember? People go in for a bag of chips and come out with no heads. Remember?" Though really, there's no way she could have forgotten. No matter how oblivious she is, that kind of thing does tend to make an impression.

But she's right that BY's is still open. It's open always and forever and its lights never go out. Even the tangerine plastic walls give off a glowing haze like radioactivity, and the windows shoot out saw-toothed beams. They never stop gouging huge holes in the darkness.

She opens her mouth to snap back, then stops and stares at me. With our dad gone and as good as dead for all practical purposes, Stephanie is the only blood relative I have left. I get up from the bed and stand facing her, only two feet away, staring back into her brown eyes. Blue light stutters across her pupils. I'm still hoping, barely hoping, that she'll think about what she's doing and back down.

Her cheeks flush scarlet and the corners of her mouth hike up, but that's it. My own sister is trying to get me killed. Knowing that—knowing it for *certain,* now—is what makes up my mind.

"All right!" I say. I sound like a very cheerful boulder. Shiny and hard. "I'll be back in fifteen minutes!" And I slam my feet into my shoes, never letting my eyes leave hers. My hands are in my pockets and Erg wraps her arms around my right thumb and squeezes.

I walk through our dark apartment: past the sagging sofa and Iliana's needlepoint pillows with their depictions of galloping horses and wild rivers—I'm obviously not the only one who dreams of being anywhere else—past the chipped coffee table and the vase I made last year in art class. I can hear the faint jitter of roaches in the kitchen. Stephanie drags along behind me as if she was stuck to my shoe. Maybe she thinks I'm just bluffing. Shows how well she knows me.

When I get to the front door I take my army jacket off a hook and shrug it on. It was getting pretty cold earlier. I turn back to her and smile brightly; there's just enough whiskery shimmer from the streetlamps outside that I know she can see my face. I want her to remember this forever. I want her to wake up sweating, years from now, and watch me smiling while I float over her bed. "See you soon, sis! Want me to pick up anything else while I'm there?"

And that's when we hear footsteps creaking up the stairs, and a key turns in the lock. As soon as I see Chelsea's face framed by the hallway's harsh fluorescence, her happiness collapsing into confusion at the sight of us by the door, something compresses in my chest. I'm not the one who has a reason to be ashamed, though.

"Hey, Chels!" I say. It's strange, I know, but I don't actually want her to stop me from going. "I was just running out." I try to move past her—let Stephanie do the explaining, if she can—but Chelsea's blocking the door. Did I mention that Chelsea lifts weights? She's what you'd call strapping, in an attractive way, but she could definitely pick me up and throw me if she felt like it.

"It's a little late for that," Chelsea says. More puzzled than angry. "Isn't it?"

"Just for a few minutes," I say. "Picking up some things for Steph. I'll come right home."

Chelsea hasn't processed the implications of this yet and she comes in and tosses her bag on the sofa. Behind the theatrical blandness I'm putting on there's a lot for her to take in, really. I'm able to scoot behind her, out into the stairwell and then down the first three steps.

"Wait," Chelsea says, looking back and forth between me and Stephanie. Stephanie's lower lip is jutting out defiantly and her chin is up; she's giving off way too much drama to convince Chelsea that this is just a casual errand. "What things?"

"All the lights have burned out," Stephanie says. She sounds insolent and, for somebody engaged in a murder attempt, weirdly silly. It makes it all worse and my knees start shaking, though I swear it's not from fear. "Vassa's just going to out to buy bulbs."

"I guess it's okay if she hurries," Chelsea says, and I realize she still hasn't figured it out. I'd be in denial too in her place. She's standing sideways in our doorway, bisected by shadow and shine.

"The corner store closes at midnight. Oh, V., can you get me some ice cream while you're there? Cherry vanilla?"

"It's *after* midnight," I tell her, moving slowly down the stairs while I'm talking. I've decided I don't want Stephanie to be able to pretend later that she didn't know. "Steph said I should go to BY's."

I can't see Stephanie from here, but I can see Chelsea's face waking with outrage as she swings around to glare at her. "Stephanie! You know she can't do that!"

"Why not?" Stephanie's voice falls out of the door and bangs around the stairwell, bouncing off linoleum and glossy green paint. "They only kill shoplifters at BY's. Scummy, sneaky thieves. Why would that be a problem for *Vassa*?"

I'm still heading down, turning at the landing now. A triangle of Chelsea's back shows overhead, sliced by banisters. Her attention is all on Stephanie. "There is absolutely no excuse for you, for your even *suggesting* this! Stephanie, you need to apologize to Vassa now!"

"Why? She'll be right back," Stephanie says. Her voice is filthy with a sick kind of sass. I'm at the second landing now and I can't see even a scrap of the girls who used to be my family.

There's a loud crack and a wail, and I know that Chelsea just smacked her across the face. It's about the best goodbye she could give me. They're both screaming now and I've reached the foyer with its corpse-colored mailboxes. And then I open the building's metal-grate door, and I'm running. I'm in the night, and for a few moments all I feel is free. Darkness drums up through my body and the streetlamps sweep my head up and away inside levitating blobs of pure brilliance.

Somewhere behind me a window flies open. "Vassa!" Chelsea screams. "Get back here!" I keep going. Chelsea's stronger than me but I'm faster, and she knows it. "You don't have to prove anything to us! Come home!"

Us? I'd like to say. *Who is this* us, *Chelsea? We're just people who got stuck in the same apartment, and there's no* us *anywhere around here.*

As for *home*, well, I'll have to borrow a dictionary.

And then I've passed enough slabby brick buildings with crappy swan planters and ugly cement lions that I can swing onto another block which is exactly the same, except with a closed auto-body shop, and I don't have to hear Chelsea anymore. She can't fix this for me. She can't, and I don't even want her to try.

I'm just getting wise now to what must have happened: I bet Stephanie unscrewed all the lightbulbs just enough so they wouldn't work. I bet they're not burned out at all. My hands are balled in my pockets as I run and something starts kicking at my right palm. It's only now I realize that I've been crushing Erg in my fist this whole time. I pull her out, half-afraid I might have hurt her. There's a cold wind winging down the nothing-stuffed streets; I feel wet trails licking my cheeks and then spilling down my neck.

"Oh, Vassa," Erg says. Her painted violet lids flutter over round azure eyes; for something made out of wood she's doing a great job of looking concerned. "Oh, you're so sad! That was so mean of Stephanie! Do you think I could bite through her jugular? If I opened my mouth extra wide?"

I'm not out of breath. I don't know why I stop running—stop moving at all—and just stand swaying in the middle of the sidewalk. There's no one around, thankfully, but the tears still feel degrading. Nothing Stephanie does should have the power to make me cry. "This is what you call *everything being fine,* Erg?"

Erg just stares at me for a moment, her little body still wrapped up like my hand is a straitjacket. She can't possibly have retinas—there's nothing behind her black lacquer pupils but a chunk of wood—but I've never doubted for a second that she really, truly sees me. "Why yes, Vassa," she says after a second. "I do call it that. Indeed I do."

My last night on Earth, with its stars fuzzed out by the rusty city sky and its rambling maze of emptiness covering every possible inch of ground. I guess Erg has a point. What could be finer? If this is all there is, well, then by definition it's the finest thing out there.

CHAPTER 3

There's plenty of nothing in Brooklyn, but BY's still hogs vacant space as if it was afraid of getting emptiness deprivation sickness. Not many stores in the city have parking lots but our local BY's franchise is surrounded by a field of dead cement that takes up a whole small block, though cars never seem to park there. As I get close the stench is like sick sweet fur in my nostrils, and I try not to look—but who can keep from looking at that? The parking lot is ringed in by poles maybe thirty feet high, and on top of every pole a severed head stares down, some with eyes and some with just gutted pits. A few heads are fresh and still have humanish colors, just a little too gray or too white. With my weird pallor I'll fit right in, I guess. Others have mossy patinas, verdigris mold, or purplish pockets of rot. I don't want to recognize Joel, but I do. He's spiked to my left and it looks like he's staring off at the sky, dreaming of bleeding into the moonlight. His smooth black skin has gone ashy and sort of prickly, as if it's covered in iron filings. I acknowledge that many intelligent people would say I'm exhibiting poor judgment, doing something so dangerous out of pride and rage, and, I mean, no doubt. But somehow looking at Joel gives me my first little shiver of hope that maybe I *will* go home tonight and fling the lightbulbs straight into Stephanie's face. With any luck they'll explode and engulf her in snow-white flames.

It's only logical: BY's can't kill *everyone* who shops there. If they did, they'd go out of business.

At the center of the ring of poles, BY's dances. Just like in the ads, the building hops and swivels on giant chicken feet, on yellow legs that manage to be at once wobbly and graceful. Its orange plastic sides glow with this relentless singeing shine that hurts to look at, and the beams lancing out of its plate-glass windows bow and scrape across the pavement. As if they were searchlights. Always looking for someone. The orange building bends with a dramatic forward swoop, a distorted trapezoid of light lunges toward my feet, and then I see that not every pole has its own personal head on top.

No: there's exactly one that is empty.

Nice touch, I'd like to say. *Good one.*

There's a growling sound that rises and falls; I've been hearing it for a while but not really paying attention. Now the source of it lashes by and I jump back so it won't crush my feet: a motorcycle, jet black, with a heavy-muscled, black-clad rider. His helmet is strangely huge, protruding like a spherical cancer from his skull, and his visor is down. He looks like a concentrated chunk of the darkness, a clot in the night's black blood. He's going fast enough that I don't have time to see much, but when he comes around again I try to make out his face. All I can see is a mouth with thin, gray-pink lips above a boulder of a chin. "Hey!" I call, but he's off.

I watch him for a few more minutes, his engine snarling up and down in pitch like somebody practicing scales on a dog. He's going around. And around. Twice more I try to talk to him, but it's like he can't hear me or doesn't care. His head never turns and his visor looks completely opaque, and much blacker than the sky with its haze of outcast light. The guy must be some kind of security guard, but it seems like he'd be more useful if he could see.

I start to realize I'm stalling. BY's prances on its horned legs, but, like every city kid on the East Coast, I know just what to do to make it stop.

The next time the motorcycle burns past I step through into the circle of those watching heads, and now the engine whines by behind me. So my muscles are tight and my legs are trembling and I feel sick and cold and stupid. Why should I care?

"Turn around," I sing. My voice comes out thin and crackly. "Turn around and stand like Momma placed you! Face me, face me!"

The building stops spinning abruptly, with a little jerk. Then, quite deliberately, it rotates so the plate-glass windows and the door are pointing my way. I could swear it's looking at me. They're just windows, obviously nothing but mindless glass, but somehow I can't shake the sense of a cynical expression and even a tweaky little smirk like the one on Stephanie's face when she sent me out to die.

Then the chicken legs crease at the knee and the whole store drops, bending forward to invite me in. I will go right in, get the lightbulbs, and leave. I will . . .

But there's something I have to do first. Knowing what I know about Erg's proclivities, bringing her into a BY's seems like absolute suicide. I don't want to leave her lying on the pavement, though. I look around for somewhere to hide her until I'm done in there. For no good reason there's a tree stump right in the middle of a parking space, and when I walk closer and peer down I see a deep cleft in the wood, big enough for Erg if I stuff her. She might have to go in headfirst, but it can't be helped.

She's howling like a siren from the instant I reach into my pocket. "No! Vassa! No, you can't do that! Stop having such bad ideas! You can't leave me!"

"Erg," I say. "You have a truly crappy track record with the impulse control. I can't trust you not to get me killed. That makes sense, right?"

"Your mom didn't say anything about cramming me into stumps, Vassa! Do you think she was an idiot? How could you even *think* about . . ." Erg can't talk anymore. She's sobbing, her little painted face all crimped and deformed. It's incredible that something so small can make such a racket. Maybe the noise is her way of compensating for her inability to produce tears.

Behind me BY's shuffles impatiently, scratching the black cement with backward strokes of its knobbly three-toed feet. "Erg." I sigh. I don't like to see her crying like this. "Erg, I'll be right back, okay?"

Erg gags, although she has no breath and no throat to do her choking with. "You cannot go in there without me, Vassa! You *cannot* do this. Bad things will happen if I'm not with you in there. You can't!"

BY's starts pitching and shaking. I can tell it's getting bored. I hold Erg up and look into her blue blob eyes, trying to see through the paint to whatever is back there. "Erg, listen to me, you have to *promise* . . ."

"I already did!" Erg sniffs. "I told you everything will be fine! We just have to stay together!" BY's door lifts a foot off the ground; it's getting ready to rear up again. I look from that deep crevice in the wood to Erg's eager face, then to the slowly ascending door. I could just give up on the whole lunatic plan. The empty street beckons, commas of amber light shining on the windshields of the sleeping cars.

And then I'm suddenly running: away from the street, toward that drowsily floating glass door. It's swinging open, clapping back and forth although there's no real wind, at least a yard above the ground now and rising fast. Erg is still clutched in my hand. It's madness, but I leap and land sprawled inside the open doorway with my legs dangling out into the night.

I can feel myself sailing up, and up.

Only now does it occur to me to wonder if singing the jingle works when you're *inside* the store? Or, um, only outside? The store cants abruptly so that the floor in front of me is sloping down instead of up and then gives a little jump. I'm jolted free of the sill and I go skimming across slippery linoleum until my head collides with a display of laundry detergent. As soon as I catch my breath I stuff Erg back into my pocket; keeping her hidden is practically a reflex at this point, but now I catch myself wondering if someone will think I'm stealing her.

Nothing happens, though. The floor settles so it's reasonably parallel to the ground and I haul myself to my feet, gaping. I expect to see horrors, hooks with dripping human hearts or something. Entrails looped around the barbecue sauce. But no: it looks like any other convenience store in Brooklyn, only much brighter and neater. The floors are neon yellow and so clean it's like they're screaming at me. The back wall is covered in the usual tall refrigerators with sliding glass doors, and then there are graded racks of candy bars, and bristling bags of chips, and orderly rows of shelves full of soup and toilet paper. Coffee and magazines and hot dogs under a glaring orange heat lamp. The same old whatever. The same assorted nothingness, now available in a pack of five tropical flavors.

I can't imagine what I was so afraid of. Pop music is playing very softly. I don't recognize the song but it's pretty, a girl's voice lilting over piano. It doesn't seem like there's anyone here but me until I turn around. A sweet-looking old lady is fast asleep at the register, her head resting on crossed arms. She's wearing a faded black dress with blotchy flowers and her pink scalp shows through wisps of pearly hair stuck full of so many bobby pins that they cover more of her head than her hair does. She looks way too old to have a job and I can't help feeling sorry for her. At her age she should be home in bed, not working the night shift in a sickeningly cheery place like this. I'm going to feel like a real bitch, waking her up so I can check out.

She snuffles a little and mutters in her sleep. Yellowish slime clumps in her snowy lashes. Deep in my pocket Erg is very still, but I can tell by her tension against my fingers that she's awake and alert.

None of the aisles are labeled, I notice. But the lightbulbs shouldn't be too hard to find. I head up one row that looks to be full of cleaning supplies. With a lurch the store starts dancing again. The stuff on the shelves must be tacked down somehow because nothing falls. Everything just pitches together, linked in the same clattery rhythm. It seems like we're dancing to that song on the radio, which is still playing as if it had just started over again.

Maybe it's the swaying, but I'm finding it hard to focus. I see the brand names honking out of their Day-Glo spirals, and just looking at them makes me feel like some kind of acrid smoke is in my eyes. Up ahead there's a blue block that looks like the packaging on our usual lightbulbs, but when I get there it's something else, some strange Lithuanian cookies maybe.

Fine. The store's not that big. I turn down the next aisle, all Ritz crackers and pinkish pastes in jars, strawberry marshmallow butter and foamed brie with the legend *It's Artisanal!* in flowery script. Under the music I hear a very soft noise, this rubbery scuffling. It's hard to believe when the place is so spotless that every surface looks lit by fever, but I guess they must have mice in here. It doesn't seem like lightbulbs would belong in this aisle, but apparently BY's isn't as immaculately organized as I thought. A stack of those familiar blue boxes is visible at the very end, on the left.

I could almost think the mice were following me. The moist whispery sound stays just behind my right shoulder as I move in on the lightbulbs. I'm starting to think that it sounds more like something dragging than like sharp-clawed little feet, but the noise is so quiet I can't be sure. Maybe it's the sound the boxes make as the floor rocks?

Those blue boxes aren't lightbulbs, either, but some kind of knock-off Pop-Tarts in a flavor called *lagoon*. For a moment I just stand there, trying to imagine what lagoon filling would taste like. The colors on the packaging are making my eyes water and burn. My lids flutter. Maybe I'm imagining things, but somewhere behind my right shoulder I hear what I could swear was a quick, spongy hop.

I might be more on edge than I like to admit, because I swing around the display at the end pretty quickly. The old lady at the register has started snoring in this feathery way, tiny ruffling snortlettes. She's obviously way too skinny and frail to chop anybody's head off. There's nothing to worry about, except perhaps for getting down, and I suppose the brawny gentleman on the motorbike.

There aren't that many more aisles to check, though, and the bulbs have to be somewhere. I hope I have enough money to get Chelsea her ice cream, too. There are more blue boxes in this aisle, and I feel like I'm starting to notice a pattern: they're always at the end, always on the left. I'm learning to be wary of fake outs and I practically run up to them, trying to catch them before they change. They do, of course. This time they resolve into cans of blue soup.

The noise on my right shuffles faster, and a little louder. Suddenly it's very obvious that whatever is there is trying to catch up. I shift back a little, looking off at nothing, and then spin around and grab a package of toilet paper standing in front of the source of the noise. I have just enough time to see a blur of something pale dropping down to the shelf below. A light flapping and smacking, and it's gone.

It's real, and it is not a mouse. Too big. A shade too pink.

Since I'm at the back of the store I decide to just check one last aisle, fast, and then get out of here. I'll wake up the old lady and buy something small, a pack of gum or a magazine. And then I think I'm never going home again.

This time I hear the sliding, shuffling noise on both sides. My heart is pattering at an absurd clip now. There are two of those things, and they're trying to make sure—of what, exactly? There's a sudden aggressive scratching on my left and I instinctively lurch right, brushing against a shelf and almost losing my balance. I let out a yelp of surprise. In my right pocket Erg kicks violently—she must bruise my hip—and then there's a thud and rumble as something falls to the yellow floor.

A candy bar in a scarlet wrapper. And on top of the candy bar there's a human hand with no body attached, rolling back and forth and slamming loudly against the metal shelf with a noise like a muffled gong.

The hand is big-boned and long-fingered. Bulging veins like indigo snakes that have gorged on too many rats. And there's an oily mauve tinge to its skin.

The tip of its thumb shows the deep red print of tiny teeth. I lift Erg from my pocket for an instant, staring in bewilderment. A trickle of blood slips from her dainty ruby mouth, and she motions frantically at my pocket for me to put her back.

As soon as I do the old lady is standing there, looking at me with wide, pitying eyes.

Something has a hold of my hair, wrenching a huge hank of it up behind me. Something strong. On the floor the wounded hand starts springing up and down, one accusing forefinger pointing my way. Its nails are painted with emerald glitter.

"Oh, little one," the old lady whispers mournfully, "you were stealing. Weren't you?"

It's funny but it takes me a moment to realize I'm the one she's accusing. "I was not! I think that sick thing on your floor was stealing. It was flopping all over that candy bar like some kind of squashed fish."

The hand's fingers all jerk straight at once and it spasms with indignation, then points at me again.

"He can't steal," the woman reproves me. One of her irises is completely veiled in some gray-white, sticky web of disease. "He works here. Keeping the shelves tidy, cleaning . . . I don't think you young people understand how much harm your thieving does. I'm all alone, and my store here is all I have. I hope you realize now that what you did was very wrong."

I try to move, and the thing behind me jerks my head back so hard that the skin of my throat strains. In front of me the wounded hand bounces excitedly, then takes off scampering down the aisle with a weird grabbing motion.

I have an awful sense of what it might be going to fetch.

"I was *not* stealing!" I'm yelling now. "I didn't take anything!" The hand reappears behind her, hopping along more slowly with a heavy axe swinging awkwardly in its grip.

"You must have been," she mutters. "That's why he was pointing you out. You could at least say you're sorry." The hand has begun climbing the shelves at her side, mashing the steel support between three undulating fingers and its palm while the axe sways between thumb and forefinger. The blade is curved and mirrored, reflecting bags of white bread as it creeps upward. It smacks against the shelves with a dull, recurrent clank. The blood in my head is buzzing and my legs start to go slack. That nasty fleshy spider has climbed almost high enough to—

"I'll empty my pockets!" I scream. Erg kicks me. "Really! How could I be stealing, when I don't have anything of yours?"

It's pathetic to realize that those are probably my last words. I'm most ashamed at the thought of what this will do to Chelsea and how she'll blame herself. The hand reaches the top shelf and swishes the blade triumphantly upright.

The old lady sighs. "No," she tells the hand. "She's not wrong."

The hand jumps in protest and knocks a pile of cereal boxes off the shelf.

"There are rules," she mutters. "Rules for everybody. Always rules. The candy would have to be on her person somewhere for it to *really* count. There's too much . . . ambiguity. You'd be getting us into difficulties with the fussy types, the sticklers and quibblers, wouldn't you? There's an element of doubt."

The hand drops the axe with a clunk. The falling blade slices a box of sugared flakes wide open and they rustle onto the floor.

"There's a lot more than doubt," I snarl. Now that I'm not seconds away from being butchered I'm ready to spit at her. "You'd better let me go, now!"

She levels her eyes at me, one gray and one veiled. The problem with staring back at her is that I start to get the sense that her sick eye is orbiting like a dead planet, and that my head is its sun.

"Not *that* much doubt," she whispers. The blotchy pink and yellow flowers on her dress look like bacteria creeping in a petri dish. "Not nearly that much. He pointed at you, after all. It's part of his job to defend my property, and I trust his word over yours. No, you won't be . . . leaving immediately."

The hand flings itself petulantly off the shelf and starts corralling spilled cereal with little sideways swipes. It's funny that something with no face can look so mad.

I'd like to tell her she's wrong. But that whatever-it-is still has an iron grip on my hair—I can't see it, but it must be the other hand. My scalp is stretched and stinging and I can barely twitch my head. Even if I could shake the hand off we're far enough above the ground that I'd at least break a leg if I jumped. And then there's the guy on the black motorcycle, ready to run me down as I try to hobble away. My odds of escape are notably poor. I'm trying to think of some alternative to screaming insults when she lets out a dreamy hiss.

"Enough doubt, I'd say, for a chance. I'll give you an opportunity to demonstrate your virtuous character. Show me that I should believe you instead of an old and dear subordinate. A chance to work off your *debt* to me, shall we say."

"This is insane!" I manage. My voice sounds garbled. "What do you think I owe you?"

When she stares at me it's her veiled eye, the one with no pupil, which seems to zoom in on my face. "More than you owe yourself. More than to mother or father. A possibility of life repossessed from the muck you've made of it. You should be grateful." She tilts her head and that web in her eye seems to drape itself over me, gummy threads feeling the shape of what it can't see. "You're pretty. Having you here will be good for business."

Erg is stroking my hip through the layers of fabric. It's clear what the gesture means: *Calm down, Vassa. Just be cool and play along. We'll figure something out.* It almost makes me angrier, but since Erg did just save my life—at least for now—I throttle my impulse to tell this old ghoul to go drink bleach. "What do you have in mind, then?"

"Three nights. Three. Do what you're told, show yourself mature and responsible . . . Why did you come here tonight?"

Her voice rasps through my head. The same song is still playing, sprinkling mournful piano notes over the air. "I was just picking up lightbulbs."

She starts nodding. "I'll throw those in. A commitment of three nights; your pay will be your survival. And a package of lightbulbs. Two packages, if you like." She isn't even looking at me anymore; she could almost be dreaming on her feet, her words coming out half song and half wind. "Three nights. You can work the register. Then I can sleep. I never get to sleep."

"You were sleeping when I came in," I point out. I don't think it will do any good to mention that three nights could be an extremely long time.

"I was not. I was working. There is always the minor maintenance to be done, the repairs to the twiddly bits at the fringes. If I were only less fastidious. . . ." She's already turning away, shuffling back the way she came. "I don't think you deserve a name. I don't see how a callow little vixen like you could have *earned* a name. But I suppose your foolish parents disregarded that and gave you one anyway?"

It's wrong to slap old ladies sideways, and then this one commands a pair of evil hands that are just dying to lop my head off. The hand behind me drops down, still dangling in my hair like some gross prehensile starfish, and shoves me between my shoulder blades to make me follow her. It's hard to believe a hand could be so strong with no body attached, but I still stagger from the impact. "I'm Vassa."

"Vassa," she whispers lethargically. "Vassa, my imp. You may call me Babs. We have a deal, then? Three nights?"

"Fine," I say. There's not much else I can do at the moment. The hands herd me up to the counter, thumping at my back and prodding my ankles. I swing my hair, trying to dislodge that hideous clinging paw, and it punches my ribs to retaliate. I'm dragged around to the back of the counter then jabbed by glitter-slicked nails until I sit down in the chair Babs vacated to come after me. Torn mustard stuffing shows through shredded upholstery. Unlike everything else in the store the chair is filthy, its cushions the color and consistency of soot-crusted oatmeal.

"You can start," Babs wheezes, "tonight. Be careful you don't make mistakes when you're counting out change. I'll expect the balance in the register to be *exact*. Otherwise, we'll have to attend to you. A reliable numerical sense is the first foundation of the mind. It lets you count the seconds you have left. It adds rigor, little one. And you seem . . . shaky."

At least the hands have finally stopped grappling at me. They're balancing on their wrist-stumps on the counter, palms facing inward and their fingertips curling. Those green-spangled nails seem to watch me like a row of quizzical eyes. Their postures are perfectly matched. "Got it," I tell Babs absently. Once she's asleep and the hands are off patrolling I can wait for the next sucker to arrive and sing the jingle, coax the store down to the ground again. Then I'll just have the motorcyclist to deal with.

"That's nice to hear," Babs says. "I'll be asleep in the back." She turns to leave, her hand on a narrow door in the corner. Erg pokes me. A reminder.

"What if I get hungry?" I ask.

"Oh . . . You can eat what you like while you're here. Just don't take anything out of my store. You understand." She glances lazily at the hands. "Dismissed, you two. Back to your duties."

And then they're gone, and I'm in a chair that wobbles with each hop and twirl of the floor below me. The first thing I do is take out my phone; I need to tell Chelsea I'm okay. The phone is dead, though, and I feel like I should have known it would be. There's nothing I can do but sigh and stuff it back in my pocket.

Almost the entire wall to my right is made of glass and in it the city dances with manic enthusiasm, the houses and stores rushing up and down as if all those glowing windows were caught in a dark tide. The light projecting from BY's waves like a flag across the parking lot, sometimes catching one of those skewered heads and making it shine: dead women and men becoming moons in my personal night. When Babs told me I owe her more than I owe myself,

I thought that more than nothing might not amount to much. Now Joel's head bounces by, gazing with blank rotten rapture through the glass, and I want to ask him: *What* do *I owe myself, Joel? What did I borrow from myself, and how on earth will I ever give it back?*

CHAPTER 4

Erg crawls out of my pocket and up my arm, then perches on the counter with her tiny legs dangling over the edge. "Nice work!" she says. The blood on her chin has dried into a garnet smudge. "I mean, that's what *you* should say to *me*, now. And you could add something poetic about your inexpressible gratitude, and how super dumb it would have been to leave me outside."

I look at the shelves; I think I might have just seen an emerald-tipped finger cresting behind some cans like a shark fin coming up in a horror movie. "You knew those things were after us, Erg?"

"Sure I did! The nasties. But I wasn't going to let them hurt you, Vassa. Oh, I taught *him* a lesson, didn't I? Chompers!" Her blue eyes are wide and, God, happy.

"And you still think *everything is fine*? Even now that we're stuck in here? Those hand things are probably not giving up that easily, right?"

I'm not fine, that's for sure, and I do like to think of myself as one minor component of *everything*. So doesn't that prove Erg is wrong? I guess there's a delayed effect from the almost-dying, because my hands have started vibrating crazily against the counter and I feel like my face is about to explode into shrapnel-sharp tears.

Erg studies me, uncharacteristically serious. "What do I keep telling you, Vassa? Just stick with me, kid. Sure, those hands will try to get you again, but I can take 'em!"

I can't help smiling at her. "They're like ten times bigger than you are."

Erg twists her head like she's shaking back her curls but the squiggles of black paint don't go anywhere. I've always wondered how her eyes and mouth can be so mobile.

"And I am ten times meaner, Vassa. *Eleven* times, perhaps, quite. As I will joyfully demonstrate if they think they can mess with us. Okay? As you can now demonstrate your appreciation for my extraordinary heroism by getting me one of those hot dogs, please. *Lots* of mustard. As in lotsandlots. And extra relish."

"Oh," I tell her. I'm suddenly so exhausted that I can barely face walking over to the case where the dogs gleam under lamplight like bright orange sweat, but she does deserve some kind of thank-you. "Sure, doll." I start to get up and the floor rears and throws me back into the chair, sending it sailing against the wall so that a few small bottles rain down on my head. Even Erg looks startled. "Oof. Okay, trying *that* again."

The store is rotating faster, grinding against the night, but I pull myself up by grabbing at the shelves behind the counter. There's some kind of clamor out in the parking lot. The building swings around like someone with a bee stinging their hindquarters and I almost pitch over again. Erg jumps up and runs toward me with her arms out, and I manage to lean close enough to grab her before we go stumbling sideways. I'm trying to get to the window to see what's going on. Erg's hot dog will have to wait.

We leap again, spin a full one-eighty in midair, and land with an infuriated jiggling. I've given up on walking and crawl toward the glass while Erg squirms her way inside my sleeve. It's a ratty old jacket with a convenient hole for her to peer through. I kneel on the slippery linoleum, careful to keep my distance from the clapping door, and gaze into the night. Thirty feet below me in the parking lot a boy is belting out the BY's jingle in a parody of an opera singer, throat arching out and arms flung wide. He sees me looking and drops to one knee. "Turn around. Turn around and stand like Momma placed you! Face me! Face—" Then he cuts off. One syllable shy of a song.

The store is just starting to kneel when the jingle starts up again, screamed more than sung, from somewhere off to the right. The melody is bansheed and hacked but still recognizable. BY's jerks to its full height as if electrocuted and reels around to confront the new singer. The light pours over the girl's face: I don't know her real name, but she goes by Lottery and we have three classes together. She's an acrid personality, always out to out-cynic and out-bitch everyone, but I wouldn't say I hate her. Not until now, anyway. She's making me seasick. The store is sinking down until her face is only two yards from mine.

Like the boy did she stops right before the last note, and someone else starts yowling on the far side of the dark. The motorcyclist zips by but he doesn't do anything to stop the latest singer, who's going for sort of a calypso effect. Now I understand what they're up to, baiting the store and driving it as crazy as they can. If I could stand up, I might get some cans to throw at them, but I'm pretty close to vomiting and besides, Babs might think that pelting these jerks counted as thieving. There are at least six or seven kids arranged in a circle, picking up the jingle and winging it around, and for a few more minutes we keep up this lunatic alteration of waltz and jolt and curtsy. I can't even kneel anymore, just lie there with my head pressed to the floor hoping my brain will stay inside it.

If you don't bother it, it won't bother you. That's what Iliana told me after I moved in with her and my sisters. There'd been nothing remotely like BY's in my old neighborhood and the heads freaked me out to an unspeakable degree. I'd imagine them floating just behind me, gibbering softly together, or those huge clawed chicken feet scraping in pursuit. Through my whole first year living here BY's scared me so much that I wouldn't walk within three blocks of the place. My evasive maneuvers were making me late for school— so Iliana marched me into the parking lot, yanked my hair back, and made me stand right between the clacking toes and stare up at BY's neon belly. *You see? Is it doing anything to you? Is it biting you? Or are you just being a baby? We all live with it, so now you better start living with it, too.*

Ah, but if you *do* bother it, then anything that happens is your own damn fault, of course. That was strongly implied. And as for the part about how sick she was of being stuck with a spoiled Williamsburg princess, that carried just fine through the walls whenever she was on the phone with her friends.

I'm mulling that over when the spinning stops dead. BY's is crouching low and a cold night wind scrolls through the gaping door. I'm trying to sit up just as the whole pack of kids comes stomping in. I know almost all of them. They're all the type who seems compelled to run in packs, like they'll get vertigo if they ever have to spend ten minutes alone with the cavernous abyss where their minds should be.

"Vassa!" Lottery says, spitting with laughter. "Hey, girl, I wondered if that was you. Hope you enjoyed the ride!"

"Want me to show you how much I enjoyed it?" I offer. "I could puke on your shoes." I make it to my feet just as the store starts rising again; I'm still dizzy enough that the movement sets me tottering. The opera-singer boy—the only one of them I don't think I've seen before—catches my elbow. I shrug him off. He should have expressed his chivalrous impulses by shutting the hell up earlier.

Lottery's looking around. "Are you here alone, Vassa? Because it's mad risky that way. Shopping at BY's is one of those *team* sports. Want us to show you how it's done?"

"Oh, I can't possibly go shopping now," I snarl. "I'm working."

That gets their attention. They snap straight and line up to stare at me. "*Working*," Lottery drawls skeptically. "As in here?"

"That would be the case," I say. I admit an impulse to elaborate on my snarkery, but the fact is that they're all in distinctly mortal peril and that makes mouthing off seem just a smidge irresponsible. "I would *really* appreciate it if you would all leave. Okay? It's a terrible idea to come in here."

Lottery mimes hacking her own head off with a sideways hand and then rolls her eyes back. Her brown hair ends in wormy bleached-out braids and she's wearing these eerie golden contact lenses. I keep looking past her, scanning the shelves for anything whitish and hopping, but the hands are keeping out of sight.

"Aw, are you worried about us, Vassa? We shop here all the time. We've all done one solo run, even, though once was definitely enough for me! But we have it down. We have what you might call *technique*."

"And *you* shouldn't be discouraging customers," Opera Boy says. "Now should you? Because I'm here to spend everything I've got. Down to the last *nickel*."

"We do offer a wide array of delectable, hard-to-find treats," I tell him. It's completely hypocritical of me, and I know it, but I can't help feeling some contempt for his recklessness. He might wind up spending a lot more than money. "Have you tried our strawberry marshmallow butter?" Behind him his friends are fanning out, one or two of them at the opening of each aisle. They're striking poses, pretending to be boxers warming up or sprinters waiting for the shot.

"I *live* for strawberry marshmallow butter," he assures me. "Want to show me where it is?"

I shake my head and step back. "I have to stay at the register. You go ahead."

He doesn't, though. Lottery glances over her shoulder to see what's keeping him and then turns back with a knowing sneer.

"So," Opera Boy says. Like a lot of people around here he's probably some crazy mix of nationalities, with golden-brown skin but gray-green eyes. Messy dark hair. "So would you do it? Chop my head off, over just some little snack pack?" He holds up a cellophane package: crackers made to look like man-in-the-moons accompanied by a mound of spreadable green cheese.

"Me, personally?" I say. "That's not really my job, but I guess if everyone else was *busy* . . ."

"Then you're not the only one working here?" He's still fiddling with his moon crackers, zipping them around like a toy airplane. Every time it flies past his hip, a small involuntary current jolts through my nerves.

"That's right, I'm *really* not." I look dramatically toward the shelves, trying to inject a clue into his foggy head. "I'm not alone, but you won't see my coworkers until it's too late."

He nods. "That's what I thought. There's something sneaky in here. You can hear the *hop*."

"So maybe instead of being a self-destructive moron," I suggest, "you should get the hell out. At least pretend you care about your life?" I have no right to be this mad, but I am. My nails are digging into my palms. He swings the crackers in midair, looping and twirling them. And then his hand dives straight for his pocket. Is he really so desperate to show off? I let out a small shriek and my heart jams into my throat. The pack is gone and his hands are rising again. I expect him to wave them triumphantly in midair, display how empty they are.

And then he laughs, loudly, and his curled right hand flips to show the crackers, tucked behind his wrist where I couldn't see them. I'd like to slap him. He pulls up the side of his jacket, tugging at the fabric. At first I don't get it, but then I realize: he's showing me that his pockets are sewed shut with big, bright pink stitches.

"Oh, I observe *basic shopping precautions,*" he says. Lottery is glaring at him again. "Okay, we'll see you in a few."

I head back to my chair and watch the children at their little game. They move down all the aisles at once, going fast, dodging and weaving as if they were hounded by sniper fire. They're giggling, grabbing random items off the shelves, and then darting forward again, sometimes tossing boxes to one another. *Technique,* like Lottery said.

Once or twice I get a glimpse of fingertips bounding after them; they're looking pretty aggravated. I almost stop worrying. Probably if Opera knows enough to sew his pockets shut, the others do, too. Once I distinctly see a hand feinting toward a girl in Chelsea's year, Felice, with something silvery clutched in its green glitter pincers. I'm just about to yell out a warning when the hand drops back, fidgeting, the silver object still in its palm. It couldn't find an open pocket, I bet. I'm starting to understand why they think this is fun. They reach the ends of their aisles and switch places, then start their shuffle back to me. They're doing well, almost at the counter.

One of the hands hops up on a stack of boxes—the damned light bulbs, though somehow I never spotted them until now. It's still holding the silver whatever and I watch it rearing up, then pause to check its aim.

Lottery's pockets might be impervious, but she does have an open hood on her jacket. It's hanging down her back like a basketball hoop, and the hand has a nice straight shot. "Lottery!" I scream. "Jump!"

She does, probably more from surprise than from anything else. There's a small *thwack* as the silver object hits her in the middle of her back, then claps down to the floor and rolls under a shelf before

I can see what it is. Lottery flings herself around just as the hand vanishes with an audible scuffling. "What *was* that?"

Her friends are clustering in front of the counter, no one laughing anymore. "That was you," I say, "coming extremely close to dying. Put up your hood."

She's a little green, but she does what I tell her. "Vassa, what the—"

"Check out," I snarl. "And get out. How stupid can you all be?"

Her lips have started trembling. "You think it's appropriate to *insult* me, when I was almost set *up*—"

"If the threat of annihilation makes you go all drama queen, then there are other fine shopping establishments that can better serve your needs," I tell her. "Are you buying something or not? Let's get this over with."

Opera Boy bursts out grinning. "Now that's what I call gracious service! My mom always complains that kids who work these kinds of jobs are so *surly*. She should see Vassa in action."

"Gracious enough to save her life," I snap. "Limit one per customer. Now if you'll bring your purchases to the register, I can have the pleasure of seeing you all leave here." *Intact*, I don't say. But in fact I am extremely relieved about that.

They drop garish objects on the counter: those moon crackers with the processed green cheese, mushroom-flavored cookies called Fun Gus's Sugar Spores, jars of pastel goo, and red gelatinous blobs in blister packs. Each blob has what appears to be a tiny squid in the middle. It's all piled up in front of me and I turn to the register. I worked in a drugstore last summer so I don't anticipate much trouble there. I pick up the crackers, tap in $1.89. The BY's raiders stand in front of me, swaddled in their own arms. They look a whole lot more uncomfortable now than they did when they got here.

Behind their back that hand hops up onto the lightbulbs again and waggles to get my attention. It jabs toward me with its gleaming forefinger, then one glittery claw swipes in a significant horizontal line. Then, in case I somehow failed to grasp its meaning, it does it again. And again. It's bad enough, I guess, that I got away, and now I've gone and cheated them of their next victim. I don't want to take it too seriously, but that green nail sweeping back and forth is kind of distracting.

I try to keep my attention on the task in front of me, entering the prices and dropping things in bags. I realize too late that I didn't ask if they wanted to be rung up separately, but they better not complain. "Okay! Your total will be nineteen dollars and thirteen cents!" I say brightly; there's one vivid green key, unlabeled, but I'm guessing it'll do the job. When I hit it there's a discordant clangor like a xylophone slapping a brick wall and the cash drawer sails open.

"Wait," Lottery says, bending down to pull bills out of her sock, "mine was just like two-fifty."

"Why don't you all just cough up and figure out the details later?" I suggest. "Who has a twenty?"

One problem with the no-pocket rule is that it's taking them all forever to get their money, worming dollars out of holes in their cuffs or reaching up under their sweaters to pull out baggies duct-taped to their guts. I find myself distinctly unhappy, watching them claw out singles and quarters and flop them on the counter. Now and then a wadded bill tumbles to the floor and someone has to go after it. Like the sagging hood this strikes me as a weak spot in their *technique,* and I don't much like having the register open, either.

"Guys, seriously. You should hurry up," I say. I start picking up bills and smoothing them out. There aren't enough.

There's a faint, dry, slithering sound near the register. I look over, expecting to see the hands, but there's nothing there. The bills in the drawer are stirring slightly. There must be a draft; the front door keeps flicking ajar and then shutting again.

Opera bends over, probably to get that last nickel he mentioned from his shoe. "Hey, here's a twenty! On the floor."

Lottery holds her hand out. "Oh, I must have dropped that! Thanks, Tomin!"

He's dangling the bill in front of his face as if it was a dead scorpion. "I don't think anyone dropped it. Weird, it's not moving now."

"Moving?" I ask.

"I seriously could have sworn that it was crawling out from under the counter. It sounds crazy, but then this place is not entirely normal."

In the corner of my eye there's a pale shimmying, and I spin to see a bill draping itself over the drawer's edge and then dropping. I catch it in time and smack it back down. "I think that came from the register," I say, my throat tight. "Look, you have to give it back." Just glancing over at him for an instant was a mistake. I can hear the whispery coasting of paper on paper and I lean in and cover the drawer with my arm.

"Ooh, I've got one!" Felice squeals. "Free money!"

I slam the drawer as a light cascade of paper flutters over its edge. Bills stick out from the top, fingering the air impatiently, but I'll deal with them later. I'm climbing onto the counter now while they're all stooped and staring, now and then stamping suddenly as currency wafts in reach of their feet. Money must be everywhere. I'm just starting to comprehend what a disaster this is, and Erg isn't even in my sleeve anymore.

"The balance in the register has to be perfect! You don't—" Felice is already stuffing money down her shirt. Right; no pockets. "I saved your idiot friend, and now you're going to get me killed? Look, please just help."

Opera, or I guess Tomin, is diving around on the floor and snagging up cash, but he—alone out of everyone—reaches toward me with the ruffling fistful held out. An offering. I'd appreciate it if I had time for anything besides tumbling over the counter, grabbing like the rest of them at the paper oblongs that skim along the floor like autumn leaves packing their own private breezes.

The store chooses this moment to start lowering itself toward the ground. As long as we're all trapped in here there's still a chance, but once they take off into the night with those stolen bills there won't be much hope left for me. We're already touching down, the glass door yawning wide, and Felice is gamboling toward the open night with laughter babbling over her lips and dollars twitching in her cleavage. I can barely think, but I leap after her and grab her arm, trying to make her *understand*—

The cash register drawer shoots open with a bang and money lofts into the air like confetti. Night breezes spiral in, and I see bills coiling up as if wrapped around invisible fingers, then whisking away. The air is dizzy with fluttering paper, and most of it seems to be making for the door.

"Vassa? You better just come with us." It's Tomin, pulling on my elbow. I can't react; my whole body feels sandbagged and numb. "I get it about needing a job, but there's no way it's worth dealing with this. Come on!"

The door is open and the parking lot glitters like a black lake. The motorcyclist growls by, never looking at anything. For some reason I'm thinking of Babs, her wispy disappointed face as she looks around at the mess, her creaking knees as she tries to bend far enough to pick up her money.

But Tomin is right, there's no fixing what just happened. I'm going to have to run for it, and I let him tow me out the door. At first my legs wobble under me, but then adrenaline whiplashes through them and they're striking at the pavement in a blur. I'm running so fast Tomin can't keep up; he has to let me go.

Babs is a psychotic killer. Why did I care, even for a second, how she'll feel?

Dark streets open up in the gaps between the houses, and the sight of them grabs my heart and pulls. The row of stakes stands just ahead. Soon I'll be home with Chelsea and . . .

"Erg!" She's not in my sleeve anymore. I start feeling all my pockets for her. God, she's still in BY's. I ran off too fast and she didn't have a chance to catch up. All at once I stop dead, hoping to hear her tiny wooden feet scampering over the asphalt. There's nothing but the wind soughing through my hair and the low snarl of the cycle ratcheting up the scale. I turn in time to see it bearing in on me, black and somehow shapeless like an oil slick pouring over the sky. I jump aside, stumbling and falling to one knee; at first I think I just happened to be standing in its path. Then it grinds to a halt and rounds on me again.

Everyone else is scattering, already out of the ring of heads and vanishing behind trucks parked across the street. Not even Tomin has stayed to see if I'm okay. I'm up and trying to run but the motor-cycle is there, somehow too big and too blobby, a seething mass that blots out the sky. Every time I try to dodge around it, it seems to grow and closes off my escape. It doesn't really look like a motor-cycle at all anymore, more like a wall of rippling cloud, and it's driving me back the way I came. "Erg! Where are you?"

I can't see the motorcyclist, just a blur like a storm front pushing me back toward the bright orange store. I must be hallucinating because I glimpse flashes of peculiar objects in the black mist: a globe on a brass stand, something that might be a lampshade. BY's is still crouching all the way down with its door wide open. Waiting for me. Somehow I've been herded within a few yards of the wide windows. They beam at me, warm and welcoming, while on my other side . . .

I see what looks like infinite space, clear and unfolding and full of stars brighter than any stars you could ever see in the city. I see what looks like a living flood of night, and I can't tell what's happening to me anymore or where I'm going.

The bright yellow floor shoves forward, knocking me off my feet as it scoops me up and carries me high into the air. The same plinky, crooning, bell-scattered song that was playing when I first came in is still on and going strong. I guess it's on repeat but no matter how much I listen to it I can never detect anything that sounds like an end, much less a new beginning.

CHAPTER 5

I just lie there on my back, breathing hard while the ground sails out of reach. The vibrations of tiny scurrying feet shake my skull and an instant later Erg is climbing through my hair. She flings her wooden arms around my ear and hugs tight, squashing the cartilage. "Vassa! Oh, Vassa, you forgot me? How could you forget me?"

"I did for a second," I admit. "But Erg, if you'd just *stayed* with me . . . Maybe if I hadn't stopped to look for you I would have gotten away, and now . . ." I can't even say it. Money is still drifting over the linoleum, gusting lazily out each time the door sways open. There's no question in my mind as to what Babs will consider an appropriate punishment. I feel too drained to cry.

"You couldn't have gotten away, Vassa. Even if you thought for a second that you were getting out, it wouldn't really be true. You made a deal, and now you *have* to stay. Okay? Don't try that again!" She nuzzles me. "Can I have my hot dog now?"

That does it. I'd like to tell myself that I'm laughing, but there are tears tagging along with the noise bubbling out of me. "Your last meal, Erg?"

"I should hope not!"

"Really? Can you survive once I'm dead? I'm so sorry, Erg. I just thought about—about making Stephanie live with herself. I didn't even *wonder* how you were going to manage without—"

"Who's this dead person you're discussing?" Erg chirps. "Because it's not you, Vassa. And a particular *friend* of yours is getting simply weak with hunger, waiting for you to observe how marvelously not-dead you are. Certainly you're not-dead enough to apply a generous amount of mustard, yes?"

"Fine." I get to my feet, balancing carefully against the oceanic pitch of the floor. We're so lost at sea, Erg and I. Money stirs at my feet. The bills seem tired now, but so many of them already went flying out the door that there's no point even picking them up. The register's disemboweled no matter what I do. Soon my severed head will be up on a pole and I'll catch airborne dollars like snowflakes on my moldering tongue.

Once I get Erg's food I set it on the counter and curl back into my ratty chair. She straddles the hot dog as if it was a horse, her tiny feet stuck in the bun, her face buried in the slop of mustard and relish. Mauling away without a care. I guess I should be hungry by now but I can't imagine eating anything. I let my head fall down on my crossed arms, just the way Babs was when I came in, and listen to Erg chewing.

"Erg?" She doesn't look up. The hot dog is starting to look like something pocked by a meteor shower. "Did you see what happened with that motorcycle just now? It looked so crazy. I couldn't really tell what was going on."

Erg twitches her face up, relish drooling over the top of her head. "What motorcycle?"

"You know," I say, surprised. "The one out in the parking lot? That keeps circling around and around? With the guy in the huge black helmet riding it? He almost flattened me. You didn't *see* that?"

"Oh." Erg nods. "Sure, I was watching you. That's not really a motorcycle." She dives back into her food.

"What are you talking about?" I demand. "It was buzzing around the place when we got here. Of course it's a motorcycle! You saw it."

"So did you," Erg observes cryptically. "Jeez, Vassa. Has working at a cash register flipped your wits completely upside down?"

"About that. The register. You know when Babs sees what happened we're toast, right?" She's gone back to burrowing, her upper torso vanished into a hole in the bun, but she pops back out to stare at me. The bread's done a pretty good job of swabbing the relish off her hair, anyway. "Are you *positive* we can't run away, Erg?"

She looks at me like she just can't believe how slow I'm being. "It's becoming quite clear that you need some sleep, Vassa. Quite clear indeed. Your thought processes are not functioning up to a reasonable standard at the present time. Really. You've gone all gurgle-brained!"

I am exhausted, so much so that my head feels like it's still falling: through my arms, through the counter and the floor, then through dreamed strata where Chelsea is crying and strangers are climbing extremely tall ladders and acrobats are dropping from the clouds on strands of rain as tensile as spider silk. "These are probably the last few hours of my life," I murmur. "It seems like such a waste to blow them on sleep."

I look up to see Erg smiling and puckering her ruby lips. She doesn't have lungs, she *can't* have lungs, but somehow I feel soft billows of her breath caressing my forehead anyway. "How 'bout if I blow you *through* sleep and out the other side? And dreaming is never a waste, anyway. It's being awake that's the riddle."

The funny thing is that her exhalations do seem to catch something in my head and send it sailing. My lids slide down and I feel as if stars whose beams end in gluey curling tentacles are climbing up my eyelashes. . . .

I don't know how it happened but I'm standing back in the parking lot, and BY's is nowhere to be seen. Nothing much is to be seen, really. The parking lot is still surrounded by buildings, but now all of them are black and fused so closely together that they might be one multifaceted block of glass, or some glossy geological upheaval. It's hard to get a handle on them, but I can make out enough to know that there's no way through. Those buildings are too slick for anyone to climb them; you'd have to fly. I wonder what Erg meant by it: *You couldn't have gotten away, Vassa. Even if you thought for a second that you were getting out.* I know I'm dreaming, but I can't escape the feeling that this is the true landscape, revealed to me by sleep and gleaming like black diamonds.

I hear the buzz, huge, like a blimp stuffed with agitated flies, and the motorcyclist rushes by. I can see him better than I did before, or maybe it's just that I understand more now. That rumbling is coming from the bike's core, sure, but also from the rider's chest and throat. And he isn't revving but moaning, or maybe even crying, in his deep motorized voice. What I'd thought before was a tight black outfit of polished leather now appears to be his flesh and it grows indistinguishably into his machine: man and bike, it's all one complex mass of shiny black musculature. His thighs and hips blend into the chassis.

His moaning seems so pitiful that I'm not afraid of him anymore. The next time his circuit sweeps near me I step directly into his path.

He stops. I don't know if he actually sees me, but he stops anyway. "Hi," I say. It's hard not to feel shy with that eyeless visor flashing back at me. "Um, can you tell me what's bothering you?"

He doesn't say anything. The mechanical engine-groan surges and falls in a rhythm like nervous breathing. The skin on his body is this inhuman ebony black, but the area around his mouth and chin and lower cheeks is ashy pale, his mouth squeezed shut and light pink. I'd like to lift his visor, but I'm afraid I might hurt him.

"It's under us," he rumbles.

"What is?"

"It's never gone. It's caught below us, hundreds and hundreds of miles below. But I can never touch it, Vassa."

I couldn't say why, but I'm not surprised to find that he knows me. I feel like I know him, too, even if I have no idea what he's talking about. "You can't touch . . . something important? Is that why you're sad?"

"No . . ." His pale mouth droops. "No, for me the sun is buried behind the Earth. Always. I know . . . it's there. But I shouldn't be here. Being here tears me apart."

There's something I'm not managing to understand. "Why don't you leave, then? Go home and get some sleep."

He laughs at me, a low choking snarl of a laugh. "You're speaking to me. I can hear you."

"Well, sure," I tell him. I'm starting to feel a little frustrated with him. I'm trying to help him, even after he almost ran me down earlier, and he's just babbling.

"Sleep is larger than any night. It's large enough to fill the mind. It's deeper than any night. So even the night can be lost inside it."

"Can't argue with that," I say, although I probably *could* argue if he made any freaking sense. "Look, if you'll tell me what the problem is . . ."

"Don't speak to me." Suddenly the dark is rumbling on all sides.

"What did I do?" Even though he's so angry, and with no real reason that I can see, I wish I could touch his face. Comfort him somehow. My hand is hovering in front of me and I suddenly notice that it's giving off a white-gold glow.

"You woke up." He makes it sound like an accusation.

It's true, though. I'm suddenly awake. My eyes open just enough to see my folded arms in their baggy olive-green sleeves and between them the garish orange formica of the counter. From close at hand comes a stubborn rustling noise, a stamp, a single giddy whoop.

I sit up, drowsy and bewildered, half my mind still trying to understand the motorcyclist in my dream and the other half watching Erg as she tussles with a ten-dollar bill, kicking it as it rears from its spot in the drawer. "Oh, really?" Erg squeaks, and jumps on it; it reminds me of somebody wrestling an alligator. "Oh, really, Mr. Tender?" It's flopping submissively under her feet as she tramples it. "Yeah, and stay there!"

"Erg?" I say. "What's going on?"

She looks up, all delirious grin and widened eyes. "What do you think? I'm a total badass, Vassa! I have taken care of what you regarded as a most *intractable* predicament. For you. To be nice. While you were being all consumed by fatalism. So, hah."

"You picked up the money," I translate wearily. "Um, great work, but it's not going to do us any good, Erg. Lottery's friends ran off with like half of it."

"They ran off with their feeble delusions, more like," Erg chirps. "With a big pile of coupons for stupid, they ran off. I hope they try to buy a shiny new car with that! And designer snailskin handbags! And a diamond-crusted pony!"

"Are you saying you got it back? Erg, they all went *running* out the door. Like seven of them. I know you're pretty fast, dollface, but there is seriously no possible way."

Erg stands in the cash drawer with her arms crossed, pouting at me. "Gosh, Vassa, I am just profoundly touched by the confidence you're expressing in me. Just *profoundly*. Perhaps I'm faster when I'm really *inspired*, like by wanting to save your life or some trivial concern like that?"

Erg has to be kidding herself, but there's no point in arguing with her. BY's spins, slowly now, and the mausoleums on the hill prance by like carousel horses, always galloping but never getting anywhere but dead. Maybe there's a violet-blue fuzz of impending morning at the bottom of the reddish sky. How long have I been asleep?

There's the soft click of a doorknob turning. Erg leaps from the drawer and throws herself up my sleeve. I slap the register shut just as Babs comes shuffling out in a fluffy lilac bathrobe. She just stands looking at me for a while with her waxy white-out eye, wheezing faintly. I could swear she's disappointed.

"Morning, Babs," I say, a little roughly. My heart is drumming at the sight of her—it won't be long, now—but I'd just as soon not give her the satisfaction of seeing me cringe.

"You're here," she mutters. "You're still here. The empurpled little vixen who did so much to distress my darling employees last night. I thought you'd be long gone."

I shrug. "It's a job. Did you sleep okay?"

Looking at her for too long still disturbs the daylights out of me; that milky eye seems like the white cue ball on a pool table pursuing me, slamming around in an intricate pattern of angles but always closing in.

"Not so well," she hisses. "Someone was dreaming out of turn. No consideration for her elders. Terrible racket."

"Sorry to hear that?" I suggest, but I don't sound especially sincere. "Is my shift over? I'd like to get home."

Her eyebrows shoot up. "Home? Home for the likes of you? Should I set out saucers of my blood for the mosquitoes as well? Whelp rats for the stray cats to eat? You can consider yourself privileged to stay here. This is home enough until your term of service ends, you half girl with your false name."

"Vassa Lisa Lowenstein," I snap. "Actually. It's real enough for me."

"So it is," Babs says, and she definitely means it as an insult. "Step aside, please. There's the balance to tally before anyone can hope to rest."

You mean in peace? I think, but I don't say it. I walk over to the windows while Erg wriggles her way to my shoulder and Babs slumps down at the register. Pops the drawer and starts counting horribly slowly. Below me the parking lot glitters, inviting me to jump and break my neck. It's a better option than letting Babs win, isn't it? At least this way I'll be in control, choosing my own destiny instead of just being played. I inch closer to the door, and it spreads itself wide and waits. For an inanimate object it's a real gentleman. Maybe it will help me off with my jacket, too, before I splatter.

Something wavers in the corner of my eye and I glance over my shoulder. The hands are perched stiffly upright on the display of detergent that I smacked into last night, bouncing a little with barely repressed excitement. One of them curls its fingers and makes a sweeping motion to urge me toward the open door just a foot away.

I step back, blood rushing through my head like a sudden wind.

If the hands were so sure I was in for extermination, I know— I'm absolutely certain—they would want to do the honors them- selves.

Babs is hunched over, licking her fingers and counting. She stops, snorts like a horse, and flicks her pallid eye at me. It seems to roll across the air, circle me, and then sweep back to its owner. Her upper lip hikes over yellow teeth and she lets out a stream of furi- ous muttering, then starts the count again.

Erg nudges my nape and gives me a tiny bite. She couldn't actu- ally have pulled this off, could she? But Babs's face is contorting with rage as she counts under her breath, almost spitting once she reaches the total, and I realize that I'm smiling so wide my face hurts. "Babs?" I say. "Everything okay? We've got no issues, right?"

"Issues," Babs says. Suddenly she's staring hard. "Issues, Vassa? We may well have them, even if I'm not yet aware of their precise character."

I pretend that I'm scratching my neck so I can curl my hand over Erg. "The balance? It's all good?"

"A nubbin of advice for you, impling. It's unwise to bring up terms like *good* or *bad, right* or *wrong,* in my store. As long as you're here the meaning of such words is entirely mine to determine, and you might not care for the definitions. But yes, the total is correct. A better sense of the numbers than I might have expected. Correct." She delivers the last word like a whip crack. She manages a tortured smile. "I'm *pleased* with your performance."

It takes all my self control not to burst out laughing in hysterical relief. Once we get out of here Erg is getting a giant hot fudge sundae all to herself. "Thanks, Babs! So if I have to stay here, where's my room?"

"Not yet," Babs says, as if a place to sleep was located in time instead of space. "I have to . . . take care of . . ." She's completely lost interest in me, her gaze about as focused as spilled syrup now. She looks off but I can hear her stamping out a complicated rhythm on the floor. It has to be important so I do my best to memorize it, repeating it again and again in my brain.

I was right, the stamping was a signal: the store starts kneeling and the cemetery on the hill goes climbing up the sky as we drop. We touch down, the door's lip scraping the pavement, and Babs shambles lethargically out into the parking lot. I watch her teeter across the sparkling emptiness, the field of illumination from the picture window sweeping over her mangy moon of a scalp while the heads of her victims gawk down at her, probably wondering why they're stuck up there in the sky. Her trailing sleeves flap like the wings of a creature too sick to get airborne.

The motorcyclist stops and Babs goes up to him, wrapping his face in both her bony hands. It seriously looks like she's pinching his cheek, like she thinks he's some enormous muscle-bound toddler. Whatever she does must unbalance him, though, because his motorcycle starts tipping sideways, and then he's falling.

And falling. Impossibly slowly. How can a huge man on a huge slab of steel fall in that soporific way, as gently as a planet turning? It makes me a little dizzy and I look away for a moment, then when I raise my eyes again he's gone. Completely vanished, though it seems impossible that he could have righted himself and sped off in that flash of an instant. Babs stands alone in the parking lot, waving her arms up and down. The first fans of dawn outline her lilac bathrobe in shaggy glow. For a long moment she just kind of hovers there, looking at the crimson fissure opening along the base of the sky. She turns and starts her slow waddle back to me. It seems to take forever, but I wait for her and so does the store.

"There now," Babs says, probably to herself, as she enters. It seems like she's forgotten all about me.

"That guy on the bike," I say. "He's a security guard?"

Babs turns my way very gradually and looks at me as if I was a talking coatrack. "Yes," she hisses and curls a smug smile. "Yes, that's right. Security guard."

I already guessed that's not what he is, but I wanted to see her reaction. "So you sent him home? Because he's just like a night watchman?"

"Night watchman," Babs muses. "A man who watches night by profession. Yes, imp, that's what he is. No need for him now that it's morning. He wouldn't know how to fix his pupil to a day anyway. Not trained for that. That requires advanced degrees."

"I guess he has to sleep sometime," I say.

Babs leers like she's just played some incredible practical joke and pushes past me. "Ah, impling. Such insight you have! It's downright scintillating. Here, now, you can sleep, too, until the night comes around again. In the back."

I follow her. She moves so sluggishly that I have plenty of time to pick out food for Erg and me. I'm famished. By the time we get to the back of the store my arms balance a jumble of packages, mostly junk, but then that's what there is. There's another narrow door I somehow missed earlier wedged between two of the tall refrigerators on the back wall, and Babs shoves it open. I step through.

Inside it's more a closet than a room, with buckets and mops and a grayish cot. A thick stench evocative of pickled dust and mummified hedgehogs. At the back a screen made of old newspapers half-conceals a grubby sink and a toilet with a cracked seat. The main thing that attracts me about this room is that it has a real door. I'm hoping it can keep those hands out. I'm sick of never knowing where they are, or when they're watching me. "Thanks, Babs. This is terrific!"

"Good night," Babs mutters even though it's morning, and then I'm finally alone. I sit on the cot and drop my packages, then grab the doorknob and jiggle it; the door seems to be securely latched, but of course there's no lock. Erg grabs the cord dangling from my hood and swings down onto my lap.

"You look sad," she observes, sitting on my thigh. "I thought stumping her like that would make you *happy*."

"I'm just thinking . . . there's no way to tell Chelsea, Erg. That I'm alive. She'll feel . . ."

"Oh, she's feeling *terrible*," Erg agrees enthusiastically. "Miserable! She couldn't sleep at all. But, hey, Vassa? About the alive part?"

"You were amazing, dollface. You were completely great. I still have *no* idea how you were able to do that. I was so sure it was all over for me. Okay?" I'm pretty sure that's what she wants, to be slathered in my praise. It must make a nice change from always complimenting herself.

"Told you!" Erg crows. "Fast and faster! And oh my gosh, Felice's *face* when she realized all that money vanished from her *bra*—she looked like a plate of splatted spaghetti, Vassa! With meatball eyes! Tomin made fun of her for like an hour."

Again there's that weird habit Erg has, talking as if she can watch people even when they're far away, but since she has a freak-ish tendency to be absolutely right I don't argue.

I'm still confused, though. "But what about the money that blew out the door? It was flying all over the parking lot, Erg. I still can't understand how you . . ."

"Well." She looks away. "Maybe I had a little help. Which hardly detracts from my personal valor in this matter. So perhaps it would be tactful for you to change the subject?"

"Help?" I ask. It's baffling. Erg never speaks to anyone but me. "What are you talking about?"

"I see you snagged those lagoon-flavored toaster tarts! Good call! I'm eager to experience their briny goodness."

"Erg . . ." But it's no use. She's clambered down onto the cot, already prodding at the cardboard.

"You have to open it for me, Vassa. May I please have my nutri-tious breakfast now?"

I give up on getting any information out of her and open the box and then the inner foil pack, taking one aqua-frosted tart for myself and setting another on the mattress. The pastry pops between my teeth like sugared seaweed. Erg is busy chomping away, and I lean against the wall and think about my dream. I know I should hate the motorcyclist—for chasing me back into BY's, for working for someone who obviously wants me dead. I know my dream was just a dream, and it would be completely inane for me to believe that I was actually talking to him and not just to some figment, some scattered detritus blasted up from my unconscious. I'm not a total idiot, and I really do know all that.

But I catch myself hoping that he was the one who helped Erg, and by extension me—that he wanted to look out for me. It would be hard to imagine a dumber hope, but there it is.

Chelsea once said that having a dad as callous, as self-obsessed, and as evasive as mine was has left me with some unconstructive ideas

of what constitutes acceptable behavior. She said it warped my judgment. Kept me from realizing when people are just plain screwed
up. So maybe that's all this is. I mean, the motorcyclist doesn't even
talk, so it's unlikely that he has much emotional investment in my
survival.

To be more precise, he doesn't talk while I'm awake. Which leads
me to the next ludicrous hope that I observe in myself, in my sneaky
reality-warping brain: that I can fall asleep soon and dream of him
again. Continue our conversation.

I deserve a good smack in the face. Something to bring me to my
senses.

INTERLUDE IN FUR

It wasn't working out. That was clear to him, but he couldn't have said what *it* was exactly. He was still handsome enough to get his way much of the time, and if there was a noticeable erosion in the scope of what he could get away with it wasn't yet all that bad. He believed that he loved his wife—as much as she could reasonably expect, anyway. She wasn't always reasonable, though. She wasn't going to deal well with his plans when he told her about them, and if he weren't such a fundamentally honorable man, he would just disappear without telling her a damn thing.

As he stepped out of the old furrier's shop to the chiming of electric bells he congratulated himself on his courage and decency. The furrier, anticipating that his client might find things unpleasant at home, had offered to let him sleep on the sofa in back. He didn't need to see Iliana at all.

He'd just handed most of his savings over, in cash, to the furrier, pressing the bills into the man's wrinkled claw. It was a not entirely human-looking hand, and he'd noticed as well that the furrier's feet were on backward, toes flapping behind him in split shoes when he walked. He'd met a few such people before, in Zinaida's company—her family had connections with them stretching back to their days in the *old country*—and if they made him squeamish, well, he had to concede that they usually knew what they were doing.

Good people, Zinaida had called these disquieting friends, with the sideways smile she reserved for speaking of them. *True gentry, persons of quality.* In that case he couldn't understand why they were so seedy and had such dubious personal hygiene and always lived in the most wretched corners of the city. *After the revolution they either didn't fit in, or they fit much too well, if you know what I'm saying.* He didn't. Smile and nod and try not to inhale. *Even some of the witches had to emigrate. It was my great-grandparents who helped my god-mother Bea get out.* Whatever he was, the furrier was happy enough to pinch the stack of hundreds between his streaked brown nails, to curl one talon in a repetitive, scratching caress. Roland Lowenstein winced and reminded himself that money would be no use to him in his new life.

The cash was a deposit on services not yet rendered; it would pay for the preparations, for the well-oiled, supple, and glossy hide, for the *very special* thread that would be used to stitch it shut. For that kind of money he expected a luxuriant coat and sharp, pearlescent claws, clean fangs, and a healthy, lolling tongue.

He felt just guilty enough to stop on the way home and buy Chinese takeout for his wife and the girls. He ordered extra egg rolls for the two younger ones, whom he thought of as *the twins* even though they had different mothers and looked nothing alike. They were twinned in his mind largely by the fact that they were both unwelcome accidents, foisted on him by chance at just the same time. The oldest girl was not technically his concern—not even his daughter—but he bought her dinner, too. And then he walked up the stairs to their apartment, feeling intense gratitude at the realization that it was for the last time, and smiled brightly at the pale one, Vassa, who furtively slipped something into her pocket.

"Suppertime, sweet pea!" He didn't actually think she was sweet.

A morose little sprite of eleven who was taking far too long to adjust to her new home and circumstances, and that annoyed Iliana, and Iliana's annoyance looped back around and annoyed him. What was anyone supposed to do with a child like that?

And after they'd all eaten and Stephanie had gone off to play video games and Vassa and Chelsea had formed discrete jumbles on the living room floor with their colored pencils and textbooks, he caught Iliana's hand and held her at the kitchen table. He hoped she would understand the force of the revelation that he'd been privileged to receive, the overpowering exigency of acting on it, but he was aware, of course, that she might respond selfishly. He explained matters gently, nobly. Now that his own father was gone, he'd come to understand that he'd never really had the old man's love. He'd come to understand that there was only one thing he could do to redress that tragedy, to heal his own long-wounded heart.

"You are telling me," Iliana shrieked, "that you'd rather be a dog than a man? A dog. Roland, a *dog*. Tell me that is not what you're saying."

Since there was no door separating the kitchen from the living room, Chelsea and Vassa had stopped their reading and drawing to sit up and listen. Vassa just looked stunned, but Chelsea was already leveling a gaze of solemn reproach in his direction—and Chelsea wasn't even his daughter, so it was really no business of hers.

"I tried so hard to win my father's love," Roland Lowenstein explained. "I did everything I could think of to impress him, Iliana, and it was *never* enough. It's only now that I finally understand why. There was only one creature he truly loved, and it was never me."

For a moment he pictured it again: his father roughhousing with Posey, the family's German shepherd, while he and his sister waited for the old man to finally notice their wistful stares.

"Your father is dead!" Iliana yelled. "Cold in the dirt! He's not going to love you no matter what kind of dog you are!"

"This is just something I have to do," Roland said quietly. "I have to try to earn his love *posthumously*. If I do nothing else in this life . . ."

"You've done nothing else is right! And now you're going to be sewed into a *dogskin* to make sure you *never* do anything!"

It wasn't working out, he thought. When he was younger everyone had taken it for granted that he would do things, and that those things would of course be magnificent; he'd simply never figured out which marvels he should choose to accomplish. And then time had flowed by, stranding him in this grubby apartment. Now Vassa had turned into a ball of trembling black hair and silent tears and Chelsea looked like a censorious owl, all wide indignant eyes.

"I hoped you would be happy for me," Roland said. "Maybe that was too much to expect, but I hoped you would see beyond these narrow concerns and grasp what's *really* at stake here. Iliana, my whole life has been devoured by longing. . . ."

"Narrow concerns?" she snapped. "You mean your daughters?"

"They're your daughters, too," he explained.

"Oh, *all* of them? Is that what you think? They're all *Iliana's* now, so no more problem of mine, that's what you tell yourself?"

There was a hint of a threat implied by that. He would have preferred not to notice, but after a moment he couldn't help responding. "Well, you wouldn't throw Vassa out now! You *are* her stepmother, Iliana."

"Why *wouldn't* I?" Iliana demanded. "You think her mother was my dear friend, that I would cherish Vassa for the sake of her memory after you run out? You do this to me and the foster-care people can take her."

He would have preferred if Vassa hadn't been right there listening to this, but at least Iliana's speech had one positive effect. Chelsea stood up—she was ungodly tall and brawny for a girl not yet thirteen, nothing like his own lithe and maidenly daughters—and her terrible stare swung from him to her mother. "No," Chelsea said firmly. "No, Mom."

"Vassa's mother never behaved maliciously toward you, Ili," Roland said. "Why *wouldn't* it be a bond between the two of you, that you both loved the same man? But if you can't see it that way, then you should blame me, not her."

"Oh, I *do* blame you," Iliana clarified. "Don't worry about that!"

"You've always been my earth, Iliana, but Zinaida was my sky. How could I choose?" He was pleased with the formulation; poetry could explain anything.

"You mean," Iliana translated, "she got you drunk at her crazy art parties, and I took care of you with the hangover afterward?"

It wasn't working out at *all*, but this was the last night he would have to endure in this particular life. Tomorrow he would begin again, with a new heaven and a new earth, and both heaven and earth would be made of fur. His life would become soft, enveloping, and dark, with no expectations of achievement and no petty hassles. A fur ocean would lap at a horizon of bright white fangs, and he'd pad soft-footed beyond the confines of the city. Every fresh scent he encountered would be as vast and hopeful as a new morning.

CHAPTER 6

There's a sickly electric blanket heaped on the cot, but nowhere to plug it in. The fibers are so thinned and clumped that the rippling white wires show through, looking like the ghosts of intestinal parasites. After I've eaten as much junk food as I can stand, sugar raking my mouth, I wad up my army jacket for a pillow and wrap myself in the blanket. A single dim light bulb smolders overhead, swinging gently with the rhythm of the dance, and I can't find any way to turn it off. It's so rare for Erg and me to have actual privacy, but now she doesn't have to stay hidden. She curls mewing around my jaw and rests her head on my cheek.

Something scuds at the door, the soft whicker of flesh on wood. I don't think it can get in, but I still find myself listening way too intensely to every scuff and thud, then to a series of stealthy hopping sounds. I picture a hand bouncing on the stump of its wrist, trying to leap high enough to grab the doorknob. I picture it inching under my blanket, the poke and dab of dry fingers, their sinuous crawl over my shoulder and down to my throat. Babs said there were rules, but I have a funny feeling that the hands might think that rules are made to be broken—just like people and their useless hearts.

"Sinister!" Babs calls. The walls must be awfully thin because I can hear her voice in all its crackling detail; it makes me think of a radio transmission beamed from another planet. "Sin, get your misshapen pinkie over here! Dex and I are waiting! Did I hack you from that stale cadaver for nothing? Shall I sew you back on to it, then?"

A rapid thumping retreats from my door. I stifle a laugh. Babs sounds so much like a cranky mom screaming at her toddler on the subway. I must have been more anxious about the hands getting in than I'd thought, because now that I know they're occupied I start to relax and drift off. I see the shadow-forms of a world where the people are locked in place, stiffened into twisting immobile clouds, while the objects around them blur with savage activity. Chelsea stands in the middle of it all, her feet on a pedestrian overpass but her head ejected skyward and frozen far above. I know she can't move, can't say anything, but a single tear glides down her cheek.

"Vassa!" Erg whispers, and I jolt back into the musty mini-room, my eyes flying wide. "Vassa! I think you'll want to see what's going on. Except it's a terrible tragedy, so maybe you'll be sad."

Babs is yelling at someone. I'm afraid to listen. "Oh, God, Erg. Is she about to behead somebody?" The worst part of it is that I really ought to do something even though there's nothing I can do.

"Nope! Not that! It's auto-da-fé time here at the Babs-and-Grill. Toasty!"

"Erg? Want to use real words?" Though maybe I did understand her, just too well for comfort.

"Today her medium is fire, Vassa. This is one of those spicy-hot executions!"

I stare at Erg in utter disbelief; even for her this seems like some pretty phenomenal callousness. "And you're *joking* about that?"

"Why, it's not like she's burning *dolls,* Vassa! I don't see the need to observe a lot of prissy emotional niceties."

"Oh? Just people?" There are moments when I could hate myself for being so attached to Erg; sometimes our connection feels almost like a string of darkness winding through us both.

"Not even people! Jeez. Chill already. You know what you should do? Sneak really carefully and look for yourself." For a long moment I stay curled there, staring at Erg and listening to Babs's voice sawing intricate filigrees of abuse. She's saying *lazy, worthless*; she's saying *I asked you to do one thing, just one.*

Very cautiously I sit up and tug on my army jacket, pulling the sleeve wide for Erg, who scrambles in. Then I turn the doorknob so slowly that I nearly forget I'm moving at all. The door tips ajar, enough for me to skim through the gap. Luckily there's the bulky cooler right there. I press myself behind it and lean out until I can catch a glimpse of the counter.

Babs is sitting on it with her legs folded; I wouldn't have thought she had that kind of flexibility. She's turned partway toward the windows so that I'm looking at the side of her crinkled face. The hands are perched up on the register, obviously watching her. I'd like to think they're the ones who are about to get executed but I know that's too good to be true.

Babs arches one spindly arm high into the air. A ten-dollar bill dangles between her fingers, squirming like it's trying to get away. She regards it with a look of righteous disappointment. "You, too? You failed me, too? And I thought you showed leadership potential. A likely candidate for advancement. Drive her to despair, I asked; scatter to the winds, I clearly instructed. A small enough task, I'd have thought, but it was evidently too big for you. Well, now that you've proved your *worth* . . ."

Her other arm lifts up and I hear the click of a lighter. A single flame appears, muddy ocher against the rough daylight. It's only now that I notice there's already a small heap of ash by Babs's leg. The bill starts torquing desperately but it can't escape, and the flame is sailing closer, the movement so light and graceful that it looks disembodied. Up on the register the hands hobble and draw themselves into fists, then flash their fingers wide, trying to get Babs's attention. She ignores them, tenderly brushing the lighter across the bill's coiled belly. A little fringe of fire bristles up along one papery edge.

If the hands could scream, they would. I can feel it from here; they've gone tense with a frantic energy.

Then one of them leaps, high and wild, and tackles Babs's bony claw in midair, knocking the burning currency from her grasp. Babs lets out an unearthly shriek and smacks at it, but the hand has already landed on the counter with a splat and it's rolling itself back and forth on top of its little monetary friend to stifle the flames. Vile as those things are, I've got to give it credit: it's a brave thing to do, what with Babs lowering and glowering and coils of smoke stretching like black rubber up to the ceiling. There's no telling what she might decide to set fire to next.

"Justice!" Babs yowls. "Who are you to confound justice, Dexter? I decide what's proper and what's immoral here, and I determine suitable penalties! You might think of how that will apply to *you*."

The hand on the counter frisks and cringes apologetically, but it's still imposing itself between Babs and the flame-crisped bill. It bends in half and makes urgent scribbling motions with its forefinger on the counter, then stretches again. I know what it wants even if Babs doesn't, and my heart goes cold.

It's the one with the bite mark on its thumb. It knows about Erg. It probably knows that she stopped the money from getting away. And it can't speak, but for all I know it's perfectly capable of expressing itself through writing. If Babs gives it a pen, that is.

Erg is made of wood.

Babs stares down at the hand's capering. It's scribbling again. "Drat you," she mutters. "What nonsense is this?"

It hops on its wrist. Up on the register the other hand, Sinister I guess, makes a sweeping bow and points toward the window.

"Indeed," Babs says. "I fully expected that half the bills in this register would effect their escape into the beyond. Imagine my chagrin at their faintheartedness."

Sin hops down next to Dex and nudges its mate, then rolls itself into a tight spiral fist. Dexter hesitates, then jitters with enthusiasm and imitates its gesture, its wrist angled up. Once they've squeezed themselves into two coils they press their knuckles together, spirals forming a unified flat surface, and propel themselves along the counter at startling speed.

I'm hopelessly confused. Babs figures it out before I do. "Him? Our servant in black?" she spits. Now I understand. The hands are mimicking a *motorcycle*. "What in the world did *he* have to do with the dismaying failures of my faithful employees?"

I'd like to ask the same question, but I might already know the answer. Sinister uncoils and pantomimes a series of actions: catching something in midair, shaking it, and bringing it back to someone. He *was* the help that Erg had, then? Babs has her mouth hanging open.

"He wouldn't dare," she rasps softly. "He wouldn't risk the consequences of defiance. Not for the sake of some half-named minx."

The hands bop up and down in a way that distinctly communicates, *Yeah, he would!*

I'm having trouble believing it, too, but the hands seem terribly emphatic and I guess they would know. I couldn't say how old the guy on the motorcycle is, but it's obvious enough that he isn't in high school. I've only seen the bottom half of his face, and that half could in no wise be classed as hot or handsome or even vaguely cute. He's downright scary-looking. He doesn't talk. He's monstrously inappropriate as a crush object. But for some reason all of these strike me as points in his favor. It's nice to have one reason that carries a hint of validity, now. *Look, the dude helped save my life! Seriously, what do you want?*

Babs jumps over the counter with incredible agility. Her teeth are bared and a spit-misted hiss comes fizzling through them.

Behind her one of the hands starts walking on two fingers, and I realize with a lump of nausea in my gut that it's imitating Erg. It's trying to tell Babs what they're up against, that Erg and the motorcyclist were acting in cahoots. But she isn't paying any attention anymore.

"*Did* he?" she snarls. "Did he really engage in such ill-considered behavior? Well, this will be a matter for discussion, won't it?" She goes storming off toward the door she slipped through earlier, presumably concealing another of these luxurious bed-and-broom closets.

From where I'm hiding the door is facing directly my way, so when Babs flings it open I get a momentary glimpse of what's behind. Whatever it is, it appears to be rather bigger than a breadbox. Or a closet, or a school bus, or maybe a blue whale.

Which makes no sense since BY's is a fairly small building, turning around and around on giant chicken legs. There's no place to put a palace-sized indeterminate cavern full of foreboding shadows and twinkling lights. I'm just absorbing this conundrum as Babs darts through and slams the door behind her. Whatever I saw is gone again.

The hands fling themselves down on that low pile of ashes, looking dejected, and I skim back into my tiny room, close the door, and think, since there's nothing else to do. What kind of person can the motorcyclist be, when he chased me back into BY's, then turned on a dime and started trying to protect me? I hope he won't be in too much trouble.

"Erg?" I say. She's still in my sleeve, one tiny wooden arm poking out through the hole. "Erg, why did he help us? Do you know?"

She doesn't answer, so I take my jacket off, trying to be gentle. She's fast asleep; her violet eyelids perfect crescents on her pale face. I bundle the fabric into a sloppy nest for her and lie down, tucking her in the crook of my arm. I guess she had a long night.

For a while I just lie there in the dirty-looking amber light, wondering about him. Babs called him her "servant," and I have the distinct impression that there's something genuinely strange going on. When he vanished earlier, where did he go? For some reason I have the feeling that he isn't far away, but I can't quite picture him living in one of those lumpy apartment buildings crowding the Brooklyn streets.

At some point I must fall asleep, and when I wake up and peer through my door it looks like the end of the afternoon. And it's snowing.

CHAPTER 7

There are places where heavy snow in April wouldn't be totally crazy, but we're not in Siberia here. The white rush of it streams through my eyes like windborne vertigo, and I suddenly have an awful sense that it might be only nominally spring. I start to wonder if we lost our summer completely, drowned it in one of those merciless nights, and now we've emerged under a slate gray sky where autumn is failing and winter is already pressing in. I'm more frightened by this blizzard, if I'm honest, than by anything that's happened so far. Brooklyn, poor Brooklyn, you're under enchantment all right, and it's cold and dark and disquieting.

Soon it will be night. I shut the door again and feed myself and Erg as best I can. I guess there's no chance of a shower so I sponge off at the sink with a wad of soapy paper towels, air-dry for a while, and then wriggle, still damp, back into my clothes. If I'm lucky, maybe I'll find a toothbrush.

"Vassa?" Erg chirps. I sit down next to her and pet her head. She seems subdued, by her inflated standards of exuberance anyway. "Chelsea is out in the parking lot. You could go wave hi to her? Through the window?"

I've jumped up before she's finished talking. "Are you kidding?

I'm going to go out there and tell her . . . apologize for being such an idiot, I guess."

"I don't want you going outside," Erg says fretfully. "Don't do it."

"Why shouldn't I?" I usually take Erg's advice—she's right more often than makes any rational sense—but I can't miss a chance to see Chelsea. I owe her so many apologies that I don't know where to start.

"Well . . . Okay, how about that it's snowing?"

"I like the snow," I say, a little petulantly, even though Erg probably knows that this snowfall is creeping me the hell out. It feels toxic and invasive; even its brittle whiteness comes across as unnatural. "It's pretty."

"You don't have a hat. Or mittens."

I stare at her. She's still sitting on the bed, hunched over, with her lips drawn into a duckbill of stubbornness. "You are being ridiculous, Erg, really? It's not like I'm going trekking in Antarctica."

"And your shift is about to start. It's almost evening."

I squirm into my jacket and offer her the sleeve. "You coming? We have to get out there before Chelsea gives up!"

Erg gives me a sullen look, but after a moment she jumps in. I pull my hood up and dash out of my room, then around the shelves toward the front of the store. Babs is slumped at the register, her face crunched and sour, the hands standing palm-forward on her shoulders like flabby twin hybrids of parrot and earthworm. I don't care what she thinks and I'm already stamping out the code on the floor. Her mouth puckers with something that might be interest or, worse, amusement. "And what would you be doing?"

"It isn't my shift yet," I snap. "You said three nights." I must have gotten the pattern right because the store is already kneeling.

"And how do you propose to extricate the days from between

them, Miss Imp? The days might be the bones running through a darker body."

"I'm just going out to the parking lot." I wish I didn't sound so defensive. "I'll be right back."

Babs smiles, her lips like crumpling paper, her white eye racing and rebounding. "Oh, enjoy your scamper. Go brisk, go far. Take wing in the snow."

The right hand, Dexter I guess, waves an unpleasantly cheerful goodbye as I walk out the door. The bite on its thumb looks a bit inflamed, like it might be getting infected.

The snow is neon orange where it reflects BY's tangerine glow, then twilight blue farther out with blocky crisscrossing shadows layered around the lot's margins. The winking of a traffic light on the corner shifts the shadows to crimson, then to electric green, and the skewered heads look worried. I don't see Chelsea anywhere but there is an isolated trail of footprints welling with indigo darkness, and I follow it. The snow is at least six inches deep already and coming in fast, pirouetting like a ballerina blown to atoms but still doing her best to play her part. *The show must go on.*

"Chelsea?" I call. The footprints run in scallops, stopping in front of each pole. God, she's been checking heads. "Chels, it's me! Where are you?" I'm starting to wonder if she's going around and around, always just ahead of me, always hidden in the huge cubic shadow BY's drops onto the snow. Then I see her standing under the last pole, the empty one. "Chelsea!"

In her thick-heeled boots she's over six feet of solid muscle, a bulky silhouette against the tent of glow spread by a streetlamp. As she turns there's a quick disruption, something like a blade passing over my vision, and suddenly I'm looking at him. What I thought was Chelsea's fantastic mound of curls turns into a huge protuberant helmet; what I thought was her brilliant smile becomes an uncanny gray-white chin. He's straddling his motorcycle as he holds up a hand in the universal gesture: *Go no farther.* I stop dead and my knees waver.

"Vassa!" Chelsea screams, and then it's her again, really her, bounding toward me. "Vassa, I don't know whether I should hug you first, or slap you senseless! If you *ever* scare me like this again, I swear . . ."

I race to throw my arms around her and she grabs me. I'm tall, too, but not like her, and I lean my head on her down-jacketed shoulder. "I know, I know, it was the dumbest thing anybody's ever done, Chels. Just imagine all the apologies you want, okay? Because I totally mean them."

"You came here for *what?* Just to show Stephanie you could go five minutes without stealing?"

"More like . . ." It's too embarrassing to admit, but I do. "More like if she wanted me dead that bad, I thought she should live with the consequences."

"Oh, so you were *trying* to get beheaded? Just so your death would be *in her face?* Okay, I'm not sure I can imagine any apologies I would consider adequate, but I'll try." She holds me back and shakes me a little. "And once I'm done with that, there's the small issue of your *staying* here this long. Were you trying to trick us into thinking you'd been killed?"

"No . . ." I say. I'm just getting my first hint of how impossible explaining is going to be. "I wanted to call you. My phone isn't working."

"This is so obvious I can barely stand to say it, Vassa. But then, uh, why didn't you just *come home?*"

"I . . ." There are certain areas of human existence that are susceptible to nice clear explanations, and then there are the shadow-zones beyond where words just won't measure up. Chelsea's still hugging me, but she's in one realm and I'm in another. "I'm working here. For a few days. I can't leave."

She reacts to this more or less the way Tomin and company did: flabbergasted, jaw dropped, forehead wrinkled. "You know what? You're most certainly leaving now. When we get home I will wallop you with a pillow and then make you cocoa, okay? And you can tell me all about how you'll never do anything so messed up again."

"I can't, Chelsea." I wish I could offer her a sensible justification for this, but there isn't one: just Babs's smirk as she told me to *go far,* that queasy, chipper wave goodbye from Dexter, and one outright hallucination that seemed like it was warning me not to leave the ring of heads. That's all I've got, and every speck of it would sound fresh-minted from the mental ward. "I . . . promised the owner here I'd help out. For three nights. And I'm not allowed to go home between shifts."

The expression on Chelsea's face is not improving.

The snow is falling more densely now, broad-winged avalanches of white plunging from the sky. In places it's so thick that it starts to seem like it's clotting into bodies, long-necked and ruffling.

"You know Iliana can't really cope with you," Chelsea says. Ominously reasonable. "She has too much on her plate. And for all intents and purposes you don't have parents."

"Sure," I say.

"So that leaves me. I could give a damn if you're only fifteen months younger than me, okay? I'm responsible for you, and if you act like you need some heavy-duty guidance I'm sure as hell going to provide it. As in, do I have to *carry* you, Vassa?"

I don't know whether to be grateful that she cares enough to bother or scared out of my wits. "Chels, I really, really need you to trust me on this. If I try to leave . . ."

"What?" She has what people call doe eyes, round and brown and limpid, but the look in them now reads more wolf. "What do you think will happen?"

"I don't actually know. But it won't be good."

Beside me a billow of snow stretches its wings and cranes its head to look at me. Its pupils are black and smart. I glance around and realize that there are *swans* standing everywhere, camouflaged by snow but staring our way. Like they're dying to know what's going to happen.

Chelsea snorts with disbelief, clamps an arm around my shoulder, and starts hustling me toward the street. "Tomorrow you can send the owner a note explaining. Say that you're terribly sorry but your family refuses to let you work for a serial killer. Blame me if you want. *Oh, my sister's so overprotective! She just wouldn't listen when I told her dismembering people doesn't bother me!*"

I try to pull away, but she's too strong. "I can't, Chelsea! I'm serious."

"I'm here," Chelsea says, "to illustrate the concept of *serious* for you. 'Cause I think it's not entirely clear to you what it means."

We're almost at the line of rotting heads. I glance back and see a flock of swans following us, their black feet flapping in the uneasy sparkle of the snow. "Chelsea?" I say. "Look behind us. There's something really not right going on."

"I'm not sure the message is getting through, Vassa. I'm worried about your suicidal tendencies. Indulging your delusions is low on my to-do list."

We've reached the border. A sharp streak of shadow falls from the nearest pole like a threat. I know for certain that I must not cross it. *"Take wing in the snow,"* Babs said. *"Take wing."*

Chelsea jerks me and at the same instant I twist sideways, spinning myself from her grasp. Her momentum sends her forward while I teeter, legs skidding apart in the slippery-wet mess of slush, and fall facedown with my arms splayed. There's a distinct tingle in my right foot. When I push up on my elbows and look, I see the band of shadow wrapping my boot as high as the ankle. I yank my foot close. My boot suddenly feels strange, constricting.

"Vassa?" Chelsea calls from just outside the circle. She looks more distraught than angry. "What is going *on* with you?"

I might take off my boot to show her, except that I can't bear to know the truth myself. "I don't want to upset you, Chelsea. Really. It means a lot to me that you came here, but I can't leave . . . until the time is up. *Please* understand."

She looks at me. And then she turns to look at someone else.

The motorcyclist is three feet away astride his bike, face obliterated by that jet visor. Apparently waiting for something, because he's not moving.

Chelsea looks alarmed. I can't blame her. He makes for an appalling spectacle.

"It's okay," I tell her. "He's been looking out for me."

She nods and straightens herself. Chelsea has a knack for dignity and she does her best at it now, extending a hand to shake. "Hello. I'm Vassa's sister, Chelsea Pascal. Do you work here, too?"

He doesn't react. I scramble to my feet, the right one cramping oddly as I put my weight on it. "He . . . has trouble talking. But he's a good guy. He works as a night watchman here, and he's been really nice."

Chelsea shoots me a look, which conveys her belief that a giant, frightening man in skintight leather might possibly have questionable motives for being nice to me. I take a stab at making the situation seem, if not normal, then anyway slightly less bizarre.

"There are three of us girls in our family," I explain to the motorcyclist, "but we all have different last names. Lowenstein was my dad's last name, and then Stephanie has her mom's name, Salvatore. It tends to confuse people who are meeting us for the first time."

Chelsea isn't playing along. "Vassa . . ." she says. She tips a significant glance toward the motorcyclist, then raises her eyebrows in a worried question. *Has he been threatening to hurt you, if you leave?*

Is that *the problem?* "Are you seriously determined to stay here? Because you don't have to."

"I do," I tell her. My foot twinges and my toes feel horribly bunched. "It's, like, a point of honor. Just for two more nights, though, and then I *swear* I'm coming home."

She won't try to force me again. I know that now. All the furious determination has drained out of her and she's left with aching sadness. "I wish you'd come now. I hate this place, Vassa. We're in the presence of something—"

Evil, I think. *Powerful. And enchanted.* Leave it to Chelsea to be very clearheaded about what we're dealing with: there's magic here, sure, but it's deeper and wilder than you'd ever imagine from a safe distance. Once you step into this parking lot the order of the world goes completely out of whack and everyday logic turns into something dark and volatile. And Chelsea didn't get to be a math and chess whiz by tolerating illogic.

"Don't worry," I tell her. "I'll be fine." She looks at me, and I look at her. I'd like to hug her goodbye, but I know I can't cross outside the circle marked by the poles, and I think she's scared to step inside it again. With extremely good reason, of course. After another long moment she raises her hand, wry and sorrowful, and walks away.

The sky has slipped all the way to dark now. It must be time for my shift, and I know I should head back to the store. Instead I look at the motorcyclist. I look at the snow behind his bike. As I'd pretty much expected there are no tracks.

"Hi," I say quietly. "I wanted to thank you. For helping me last night."

I'm half-hoping he'll finally talk to me, but he doesn't. Everything has been so strange that it's making me lose my grip on reality. There's a part of me which is convinced that my dream of him was absolutely true, that we really talked, that his motorcycle is actually joined to his body. But now that I'm looking at him again what I see is a basically regular, oversized guy, dressed in black leather, sitting on a regular bike. Of course that's a leather suit, thick leather gloves, and not his own personal skin. What was I thinking?

He's just inside the circle of the heads, so I walk up to him. He doesn't react at all. Right behind me I can hear the bustle of the swans, following me like the train on a long, snowy dress.

"Can you even hear me?" I ask. "I'd like to talk to you. Look, the hands told Babs what you did for me. I'm afraid you might be in trouble."

No response. Snow is piling like a huge eggshell on his tuberous helmet. Frost-webs pattern his visor. I raise my hand to wipe it clear.

He lets out an awful, rumbling groan—the first sound I've heard from him, but so *much* like his voice was in my dream—and I flinch back. The swans shuffle restlessly, and I hear slow, snow-muted footsteps padding closer. I turn to see Babs only a few yards away, coatless and with crystals clustering on her dress and hair; it's a different dress today, a summery blue gingham, but she doesn't seem cold. Now that she knows I'm watching her all the agility I saw before is gone, and she's reverted to her old interminable waddle. "Impling," she says, shaking her head. "What a mess you've made."

"What are you talking about?" I ask. And then I see the crimson spatter all over the snow. Dark abstract blotches follow in my footsteps. I can't understand it until I look at the swans huddling together like a feathery iceberg. They're bleeding, all of them are bleeding, but it doesn't look like there are any specific wounds. Ruby droplets weep from their feathers everywhere I can see and rain down, pocking the snow with red holes and then wicking outward into sparkling cherries. "What's *wrong* with them?" I almost scream it, and Babs chuckles a little.

"Such filthy birds," she says, and then grins. "Like rats with wings. You won't be working the register tonight, will you, imp? Dex and

Sin will handle that. For you there's all this muck to clean. How I hate dirty snow."

The swans twist their necks, scattering blood with every move, and I can't focus on what Babs is saying. "They're hurt! We have to . . ." *help them,* I want to say, but it seems absurd. It's as if every feather is a needle driving into their flesh.

"Naturally they're hurt. They thought they were about to have a new friend. A downy companion. They came to collect her. They prepared themselves. Then somehow their friend turned *back*. She betrayed them. Wounds such as that don't easily heal, do they?"

"You're blaming me for this?" I'd like to smack her. Her white orb rushes forward like it wants to knock me sky-high. The eye feels immense, an icy meteor swinging straight at my face, and I almost throw my arms up to protect myself. Every cell in my body urges me to buckle, to cringe, and then run stumbling away from here. Which is exactly what she wants, of course.

I can't manage to be completely brave. I flinch, and Babs leers. But at least I stand my ground.

The swans leap fluttering into the air, spraying wide fans of red across the snow, then settle again in a dense mass at my legs. They snake their necks around my waist and stroke me with their blood-streaked bills. Babs turns downright gleeful at my discomfiture, which is admittedly intense. "You'd best get started, then, hadn't you? I'll expect to see it all pristine and gleaming by morning."

"Fine," I say; it might be better than working that lunatic register. The air out here is fresh and free, even if I'm not. I can feel swan blood seeping through my clothes. "Got a shovel?"

"Now how would you clean snow with a shovel? Better a small brush . . . a speck of fluff from your friends here . . . a hair from your own head. *That's* the way it's done, my girl."

The meaning of this escapes me at first, because it's incomprehensibly crazy. Babs stands smiling patiently, but at least her rolling eye is minding its own business for now, sticking in her head like it ought to. Then I get it. "You're asking me to clean *individual* snow-flakes? One at a time?"

"Mind you don't break them. They can be fragile at the tips."

"You do know that's impossible." My voice has gone flat with disbelief.

"Oh? Then Sin and Dex can terminate your employment here right now. Would you care to step inside?"

I suppose I could freak out. Start screaming in hysterics. Erg saved me before, but this is beyond insane. If I'm doomed, though, then I might as well crack up as stylishly as possible.

"Oh, I'll get it done," I hear myself saying insolently. "Is it okay if I take cleaning supplies and stuff from the store?" I look at the swans, still squeezing around me like pillows on legs. "Maybe some first-aid supplies?"

That catches Babs off guard, I can tell. "Certainly you may. Take whatever you need. Just so nothing leaves my parking lot."

"Great!" I say as cheerfully as I can manage. She's looking almost worried now and I have to admit I enjoy it, even if that makes me a bad person. "You'll tell Dex and Sin, then? Not to get all jumpy if I come in and collect a few things?"

"I'll tell them that you have permission to carry our things as far as the border." Babs hesitates, glowering, and opens her mouth to say something else, then lowers her eyes and bunches up her ashy lips.

"Yes?" I say. "Something on your mind?"

"*Everything* is on my mind," Babs retorts. "That's why your ilk is spared the burden of having anything at all in yours."

"And we do *so* appreciate that," I snap, but she's already dragging her feet through the blood-mottled snow. It takes me a moment to realize that she's not heading back to the store, but toward the motor-cyclist. He hasn't moved at all. I have a sick sense that, whatever is coming next, she wants to make sure I see it.

"Which came first," Babs hisses to him, "night or day? When the first eye cracked open the first egg what hatched from it, morning or evening?" He doesn't try to answer, but to be fair I wouldn't, either. She raises a bony hand and takes hold of his visor. "Shall I show you?"

From where I'm standing I can't really see his face, just a sliver at the side where Babs is holding him. She lifts his visor partway, still staring at him.

He gives an unbearable wail. It begins low and guttural then careens higher, turning shrill and frenzied. His right hand shoots for the sky in a gesture of appeal. I try to get to him, to help him somehow, but my legs are squeezed by swans and I stumble.

Babs lets him keep screaming for several long beats then lowers his visor; his howling fades into a whimper. His outstretched hand drops limp onto the handlebar. He's so big, so strong-looking; I can't understand why he would let her torment him.

"Remember," Babs growls, "you've already lost. But loss is, let us say, a process. Don't assume you're done." With a few deft motions she starts the bike's engine and the loud growl trembles across the dark. "Go!"

He goes. Obediently, weakly, he follows orders, his motorcycle accelerating into its familiar loop. Around and around. When he passes by again I have to fight the urge to pummel him with bloody snowballs. He could have flattened Babs with one swipe of his hand and instead he waited patiently while she tortured him.

Babs looks from him to me with leering satisfaction. "He doesn't enjoy that, does he? Well. I'll be off to bed, then, my imp. We'll speak again in the morning."

The blood has spread into wider blotches, near black against the snow's glimmer whenever the store has its windows averted then brightening into rosy outbursts as the light sweeps by. Babs is waddling away with her arms spread. As long as she was in front of me it was easy to act brazen and confident. I was so angry at her that all I wanted was for her to squirm, to doubt that she really had me cornered. But now that she's gone I'm left with nothing but blood-ribboned swans and breathless dread.

I feel the delicate slide of tiny lacquered hands climbing up my shoulder. There's no one around. "Erg?" I whisper. "What do I do now?"

"You get started," Erg says from under my jacket. Completely matter-of-fact. As calm as a bar of soap.

"The swans are still bleeding, though. Every time they move there's more blood spattering around. It's hopeless."

"Well, why don't you start there?" Erg suggests. "Poor swans. That's got to hurt, right?"

Start there, I think. *Here's your new calling. Go be a swan doctor.* Instead I wander over to that old cracked stump, moving carefully so I don't step on the swans' webbed feet, and collapse. They follow me in tight formation, my own private swan-cloud. I can feel tears crowding just behind my eyes, shoving to get out, while the swans bundle themselves around me in feathery heaps. They're warm and soft and I don't even mind the blood anymore because it's so comforting to have them pressing close. A long neck wraps like an arm around my shoulders and wing tips brush the tears from my eyes. My lips taste tart and metallic from the smears of their blood. I hug the white bodies nearest me, and then all the final scraps of my self-control flurry away and I'm crying so hard I can't breathe.

The motorcyclist whizzes around and around. Apparently the hands were lying about him helping me before because he sure doesn't seem to care now. He won't help me anymore than he helped himself when he stood there like an empty shell while Babs reduced him to squealing pain. He could be a robot programmed to be maximally pathetic.

It's his bland dull silence, I realize now, that let me dump all my fantasies onto him and pretend he was somehow interesting. As I cry I'm shaking and I don't know if my body is buffeted most by cold or fear or rage.

"Vassa?" Erg says. "I can see you're upset. But it's time to get up and do something."

I feel like pulling her out from under my clothes and flinging her across the street. "Really, Erg? You think I should start polishing snowflakes? I'll get right on that."

"Cool!" Erg trills excitedly. I guess her wood must be extra hard since it's clearly impervious to sarcasm. "I'll help! Though really you might want to take care of the swans first."

Right. Their feathers are still wrapped in curving rivulets of fresh blood. Just because they don't have voices it doesn't mean they aren't in pain. If this is really my last night and my last moments are jangling like coins in my pocket, then I might as well spend them on wishes. Throw those moments into the darkness always rising like the jets of a fountain and whisper, *I wish that all of us together in this night could stop hurting. I wish we'd finally cease to bleed.*

CHAPTER 8

When I get up the swans come with me, covering the snow in webbed prints and blurred red stars. An eddy of white wings swishes out and then squeezes close again with every step I take. With my baggy blood-blotched clothes and snarled purple hair I know I must look like an axe murderer, but the swans swirling at my feet make me feel more like a princess dropped from the moon.

As I approach the store it stops dancing and kneels down. I don't even have to sing the jingle. The privileges of being an employee, I guess.

"All right," I tell the swans, "you guys wait out here, okay? I'll be back in like two minutes."

They ruffle their feathers and stroke me with their bills, pressing closer. I get the impression that they're not keen on being left alone. They'll make a terrible mess in the store if they come in, though. "Really," I tell them. "I want to take good care of you. Just be a little bit patient and I'll come back as quick as I can. Please?"

The biggest of them stands as high as my waist even with its head tucked down. Now it steps back and stares into my eyes. It has a look of disquieting, distinctly unbirdly braininess, which tends to support my theory about these swans and also about what might have happened to my pinched right foot. After a moment it actually nods, human-style, and steps aside to let me through. The others look like they just can't believe it, but then they follow suit. "Thanks," I tell them softly, and walk through the wide-open door. They stretch their necks out to keep touching me for as long as they can.

The hands are on the counter. One of them, Dex I think, is giving the other a manicure. They've chosen a smoky-lilac iridescent polish this time. I liked the glitter better. It doesn't seem like they're paying attention as I turn down the second aisle; I have a vague sense that I noticed a first-aid section on a bottom shelf the first time I came in here. It takes a while to find—it's down the third aisle, not the second—but it's not as bad as looking for lightbulbs. Eventually I come across brown bottles of peroxide, and, tucked behind them, rolled gauze bandages in small red boxes. There are a lot of them, but no matter how many I load onto my arm I probably won't have enough. My flock might consist of a dozen birds, all scary big and spangled with wounds from head to tail.

I keep digging along the back of the shelf, finding more bandages. Once they're spilling out of my arm I start taking them out of the boxes and stringing the rolls on the cords dangling from my jacket. Then I grab a pack of paper towels, too, to try to mop the swans clean, and a candy bar for Erg, and head back to the door. The store has considerately stayed kneeling for me, which I appreciate. As I go the bandages start unspooling. White wispy streamers trail off me and tangle in my long hair. Dex and Sin are spread flat waiting for their enamel to dry, but as I walk by Dex can't resist clicking out a menacing staccato on the counter and then grabbing a loose twist of gauze. It unravels with a jerk and lands in an airy mess on the floor.

"You smudged your polish," I say, and step back into the night.

I'm finding the relentless darkness less oppressive than I used to. Night is beginning to feel like my own heart dissolved into a black solution, a tender medium holding me close. The swans flutter in greeting, more outflung blood speckling the snow, though at this point it hardly matters. Crimson spreads in plumes; it feathers into shapes like smaller scarlet birds as if everything the swans have ever lost will rise up and live again. If my survival depends on restoring the snow to papery blankness, I may as well get resigned. I still have the option of breaking the border and, I'm pretty sure, living as one of them, white and winged. We'll be a kind of family.

The flakes have stopped falling. The night is one thick mass of shadow only disturbed by the distant streetlamps and a few gleaming windows. I lead the swans back to the stump and take the nearest one into my arms, stroking the sleek white head to calm it. The peroxide is going to sting, but I don't want to risk the wounds getting infected.

Once I've moistened a paper towel I start dabbing as gently as I can. The swan I'm cradling bristles with discomfort and snaps at the air while its feathers streak a slowly paling pink.

"It's okay," I croon, "you'll be okay."

I'm not used to being this sweet, but right now I can't help it. Once the swan is reasonably clean I take a bandage and start wrapping, doing the wings separately so it won't feel trapped. Once the first bird looks well swaddled I move to the next. The motorcycle growls by like the hand of a clock with no time left to tell and I tend to the swans until I forget everything beyond white snow and white feathers, the cold stiffening my hands and the darkness surging above.

"Miss Yagg?" a brusque voice demands. The swans scatter in a panic and I look up, well beyond annoyed. Whoever he is he's wearing a beige suit, he has a long tapering snout, and his visible flesh is covered completely in pointy scales colored a nasty cockroach brown. Not human, obviously. But after everything that's happened I may have reached the point of terminal *whatever*, and I give the shocked recoil a pass.

"What are you thinking?" I snap. "You scared the swans!"

He doesn't take that up, just peers through small round glasses at a sheaf of papers bristling from a folder. "Miss *Babs* Yagg?"

"She's *asleep*," I snarl. "It's the middle of the night, or hadn't you noticed?" Maybe once he leaves the swans will come back to me; at least five of them still need their bandages.

He raises one clawed hand, or maybe more accurately paw, and taps a long conical nail against a plaque that hangs on a heavy chain around his neck. It's a large mahogany oval topped with a layer of brass, and on the brass is engraved:

PICNIC AND PANGOLIN
ATTORNEYS AT LARGE

"Night or never," he grumbles, "to me it's all *business* hours. *At large* encompasses even the most eldritch obscurities, does it not? *Large* takes it all in. So you can see that the dim hours, like all others, fall within my purview. I have a matter to bring to Miss Yagg's attention, if you'll be so kind as to fetch her?"

"Look," I try, "Mr. Picnic—"

"It's Pangolin."

"Mr. Pangolin—"

"Just *Pangolin*." He practically grinds out the words. "If you please."

I could swear there are more papers in the folder than there were a moment ago. The pile thrusts forward, and now a single page slinks free and flutters to the ground. "I'm sorry, Pangolin, but I'm not going to disturb Babs this late. If you'll tell me what this is about, though, I can give her a message."

He shuffles closer, his long tail gouging the snow, and leans in to snuffle at me. The end of his snout is moist and pinkish, and he examines me through his glasses with bright black eyes. "Am I to understand that you are currently in the employ of Miss Yagg?"

"Of course I am," I tell him curtly. "That's why I was bandaging her swans that you scared away."

He's shorter than me, maybe five feet tall. His nose traces an arc two inches from my shoulder, sniffing methodically. "And would you perhaps characterize yourself as a *trusted* employee?"

I'm getting curious, I admit. "Oh, I'd say Babs trusts me *absolutely*. She's even been encouraging me to open my own BY's franchise."

Pangolin's free paw jerks up and then starts scrabbling nervous circles in the air as if he was trying to burrow through it. "Oh! Dear girl, that would be most inadvisable! Don't consider it for an instant, please!" He snuffles again. "You smell too nice for such an unsavory business. And then the legal difficulties . . . you don't want any part of all that, I assure you!"

"Thank you for your advice," I say carefully. "What are the legal difficulties? Babs—Miss Yagg—she really wants me to open a store, so I'm not sure . . ."

"Don't listen to her," Pangolin snipes. He draws himself to his full height, such as it is, and sticks his snout in the air. "My partner Picnic and I are serving papers. A class action suit brought against the whole BY's chain on behalf of the denizens of . . ." He stops and shuffles his papers and they fall like tears, skating away on swirling currents in the air. "The denizens of Kings and Queens counties, Staten Island and the Bronx . . . Newark, Baltimore, and much of Pittsburgh . . . Detroit, certainly . . . There may be other districts implicated in this scandalous exploitation of circadian vulnerabilities as well, before the matter sorts itself out. Such an association would taint your prospects irreparably, I'm afraid."

"Circadian vulnerabilities?" I say. "Are you by any chance talking about how crazy the nights have been getting?"

Pangolin isn't looking at me anymore. His tail scrapes a fan in the snow as he turns to watch the motorcyclist in his endless loop. "And who would *that* ungentlemanly apparition be?"

"Him?" I say. "He's the night watchman. I'd introduce you, except he doesn't talk, so chatting with him is pretty unfulfilling." That's putting it mildly, of course.

"He looks coarse," Pangolin observes. "An ill-favored reprobate. Can you tell me his name?"

"I don't know it," I say. "So you're bringing a lawsuit against Babs because you think she has something to do with what's been happening to the nights around here?"

It sounds insane at first, but as I think it over I have to admit I wouldn't put it past her. I'm looking for the swans, and at last I spot them: they've formed a new huddle on the store's roof, a white bulk that seethes with every leap and jiggle. They're watching me and I wave to them.

"We've done the calculations," Pangolin assures me, and I turn back to him. "We've cast bones and analyzed hidden secretions from the bellies of bridges. Everything points to this location as the epicenter of the stark auroral limitations under which Kings and Queens counties presently labor. This *location*, miss. And by a *most* peculiar chance a branch of BY's has been likewise found at the heart of the distended dark in every city we've investigated thus far. The situation threatens to upset certain balances . . . between certain communities . . . that Picnic and I are charged with maintaining, if you will." He scowls as the motorcyclist sweeps by again. "There was another of these blind, hodgepodged watchmen at the crux of the trouble in Pittsburgh. In Newark as well. I saw them myself."

I guess by *blind* he means that no one could see through that visor? "So—just to clarify—can you explain exactly what I should tell Babs?"

"I have to press the papers into her own hands. Into her hands *personally.* I have to see to it that the words leave an indelible imprint on her palms. Perhaps scars. Then she can peruse them at her convenience." Pangolin sounds fretful now. "If only Picnic were here—he's *supposed* to be here, but punctuality is hardly his—and the lawsuit isn't only against your Miss Yagg, my dear, although to be quite frank we suspect her of being something of a ringleader. A guiding spirit, if you will, who's incited her fellow BY's owners to imitate her rather regrettable course of action. Oh, no, our suit is against the entire organization. We propose to bring BY's to its knees!" I might not have realized this was a joke, but he laughs; it sounds like someone scraping a bucket with a saw blade. "Its *fowl* knees!"

Laughter jars his body enough that his papers finally slop free in a pale cascade. I bend down to gather them for him. "Those are *legal* documents!" Pangolin calls reproachfully.

"I know," I say. "I'm just picking them up for you. I won't read them!"

"And are you an attorney, miss? You look rather juvenile for the part."

I'm just standing up with a mass of papers in my arms when I feel an awful prickly burning in my palms, my wrists: all the skin that isn't protected by my jacket. It sears into my flesh like a parade of blazing ants, and I scream and dump the papers onto Pangolin's outstretched paw. He drops half of them again.

"Oh my God, what *is* that?" I hold up my hand and see the skin emblazoned everywhere with backward letters, too mushed and muddled to read, but bright scarlet and already blistering.

"I take it you haven't yet passed the bar," Pangolin says. "You should have known better."

"The ink is like *acid.* . . ."

"Those are legal documents! I did inform you of that fact, but you saw fit to throw caution to the winds! Ah, Picnic, perhaps you'll have some remedy to offer? This young lady was reckless enough to handle legal documents without obtaining the proper qualifications first."

"Snow first," a voice informs me. "Cry later." Someone grabs my wrists and pulls me to my knees, then plunges my hands into the snow. I'd be angrier if I weren't so relieved to feel the pain receding.

I look at the stranger, Picnic I guess. A weedy, seedy middle-aged guy with pale orange tufts of hair and a long, pink face. A plaque identical to Pangolin's sways from his neck. He's wearing a truly hideous red-and-white-checked suit. It seems kind of unprofessional. Pangolin looks a lot more like my idea of a lawyer.

"I was just trying to help," I say. "Pangolin kept dropping them."

"Was *that* your concern?" Pangolin says in astonishment. "Oh, but I've trained them very well. I've devoted endless hours to teaching them *beck* and *call, beck* and *call* . . . they'll turn somersaults if I ask them to. They'll wipe the perspiration from the night's own brow and then swift their way back to me. Loyal to a fault, are my documents!"

"Fly first," Picnic says in tones of warm agreement. "Write later." His long flabby nose is running copiously and he bends down to rub it on the snow, then straightens up snorting. I'm still on my hands and knees trying to quench the burning pain. Behind me BY's dances, tramping chicken-prints into the slush.

I suddenly feel like I might be getting the hang of things.

"Pangolin," I say, "if *at large* encompasses the night, then it must include sleep as well? You can operate among the sleeping any time you want, I guess."

Pangolin stares at me. "Sleep *and* dreams. Certainly. *Large* is a very inclusive territory."

"That's not my expertise," I say. "I don't have the right qualifications, so I can only deal with people when they're awake. That's why I can't disturb Babs now and fetch her for you. But you can go in and knock on her door yourself. Because for you it doesn't matter if she's sleeping." Babs might hack my head off for bothering her, but I'm guessing Pangolin can hold his own.

Picnic and Pangolin give each other significant glances of the she's-not-as-stupid-as-she-looks variety.

"I'll walk right *through* her door and teach her to festoon our lives in blocks of darkness! I'll hand her papers that will explain matters directly to her epidermis! Miss Yagg will rue having brought matters to such a pass that Picnic and Pangolin were forced to take notice! Ah, she thought it was enough to foil those authorities of a—shall we say—woefully prosaic nature! She thought that befuddling those law firms of a—shall we say—quite restricted mentality would be enough! Ah, but she forgot about Picnic and Pangolin. *We* are not so constrained." He claws the pavement triumphantly. No shoes, of course. "But there is one small matter where we might . . . be grateful for your assistance." He looks up, vividly expectant.

"Yes?" I say. Neither of them says anything, just stare wide-eyed waiting for me to understand what they're talking about. "What would you like me to do?"

They don't say anything, just smile a little more brightly. It reminds me of how cagey and weird Erg gets when certain subjects come up, like anything about the motorcyclist for instance.

"I'd be happy to help," I try, "but I need some specifics on what I can do for you. Like, in word-pictures."

Pangolin's face splits in an unnerving grin and he curls his long-clawed toes. Picnic swings his pale eyes toward BY's, dances a few fidgety steps, and then stops. Pangolin turns and glares at him in a manner suggestive of just-shut-up-you-fool.

"I see," I say. I haul myself to my feet; the right one still feels all wrong, but the pain in my hands has faded to a dull fizzling. "Come

with me." I'm ready to bet a ventricle that they're somehow not allowed to stop the store from dancing, but they're too embarrassed
to admit it. "I'll escort you to the door. And while we walk maybe I
could ask you for some professional advice?"

Pangolin flusters. I'm walking at a decent pace and his claws
scrape rapidly beside me. "Advice? I suppose . . . as long as protocol
was *precisely* observed, we might . . ."

"Babs is planning to chop my head off in the morning," I explain, "unless I can get every trace of blood out of the snow. I'd run
away, but if I try it I'll turn into a swan. So I just wanted to ask, is
it legal for her to kill me?"

Pangolin starts and paws his own face as if I had just presented
him with some sadistic riddle. "Are you asking me this . . . simply
to mock the limits of my legal perspicacity? To cast me in a labyrinth
and laugh while I strain to decipher each flex and bar of the way?"

"No, no," I say. "I'm totally sincere. I'd really like to know."

He flicks a worried glance from the corner of his eyes and his
snout twitches. "I'll . . . give the question my most careful consideration," he promises, and I nod. I didn't really imagine that he'd
be any help. We're deep in the store's orange glow now; it's com-
pounded by the snow's reflections, almost buzzing with brightness.
Joel's head is nearby, watching me with sad dead eyes.

"Hey!" I call to the store. "Are you really going to make me sing
the jingle? I thought we knew each other better than that." The store
stops and pivots, bending until its big window is practically brushing
the tops of our heads. I get the feeling it's not so sure about my
companions. "Oh, they're not *here* as lawyers," I explain. "They're
bargain hunters. It would be bad for business not to let them in!" It
hesitates, straightens up, then gives a kind of brusque nod and
kneels in front of us. I'm starting to feel pleased with myself. It's all
in the wrist and so on. "So, Pangolin? The entrance to Babs's . . .

apartment is just past the counter. On the left, kind of back in the corner. You'll see it." I hope he will, anyway; sometimes things in BY's can be hard to spot.

Pangolin turns to me with a grandfatherly smile and whaps me gently on the head with his spiny paw. "Nicely done, miss. You might strive to improve your qualifications so that sleep slips within your ken. I believe you show promise enough for that if you practice."

"Dream first," Picnic suggests fondly. "Die later." I'm not sure how helpful that is. I watch while they go shuffling hand in paw through the glass door. Then BY's stands again and cuts off my view of them.

As soon as they're gone the night feathers itself in falling white and the swans coil around me. I stroke their elegant throats, their sleek black bills, and they nuzzle me. The gauze wrapping the bandaged birds is dotted in red, but it does look like the bleeding is finally slowing down. They'll be okay; I wasn't lying when I told them that. I lead them to the stump and get back to work, cleansing and wrapping the ones that are still bare and dripping. The bandages are getting a little thin, but since they're not bleeding as badly now I might have just enough after all. The motorcyclist growls around and around; his tires have crushed blood into the snow so that he follows a track of slurred pink soup. I imagine he's cracked the tips off a few snowflakes, too. Babs will be horrified. I wonder if Pangolin is right about her, but when I think over everything he said I'm not actually surprised. Maybe he's right, and I'm entombed in the night's perfect center, stuffed into its core.

As for me, I care for my swans, because they're warm and hurt and, unlike Pangolin, I'm not *at large* at all. I'm not qualified to batter down the night or handle legal documents. It might even be the case that I'm *at small*, imprisoned by a ring of severed heads and a pile of rustling birds; my territory is an island of blood and snow shimmered by the sunset-colored light misting out of BY's. My country is the stump where I unwrap the candy bar for Erg and set it on my thigh. She eats in a living, shifting cathedral of arched white necks.

Maybe it's small, my territory, but inside it I can still love what's in front of me with all the heart I have left.

CHAPTER 9

By the time I'm done bandaging my whole flock I'm getting sleepy again. After all her talk about helping me Erg's already passed out in my pocket. I've been out here in the cold for what, by conventional standards, would surely amount to hours. My swans stay close, batting me with wings made clumsy by their bindings, and in their warmth and gentleness I start to nod.

"Don't your parents worry about you?" a voice says behind me. "Working here?"

Tomin, of course. I kind of figured he'd be back. "Parents?" I say, snapping awake. "I think I might have had one or two of those once. I can barely remember."

He walks in front of me and sits down right on the bloodstained snow. "What happened to them?"

It's an uncomfortably direct question, but that's kind of admirable. The easiest thing, for him and for me, would have been to keep on playing it as a joke. "One dead, one gone," I say. "Not that I can recall the details or anything, but those are the usual options. How about yours?"

Tomin tips his head and considers that a lot more seriously than I'd anticipated. The motorcycle growls along its arc, and the rider's head never turns. Now Tomin, unlike that pitiable freak, is definitely somewhere on the way to gorgeous, if not exactly arrived there. Probably a senior. He talks, and in *sentences*. All I really have against him is that he's idiotic and reckless enough to walk into a BY's, which is to say, quite precisely as idiotic and reckless as I am myself. Between the two of us that has to imply some dubious brain chemistry in addition to deep-seated emotional problems, but it's not like we'll be getting married. With all of that in mind, I smile at him: a shiny, artificial smile that would make me want to punch myself in the face if there was a mirror handy.

He smiles back and I stroke my swans; the conversation seems to disturb them a little. "My parents? I can tell you don't actually care." He doesn't seem to mind that, though. "They're at home, on a sofa, being so well-adjusted that they can barely have a conversation. They've worked hard to give me an upbringing better than what these *ghetto* kids get, and I should show I appreciate that. Constantly. See why I'd rather hear about yours?"

I see too well, really. "Oh, like tourism? A visit to the far-off land of dysfunction? Seriously, don't you get enough of that with Lottery?"

I expect a burst of pissy defensiveness in response, but no. He smiles serenely. It occurs to me that he didn't ruffle much during the chaos last night, either. "Actual person actually talking about stuff that matters. *Not* what you get with Lottery. So which is the gone one? Parent, I mean."

"You don't see fit to ask why I'm sitting in a pile of bandaged swans?" I say. "Just wanna cut straight to the gruesome biography?"

"Swans," Tomin says, grinning outright now. "I noticed that. We *are* in the BY's parking lot, though, so it's kind of how things go. So about the parents?"

"Mom dead, dad gone," I concede. "Unless you can think of other ways I might have come to misplace them. I'm totally open to suggestions."

"Prison gone?" he asks. "Or girl gone?"

I feel confident that he does not really want the answer to that question, and I don't particularly want the story getting around, either. If my dad is still alive—and I've got no way of ever finding that out—then what is he doing tonight? Knocking over a garbage can, sniffing a poodle's ass? Lottery would probably find the whole business very entertaining indeed. "Absent gone. Long gone. Hey, ask about our bandaged swans! They're on special!"

He just tips his head and considers me; warm, but still serious. He seems a lot nicer now that he's away from his asinine friends. "I'm wondering what I'd have to do to give everyone total amnesia. I mean something bad enough that they'd forget me completely, and they'd even forget what I did to *make* them forget. Maybe they'd just barely know that there had been someone around with my name, but it would all be kind of vague. . . . That doesn't sound easy."

"It's easier than you think," I say, and there's a little spike of bitterness in my voice. "My dad left all of us highly motivated to erase him from our minds as thoroughly as possible." I'm slipping, saying too much; in a night this deep and strange the boundaries start to blur. Something about the glimmering crimson blots and the relentless dark makes it hard to believe that either of us will remember a word of this conversation in the morning, and anyway I'll probably be dead before breakfast. That makes tonight pretty special, but even so we're overdue for a new subject. "What brings you to BY's, anyway? You're not going in there again, are you?"

He's still studying me, and since he's facing toward BY's the sweep of its windows lights up his gray-green eyes, luminous against his dark skin. Like a lot of girls I have a soft spot for the tousled hair, too. The snow around him glows neon blue. "I was planning to go in. Because that's where I thought you'd be. Even though . . . Was that as close as I think it was? With Lottery?"

"Lottery came within a hair of improving New York's gene pool," I agree. "And if I'd known the crap your crew was going to pull with the money I absolutely would have let nature take its course. It would have been kinder in the long run, right?"

He doesn't take that up, but his mouth tenses like there's something he's not sure he should say. "I asked her about you."

"Right." Of course he did. "Why do I feel so confident that she didn't have anything good to report?" I'd like to ditch this subject, too, really. There are so many topics I'd rather avoid that sometimes it seems like I can't talk for more than five minutes with anyone—except for Erg, of course. And maybe Chelsea. I can never afford to make friends since they all have this awkward habit of asking questions. Should I be worried about that?

"Not much of it was good," Tomin agrees politely. "She talked about what a klepto you are. And she said no one at your school likes you and that you ignore everybody anyway, because you're so stuck up. And that your mom was some kind of big-deal painter." He delivers the last line cautiously, watching to see how I'll react. "Am I bugging you? Talking about this?"

Nice that he cares, I guess. Chelsea and Stephanie accepted ages ago that questions about Zinaida were strictly off-limits. That I might freak out and start yelling or crying if anyone even said her name where I could hear it.

But tonight might be my very last chance to talk about her, and maybe Tomin will remember just a little bit of who she was when I can't anymore. Whenever I manage to forget for a moment what's coming in the morning one of those corpse heads seems to float across my vision like a balloon for a baby demon. Talking is a welcome distraction. It almost stops me from noticing how truly scared I am.

"Zinaida," I say aloud. It's the first time in years I've let that name escape my lips. Reckless and raucous and wasted and traffic-stopping Zinaida, who just barely got it together enough to give me a magic doll before she died. "That was her name. And I know my stepmom thought I was stuck-up after I moved in with her and my sisters, but that was really just culture shock. See, if there isn't someone in a pink velvet suit passed out in a pool of vomit, it just doesn't feel like home to me." I'm trying to be funny but my voice is all wrong, strained and skittish. "She really wasn't that good of a painter, but she did get shows and stuff. I wonder why?"

"You mean she looked like you?" He's smiling again.

"Prettier. Art critics used to follow her around on their knees, salivating. And she was . . . like, charismatic. Made a lot of noise, knew everybody, kind of all over the place when she was talking. Full of ideas, wore crazy outfits. Rainbow-glitter eyelashes. Guys swooned."

Zinaida is such a vivid presence, even in memory, that for an instant it feels like my words could become a current strong enough to sweep me away from here and back to the past.

Tomin nods, taking in my baggy, battered, blood-spattered clothes, the huge cargo pants and huger jacket, my snarled filthy mass of purple hair. "You don't actually like looking like you do, right? That's why you try to hide it."

"Why *would* I like it? Both my parents were knockout gorgeous, and it was basically like they went around with death rays shooting off them. Their faces were totally a destructive force. They screwed other people up and they screwed themselves up. So even if I've only inherited a fraction of that, I mean, it still doesn't seem all that fabulous." I'm talking too much, too fast, too angrily. It's as if even mentioning Zinaida makes me act a little like her. "I should probably only date blind guys. That way it wouldn't be an issue."

I'd kind of forgotten about the motorcyclist, but now when he buzzes by I have the distinct impression that his orbit might be shrinking a little. His opaque visor reflects curls of BY's tangerine light. Pangolin called him the *blind watchman*, but I wasn't thinking of him, I swear it.

"Or, you know, you could give somebody credit," Tomin suggests. It takes me a moment to remember what he's talking about. "For trying to see past the obvious shit."

"No one does," I say, a little bitchily. "Not just with me. I mean in general. It's like the obvious shit cancels out everything else. Why else does everyone put on such a big show of being *somebody*?"

"Is that what I'm doing?" he asks. "Putting on a show?"

"You were last night," I snap. "The moon crackers? Remember? To prove how well you fit in with the most messed-up people from my school, and that you were just as much of a jerk as the rest of them? Good job. You had me totally convinced."

For an instant he looks embarrassed, then in the next his face changes into a don't-go-there smirk. "Extreme Shopping. Not that many people are into it. It's dumb to try it alone, so when Lottery says they're going on an expedition I say I'm in."

"Or you could just not do it at all," I suggest, and nod toward a particular head hovering over us. "You see that kid up there? Joel Diallo? I knew him. I bet some asshole dared him to go in and buy something, and he was desperate to prove that he wasn't just a repressed geek after all. Because that was what was *obvious* about him, and who was going to bother, I don't know, actually finding out—" *who he was*, I'm going to say. But I don't, because Tomin hasn't even glanced toward Joel. He's staring down at his knees instead and his face is going greenish. "Um, Tomin?"

A truly nauseating idea bobs up into my mind: maybe the Extreme Shopping kids have some kind of initiation ritual. Lottery did say that they'd all done one solo run, and what else would that mean? Maybe Tomin was there. Maybe he was part of what happened. I suddenly picture him laughing with Lottery out in the parking lot, waiting for Joel to come back with his damned trophy. Until they heard him screaming, and ran home to pretend they'd had nothing to do with it.

God, and I'd almost started to like him. "Did you know Joel, too?" I ask, and the sick edge in my voice makes it really, really clear what I've been thinking.

"Vassa . . ." Tomin starts. Ooh, is it confession time? "Look, why are *you* here? You know the score. And don't tell me you need the money that bad."

Ah. Changing the subject. My upper lip hikes. "I'm not here for money. It's kind of an unpaid internship."

"At first I thought you just wanted to be, like, part of something magic. Even if it was dangerous. But that's not it, right?"

His tone is vulnerable, searching; it almost makes me think that my suspicions are horribly unfair. But I don't feel like explaining my situation, especially since it might become tricky to skirt the subject of my impending execution. My swans almost seem like they know what I'm thinking because two of them rear up from the drowsy huddle to wrap their long necks protectively around my shoulders, touch my lips with their bills. I look back at the feverish orange glow of BY's, dancing as always with brisk swaying steps. It seems like Pangolin has been in there for kind of a long time and I'm starting to get worried.

"I'm here because I have to be," I tell him, pretty curtly. "And considering that you're all about having *actual conversations,* I can't help wondering why you haven't answered my question. About Joel. Or does he not count as *stuff that matters*?"

Tomin looks at me with widened eyes. His jaw is clenched, his knuckles pale and bulging. Through all the insanity last night he never once got this rattled.

If he didn't help kill Joel, then I'm pretty sure he knows who did.

Something roars past us, much too loudly: the motorcyclist is definitely circling in a much tighter loop than he was before.

"Joel counts," Tomin says at last. "He mattered."

"Yeah?" I say. "Care to elaborate? Or, you know what? I honestly don't expect to survive for too long myself. Why don't you go find a girl who has a life expectancy of at least a week? I mean, at a *minimum*." Then I stop talking abruptly because I've spotted something disturbing. Just beyond the borders of my personal swan heap a trail of tiny oval dents leads away into the night.

Footprints. I feel for Erg automatically, even though I already know she's gone. I'll have to extricate myself from my swans and try to follow her.

Tomin's on his feet, looking in a different direction than the one where Erg disappeared. "Vassa!" he yells suddenly. "Watch out!"

I see his hand reaching down, trying to catch my arm. He doesn't manage it, though, because the swans are suddenly rising up in a buffeting cloud around me, their broad strong wings wheeling in all directions. Enormous pulses of air drum at my face and there's a noise like flags in a storm. I throw my arms over my head and try to stand, but I'm too wing-pummeled, white-blinded, disoriented by the thrash of their necks. Black webbed feet scrabble at my face and I hear Tomin shouting desperately over a growling blast, and then the swans sort of peel back and a seething wall of black takes over my vision. It's coming right at me and there's no time to run.

The motorcyclist. He's about to crash right into me.

INTERLUDE IN WOOD

WINTER, SIX YEARS EARLIER

"Maybe your daughter would be happier with the money?" the old woman suggested roughly. She turned a crude wooden cylinder in her hands. It was the heart of a cherry tree that once grew on a stillborn girl child's grave, then the wood had been boiled in her parents' tears until the salt blanched it to a pale gold. It was already imbued with tantalizing power, and she wondered how her visitor had gotten hold of it. "You invest your money in some nice stocks for the little one now, she grows up, and for a surety it comes in handy. She sees you were thinking of her. That's what a smart woman would be doing, Zinnie."

"My daughter," Zinaida proclaimed, "will have the kind of life whose obstacles can't be conquered by money! I know it. She needs something much stronger. Bea, you can't really believe that a child of mine will be *ordinary*. With the traditions in my family, Vassa is certain to be pulled into—into the affairs of your sort of people eventually. And I won't be there to help her. Naturally I'm worried."

The room was lacy, dusty, and cramped, and in her embroidered boots Zinaida dominated the upper strata. She wore a wasp-waisted, flaring frock coat of celadon brocade over caramel leather shorts, and her black hair was pinned up in complicated soft-serve coils. On a

woman less striking the clothes might have seemed fussy and osten-
tatious, but on her they looked utterly stylish. Her beautiful face was
turning gaunt and faded, but her presence remained so forceful that
almost no one could have guessed how ill she was.

"You know that how?" Bea asked. "You've been looking into
things you shouldn't?" Zinaida didn't answer and the old woman
sighed. "What you call your worries, I can tell they're actually your
wishes. You do this, you'll make them come true by your own act.
You're too proud of those *family traditions* of yours, aren't you? You
want your Vassa tangled up in magic so badly that you won't attend
to what it might cost her. You don't have much time, Zinnie, but
it's pure truth that you've got time enough to think better of this.
Change your mind. Let your Vassa grow up without *persons of quality* dragging her into their business. Forget the doll, and I'll make
sure of it. I'll make sure she's as ordinary a girl as you like."

"The doll will protect her. God knows her father won't. Why
wouldn't you *want* that for her, Bea? You remember, don't you, how
my great-grandparents helped you escape from Russia? How you
lived with them in Paris, when you had nowhere else to go? Raised
my grandmother almost as if she were your own? You've been a
friend to my family for generations. I know you'll be a friend now
when I need you most!"

"I've been a friend to your family, and I've been other things, too.
You know it. The doll will protect her, surely, but it will also bind
her, and to a side of life that might be better left apart. You *know*
that, Zinnie. Don't tell me you don't know what you're doing.
What do you tell yourself, that your pretty Vassa can dabble about
with persons of quality, waltz at our parties, and somehow avoid
the dangers we bring with us? You think she can do that, when *I'm*
the one you ask to do the binding? Ah, but you know full well what
I've been. I don't put that past down when I take up this wood in my
old hands."

Zinaida pursed her lilac lips and paced. Bea was still sitting calmly with her teacup on her knee, but to her the idea of serenity and stillness seemed oppressive, a precursor of the unwelcome peace to come. "But that's why you can help us, Bea! You've seen so much, dreamed so much, *been* so much. You can give some of that to my little girl now, can't you?"

Bea stared down at her teacup as if she hadn't heard. The tea was cold and milky, full of obscure clouds and dangerous sediments, and with every word Zinaida spoke she grew sadder. Even after sixteen years in this dark apartment its immobility sometimes made her dizzy, a bit nauseous. She wasn't meant to be a damned barnacle.

"My past, Zinnie?" Bea finally whispered. "You want me to give her my past? What I hated then I hate now, and the wood will pick up the scent. And where the wood hunts, so will your Vassa. You might ask yourself if I have reasons of my own to make this doll for you. You might ask if reasons like mine can bring any good to anyone."

"You mean Babs?" Zinaida asked flippantly. "To hell with that old witch."

"Be it so," Bea Yaggen murmured. But she didn't look up and a tear splashed on her knee.

CHAPTER 10

There's no impact as far as I can tell but there is a whole lot of pitch-black nothing, more than I've ever seen before, though as a Brooklyn resident I might have considered myself something of a nothing-ness expert. It takes me quite a while to understand that I'm moving, and at terrific speed. Stars flare in their multitudes all at once as if the night had suddenly opened a billion eyes, all of them watching me.

It's actually kind of awesome. I'm racing through this brilliant infinity, and, there in the distance, I catch sight of a star that I some-how know is our own sun. In the span of a gasp I can see Earth rolling up at me, the blue curves stretching and flattening, continents bursting with detail and mountain ranges heaving into view. Waves start to scatter sequins of light and cities lie like scabs. I'm approaching the sunlit side, but as I draw closer there's an involuntary swish and bend to my flight and I'm sailing over a dark boundary. Winging my way into night.

Cities appear now as stippled blaze on the charcoal land, and a flourish of wind wraps my face. There's a strange lull while I seem to be in movement but not in time, and then I realize I'm not alone. I'm riding on the back of a black motorcycle and my arms are wrapped around a surge of darkness, sometimes loosely humanoid and sometimes shifting into cloud forms, minotaurish or serpentine. If I look into it deeply enough, I can see wandering stars.

We're streaking along fifty yards above a harbor—yachts wander, too, lights swaying on their masts—and then a city; I don't know which one, but the redbrick row houses make me think we're on the East Coast of the United States.

I lean against the motorcyclist's broad starry back. He looks shapeless and wild but I can feel cold leather under my cheek, and there's definitely something more or less person-shaped closed in my arms. I might laugh if I wasn't breathless with beauty and velocity; I might cry if I wasn't trying to laugh.

We're heading inland over darkness carved by roofs and scripted in blinking signs, and the motorcycle curls and leaps as if we were driving along a road in the hills and not through smoke-black air. We've left what looked like a pretty fancy neighborhood and now we're sweeping over grittier districts where hunched men miss the steps as they emerge from stinking bars. Girls no older than me stand knock-kneed in tiny glittery dresses, staring at nothing. No one seems to notice us; it's like we're webbed into the wind, the roaring night.

Something tangerine and boxy jiggles ahead. It doesn't take me long to realize it's another BY's franchise, waltzing and scraping away in the silence. The heads here must not get changed quite as often because a few of them have decayed all the way to bone. Skulls bounce back light the color of setting suns. I tug on the motorcyclist, to ask him to take us anywhere else. Instead he dips lower, curving in. He looks human again, black and shining, but with obvious shoulders and head and arms. It's strange, but seeing him *look* human is what brings it home to me that he really, definitely isn't.

A second motorcyclist circles below us, endlessly rounding the parking lot. He looks smaller and lumpier than my friend, as if somebody'd done a sloppy job of putting him together out of scraps. But he's also encased in tight black leather, and his bike is black and growling, and his visor looks much too dark to peer through. I don't think he can see us but he might sense something, because unlike everybody else he cranes his head our way. A wordless, guttural cry shakes from his throat. It sounds so pitiful, like something half machine and half child calling for help.

My motorcyclist calls back to him, the same rumbling howl. We weave around the circling bike below us, dancing a smaller orbit. I wanted to run away before—*anyone but me, anywhere but here*—but now I've changed my mind.

I want to help them. I don't know *what* they are, but I do know that they're desperately unhappy and very, very alone. Even more alone than I am. I catch a glimpse of an old lady scowling from the window—probably every BY's franchise has a witch in charge—and I wonder if she's as cruel as Babs.

"Vassa," the motorcyclist drones; his voice trembles from his whole body, even from the motorcycle's core. "Vassa."

"You can talk again!" If he can speak, then doesn't that mean I'm dreaming? Of course, I must be. Of *course* I'm not dead.

"You can *hear* me again. I've talked to you, so many times, but you can't hear."

I think about this. "You mean I can't hear you when I'm awake? Conscious?" I mull the problem a little more, but now the solution seems obvious. "Then does that mean you're sleeping, too? Are you *always* asleep?"

"So I don't feel."

"So you don't feel what?"

"What I was." The motorcycle gives a sudden lurch and we're ascending again, the rider below us straining in our direction, one lonely arm reaching our way. "What I was, was the all. The all above us."

Right. I'd managed to forget that talking to him is one thing; understanding what the hell he's trying to communicate is something else. I'm so distracted by the thrill of flight that there's a pause before I arrive at the obvious question. "So what are you now? Because I'm getting the feeling that you're not—" I don't want to say *not human,* just in case that hurts him. "—not the same kind as me?"

That seems to stump him. He slides into silence again, our wheels whipping up a scrum of leaves from an especially tall oak. It's weird but I'm also starting to think that I can feel his emotions coming through the places where my arms wrap his body, where my torso leans against his back. Sadness seems to seep through my skin, and I know I'm making him think about things that he finds bewildering and unbearably painful.

"I know what I *was.* Now that I'm not, now that I'm separate . . . Can there be any word for me, Vassa?"

"Most people would say you're a man. That doesn't seem quite right, though. Does it?"

He answers me with a strange rattling growl; definitely not a sound a human could make. We skid through the fringes of black forests, curve away from fire-hooting factories, and then, although it seems impossibly soon, we're sliding above the sparkling margin of another city. I know where he's taking me, so this time when my hair whips back like a curtain pulled by the wind I'm not surprised to see the orange bobble of another BY's, this one in what looks like a shabby district of vinyl-sided houses with feeble smoke-choked gardens. We dip down, air surging up my jacket, and below us another motorcyclist cries out and flings his arms wide in appeal.

We head right for him. At first I think we're going to pull up at any moment, but as the parking lot's dark shimmer spreads like a cancer over my vision I start to have my doubts about that.

I'm dreaming, just dreaming, I tell myself, *none of this is real.*

But at this speed it's hard to have much faith in the distinction.

The strange motorcyclist below is even more wind-warped and goblin-twisted than the one I saw in the last city. He's hunchbacked, his arms absurdly long and rippling like the boughs of a cypress tree. He yowls in animal terror at our approach, his grotesque arms and huge flipperlike hands winging up to ward off the blow. Beneath his black visor I see a wide-open mouth with a pallid tongue and pointy teeth. His spherical head seems to be inflating until it could burst, so huge that I can't understand how we haven't hit him already. I cringe back as a raspy scream tears from my throat. . . .

And then I'm still screaming, but I don't see the parking lot or the howling mouth or my own motorcyclist in front of me. I'm not perched on the leather seat or holding onto his muscular body. I'm just completely and entirely alone in star-struck darkness. What's funny is that the darkness feels so claustrophobic, so tightly confined. My panic undergoes a tonal shift, from fear of being splattered across the asphalt to fear of being imprisoned forever. The scream in my throat twitches half a note higher before I run out of breath and stop, gasping, with the miserable feeling that I'm being ridiculous. I'm dreaming, and I wonder if my dream is nested inside someone else's dream, which is maybe inside a bigger dream yet.

Sleep is larger than any night, he told me. *It's large enough to fill the mind.*

I reach out a hand; touch a surface wet and rough and concave. As if I was standing inside . . .

A skull. I suddenly have an awful, knee-buckling sense of where I am and why there was no crash a moment ago. My feet rebound from something spongy and I look down and see my boots darkly silhouetted against a pale morass. I know, I know beyond any rational knowing, that I'm standing on the other motorcyclist's tongue, and yes, that is just as creepy as it sounds. I suddenly miss Erg so much it twists my guts. Even in my dreams she's nearly always with me.

"Erg?" I try. Grumbling shudders under my feet in answer.

Whatever that is, it's sure not her. But if Erg was here, I know what she'd tell me: *Get started.* She doesn't have much patience with cowardice. And in a place like this, there's only one thing that getting started can mean.

I walk, my eyes slowly adjusting to what looks like a dim dusting of starlight. If I'm standing on a tongue, then it seems like there ought to be a brain above me, but when I look up there's nothing but yawning space and, high above, these two jagged golden crescents that I can't figure out. They look like they're spinning, sharp points wheeling at their edges. I'm still staring up at them, trying to understand, when there's a kind of unctuous squirm under my feet. It sends me sliding toward an even darker depression up ahead, slithery lumps knocking my legs from under me as I go. After a moment's denial I get it: I'm being swallowed. My hands swing out, trying to grasp at anything, but there's nothing except for the fleshy wallow of tongue and throat. And then I'm going down.

It's not slimy and constricting like a throat—even a giant one—ought to be. I'm in free fall and when my fist hits the wall there's a metallic clunk like someone dropping a tin can. A buffeting gust comes from nowhere and sends me rolling through the emptiness, and then I land. On something very soft, even furry. My hands sink into pillowing fluff, then stroke a floppy outcropping as long as my arm. In the hazy light I can just make it out.

A rabbit's ear. Too cold to be alive, though.

This is now, officially, the absolute weirdest dream I have ever had.

I stand up on a landscape of enormous taxidermy rabbits, all heaped and mashed together into bulky forms vaguely reminiscent of human organs. I wish I could say that I have the foggiest clue what it all means, but I really, truly don't. There's nothing I can do but shrug and say, *Yeah, well, dreams are like that.*

As quick as that thought, I'm back on the flying motorcycle and we're starting to lift off. My motorcyclist stares straight ahead, but as my arms squeeze him reflexively from sheer astonishment he lets out an odd sound, one I'd never expected to hear from him. I'm pretty sure he's laughing, but he still seems sad.

"Vassa," he says after a moment. "Vassa, do you see?"

"No," I tell him bluntly. "What the hell *was* that?"

"One lost from the all. We are made so."

I'm feeling a little pissy at how mysterious everything is, but I make an effort to puzzle it through. No matter how crazy everything seems, I'm pretty sure that he's doing his best to explain. He said before that he had been *the all above us.* "You mean like you?"

"Can that be called a man, Vassa?" His tone is strained, expectant.

"You mean what I just saw?" I say. "It was definitely not a man. It was more of a mess." As soon as the words slip out I'm sorry. He gives a low, wounded cry and I know it's because I was so callous, so careless of his feelings.

Because maybe he was showing me things he doesn't know how to explain in words. Maybe the other motorcyclist was actually, physically constructed out of tin cans and stuffed rabbits—and if that's true, if that's not just some lunatic idea of mine, then I can see how it might be a sensitive issue.

We're flying up over a blocky field of warehouses, streetlights casting random nets of illumination.

He seems like he's still thinking it over. "Then it shouldn't *seem* to be a man," he says at last. "What can't be should not seem. It starts to seem, even to itself. Caught by the lie."

I think I'm getting what he means, and I feel so sorry for him that I can't speak at first. I've been doing a lousy job of saying the right thing so far, but after a while I give it another try. "You don't have to be human to be a *person.* I mean you don't have to be human to be *somebody.* I don't know you that well, but you seem like way more of a somebody than a lot of humans I know! Really."

Above us the clouds sag like a thousand dark eggs. I feel like he's trying not to cry. I feel like he doesn't even know what crying is exactly. For a while we rise and fall together along slopes of midnight and the only sound is the stuttering wind.

"Night sees you, Vassa," he tells me at last.

Is he trying to change the subject? "I guess the night sees everything. *If* it sees."

He shakes his head, the huge helmet rocking from side to side. "Night sees that you . . . mean to be kind. To help. At first it saw only that she hated you, and that was enough . . . to reach out a breeze in the dark for you, to gather what was lost. Now it hears the messenger. Now it knows more." His speech is getting more laborious, fighting its way through uncertainty. I'm not sure how I'm supposed to respond. What messenger?

"Well, I try not to be *mean,* anyway," I tell him. "For whatever that's worth. I don't honestly think it's good for much."

I don't think my help is good for much, either, but there's no point in telling him that. Now I can see the horizon breaking into the silver scribble of Manhattan; at this distance its skyscrapers aren't much more than splinters, but I can still recognize the general outline of the place. Maybe we're heading back to Brooklyn now. "Do we have to?" I ask him. "Go back?"

I didn't think that was an especially hard question, but he takes a long moment to consider it. "To go on dreaming . . ." he says softly. "Forever, Vassa?"

"It sounds like more fun than getting my head chopped off!"

Suddenly we're in the thick of Manhattan, passing between mirrored skyscrapers. Our reflections are broken and reformed into a field of scattered arms, bent legs, random scrolls of violet hair, all endlessly repeating. Then we're through and the East River slides, dark and glossy, under a dozen bridges. We dash directly above the gray spine of the Williamsburg Bridge, then over the loft building where I lived with my mom when I was small. The puddles on its roof reflect a mosaic of stars and shattered clouds. She used to take me on late-night walks across that bridge, long after all the other kids my age were fast asleep. If it was one of the times when my dad was crashing with us—which he did sometimes, for a month or two—he'd stay home sulking by the TV until we finally drifted back, bringing ice cream and champagne and wildly exaggerated stories of our adventures in the night.

It feels like she should still be here: on the roof, maybe, watching the river with a cocktail in her hand. Zinaida, more than anyone I've ever known, seemed like somebody who ought to live forever, like she was just so vital that death might decide to make an exception for her. I have to suppress an impulse to call her name.

We cross Williamsburg and then Bushwick, the J train briefly keeping pace below us on its elevated track. He's taking me back, and there's nothing I can do about it. As soon as I think that there's a quick slide to the city and BY's lunges into view, swaying on and on above a snowfield so garnet-blotched that you'd think the earth itself had started bleeding.

It's only now I realize that there was no snow in all the other places we've visited tonight. It's just here in the immediate neighborhood of my own BY's, stretching for a few blocks beyond the parking lot. I should have known. My swans have settled into a sleepy drift of feathers at the foot of Joel's stake. After all the wild disturbing bliss of the night I'm shocked by the force of my own despair as I look down on the red-ripped snow. "Don't you understand?" I ask the motorcyclist. "If I'm stuck here again, it's all over for me. Babs has me cornered."

"Night knows you, Vassa," he repeats; this time he sounds almost impatient.

The ground below us is starting to shimmer: faint waves of motion so subtle that I can barely make them out. It looks almost like wisps of red sand coiling through the wind. We dip lower, circling the parking lot again, but still not touching down, and the red flickering grows denser. It lifts in sinuous billows like airborne shadows or like ruby horses galloping in midair. Whatever it is, the lamplight catches it in delicate flights of sparkle. I hear myself crying out from the force of its beauty. A red wave flies across my eyes and I reach out my hand; when I peer close I can see a bright speck on my palm bizarrely magnified. It's a translucent crimson round with an indented center.

A single blood cell. Frozen into a perfect jewel.

The snow below us is paling, first to a deep raspberry pink, then to the color of seashells, then lighter still, only a waft and a breath of pink lingering in the white while around us the air scintillates with flocking rubies, all whirling up and away. There's a slight thud as we touch down and I hear myself half-laughing and half-gasping into the glimmering storm.

"Vassa," someone says in my ear. "Vassa, you can wake up now."

It's Erg. She's clinging in my hair, and I feel my eyes opening even though I never knew they were closed.

We're in the parking lot. I'm still sitting on the back of the motorcycle and we're going around and around on the same old clockwork course. We never left, I bet, except in our shared dream. I don't have to try to know that if I speak to the motorcyclist, either he won't be able to hear me, or I won't register his replies.

And all around us, the snow is as clean and white as the light of a brand-new sun.

CHAPTER 11

I'm still entranced by my dream and maybe not thinking super clearly. I watch hazily as Erg leaps onto the motorcyclist's shoulder and croons or chirps or whispers something in his ear. The sheer oddness of seeing her speak to someone who isn't me makes me wonder if I really woke up at all.

Even more surprising is that he must hear her, because we stop long enough for me to clamber off the bike while Erg crawls up my arm. I stand there in the snow, my legs and back so stiff that I know I must have been riding for ages. But I don't seem to have the serious injuries you'd expect from a collision with a moving vehicle. Did he somehow catch me and throw me on the seat behind him as he rushed at me?

He takes off again before I can even say goodbye.

"Erg?" I say, confused. "What just happened? How did you get up here?" Could Erg really leap onto a speeding motorcycle?

"It's almost morning, Vassa," she says from just under my collar, as if that answered either question. "You can take a break soon. See, the sky is getting lighter over that way?"

"You were talking to him?" I ask; I know she wants me to drop the subject, but I can't. "Since when do you talk to other people?"

God, I sound jealous. I'm sure she can hear it. It's not super rational, maybe, but Erg is the only thing in the world that's ever
been truly and entirely mine. No matter what crazy things she does
sometimes, she's always been loyal to me in a way that I can't even
be to myself. The thought of that ever changing is enough to shake
me with suppressed panic.

"I never talk to other *people*, Vassa," Erg coos. "You know I don't!
I'm your doll all the way!"

This time I think she wants me to catch the subtext: my idea
that the motorcyclist is something besides human wasn't just an
artifact of my dream. It's the truth, and Erg wants to make sure I
know that. "You know you *could* just tell me what you know about
him, Erg. I promise I can handle it."

Erg makes a face. "There's Babs, coming to check up on you!
Oh, Babsie, the snow sure looks *pretty* this morning, doesn't it?"

"Why are you always changing the subject?" I snap, but she's
already burrowing back inside my jacket. And of course she's right:
I look to see Babs in her lavender bathrobe just outside the door of
BY's. She's standing stock-still, gawking around at the flawless
glitter of the snow, and to say that she looks perturbed would be an
understatement of unprecedented size. I can't keep a grin off my
face. She looks over just in time to see me beaming like a search-
light. It's probably an extremely bad idea to gloat, but I can't resist
giving her a cheerful wave. Her face contorts, rolling through a
whole sequence of tortured expressions before it arrives at a feeble
simulation of a smile.

I smile back and run over to her, bouncing as I go. Like almost
everything I do it's ill-advised but impossible to resist, at least in
the moment.

"Hi, Babs! Isn't it a beautiful morning? I love the sky when it's
just getting purple like this. It goes so well with my hair."

One thing I'll give Babs: she's never been short of a snappy comeback. But now she just stares silently, keeping her white eye tucked in her face. It's like she's decided that her usual kind of cheap intimidation isn't enough under the circumstances and she's calculating what to try next.

"Vassa Lisa Lowenstein," she chirrs at last. "But where's the rest of it, I'd like to know? Ah, and who was it performed the *operation*, for that matter? You didn't sever yourself."

"Excuse me?" I say. "Have you not had your coffee yet? I could get you some."

"Half is missing," Babs says. "Half is what throws it all off. You can't do the math when you can't see the numbers, imp."

"Half of what?" I ask, and I make kind of a show of being bored.

Babs glowers at me like she's daring me to keep playing dumb. "Your name, *Vassa*. Half of it is missing. Not what we might call in evidence. But I do believe I'll find it soon."

I'd prefer not to have the slightest idea what she's talking about, but in fact there's a bare inkling in the back of my brain. I turn on the obliviousness full force.

"Oh, you mean how Vassa's not a regular name? You're kind of right. My mom made it up to be, like, a more American-sounding version of Vasilisa, or Wassilissa, or however you spell it. After her grandmother. I guess you could say the second half is missing, except she turned that into the Lisa part."

Babs makes a face halfway between a wince and a grin. "Oh, *that* must be what I was talking about, then. I didn't know. Ah, you're becoming a bitty nuisance to me, but now the rule of three nights applies and quibbling won't avail. Can't simply pack you in a crate and ship you away. *Somebody* was counting on that, sure as entropy. Well I can assure you, imp, that I'll be making full use of our time together."

And she turns her back on me with a theatrical pivot, heading toward the motorcyclist; he's already stopped, waiting for her.

I get the distinct impression that Babs is walking faster than usual, not bothering anymore to put on her doddering act for me. Maybe she's decided that there's no point in pretending with me now. We both know that a regular human girl couldn't have cleaned the snow without serious help, even if I'm still having trouble accepting that my dream could be real. I mean, the *night* saved me? Night sucked every blood cell out of the snow for me? It's not like there's any sane explanation available, though, so I might as well start believing the crazy one. Babs doesn't try to hide what she's doing once she reaches the motorcyclist, either. She lays both hands on him, rocking him lightly back and forth while he sits there impassively. His giant head wobbles from side to side. Then she gives a little push, and he's falling. Falling slowly as the moon turning its dark side to the Earth.

A kind of heavy impulse catches my eyelids, trying to close them at the crucial moment. I resist, determined not to let my gaze waver this time, and I'm looking straight at him as he vanishes with something like a wink in the texture of the world. He's gone.

Babs turns back and her stare is ragged and challenging, reminding me that she's got him under her power. Well, mostly she does. She can't control what he does in his dreams, or where we go together, or what he tries to reveal about her secrets. She can't stop us from learning to understand each other, at least a little.

Night sees you, Vassa, he told me. *Night knows you.*

I turn my back on Babs just as ostentatiously as she turned away from me a few moments ago. I turn away from the dawn, crawling up the horizon like mauve smoke, and look toward the darkest fold of the sky. "Hi, Night," I whisper. "I hope you can hear me. You were amazing! Thanks so much!" And I blow it a kiss. Then, without looking around again, I stalk up to BY's open door, climb through, and head back to my own little closet-room, grabbing some random food on the way.

I know Babs was watching the whole thing. I know she's positively fuming and that she'll do whatever she can to get back at me. But I just can't make myself care.

Even so, I'm relieved to reach my room again and shut the door.

There's still the small matter of my right foot, cramped and bunched-feeling in my boot. I can't really avoid the truth any longer, and anyway I already know it. Erg is sitting next to me on the cot trying to lick strawberry marshmallow butter out of a jar lid, but the stuff proves to be so dense and viscous—like a puree of pink tires—that she can barely dent it.

I unlace my heavy, studded boots and pry them off; it takes some work to tug the right one free. Black, sharp-pointed toeish protuberances have gouged through my sock; when I peel that off the whole webbed, knobby swan foot splays across the blanket. I know I've always said that I don't want to be this pretty, but this isn't really the kind of uglification I had in mind.

Erg looks at my transformed foot, her blue eyes morose—but not at all startled—above the gluey pink streaks on her face. "I knew that would happen."

I want to feel surprised, but I can't manage it any more than Erg can. "Then why didn't you warn me?"

"I did warn you! I told you not to go outside! Because I knew! You wouldn't listen to me!" I don't think I've ever heard her sound so genuinely angry.

"You didn't tell me *why*, though. How was I supposed to take you seriously when you just talked about mittens?" She's scowling at me, but the pink sludge gummed all over her front makes it hard not to laugh. "Erg, I mean, it would *really* help sometimes if you would just tell me straight out what the deal is. Right? How frustrating is it that you obviously know who that motorcyclist is, and you won't tell me anything?"

For a long while Erg just stares at me in disbelief. When she talks again it's slow and measured, as if she was calculating the best way to get through my thick head. "Vassa? You have had occasion over the years to observe the fact that I'm not human, right? You've thoroughly absorbed that? No lingering doubts?"

"Do you have a point, Erg?"

"Well, what *do* you think I am, then?"

A pain in the ass, perhaps? A flurry of sarcastic replies wings through my head, but she's upset enough that I decide this isn't the moment.

"A magic doll. From my mom." I don't admit the embarrassing part, though: that I've sometimes wondered if just a trace of Zinaida is still alive, deep in Erg's little wooden chest. Erg came alive at the same moment that my mom's heart stopped beating, so the conjecture's not as crazy as it sounds.

Erg sighs dramatically; very Zinaida-style, in fact. "Well, so maybe there are certain flavors of beans that we aren't allowed to spill! Did you ever think of that?"

We.

I have never before heard Erg use the word *we* to mean anything besides her and me, together forever. A doll and her girl, bound by the fact that they both appear to be pretty, brainless toys. My heart jars in my chest.

"Who's this *we*, Erg? The magic dolls' club? Or do you mean you and the motorcyclist?"

I saw her talking to him, so that's as good a guess as any—though I'm pretty sick of guessing. This business of her not being *allowed* to tell me what the hell is going on seems awfully convenient.

Erg hears the edge in my voice and wipes her sticky face on the mattress before scampering over to me and hopping onto my knee. "I'm your doll, Vassa. Even if you died, I couldn't belong to anyone else ever!"

"Does *we* mean the motorcyclist? Or are you talking about somebody I don't even know?"

Erg hesitates. "*We* means . . . the whole big category. Like me."

Maybe I'm being unfair, but I still feel angry with her and her self-indulgent obscurity. Zinaida liked putting on displays of mysteriousness, too. "And that category includes the motorcyclist?" Erg just stares at me. "Erg, come on. How can he be the same as you? He's not a doll!"

"Actually," Erg mutters, "he kind of is."

As soon as the words are out her face changes. A look of absolute horror comes over her. Her golden wood seems suddenly paler, her blue eyes go wide and she flings her tiny hands over her mouth.

"Oh, no!" Erg moans. "Oh, nonono! Oh, I didn't *say* that! I was just thinking it and it came out! I didn't . . ." She's begging, whimpering, but I get the feeling that she's not actually talking to me anymore. Her eyes dart through the corners of the room. "Please. I was just thinking too loudly! I didn't want Vassa to hear!"

"Erg?" I say. "What's wrong?"

She throws herself down on my thigh, howling, and starts pummeling me as hard as she can, though it barely stings. Maybe those were some of the extra-special beans that she's not allowed to spill, but I still don't see why she's so upset about it. "It's your fault, Vassa! You wouldn't stop asking me questions!"

I stroke her slick back while she flails at me. It seems like she's mostly just generating drama for drama's sake, but I still don't like seeing her freak out this way.

"I don't actually understand what the problem is. But I'm still sorry. Okay? I won't ask you about him again. Okay, Erg?" I'm still puzzling through everything I've learned. He's not a man, but he seems to be, even to himself. He's caught up in the lie of *looking* like a man. He was part of *the all above us,* but now he's a kind of doll. He sleeps all the time; he flies in his dreams and he can bring me along. He seems to be on pretty friendly terms with the night, enough to understand what it's thinking anyway. But what can all that add up to?

Erg knows, but I can never ask her again. She's done a great job of making sure I can't ask her, unless I want to cope with her launching into a nervous breakdown.

She's a little bit calmer now, whimpering steadily. "Not just about him! Don't ask me anything about—"

"About things in the same general category as you? You mean, magic things?" I say. I realize too late that that's another question, even two questions, but Erg only answers me with renewed sobbing. "How about this: where did you sneak off to last night? Is that a question you're allowed to answer? I saw your footsteps in the snow, but before I could look for you the motorcyclist came right at me. And then I guess Tomin ran away like a wuss, and somehow I didn't get pulverized?"

Erg just rolls her face against my leg and keens, but suddenly one of those loose bits of information finds the right slot in my brain. The motorcyclist told me that Night *hears the messenger,* and all at once I'm pretty sure I know who that messenger is. She can talk to the motorcyclist. He obviously hears what she's saying even when he can't acknowledge me at all. She can probably talk to Night, too, and understand its language. They're all basically on the same team, and a pitiful little human like me can't expect to comprehend what they're playing at.

And—God, how obvious is it now?—that's where she disappeared to while Tomin was hanging around.

"You went to get him," I say, and this time it's not a question at all. "The motorcyclist. That's why he drove at me like that. You were already riding around with him. You set up the whole thing."

I don't mean for it to sound like an accusation, but it kind of does. Erg won't stop crying, it's awful, especially since I don't know whether to blame her or myself. "Want some breakfast, Erg? That marshmallow butter isn't nearly enough to fill you up, right?" I nudge her, trying to coax her to look at me. "Now, *that's* a question I know you can handle! Dollface?"

Finally, finally she turns her head enough to glance at me, her tiny lips trembling. "I'm not hungry."

That's a new one. And it's perfectly calculated to make me sick with worry. "I bet you'll feel better if you eat something solid. We still have some of those lagoon toaster tarts. Let me open one for you?" Erg just turns her face back to my leg and snuffles; I tear into one of the foil packets anyway. "Erg? Pretty blue frosting? And when we get out of here I'll take you out for ice cream or whatever you want. Okay?"

"I don't feel well," Erg murmurs. "You should let me sleep."

I stare at her for a moment; I don't think it's even possible for her to get physically ill. This has to be an act. "Fine," I say after a lull. "I guess we're both tired." It's true, too. I was unconscious for a good chunk of the night, but somehow it wasn't restful at all.

I lie down and look at my feet, one pale and human with chipped silver toenails and the other with thick, coal-colored skin webbed across a fan of bones. Erg is still clinging to my leg. I'd like to hold her, but I'm guessing she's not in the mood to be cuddled.

Looking up at the peeling ceiling, I remember the stars that raced around me and the cities that glinted below. He was once part of *the all above us,* but now he's separated from it. Lost from something above, turned into a doll and a slave, blindly watching the stars inside his own mind. And didn't he say once that for him the sun is always buried under the earth?

So, what's above us when the sun is below? The cot creaks as I crane my head back. I almost expect the ceiling to open and reveal the answer to me, but in fact I know it anyway. I would have figured it out earlier, maybe, if I didn't have this silly habit of being more or less sane.

He used to *be* the night, or a piece of it anyway. And now that it's day again I miss him way too much for comfort.

When I see him again I'll know there's only one more night between me and survival—but it's starting to feel like I have way more to do here than just get out alive.

CHAPTER 12

It takes me a long time to fall asleep. I stare up at the ugly vacancy of my tiny room with its dim lightbulb always smoldering above. I keep wishing that I was back on that motorcycle, holding him close, my hair merging with the wind. I mean, I know a night-doll-monster-beast isn't the most conventional choice for a boyfriend, but does his inhumanity really have to be a deal breaker? I've never cared much about what's normal before—being Zinaida's kid meant that *normal* was always a pretty alien concept for me—so why would I start now? Being not-human must give him a unique perspective on life, and I could learn way more from him than from your standard-issue guy. Tomin would be the socially acceptable choice, but he put all his energy into saving himself while Night and the motorcyclist were busy helping me instead. Right?

Right?

I wish there was someone here to argue with me. I wish somebody would barge in and lecture me on what a big mistake I'm making; then I could flip out. Yell at them for being so uptight and narrow-minded that they can't appreciate a really intriguing, sensitive night-doll-monster-beast when they meet one. Erg is out cold on my leg, though, and nobody else shows up to oblige me. I can hear whispery shuffling noises on the roof overhead; it must be my swans snuggling as close to me as they can.

I'm still arguing feverishly with my judgmental imaginary friend when the air seems to phase into gray, and I realize that I'm not in bed anymore. I'm walking—it's clear that I've been walking for quite a while now—through a dull gray forest with light much too unfocused to come from any sun.

"Just because somebody starts *out* human it's no guarantee they're going to *stay* human, anyway!" I proclaim. Even to myself I sound pretty ridiculous. "Look at my dad!"

I wave my hands in the air, but they don't go very high because I'm holding a leash on each side. The leash in my left hand leads to an enormous swan, waddling patiently even as it cranes its neck to stare back at me, and the leash in my right . . .

I'm walking my dad. I know it's him even though I never saw him again after he left us for his *appointment*. He was in such a hurry to get away that he didn't even hug me goodbye, just waved from the door—with an expression on his face like he was desperate to reach a bathroom—and bolted. Chelsea's told me a million times that it really wasn't about us. She thinks that what he was running away from was his disappointment with himself, with the way he hadn't lived up to his own inflated expectations; he came from a family of big shots and he took it for granted that he'd be one, too.

Still, it's pretty hard not to take something like that personally. He looks like an oversized German shepherd now. I knew about the dog part, of course, but not the specific breed. He has a lovely thick coat, if I say so myself. His pink tongue sways as he pants up at my face; I can't tell if he remembers me.

"Ah, yes," Pangolin says, and reaches down to scratch my dad behind one floppy ear. "An elegantly composed metamorphosis, his. I'd imagine he went to considerable expense to pull it off so handily. What fine, fine claws he has."

"Hi!" I say, startled. "I was getting worried about you." As soon as I say it I know the truth: I wasn't nearly worried enough. He and Picnic should have left the store last night. At the very least I should have checked for their departing footprints in the snow; I'm the one who encouraged them to wake up Babs, after all. "Are you okay?"

Pangolin scuffs at the path's dead silvery leaves with curling toes. His moist snout waggles up at me and his tail thrashes. "I regret to say that Picnic and I are not . . . entirely content with our present circumstances. Though if I may say so, we would be far less satisfied if we were members of that peculiar species you mentioned just now."

"Human, you mean." I'm getting used to how things work now; he doesn't have to answer. Picnic looks reasonably humanesque, but I've learned that doesn't necessarily mean much. "Seems like it's really going out of style. Getting downright passé. So I guess you think what my dad did counts as self-improvement?"

"Perhaps I would describe that as a, shall we say, a *lateral* move. Believe me, I don't mean to impute any truly crippling inadequacy on the part of those . . ." Pangolin pauses and snuffles with embarrassment. "No one denies that such creatures can attain . . . a small measure of dignity, miss, despite the limitations of their nature. Certain modest accomplishments can be theirs. You, for example, are currently operating in a milieu that quite recently was denied to you. I did tell you that I thought you might manage it with practice."

It takes me a few moments to get past his explanation of my non-crippling inadequacy and sort through the rest of it. "You mean we're asleep?"

"You seem to have improved your qualifications with considerable dispatch," Pangolin agrees with approval. "Sleep *and* dreams now fall within your compass, miss. I thought you showed a certain potential, but I hardly hoped you would develop so much in such a short time. I won't make any *personal* inquiries, but I do suspect you may have had some assistance." He stands on tiptoe, leans in and sniffs close to my neck, huffing humid vapors at my skin. "I smell a formal connection that might explain how you exceed the limitations usual to your kind. A bond. Indeed, you are not legally free *not* to exceed them. You are subject to certain obligations."

The countless trees suddenly give a synchronized shake in the unmoving air and silver leaves wheel down on all sides. My dad whines and I reach to pet him without thinking. His fur feels coarse and oily. On my other side the swan glows with snowy light against the hunched shadows among the trees. Pangolin's giving me a lot to think about, and after brooding for a moment I'm not sure I want to understand what he's telling me any better than I do already.

"What's wrong with your present circumstances, anyway?" If Erg's taught me one thing, it's how to change the subject.

"Ah," Pangolin says, and shuffles. His claws shred the leaves into whispering confetti. "Ah, well. Our current habitation is not the most choice. Lacking various comforts. Picnic wished me to tell you that we find it less than perfectly congenial. We might prefer to relocate."

"Are you asking me for help?" I say. Then in the next instant I'm sorry I said anything. My situation is crazy enough as it is without throwing in a rescue mission. So why can't I just shut up?

Because it's my fault they got busted, is why. I'm responsible. Shutting up is a luxury I don't deserve.

"Are you trying to tell me that Babs has you trapped somehow?" I ask.

Pangolin sort of ruffles his neck, scales rippling. His glasses fall off his snout and vanish into the leaves, and he dives down and starts rooting for them. Of course he's asking me for help. That's why he's here. My swan snakes its head down through silvery drifts and comes up with the glasses askew on its beak and a wicked expression, maybe even a *smile*, on its face.

"Pangolin?" I say. "Can you tell me where you are?"

He doesn't even look up, just keeps snorting around on all fours, the tails of his suit jacket flapping. It's apparently one of those difficult questions, the kind with wrong-flavored answers. The kind that Erg would say *we* don't discuss. Beside me my dad suddenly barks. His voice seems weirdly shrill for such a big dog. Then he bursts out whining and tugs hard on the leash.

Every direction in this forest looks exactly the same as every other direction, but I still know where he's trying to take me. *This isn't the dream I wanted,* I want to say. *Can I please send it back?*

I wake up sweat-slicked and shivering, the tatty blanket knotted around my legs. Tea-colored light smudges the walls and I lie there, too queasy and tense to move. Unidentified shadows creep along the newspaper screen that hides the toilet, clouding the faces of dead presidents. I have to do *something*, and there's nothing I can do—except, maybe, go in for futile, random, completely half-assed heroics, and fail dismally, and get myself killed. Best plan *ever*, Vassa!

I push up onto my elbows and see Erg's head sticking out of the silver packet that held those lagoon toaster tarts, her little glossy face haloed in crumbs, blue filling gobbed onto her slick black curls. That's great that she got her appetite back so quickly. For a while I just stare down at her as she sleeps, thinking about what Pangolin told me. That "formal connection" he mentioned can only mean one thing, but I'm not as clear on the part about my obligations. Feeding Erg, sure, but what *else* am I required to do? Erg's been working hard to keep me safe since we got here, but she didn't actually try to discourage me from entering BY's in the first place. On reflection, that does seem kind of out of character.

I can't stop myself from wondering, suddenly, if her real agenda has anything to do with me at all. But there's no point in asking her; I'll never get the truth. And she has her excuse perfectly prepared. Why, of *course* she can't tell me anything important, of course she goes into hysterics if I need information. Jeez, Vassa, don't you know there are *rules*?

I don't want to resent Erg. Really. I don't want to distrust her. She's done so much for me, and in my own useless way I totally love her. But considering that there are *certain obligations* that I'm not *legally free* to blow off, it does kind of feel like she owes me a lot more honesty than I've gotten so far.

"Erg?" I say. I shake the packet gently, listening to its metallic rustle; it sounds like the leaves that kept falling in my dream. "Erg, wake up! I need your help with something."

Erg's blue eyes are instantly open, the look in them sad and skeptical. She wasn't asleep at all.

"I *always* help you," she says, and for the first time ever I realize that she might resent me, too. "Don't I, Vassa? I carry things around for you that you sure couldn't handle by yourself!"

I'm not clear on what that last part is supposed to mean, and right at the moment I'm not much interested. "Picnic and Pangolin are in trouble. I think they're in that apartment or whatever it is where Babs lives. And it's kind of my fault, since I told them to try it? I don't know why I thought they'd be safe, but I was totally wrong."

Erg just stares up at me from her foil packet, utterly unsurprised. If she knows so much, then why do I even bother speaking?

"So can you help me get in there?" I continue after an awkward silence. "It's going to be tricky with the door so near the register and everything. Babs is probably right there, and then there are the hands to watch out for."

Erg still doesn't say anything, but her lips are curling into a funny half smile.

"I thought maybe you could distract them," I finally say. "So I can sneak in?"

Erg wriggles out of the foil packet and bounces onto the back of my arm where it rests on the mattress. "Wow, that's so sweet of you, Vassa! To do something that totally dangerous just for Picnic and Pangolin. Because *naturally* that's the only reason you would even dream of going in there. I mean naturally. It would never, ever occur to you that you might find out something about your boyfriend."

"My what?" I say, although we both know that we both know. "Who are you talking about, dollface?"

"*Vrum, vrum?*" Her little face is twisting. "Golly, where does Babs keep him during the day, anyway? I can't *begin* to imagine."

She's bringing him up for a reason, I'm pretty sure. Letting me know without saying it in so many words. "So . . . do you think we *could* help him? Is that . . . I don't know, is it possible?"

"Help him do what? That's the real question," Erg observes cryptically.

"Get free. All those guys on the motorcycles are trapped. I *know* they are." Like me. What makes me think I'm in a position to free anyone when I obviously can't free myself? "Doll, you want to help him, too, don't you? You *seem* like you like him. Do you?" If anything I'd guess that she likes him too much; she seems just a shade too interested whenever the subject comes up. Could Erg be capable of getting a crush on someone?

Erg considers that, and I realize I've never heard her say that she personally likes or hates anyone. She only ever says what *I* feel.

"Well, I *understand* him, anyway," Erg says at last. "I guess you could say that I relate to him?"

"Do you feel trapped with me?" It's never occurred to me to wonder that before.

Erg looks away. "So you need me to create a diversion? I can do that for you, Vassa. Sure I can!" She pauses and then stares back at me, her blue eyes hard and wounded. "Since everything *else* I've done isn't enough for you. Is it?"

Now it's my turn to glance away. Maybe I was being really unfair to her. Maybe I've been unfair to her for years. A streak of feverish yellow floor gleams under my door and I can just glimpse a sliver of gray-pink wrist through the gap. Skin whispers on wood and a frosted nail bends down to peer in at us. When it sees me looking back the hand hops away, willfully casual, just as if I hadn't caught it spying. "Do you have a better idea? Because right now—even if I *do* get away tomorrow, I'd be leaving everyone else here completely screwed. I really don't see how I can do that!"

She bends down and nuzzles the back of my hand with her cheek, sticky with swimming pool–colored gunk. "Babs thinks she's *always* the one who wins," Erg observes, and again I'm surprised by how caustic she sounds. "She thinks she can get her way every single time. But we'll show her!"

"So you do think it's the right thing to do?" I ask, and I realize that I really, intensely care what she thinks about this. "Trying to get Pangolin out—and maybe—"

Erg pulls herself up and gives a quick shake, dislodged crumbs flinging off her tiny body. "I wish it wasn't going to be you, Vassa. Going in there. It's not safe for you at all. I mean, there might be some things in there that aren't very friendly."

"But you won't tell me *not* to do it?" It's only now that I understand she won't be coming with me. Even if it's risky for me, Erg can take care of herself just fine. Right? She can outsmart Babs and the hands, no problem. Can't she?

"I won't tell you not to do it," Erg agrees somberly. "Because that's why we're here."

INTERLUDE IN SCALES

THE PREVIOUS FEBRUARY

Icy pockmarks hollowed the snow so it shattered under the scrabbling of conical claws and the thrash of a heavy tail; the alley was narrow and inconspicuous and no one had cleared away the drifts. The windows on both sides were sealed with cement blocks and gray icicles dripped from their frames. The corpse—an old man swaddled in rotten furs, his gaping mouth showing two ragged curves of bone in lieu of ordinary teeth—had been left tied to a streetlamp. His neck was badly bruised, his tongue swollen. The body drooped against its bonds and its feet had skidded apart on the icy ground: feet that were almost entirely concealed by extremely long, voluminous pants. Wads of filthy cloth hunched around its shoes, and Pangolin bent to look closer. It was an unnecessary gesture. He was already perfectly aware that those feet in their broken shoes pointed back toward the lamppost: that is, in the opposite direction from the face.

He straightened and peered at a curling note pinned to the old man's mangy lapel. The red ink was snow-smeared but still faintly legible.

Pangolin glanced around for Picnic, who was hugging a corner of the nearest building and tenderly nuzzling the brick. "It appears that poor dear Candlewax has borne the brunt of some overly excitable humans' displeasure. Regarding a certain nocturnal stubbornness, which Candlewax himself assuredly did nothing to instigate." Picnic tipped his head back and regarded his partner with sleepy eyes, then gave the wall a slow, exploratory lick. "*We will slaughter all you unnatural scum one by one until we get our daylight back,* it says here. Regrettable ignorance, is it not, Picnic? The writer would benefit from instruction on the subject of *nature.* Both what it encompasses, and what it excludes."

"A fish will balance best with both its feet planted," Picnic observed gravely. He stood on tiptoe to nibble a soot-blackened icicle.

"Indeed," Pangolin agreed. "And I fear that persons unknown—though manifestly they can only be *persons of quality*—have rather unbalanced the fish in question, distending the nights as they have. Dreadful selfishness, tinkering with the dim hours in this fashion. Most irresponsible. Well, we have our mandate: to ensure harmony between our community and what one might describe as, perhaps, the society of the not-up-to-snuff. And harmony has no better preservative than obliviousness. I fear the persistent nights are encouraging the lower orders to pay us rather too much attention. They certainly paid too much to poor Candlewax. An appalling bit of vigilantism, this! I expect that some *human* took note of his feet and saw fit to blame him unfairly. And now we must guard against further attacks on others of our society with, ahem, salient characteristics." A ripple passed through the tip of his snout.

Picnic padded over, his checked suit flapping in the frigid wind, and examined the corpse for a moment. Then he reached out and gave it a gentle shake. Firefly glints began to creep over the snow, gathering from all directions. Soon the backward feet and flopping trousers were covered in twinkling swarms, and Picnic snuffled with satisfaction. The brass plaque around his neck gleamed with unsettled reflections. "Cracked eggs still have yolks," Picnic said thoughtfully.

"And as this nightfulness appears to thin with distance, it should be entirely possible to pinpoint its epicenter? I find myself very much inclined to agree, Picnic. Well, then, we must take it upon ourselves to bring the full weight of the law to bear—on these persons of questionable judgment—until balance can be restored. We will track down the source of the expanding darkness and identify the perpetrators! We will," Pangolin added, "bring a *suit* against them. In the court of possibilities!"

Picnic's eyes widened as he turned to stare at his partner, and he gave a high-pitched whinny.

"We will indeed!" Pangolin affirmed. "We will exert our full authority! No measure is too drastic, Picnic, when we find ourselves faced with such perversity!" Behind him the seething lights had already devoured nearly all of the old furrier's flesh; ribbons of worn pelt dripped from exposed bones. The living sparks gathered in dense rings around the skull's empty eyes and the sockets began to widen. It was clear that by morning no trace of the body would remain.

Picnic stood for a long moment with his head tipped, then nodded. A full moon was just rolling into the crevice of sky overhead, and Picnic flourished one long hand in its direction. "The Brooklyn Bridge sweats birds tonight. Wet as fresh-washed socks."

"So it does," Pangolin agreed, and proffered his paw.

CHAPTER 13

That's why we're here. I try repeating that in my head a few times, getting used to the way it sounds. *That's why we're here.* Clueless little humanette that I am, I thought we'd gotten stuck here because I came in for lightbulbs. I thought Erg was here to protect me, not to make sure I carry out some vague mission to do with *showing* Babs. How naïve of me.

"You mean we're here to . . . put Babs out of business?" Maybe I'm semi-enchanted even now, because when I put it like that it sounds awfully mean. Babs has her issues, no question, but for some reason I don't actually want to do her harm. She's like the hopelessly pathological grandmother I never had.

"You don't *like* what Babs is doing, Vassa," Erg explains. Ah, so we're back to speaking exclusively in terms of how *I* feel, as if Erg's feelings weren't at least as much of a factor in getting us into this mess. As if she didn't have a whole slew of emotions independent of mine. "You're still really upset about Joel. And you don't like the way she treats your boyfriend, or the swans, or those two lawyers. You'd love to stop her from hurting anyone else ever again! Right?"

"Sure," I say. *What do I owe myself, Joel? What did I borrow from myself, and how on earth will I ever give it back?* "Every time I see

Joel's head out there . . . Somebody should stop Babs from doing that."

Erg arches her black eyebrows at me. "*Somebody*. Oh naturally, Vassa. As in somebody-who-isn't-Vassa should stop her? Some big, strong not-Vassa hero-person should come along and make everything better, and fix the nights, and help your boyfriend! And maybe after this somebody *else* gets around to fixing everything, *you* can bake them some nice cookies to say thank you! Oh, except by then you'll be too old to stir the batter."

Maybe she has a point, but she doesn't have to be so snide about it. "So Pangolin was right? Something Babs is doing is making the nights last so long?" This is probably one of those forbidden questions because Erg just fixes me with a sardonic stare, her flat blue eyes weirdly brilliant. I twist the scraggly blanket in my hands. "Well, BY's *is* the only store around here that stays open all night! I guess stretching the nights out must be good for business." I think I'm only kidding until I hear the words settling on the air. At first they start sounding kind of true, then as Erg keeps on gazing at me they sound absolutely true, unbearably true.

"Ooh, what good thinking, Vassa!" Erg lilts. "Gee, maybe that *is* Babsie's motive. I mean, *you* never would have come in here if the nights were just normal-length, right? And Babs would get so bored if she didn't have customers to play with."

Every single thing I figure out just sends new questions avalanching down around me. "Okay. But how? I mean how the hell could Babs do that?"

Erg gives me one of her how-dumb-can-you-be looks.

"This has something to do with the motorcyclist," I say after a moment. "It's crazy, but I think he might be . . . connected to the night? Is he like a hostage?"

Erg doesn't answer, but she does lift the corners of her mouth just a hair. Letting me know. "So, about how you want me to create a diversion? Babs will stay at the register if she thinks that's what we're doing. So what you need to do is go talk to her and act really hard like you're trying to *keep* her at the register, okay? Ask her lots of questions. Pretend like *you're* the diversion. Then she'll go to see what's happening in back. Okay? Does that make sense? *Then* you run for her door."

"You sound worried," I tell her. "No faith in me, Erg?" I'm not too sure I can pull it off, either, really. And even if I *do* get into Babs's rooms I won't have the foggiest idea what to do next.

Even so, I start wriggling my swan foot into my boot. If we're really doing something this crazy, then we might as well start now.

"Well." Erg has the grace to look embarrassed. "It's not like you're a *doll*, Vassa. I mean I think—compared to a lot of humans, you'll probably do fine? I mean you're used to being *around* a doll, right? So I'd think that would have to help some!"

"Keep digging that hole, Erg," I tell her. But then I scoop her up, and wipe the gunk off her hair, and kiss the top of her little head over and over. And she doesn't even try to bite.

I'm not actually doing this, I tell myself as I straighten my jacket and make a haphazard effort at untangling my hair a little. *I wouldn't do anything this stupid.* But I'm leaning down over the cot, holding out my sleeve for Erg. *Anyway, what about Chelsea? You promised you'd be home tomorrow.* It feels like I'm acting out gestures that have been waiting for me all along, like my movements are grooves cut into the air and I'm suddenly flowing inside them.

I open the door and step out into the orange and yellow of BY's, the colors sizzling around me like hot grease. After a few steps Erg taps my arm, and I lean against a shelf for a moment to let her out. I feel the skid of her tiny wooden hands on my wrist; I hear the faint clang of her feet hitting the metal. The tinkling piano music almost covers her chiming footsteps, but not quite. I don't let myself look down to watch her darting behind the jars of green-blue salsa.

That means I'm on my own, of course. I hadn't realized until right now how completely I'm accustomed to relying on her. The idea that Erg would deliberately send me into danger makes my knees waver just a bit with each step.

I walk lazily down the aisle, picking up boxes—one is a cereal called Weasel Bites!—and putting them back in the wrong spots, stuffed in at the wrong angles. It's enough to bring the hands thumping after me, indignantly straightening the things I've mussed; that should give Erg enough time to start whatever she's got planned. I turn away from the hands, knocking a display of hot pink canisters with my elbow. Half a dozen of them clatter to the floor; I absently pick them up, shove them in odd corners, and put one on top of the refrigerator.

Dexter leaps on top of my head with a sickening soft slap, then scrambles in my hair until he's swinging right in front of my nose, jiggling furiously all the while. I wouldn't say I'm used to it, especially not to the feeling of his skin, like hot, dried-out dough, when he drags against my nose.

This close I can smell him, ashy and slightly rotten. He swats at me and then drops heavily onto the floor. Then he just stays there, weak and worn-out from attacking me, so I get a good look at his thumb. It's swollen as fat as a crimson leech and the inflammation has spread up past the joint; there's an edge of dirty green around the ragged imprint left by Erg's teeth.

Without thinking I bend down and grab him by the pinkie then saunter over to the register. He seems too sick to fight back effectively, and Sinister is still in a fluster of neatening up. Babs looks at me groggily, her head lifting up from her crossed arms.

"Hey, Babs?" I say. "I think poor little Dexter here needs a vet. He's looking pretty gross." I hold him up as he twitches angrily and claws at my palm with his free fingers, then I plop him right on her sleeve.

With a quick, spastic sweep she sends him flying. He collides with the shelves behind her and tumbles down in a rattling mess of tiny bottles. I perch on the counter right in front of Babs, ostentatiously casual, as if I wanted to block her view of the store behind me.

"Vassa," Babs hisses. "You're not a girl at all, are you? You're the noise of a car crash, perhaps. A broken toaster. Bea should know better than to send the likes of you. I'll be seizing the opportunity, though, since it's gone and stuffed itself into my store. I'll teach her how futile it is to harass me!"

I decide to ignore that; the name Bea does sound dimly familiar, but right now I can't place it. I peer around Babs to see Dexter wallowing among scattered stars of broken glass. He's bruised and there are flecks of fresh blood on his sallow skin; if he had a voice I'm pretty sure he'd be whimpering.

"I mean, Dex *is* your pet, right?" I say—and the funny thing is that I really mean it. Watching him flopping in that miserable way sends an angry flush through my face. "Don't you think you should take better care of him?"

She stares at me, maybe too irritated to speak, and I glance out the window. Of course every trace of snow has melted away—you know, now that it's served its purpose—and the parking lot is darkly glittering like a bald gray head in the vibrant sunlight. It looks like it's still early morning. "Dexter is an *employee*," Babs snarls at last. She aims her rolling eye at my right hand where it rests on the counter. "Plenty more where he came from."

"Oh, Dexter!" I say. "You hear that? There you are, injured in the line of duty, and Babs is already scoping your replacement. Poor baby, that must really hurt."

From the back of the store behind me comes an unexpected sound, high and resonant. A weird fizzling noise invades that endless crooning pop song. I lean closer to Babs's face and take hold of her bony shoulders like I want to stop her from getting up. Dex is up on his wrist in the wreckage now, fingertips curled as if they're looking at me. I'm absolutely sure now that those painted nails function as eyes. Then he pivots toward Babs. For a disembodied hand, he does an outstanding job of looking plaintive.

"Dexter," Babs snaps. "Get up here and remove this parasitic toilet plunger from my person."

"You mean me, Babs?" I say. Erg did tell me to keep asking questions. "Aw, you used to think I was pretty! Who's this Bea you were talking about, anyway?"

Dexter dutifully hobbles over and starts climbing the wheeled base of Babs's chair, but he's obviously having a hard time of it. The music keeps getting more distorted, the singer's voice warping into a painful throb. Erg must be doing something horrible to the speakers. Then the store gives a little jump, and Dexter loses his grip and splats back onto the yellow floor. His infected thumb convulses. It's truly pitiful.

Babs cranes her head and shoots him a withering look. Then she stands, strength surging through her wasted-looking body, and shoves me hard enough to send me toppling onto the floor. By the time I'm back on my feet she's already swinging around the counter and heading up the aisle on the right. The speaker at the back emits a tortured squawk and goes dead. Dexter comes creeping after her, but in his battered condition he can't keep up. He's still way too near the door to Babs's rooms. I make myself walk slowly and calmly in that direction. The sound of running footsteps would be sure to bring Babs and Sinister down on me in a heartbeat.

Dexter turns to watch me as I slip up to the dull orange door just past the counter. There's no way I can stop him from seeing me go in there. Then I notice the axe hanging on a hook just to my right: the same axe he was ready to swing at my neck when I first arrived here. Given his weakened state, I could probably chop him in half without even trying that hard. Bring the sluglike chunks along with me and tuck them under Babs's pillow for the dead hand fairy. Maybe Babs will get a dollar!

He looks at me with his hazy lilac nails, somehow managing to seem sad and sheepish. Then he raises his nails toward the axe. It wouldn't be like killing a person or even a squirrel. Whoever Dexter came from was hacked to bits long ago. Probably the head once associated with Dexter is decorating a pole right now. I take the axe off its hook, balancing the weight of it in my grip. When I glance toward the back of the store I see Babs oozing up the shelves like an inchworm to get at that malfunctioning speaker. I can get away with this.

Dexter waits, his skin tone even grayer by contrast with the screaming yellow floor. Mournful and resigned. Maybe he misses the person he once belonged to. Maybe, for a hand, losing your person is the loneliest thing that could possibly happen.

I hang the axe back up. Dexter flexes a little in surprise.

"Can you keep a secret, Dex?" I whisper. "Tell her I went back to bed, okay?" And I open the door, skimming through without even looking where I'm going. As it closes behind me I have just enough time to see Dexter bobbing his nails up and down.

Like he's nodding.

CHAPTER 14

It's dark inside—no surprise there—but the darkness is prickly and uneven. It seems to shuffle and rearrange itself like a deck of cards as I turn to face it. Fine; I didn't expect this place to feel comforting. I can't make out the floor so I slide my feet along, my hands stretched wide to hold the shadows. There's nothing anywhere that hints at walls; I could be on a football field, albeit a field shrouded in ash-clouds from a convenient volcano. My breath is fast and shallow and I keep half-jerking back, sure that I'm about to fall. After a moment, as if on cue, a light appears in the distance. Small and amber, an antique star floating all alone. Beckoning me. Probably the smart thing would be to go in any direction but that, but *smart* doesn't appear to be my outstanding characteristic these days.

It feels like I'm shoving my boots along shag carpeting. The light waits patiently in a dim expanse. Once I get closer I can see amber reflecting off the sharp point supporting it, angled lines sweeping below. It's incomprehensible until I'm right in front of it, running my hands down its beams, looking it over in the dull orange glow. My eyes must be adjusting to the dimness, because suddenly I can see it fairly well.

Why, of course. It's a five-foot-tall tin model of the Eiffel Tower with a twinkling bulb on its summit. A placard on its front reads *Ooh La La!* in garish pink enamel script.

Gosh, Vassa, what else *would it be?* I let out a sputtering laugh—a little hysterical sounding, honestly—and turn away fast enough to stub my webbed toes against something lower down.

On inspection the something looks like a glass ashtray, except bigger. It would be the perfect size if you were smoking kitchen sinks, maybe, or kindergartners. In the middle I can make out the words *Las Vegas* in gleaming gilt letters surrounded by chaotic images of dice, shooting stars, playing cards.

Now I'm definitely getting hysterical, but I can't seem to stop the gasping, manic laugh in my throat. I'm not moving nearly as cautiously now and I stagger into a waist-high, porcelain blob painted to look like the Brooklyn Bridge. Babs has quite the souvenir collection.

On the far side of the bridge I suddenly notice a wall trying to pretend that it was there all along. And in the wall, another door with a welcoming golden light just above it. "Yeah, right," I say aloud. "Like you're not a trap?"

Maybe it's my imagination, but I could swear the wall looks offended.

"Don't worry," I tell it. "I'm coming in anyway." I don't see how I stand a chance of finding Picnic and Pangolin—or Mr. Night-Doll-Monster-Beast for that matter—unless I explore every last possibility. Even the possibilities that are just here to mess me up, since in a place like this that's probably all of them. I leave the bridge and walk over to the door.

It sounds like there's a seriously wild party going on behind it. And they're playing that damn song with the cascading piano, the whispery girl's voice. It's the same melody, piercing and relentless, but somehow more beautiful than ever.

If there's one thing Zinaida's daughter should be able to handle, it's a party. My clothes are stiff with dried blood and my hair is so ratted I might end up cutting off half of it, but that never would have stopped her from raging. On Zinaida, swan blood would have been a *statement*. After a moment's hesitation I turn the knob and strut right in like I own the place, tossing my head the way she used to do.

The instant the door opens the music vanishes.

The room in front of me is better lit than the last one, and it appears to be perfectly empty. There's a faint receding babble of drunken voices and then that fades out, too, like tumbleweed rolling into the distance.

"Fine," I say aloud, but my heartbeat is careening through my head and waves of cold prickle my skin. I force myself to walk forward. Apart from the uncanny disappearance of the guests it does look like a party, the kind where Zinaida would have been right at home. The room is huge and high-ceilinged. There's one wall of exposed brick and another with dramatic squiggly wallpaper, old gold and caramel and violet. Half-drunk cocktails are perched precariously on velvet sofas with slithery curves. Confusing chandeliers with stuffed exotic birds flying among the crystals sway overhead. BY's must be a whole lot more profitable than it seems, if Babs can afford this stuff.

When I was seven I would have been left in the corner with a plate of stinky cheese and a comic book. Somebody would have given me a glass of champagne as a joke. Now and then I'd glance up to watch my mother, fascinated by how lovely and vivacious she was, the way everyone stared at her. If you'd asked me at the time, I'd have said that all I wanted out of life was to be as much like Zinaida as possible.

Then by midnight I would have been asleep on the floor, and at three a.m., one of her coked-out admirers would have carried me down to a taxi.

I wish I could go back to being scared. Even frenzied terror would be an improvement over what I'm feeling now. Just for an instant I close my eyes, trying to will away the icy sickness in my stomach.

When I open them again the room seems distinctly bigger, its ceiling higher, its furniture bloated. A long buffet table has materialized on the far side; it looks picked over and abandoned, with oysters slopping in half-melted snow. And hanging over it is a huge oil painting, all sweeping yellow waves and small purple figures caught in tidal swirls. I know that painting.

It's by my mother. I personally *posed* for those teeny drowning people by rolling around her studio floor. It seemed like a blast at the time and it never occurred to me to wonder why she always painted me dying.

Traps don't get more obvious than this. And they don't get more irresistible.

I'm halfway across the room before I even have time to notice that my hands are trembling.

"Champagne?" someone says when I'm still fifteen feet from the painting. I take the proffered glass by reflex—the bubbles look strange, knife-bright—and only then twist around to see who's there.

Ah. No one. Just that serpentine wallpaper and a Venus de Milo completely covered in scarlet glitter on a pedestal. Even that's pretty far away, and what with the lack of arms she'd make a rotten waiter. I can't repress a yelp.

"Nice touch," I tell the air once I've recovered a little. "Really, you're doing a great job!" I'm a long way from legal drinking age, of course, but on the other hand I'm a lot closer now than I was the last time someone offered me champagne. I lift it up, inhale its scent. It smells intoxicating, fresh and deep and floral all at the same time. My nostrils dilate and saliva floods my mouth.

Even I'm not stupid enough to fall for this one. I let the glass drop, dreamily, as if it had just slipped from my fingers.

There's no tinkle of breaking glass on the polished floor. No sound at all. I don't let myself look. Doing my best Zinaida, I pretend I'm not shaking and saunter toward the buffet. I wish I wasn't so hungry suddenly. That platter with the oysters is right in front of me, next to a cake that would be gorgeous if it didn't have a crater in the top. Was there a meteor shower just now?

Somebody attached pairs of shiny black leather doll shoes to each and every oyster. Cute.

And, uh, somebody is polishing them.

He's about a foot tall. A distinguished-looking gentleman with short silvery hair, but his clothes are dark and rough as if he'd fallen on hard times and had to go to work shining boots in the subway. He's certainly working very hard, stooped over and buffing maniacally, his rags and waxes spread out beside him. He doesn't look at me as he finishes with one oyster and moves on to the next. "Um, hi?" I hazard. "Sir?"

He glances up in alarm. At least he can hear me.

"I'm, uh, my friends were supposed to meet me here, but I can't find them. Picnic and Pangolin? Picnic would be wearing a red-checked suit. Pangolin has scales. Have you seen them?"

The miniature man is backing away from me in terror. He collides with the cake behind him—it's taller than he is—and starts sort of insinuating himself into its frosting with a slow twisting motion. Like he could burrow his way inside it and I wouldn't have any idea where he'd gone. It's so ludicrous, and I'm so on edge, that I give in to an impulse to mess with him. Staring right at his face, I grab a plate off a nearby stack, pick up the ornate cake server lying there, and cut myself a big piece that just so happens to be the piece he's wallowing against. The blade slides down to his left, then to his right. His eyes go wide, but he doesn't stop squirming against the cake-wall. It has beautiful frosting, striped lilac and metallic gold, with clambering blue and purple vines. When I slide the server under his feet he jumps sideways and sits down with a thump in a swamp of crumbs and slippery fudge.

The slice falls in half as I carry it to my plate, burying his legs in a cakevalanche. An azure sugar rose lands right on his lap.

"So, as I was saying," I continue, swinging a fork in midair. "Picnic and Pangolin. Have you seen them anywhere?" The cake, I have to admit, looks delicious, with fat cherries layered in custard and dark chocolate pastry. A forkful of it is halfway to my mouth even as the petite gentleman gapes at me. He's started shaking so violently the forks rattle. "Or a huge guy in black on a motorcycle? I'd like to find him, too."

I stare at him as I open my mouth to take a slow, theatrical bite.

He's shuddering so hard that I can't see him clearly, but I can tell that his head is inflating and turning magenta. His arms spindle outward, suddenly flailing far across the table, and he bursts into an explosive scream that hammers at my eardrums. My hands fly up by reflex to cover my ears and the cake flops onto my chest, sliding down and adding a trail of custard and frosting to the bloody mess already covering my jacket.

Then I realize what a close call it was. It doesn't take a genius to know that eating the food here would be a very, very bad idea— even if I'm so hungry now that it's making me a little unbalanced. It's been a long time since I had a meal. Still, if that's all there is to the trap—*lay off the food, girlfriend*—then it's not nearly as tricky as I expected.

By the time I've recovered from the shock he's already tunneling deep inside the cake. It's my fault for being so mean, of course. What's wrong with me?

"Sorry!" I call softly, but he's gone.

The music, on the other hand, has come back, just as suddenly as it vanished. So has the chaos of laughing, chattering voices. I twist around in confusion and the sound shifts, too, traveling as I turn, so that it always seems to be coming from a spot directly behind my head. I spend a few moments jumping around like an idiot, trying to find the source of those voices, before I get a grip on myself: just because someone's playing me, that doesn't mean I have to act like a toy.

Just ignore them, Vassa. Then they'll get bored. I make myself pretend I don't care and pace over to the painting, studying it with my head cocked sideways as if I'd never seen it before. I even fold my arms, looking at the ocher tidal wave engulfing a city, blurry abstract buildings toppling, and little purple Vassas being swept away.

It's actually kind of a beautiful picture, though. Maybe my mom was a better painter than I thought. The music and voices surge right behind me, trying to get my attention, but now I don't even want to turn around. Instead I forget all about pretending to be blasé and reach a hand out toward the swirling paint.

Zinaida. I haven't seen one of her pictures in years. Iliana won't allow them in the apartment, not even reproductions, and maybe I tend to avoid them, too. Now that one is in front of me I feel like Zinaida's very close, watching me and maybe even smiling. *Mom?*

I don't let myself say it, but my mouth feels thick with the urge to call out for her.

Once when I was eight she did my jet-black hair in elaborate curls, put me in a fluffy lace dress, and had me pose for a portrait holding a gun in my mouth. Red roses in the background suggestive of spattering blood. The gun was just a realistic-looking fake, but the painting still caused quite an uproar when she exhibited it. I think there was a congressman who had something to say about that, and *The Post* published a crazed denunciation, which my mom read out loud to me in her silliest bombastic voice. How could I have a problem with anything she did when she always made sure we were both on the same team, laughing together at the dorks who were uptight enough to be outraged?

See, like Lottery would say, Zinaida had *technique.*

We both giggled like lunatics and the painting sold for a stupefying amount. I wonder if Babs owns that one, too.

Now that I come to think of it, I'm pretty sure she made my hair purple in that picture. How did I manage to forget that?

Now that I come to think of it, I really need to sit down.

All the sofas seem too far away—the room still appears to be growing bigger, and as it grows the sofas are getting dragged into the distance. After wobbling for a moment I give up and just splat down on the floor, the white hem of the tablecloth swaying in front of my face.

And that's when I see the missing party. Everyone is about the size of the shoe shiner, dressed in oddball hats with spiraling feathers, drapey silk dresses, eccentric spiny shoes. The men wear tuxedos in neon colors, some with shorts or even just polka-dot underpants. They're under the buffet table, all dancing frantically and getting wasted, lugging glasses of champagne half their own size. And there's a miniature piano where a scaled-down, elegant woman in a low-backed black dress is playing that song—always the same song—and singing so sweetly that it hurts to hear her.

Duh, Vassa.

Given the way the shoeshine man reacted to me, I decide not to say anything. I'm so dizzy that it feels like my head is filled with bursting bubbles, I'm almost nauseous from hunger, and my legs are quaking so horribly that I'm not sure I can walk. I might as well watch them for a while, then, and see if I can learn anything?

I lean my head in my hands, breathing much too hard. I find myself examining the women with special intensity, but for a while I don't admit to myself why I'm doing it. I mean, their fashion sense is pretty interesting, and their makeup is just insane: I see one whose visible skin is all pale green with crimson lines that make her look like a topographical map. After a few moments, though, I have to acknowledge the truth: I'm looking for *her.* Everything about this place screams *Zinaida*; it's baited all over with memories. So, I mean, what if she's right in front of me? What if death just made her very, very small, but she's still dancing?

What if I see her and I don't even recognize her?

When did I start crying?

"Pigsty, wombat," the tiny pianist sings passionately, her hands like wind on the keys. Are those really the right lyrics? "Day-ay-ay of the week, oh washing machine on the street! Oh, how I don't know which way is blue, and who-hoo were you when the storms fell through?"

Her voice is so beautiful that even those absurd words bring a lump to my throat. *Who was I when the storms fell through?*

Once I got wise to Zinaida—or, at least, *wiser*—then I didn't want to be like her anymore. Then there was no one left for me to want to be. I wanted to cancel everything, live as a negation: not-Zinaida, not-myself. What was *Vassa* after all but a pretty accessory for her wild mother? So who was I when the storms fell through? Why, nobody really. That girl with the purple hair. A noted kleptomaniac who didn't even steal. I try to calm down. I try to breathe deep to stop the tears coursing down my face, but I can't manage it. And Erg isn't here to order me to pull myself together.

In front of me I watch as one of those pint-sized people—this one an old, graceful woman wearing some kind of Elizabethan ruff with no shirt under it and a pair of poofy white bloomers on her bottom half—suddenly gasps, staggers, and then topples sideways. Partiers dodge her falling body and then go on dancing. Her eyes are as empty as quartz. Dead, she's obviously dead. Maybe she had a heart attack?

Then, toward the back, a weirdly slender man starts to pitch from side to side, his hand at his throat. His throat stretches out, getting queasily long, until it arches out over a nearby champagne flute with his head twitching upside down. He crumples, too. God, there's some kind of epidemic. I see a substance like silvery sand sifting out of his nose and open mouth. I see the grains lift up, hovering in midair like flies, and then start circulating purpose-fully among the dancers. Everyone's going to die. And I can't shake the idea that one of them might be her.

I lean forward, ready to grab armfuls of tiny spangled people, run with them somewhere, anywhere that they might be safe from the spreading contagion. My heart is drumming like mad as I stare around, trying to track every floating silver mote—if even one of the little people I try to save is already infected, I won't be helping at all. But my eyes can't move fast enough to follow all those specks, and I'm ready to scream from frustration. Glitter swarms in the corners of my eyes, specks invading laughing mouths and then gust-ing out again as the same mouths sputter and choke and lapse into horrible stillness. My breath has stopped, too. I lean deeper in, my forehead brushing the hanging tablecloth, watching as one dancer after another drops with brilliant tiny shoes kicking in midair. . . .

Someone grabs hold of my collar and hauls my head back. "Vassa," a melodic voice coos. "Vassa! Don't go under there!"

"I have to save—*someone*," I answer. "Anyone!" Then, without thinking what I'm saying, I give myself away in a failing murmur. "I couldn't save her before."

"Not here," the voice assures me. "Vassa, she's not here."

"They're *dying*." The plague is worse now, neon-suited miniature gentlemen gagging in pools of champagne, small women shred-ding their feathered dresses with convulsive hands.

"*They'll* be fine," the voice tells me—in a way that distinctly con-veys *and you won't*. "*They* are playing." It's speaking from just behind my left shoulder now, so I catch my breath and look back.

It's the singer in the black dress, my view of her smeared by my tears. She's standing right beside me, and she's growing rapidly. Already she must be at least three feet tall. "Why do you care what I do?" I ask. I'd wipe my eyes with my sleeve if it wasn't so filthy; I settle for the back of my hand, which isn't much better.

The singer looks at me: she seems more cute than pretty now, with a button nose and curly brown hair, and apart from the trivial matter of her size she looks a lot more ordinary than her friends. "Zinaida," she says at last. "I see her again in you."

That name works on me like magic, as she must have known it would. Suddenly I'm ready to follow the singer—who's now a whopping three-foot-eight at least—anywhere she'd care to take me. When I glance toward the party under the table again I notice the old woman in white, the one who fell first, peering slyly at me out of the corners of her eyes. If I'd inhaled that stuff I wouldn't have opened mine again, though, I bet; my insides lurch as the realization sinks in. "Do—*did* you know Zinaida?" God, how it hurts to say that. I feel like my ribs might split.

The singer smiles at me, dreamy and speculative. She looks about twenty-two, but I'd guess that can't be her real age. "Who didn't?" Irrationally, the past tense comes as a terrible disappointment to me, but she doesn't give me time to dwell on that. "Vassa, Vassa Lisa, come with me. I want to show you something."

I get up, still way too unsteady, and follow after her. My capacity for surprise is pretty well exhausted by now, so I feel only the vaguest possible wonder that she recognized me so easily. She seems to have settled on being about five foot three and her exposed back is pearly and freckled.

We wander through a messy but very fancy kitchen, all strawberry marble and chartreuse lacquer, then past an open bathroom with brass faucets in the form of impressively sinister swans with gaping maws. These swans really do resemble rats with wings, like

Babs said, and probably with rabies to boot, but even so I wish I had time for a shower. Then the singer opens another door, and we're in a small parlor with stuffed peacocks on stands and so many brocade chairs and mahogany end tables that I can barely move; some of the chairs are even heaped on top of one another, and glass-fronted cabinets are stacked on top of the heaps, all the way to the ceiling in places. The singer doesn't have any problem navigating through the mess. She just kind of slices across the room and turns to face me, smiling wryly, beside a table supporting a dozen snapshots in glimmering frames.

Her slender hand drapes along the top of one photograph in particular. She doesn't say anything but I have the distinct impression that there's nothing accidental about her pose. Once I've made it over to her, half-squirming and half-climbing, I pick the picture up. The frame is especially gorgeous on this one, gold and enamel set with opals, so it must be extra important.

At first glance, though, the image is nothing special. Two women, maybe in late middle age, wearing sloppy flowered dresses and squinting into the sun. I wouldn't recognize either of them if it weren't for the inscription: *Dearest Babs, memories of you are realer to me than present hours spent with anyone else! More love than tongue can tell, Bea.*

Bea. Now I remember her. Zinaida used to brag that while other girls might have fairy godmothers, her own godmother was a *witch*, and that was obviously much cooler.

Once or twice we visited Bea's apartment, where she served us acrid tea and cookies so stale that they crumbled to grayish dust when I tried to pick them up. Since my mother talked so much about Bea's spooky powers I'd sit there fidgeting, too scared to make eye contact. But whenever I did steal a glance, Bea would be staring at me. It didn't take many visits like that before I started bursting into hysterical tears whenever my mom suggested another one.

If Bea and Babs were witchy best friends once, it seems pretty clear that they aren't all that crazy about each other now.

"Babs said something about her," I tell the singer, a little breathlessly. Her eyes seem to float in front of me, wise and gray with caramel-colored streaks radiating through their irises. "Babs said that Bea *should know better* than to send me. But I haven't seen Bea in years."

She doesn't say anything, because giving people solid answers just isn't the way things are done here. But she stares in a way that's as vivid as speech.

"But I guess that doesn't mean that she *didn't* send me here somehow," I say after a moment. I think it works better if I speak to these people in statements rather than questions. And in fact the sweet-faced singer manages to tell me *Yes* without saying anything.

The next thought that occurs to me is so awful that I wish I could blot it out of my brain before it has time to register. Maybe the solution to all of Erg's mysteriousness is a lot simpler than I thought.

Maybe Erg is working for somebody else, and she has been all along.

That's why we're here. Oh, right.

"Actually," I tell the singer, "maybe I do know how Bea sent me." My voice sounds choked and sweat slicks my forehead. I don't know what I'm hoping for. Maybe I'm still clueless enough to hope she'll contradict me, tell me something that proves Erg is totally innocent and hasn't betrayed me—hasn't been betraying me nonstop since I was ten years old.

"Of course you know how, Vassa," the singer says simply. Then she turns and starts burrowing into a pile of chairs and ottomans so densely jumbled they look like a thicket; I wouldn't be surprised to find that the seat cushions were sprouting thorns. Her body seems to glide into the empty spaces, fitting itself to every shadowed gap. I'm trying to follow her, but by the time I've found a crevice big enough for one shoulder she's already gone. And I'm stuck behind in this room of expensive junk. It's just me, and the photo still in my hand, and some truly hideous thoughts.

"Where are Picnic and Pangolin?" I yell after her. God, I almost forgot to ask. "I have to find them!"

"Oh, Peek-neek and Pan-go-leen," her voice croons back from the jagged shadows; she's assumed a grotesque fake French accent and she already sounds far away. "Oh, Peek-neek and Pan-go-leen, oh vhere can zey be?"

I know I have to move. I know I have to find my mutant lawyer friends and the motorcyclist and get the hell out of this place, where every last thing I see beats at my brain and sends my emotions reeling. I can't escape the realization that I'm way too close to cracking. But for a long time I just sit on the carpet, wondering about Erg, raking my memories for clues that she's some kind of double agent and always has been. Maybe all those times when she snuck away her thieving was just the cover story, and she was actually off conniving with Bea.

Then my thoughts veer again, and I'm rocking and clutching my knees and telling myself that it *can't* be true. If I'm right, then Erg has a spark of my mother's life inside her, and, as crazy as Zinaida was, I have to believe that she did love me—I mean, more or less. You know, in her selfish and oblivious and hopelessly ambivalent way. You don't paint portraits of your daughter as a suicide, do you, unless you have some seriously mixed feelings about her?

Erg practically came out and said that she feels *trapped* with me, and maybe in some twisty underground way that's Zinaida talking. I know I was an accident—that was never a secret, not even when I was tiny—and my existence was pretty inconvenient for both my parents. My dad sometimes talked about how much more *fulfilled* he would have been if Steph and I hadn't come along; he didn't say it to our faces but he wasn't super careful about being overheard, either. Maybe my mother wouldn't have totally minded getting rid of me, and now Erg feels the same way. She could never belong to anyone else, Erg said, not even if I died, but it's possible that she'd survive just fine on her own—and have a lot more fun doing it.

This line of thought is not helping me feel especially motivated. I'm supposed to care what happens to Picnic and Pangolin—why, again?

And then Night and the doll-monster-beast in black leather— I'm going to get all bent out of shape worrying about them? What did they ever do for me—besides, you know, save my life repeatedly? Which Erg has, too, now that you mention it.

Get up, Vassa. Ugh. It's like Erg is talking in my head; we're bound together, formally *obligated,* and I can't ever get completely away from her.

"Get up and do what you have to do, Vassa," I say out loud, and this time the voice is all mine. "Whatever that is. Erg was right that there's no big hero coming to do it for you."

I stand up, shove the photo into my pocket, and stare at the nearest wall, daring it to play the next trick. A flicker passes over the plaster, visibly hesitates, and then resolves itself into a door. No matter what happens, I'm going to go through.

CHAPTER 15

As soon as the door falls ajar I'm engulfed by darkness, as if some light-destroying force was rushing through and obliterating the parlor where I've been standing. The shock is enough to freeze me in a defensive hunch, but after a moment I draw myself straight and inch forward into empty black, my eyes wide and my breath shallow and jerky. There's an awful sense of void, of echoing depths always half a step away. Behind and forward and sideways all seem to have their own awful suction, all pulling on me at once.

After a few moments the anxiety gets to be too much and I drop to my knees, sweeping my hands across the floor in front of me. Random tiny drafts come and go against my cheek, a hush and whisper like breaths migrating from one throat to the next. Panic impales me like an icicle and I stop dead, staring everywhere in the utter nothing. I have to go back, but there is no back.

This whole bravery thing was a terrible idea. I'm not cut out for it. The disorientation dragging on my limbs gets so bad that I finally lie flat on my belly and try to slide along in that way. My arms seem cold and rigid. I feel like I'm gliding much too fast, and simultaneously not moving at all.

And then someone groans. Low and tremulous, and very close, and on all sides of me at once.

I stop dead, my breath held so tightly that it feels like my lungs are trying to crush some small animal.

The groan comes again, and this time the voice catches at my memory. I've heard it before, deep and growling, but my mind's so deadened by fear that I can't place it. The voice murmurs a little, incomprehensibly, like someone talking in their sleep. Like someone in a dream, trying desperately to get through to anyone on the outside of his unconsciousness.

It sounds like the cries of someone who never wakes up.

The floor thuds fiercely. For one disordered moment I think it has a heartbeat, but it's only my own pulse recoiling off the cold surface and shivering back through me. That voice is his, or else it's something pretending to be him, and for a long while I can't make up my mind to speak and give myself away. But, as usual, I don't seem to have much choice. "Hey," I whisper at last, "is that you?"

No answer. Of course, even if he's close by he won't be able to hear me

But he *is* here, I'm suddenly sure of it, and I'm damned if I'm going to leave him alone in this place.

Babs isn't winning this one. She doesn't get to keep him. He can't be far, and at any moment I'm sure I'll touch him, catch his hand in mine.

He groans again. I stop to listen, but the space we're in must have horribly tricky acoustics because he seems to be everywhere at one, blurred and scattered. "Hey," I call. "Hey, it's me, Vassa! I've come to get you out. Why can't you *hear* me?"

The problem with talking out loud is that I have to listen to my own voice, understand how childish, pathetic, and weak I sound. Anyone would think that I was begging someone to come and rescue me, not the other way around. He's here, he has to be, but at the same time he's nowhere; my breath starts to rasp and my eyes go hot with pure frustration. "I can't get you out if I can't find you! Please, *please* just tell me where you are."

And then finally I see something: a kind of golden wink in the distance, jagged and radiant. It's there for one instant and gone the next, but I'm almost sure it was real. Maybe he heard me after all, as a cry sifting into his dreams; maybe he's trying to wake up, or to signal me. I stagger upright, making an effort to slow my breathing, and push into a void whose only landmark is my own misplaced hope. No matter who I couldn't save before, no matter if I'm stuck being a random mess of a girl, I'm still going to save *something*.

The sensory deprivation must be bringing on hallucinations, because just for a moment I'm not the flesh-and-blood Vassa. Instead I'm eight years old and made entirely of living paint, my head heaped with a tottering mass of purple curls that could shame Marie Antoinette. There's a gun in my mouth; I can taste the sour steel. I can feel my finger tightening on the trigger.

And then, just like that, the image is gone and I'm back in the dark, sixteen and basically human and no one in particular. That spark comes again, a golden star with rotating blades. Then my vision seems to double, and I see two of them, blinking parallel lights high up and still far away. Haven't I seen something like them somewhere before?

I must not be afraid of falling anymore, because I'm running toward them.

If the motorcyclist had a name, I would scream it. All around me the air rumbles with his voice, and this time I know he's calling to nobody but me.

I run for what feels like a long time. After what seems like about ten minutes or so, though, I start to feel like I really should be getting someplace besides the same dark, the same rhythm, the same jagged stars, which still look exactly the same distance away, even though I must have covered well over a mile by now—in an old lady's apartment in the back of BY's. Who can afford this much space in New York?

Something tugs on my pant leg right by the ankle. Erg, probably. "Is that you, doll?"

There's no reply. Just another tug toward the left and then a sluggish shuffling sound. Definitely not the clip of tiny wooden feet.

It could be almost anything, out to lure me almost anywhere. After a moment's wavering I decide to follow. I've gotten so used to the perfect emptiness here that I've stopped holding my hands out in front of me, and after all of a dozen steps I smack nose-first into something hard. A little fumbling investigation, and it reveals itself as a door.

A way out of here, which seems like a good thing on the face of it. Except, you know, that the motorcyclist might still be trapped somewhere behind me, and I told him I'm here to help him escape. My hand tightens on the knob; now that there's finally something to hold on to, I feel sick at the thought of letting it go and stumbling blindly away again. There could be a tiny coward in my chest, chattering at me to open the damn door and get myself out of here, no matter who I leave behind.

The knob is cold and damp. If I walk back into the dark, I know beyond all doubt that I'll never find the exit again. "Where are you?" I try calling—stupidly, selfishly, hoping that he won't answer so I'll have an excuse for saving myself. "Um, motorcyclist? Where are you? I really *tried* to find you!"

Ugh. Just shut up, Vassa. If you're going to be your father's daughter at least have the class not to pretend you're justified.

The tugging at my ankle comes back, more urgently now. I could take that as another excuse, and we all know how I just *love* excuses.

I make myself turn to face the dark again. Those sharp-pointed stars are still there, their jags cycling slowly high up in the dark. In a regular place, of course, I could walk a few steps forward and feel confident that the door was behind me; here it'll probably vaporize as soon as it gets the chance.

When I push off my stomach clenches so hard that I nearly double over. My hand still reaches behind me, clinging to the knob. When I finally let go cold waves of trembling surge through me. But at least I'm not acting like a heartless traitor. I'm doing *something*.

Behind me there's a quick scrape of sound: the unmistakable rasp of a match, low down, and then light brushes around my boots. I turn to look. Dexter is there holding the match up; in its jaundiced light he looks sicker than ever. He was the ankle-tugger then, but he sure doesn't seem to have his old strength. He stands limp, his fingers sagging. Incredibly enough, though, I'm happy to see him. "Hey, there, little guy. Do you need something?"

He lifts the match up stiffly, and I realize he's waiting for me to pick it up. I crouch down and take it from him, and he nods his fingers at me, casting enormous bobbing shadows on the door, which is still inexplicably right where it was two minutes ago. Then, with what looks like a really painful effort, he flips himself and walks on two of them, just the way I saw him do once before.

Erg. He's telling me something about Erg. "Dexter? What happened?"

He throws himself palm down with a resonant splat. For a moment he lies there as if the breath had been knocked out of him—not that he has any—then hauls himself back onto two rigid fingers and acts out the whole pantomime again. Much as I might prefer not to, I get it.

"My friend is . . . down. Is that it? Did . . . ?" I almost can't say this. "Babs didn't *catch* her!"

Dexter twists back onto his wrist-stump and nods his fingers solemnly just as the match burns out.

It might be a trick, of course. Dexter has every reason to hate Erg with a passion, considering that he might be dying from the septic bite of her little wooden jaws. But somehow I can't think about that.

I can't even think about my *own* possible reasons to hate Erg. All I can think is that she needs me, and how much I still, always and absolutely, need her. For just a moment I wobble in uncertainty, then I pivot toward the pitch-black void where the motorcyclist might be desperately waiting for me.

"I'll come back!" I call wildly. "Just as soon as I can, I'll come back for you!" Without thinking about it I reach out in the dark for Dexter; he's way too weak to run.

I hear the sound of him hobbling over, then scuffing indecisively for a moment.

And then he gives a little hop, and holds my hand. I can feel how sick he is by the touch of his skin, ashy and sticky and smoldering with fever.

We're through that door before I can even feel grossed out.

Even after all the distance I covered, I recognize the room in front of me immediately: it's the dim space I wandered through first, the cavernous room with the giant souvenirs. That amber beacon still flickers on the top of the Eiffel Tower, and it must be brighter now because I can see more of those overgrown knick-knacks scattered around a gray field: a shoulder-high St. Louis's Gateway Arch, a particularly awful Colosseum sculpted in mint-green plastic; as I run past it I notice tiny model gladiators gutting one another inside it, and I look away before they can start moving. What I *don't* see, predictably enough, is the door back to BY's.

"Don't you get tired of playing the same lame tricks all the time?" I ask the room. "How about something new?"

Dexter give me a little tug toward the vacancy to my right, but I ignore him. There's something just a little bit different about that Eiffel Tower now, a kind of rag hanging from one of its beams. I veer toward it and halt, reaching to touch it with my left hand: a loose flap in red and white checks. On inspection it proves to be the corner of a suit jacket. My first thought is that Picnic and Pangolin were dragged this way and Picnic's jacket caught on the metal and tore, but the scrap is pretty high up for that. And it's hanging from the *inside* of the beam, caged in the metal grid. Picnic would have had to be yanked up inside the tower for his jacket to snag in that spot.

I've been pulling on the scrap for a while now, and it's not coming loose. I feel along the edge where the fabric meets the metal, and, weirdly enough, it seems like it keeps going straight into the beam. Dexter scratches impatiently.

All at once I remember what the singer said: *"Oh, Peek-neek and Pan-go-leen, oh vhere can zey be?"* That horrible phony French accent. Oh, *there's* your answer, Vassa.

Erg might just have to wait.

"Dexter?" I say. "Can you sit on my shoulder for a minute? I need both hands." The irony of saying that to him hits me as he thumps my palm with his fingers, which I think translates as, *We don't have time for this.* But when I lift him up he obediently disengages and flops over my collarbone like an animate pancake. I wish he wouldn't fidget. "Thanks, little buddy," I tell him, even though the sensation of him snuggling against me is fairly disgusting. But after living with Babs, poor little Dex probably needs all the positive reinforcement he can get.

I work on freeing that flap of suit. The metal holding it has a narrow slit down the center, and I pry at that as the sharp edges gouge my fingers, then I haul on the cloth again. The tin is starting to bow back and enough of the suit is through now that I can wrap both hands in it. The checks are dotted with blood, presumably mine. *Ooh La La!* I lift my feet off the floor for an instant, dragging on the suit with my entire weight, and I hear a kind of yelp.

From, that's right, *inside* the metal beam. It's maybe an inch and a half square.

"Mr. Picnic?" I call. "Are you okay?"

"Just Picnic," Pangolin's voice grouses, "if you please." And at the same time Picnic says, "From self to other to self again creates, by its dizzying oscillation, that dialogic commingling of spirits that we most aptly term *empathy*. . . ."

I've never heard him say more than a few words in a row before and I'm not sure this counts as an improvement.

"Empathy," I say. "Right. That's why I'm here to get you out. Because I'm pretty sure it must suck to be jammed inside a metal beam like that."

As I talk I'm twisting the tin back, using the flap of his jacket to keep my hands from getting cut any worse. There's a thin squealing sound and something comes flopping through the opening.

A tail. Cow-style and covered in what looks like freckled pale skin, with a luxuriant tuft of ginger hair at the end. Neat confirmation of the whole not-human thing. I keep tugging on the suit and twisting my fingers into the gap in the tin, and it spreads wider and wider. One of Pangolin's conical claws sticks through, and then with a rapid drubbing sound Picnic gets a foot out. The metal's giving way more quickly now, and soon impossibly large limbs are dangling out of that narrow beam. Then, with a wild thrashing, Picnic pulls himself all the way out and lands on the floor with his arms fluttering vaguely. We each get hold of one of Pangolin's clawed feet and work him loose as well. Sheepishly, Picnic tucks his tail back inside his checked pants.

"Have you any parasites, miss?" Pangolin inquires courteously once he's standing square on the floor. "Lice or other vermin?"

"Excuse me?" I can't honestly say I saw that coming.

"I thought I might devour them. As a small token of our appreciation."

"I'm cool for now," I tell him. Just like in my dream, he seems to have lost his glasses and his beige suit is torn and bloodied. "Maybe later there will be something you can do for me, though." I don't know if they can help rescue Erg or the motorcyclist, but it's worth asking.

Dexter twitches impatiently on my shoulder and tugs a lock of my hair. Pangolin eyes him suspiciously. "No parasites, you say? That one might be too bulky for the orifice available, but he could be minced."

"You can't eat him," I insist. Apart from how totally nauseating the idea is, I feel a weird twinge of protective loyalty for the live-dead thing perched on my shoulder. "We're friends now. I mean I think we are."

Dexter gratefully nuzzles me. I'd prefer if he didn't.

Picnic leans very close to my shoulder, peering at Dexter from all sides. "Five fingers," Picnic observes sagely, "but only one points to the heart."

"That's great," I tell him. Now that I've finally done something useful I can't keep the impatience out of my voice. "Look, I'm really happy that you're both okay, but we need to get out of here." Erg is back in my thoughts like a shooting pain. "I . . . another friend of mine might be in trouble."

Technically we're all in trouble, really. It suddenly occurs to me that Babs will be under-thrilled to see me stomping into her store, through her private door, with her prisoners in tow. I'm not in the business of making Babs happy, but this seems extreme—and since she's got Erg in her clutches it's not an ideal moment to be driving her wild with rage.

Dexter yanks my hair hard enough that I start walking in the direction indicated, and Picnic and Pangolin trail along with me. A door asserts itself out of nowhere, a charcoal smudge on the dark, and Dexter prods me to go faster; Pangolin skitters to keep up, claws clacking like an old typewriter.

"You'll be pleased to hear, I hope," Pangolin tells me breath-lessly, "that there has been considerable progress made on the case."

I stifle a hacking laugh. Being imprisoned in a model of the Eiffel Tower isn't my idea of progress, but it seems rude to say so. "Awesome," I tell him absently. An image of Erg on fire flashes through my mind, and I'm half-running. "What kind of progress?"

"That is to say," Pangolin intones emphatically, snuffling just behind my shoulder, "some very significant motions have been en-tered. In the court of possibilities."

"How cool that you could still enter motions," I say, trying not to reek of sarcasm, "while you were stuffed in that beam."

"*I* did not enter them, miss. You of all people should be aware of that."

This would be interesting if I had any damn time for it. We're almost at the door and I pause; it might be a truly stupid move to just barge through. Dexter jumps off my shoulder and vanishes into the shadows; of course, he doesn't want Babs to know he's been helping me. That's fine for him, but I can't think of any good way to hide the fact that I seriously invaded her space.

"I guess we just have to wing this. Look, Babs is holding a friend of mine hostage; it might get ugly. . . ."

Pangolin makes a noise that I think is a chortle. Personally I don't see what's so funny. I hold the doorknob, pondering my options: leaping out shouting, sidling furtively. I decide on Zinaida-style entitlement, turn the knob, and stroll out into the store, fake-confident, pretending I'm not blinded by the scream of citrus light.

CHAPTER 16

I almost smack into Babs. She's standing very close, facing the door. Obviously she knew I was in there and she's been waiting for me.

"Half Vassa," Babs hisses as my eyes adjust, her crinkled face emerging from the glare. "Half Lisa, half Lowenstein. I told you I would find the missing part, you broken plate of a girl. I have that leftover shard of you screwed up in a jar."

I can hear Picnic's shuffling feet behind me and the heavy clack of Pangolin's claws. "Then you should give it back." My voice jerks as I speak. What exactly does it mean to say that I'm broken, to call Erg my missing piece? I'm not about to correct Babs, though I think it: *You're wrong; Erg's not some leftover part of me. She's all that's left of Zinaida.*

"Name *it*," Babs suggests suavely, not even glancing at her escapees, "and I'll hand it right over to you."

I may have mentioned in passing that I am not quite as stupid as I look; telling Babs anything at all about Erg is clearly a horrible idea.

"Not happening. It's mine no matter what name it has. You've got no right to ask me anything about it."

There's a sizable bulge in the right-hand pocket of Babs's dress, this one a shabby gray eyelet number with big pink buttons. There's a subtle clunking sound like a small wooden foot kicking at cloth-damped glass. I fake a bit in the opposite direction, pretending to gaze out the window, but actually getting ready to lunge for that telltale bump.

"Just try," Babs hisses. "Sinister is keeping *it* company. Make a nuisance of yourself again, imp, and he'll twist its yapping little head right off. Then he'll get to work crackling its twiggy limbs to splinters. And then . . . I'm certain we'll think of something else equally agreeable. I'd say that your morals and disposition are about to show startling improvement. You'll bring an entirely new level of dedication to your work, won't you, *Vassa?*"

Hearing her say it in that tone almost convinces me that it *is* only half a name, a label suited only to a hopelessly incomplete person. My neck aches at the mention of snapping Erg's, and as she goes on rattling off threats strange fibrous masses of pain start to nest inside my arms and legs. It takes all my strength to keep from crying Erg's name, over and over again.

Picnic has wandered over to the magazine rack. He seems to be perusing the horoscopes in the back of some fashion magazine with total absorption. Babs spares him a brief scowl. Pangolin is sitting on the yellow floor, clawed toes curling as he tries to balance a dozen sticks of gum in a single straight tower. Could I possibly have rescued anyone more useless?

"Ugh," Babs says, "the mess of it. Out now and what a bother it would be to stuff them back. Well, I snapped up something more valuable, imp, so it seems you got the worse of the trade. So, what do you say? Is the mouthy little toaster suddenly shy of words?"

Babs arches her eyebrows and waits for my reply. I stand there brooding, looking for some alternative to improving my morals and disposition the way she said. There doesn't seem to be one.

"Okay," I say in a long exhalation. "Okay, I'll do whatever you tell me, Babs. Just don't hurt her." It's like I'm a doll myself and

Babs pulled the cord in my back, knowing exactly what words would come out of me.

"*Her,*" Babs says, savoring the sound of it. "*Her.* A poppet, a bobbin, a crunchy fortune cookie made to hold a slip of human soul. Oh, you'll do a good deal for me, Vassa. And I'd say our new arrangement will last as long as you do. That'll show Bea, won't it? Why, if she insists on throwing her toys at me, I might decide to keep them."

And she pulls the jar out of her pocket, just long enough to rub it in. I see Erg wrapped up in Sinister's fingers as if he were some kind of flabby boa constrictor, her blue eyes staring over the top and her miniscule black Mary Janes protruding from under his thumb. They're both sealed up in an empty jar of strawberry marsh-mallow butter, imperfectly cleaned, so that pink smears hide just a bit of the awfulness inside: Erg crushed and gagged by sick dead flesh. A memory of Sinister's grotesque strength comes back to me, a sensory echo of the way my throat ached as he hauled on my hair.

Even though the rest of her is stifled, I can see Erg's eyes. Azure and flat and confrontational. Paint that might as well be poison, since there's so much hurt in them. I can tell at a glance that she knows everything I've been thinking, all the cruel accusations against her that roiled through my heart. She doesn't have to talk to tell me that; the bitterness in her gaze is more than enough.

She knew all along what would happen. Erg always knows far too much for anyone's good.

She knew, and she sacrificed herself to help me—because I asked her to.

Who the hell am I that I should stand here breathing in a human body, wearing a face like a flag for a nation of spoiled, glossy idiots? If you look at the face and the body, you'd probably assume there was someone inside them, maybe even someone you'd like to know. But by betraying Erg I've made myself empty.

INTERLUDE IN SEA

Bea leaned on the railing looking out at an ocean colored graphite by the November haze, a bagel and cold coffee clutched in her hands. The Rockaway boardwalk streaked for miles in both directions, backed by an elevated train and then ranks of forbidding apartment buildings. On the beach below, Hindu women in flowing scarlet threw flowers into the ocean. When they noticed Bea they shrank away instinctively, glancing at her over their shoulders and muttering. They didn't know what Bea was, only that there was something about her that they didn't like at all. Superficially she was only an aging woman with a sagging camel coat, goose-pimpled bare legs sticking out of hot pink sheepskin boots, and a beret covered in absurd crochet flowers. Just another shabby immigrant grandmother, but one somehow haloed in unnerving power.

Slow footsteps tapped up beside her but she didn't look, not even when a bony hand caressed her shoulder.

"Bea," a voice implored. The sea rushed up and then folded into itself with a sigh. A gull circled, gawking wistfully at the untouched bagel in Bea's hand. "Can't we come to understand each other once again? Must you really take this little complication in such an unforgiving spirit? Bea, love, listen . . ."

"Don't *love* me," Bea snapped. "Don't like me while you're at it, if you would be so kind. *Love* you're dribbling at me, and after all you've done? I'll slap the word straight back down your rotten throat."

"It's not as if you'd left us much choice." Babs's tone had already altered, turning smug and haughty. Her lips puckered in a complacent smile, but Bea glanced over in time to note the shifty discomfort in her eyes. "You think we should trust you? Too many conflicts of interest you've been coddling to your bosom, Bea. Too many words gone astray to those bitty friends of yours. You've told me yourself that you feel *indebted* to those creatures. *Grateful* to them, and solely because a pair of them let you tag along when they fled from St. Petersburg—as if they didn't have plenty reasons of their own to want someone with your abilities along for the ride! You might as well feel grateful to a baked potato. They aren't our kind of people, are they? But there you are with your pretty goddaughter, no less, in art school, and *what* were those drawings in her senior show? How has she met so many persons of quality, I ask, if not with your help?"

"Ah, but Zinnie's show was only a month ago," Bea sneered. "You'd been hard at work for years before that to worm me from my store. There are only so many franchises to go around, and you weren't best pleased to be left out of the game, were you? Who was it that called the board together to discuss my *conflicts of interest*, Babs? The sneaking, the conniving, the playing on my loyalty so I wouldn't blink my eyes and see the cold truth when I opened them again! Ah, Babs, how I tried to defend you when the rumors first drifted my way! *Don't say such things of her*, I told them. *Not Babs. I won't hear another word.* It's bitter to bite my old tongue now, and taste a fool."

"I did you no harm, Bea," Babs insisted. "Not a thing but what was best for you. You'd be torn between your feelings for them and for us. No rigor, no cleanliness of mind. I straightened matters up so you could be at peace. You think we haven't heard reports of your chatter about a *different economic model*? You think we can't sort what that means? A full dozen franchises we have now, Bea, and the owners of every last one have come around to accepting my wise proposals for a sounder and more profitable future. Oh, but you're not much of a team player, are you? You want to leave those creatures intact. It won't do." Her smirk pinched for a moment. "And will those little persons you romp with be showing you their loyalty now? Will they be dearer friends to you than—"

Bea waved her coffee dismissively. "You sit at my register now, Babs," she said, "but the keys will add up your heart. You know it. You live inside my walls, and the day will come when they will turn themselves inside out to shake you to the ground. Everything I've held in my hands will remember me, so all you touch will know you for what you are."

Babs stared at her. Her eye was just going gray and it tried to leap from her face, to roll forward in attack, but she hadn't yet mastered the skill of sending it out and it only seemed to bubble. Bea's nostrils pinched in contempt.

"Are you saying that you mean to send your bits and pieces with their pitchforks to seek your revenge for you?" Babs hissed at last. "Or conjure up the teakettles to assault me? That's not the world we're in now, *love*. I'm a respectable woman of business, and you've fallen down to being a soggy old nobody. Ah, but you think you can come after me anyway? Is that what you're saying?"

"*Come after you*, Babs? I'm saying no such thing." Bea finally smiled. "I'm saying I won't have to."

CHAPTER 17

It's still midday with a glowing haze filming the sky: a hot, grayish cast to the view beyond the windows. It's not time for my shift yet but Babs brusquely orders me to take over the register anyway, and of course I do without a murmur. Babs has hinted pretty hard that she won't be letting me leave tomorrow after all, even assuming I make it that long—and I could never go without Erg anyway. So like Babs said, this will have to be home enough.

The funny thing is that she seems to have lost interest in Picnic and Pangolin, ignoring them as they shuffle around her store examining the screws that hold the shelves together and peering into the refrigerators. Picnic even buys a charcoal-colored soda called Professor Pepper's Sippable Shadow. Ringing him up scares the daylights out of me, but this time it all goes smoothly and the money stays put in the register. A few bills twitch lackadaisically, but that's it. Pangolin wanders over and beams at me as if this was the happiest day of his life; things might be going just fine for him, I guess.

"So aren't you guys in a hurry to clear out of here? You know, escape? Before Babs decides to do something worse to you?"

A fly buzzes past Picnic, now idly slurping his Shadow and gawking out the window. He catches it with a flick of his hand and wads it up, the tiny carcass dropping to the floor.

Babs appears to be busy restocking, though as far as I can tell we haven't sold much since I've been here. Somebody must have fixed the broken speakers: that song is back, with the whispered croon and the notes raining down. But this time I can make out the lyrics, and they don't seem to be the same ones I remember. *Centralized breathing, tuned to your shoe,* the singer sighs, *oh how the candle in knots.* Picnic amuses himself by drizzling a bit of his soda onto the linoleum then takes another gulp with a satisfied snuffling. *Please don't believe that the shadow dropped far, or who-oo will you find if you open the stars?*

"Ah," Pangolin says languidly, and I jump a little. I guess my mind was drifting off with that song. "No, no, that isn't necessary. We can remove ourselves at our convenience, you see. We've served up our papers like so many tasty roast beetles, and now our principal occupation is to wait for the inevitable unfolding of events."

Now that he mentions it, he's not clutching his file anymore.

"So you mean you didn't need my help at all?" My voice spikes, high and furious. "Do you really not understand what happened? Babs caught my friend because I went in after *you.* And now you and Babs are both acting like you don't give a damn about each other. I don't—"

Pangolin flourishes a paw, cutting me off. "I did think I was careful to elucidate matters for you, miss. Certainly we never could have managed without your kind assistance. No one else ever would have sought us out; we could have expected to stay in those uncomfortable environs for quite . . . some time. Several centuries, perhaps. But as I informed you there has been *significant* progress, and Miss Yagg is unlikely to concern herself with our whereabouts henceforth. That is, the movement in the case has been, one might say, redirected. Picnic and I are no longer relevant to her concerns."

"I don't get it," I tell him. "You're the ones who are trying to bring BY's down. What's not relevant about that?"

Pangolin ripples his snout incredulously, but doesn't say anything. He offers me a condescending pat on the head and strays off again, and at this point I'm not sure I care what he does. When I glance back at Picnic I notice the fly reviving in a splash of gray froth; I guess it was just stunned.

I go through the motions numbly, hating the coarse light outside, the unctuous song that never stops playing, the store's relentless jerk and sway. It's only now I realize that I didn't feel the floor heaving the whole time I was in Babs's apartment. Now and then I try to think of some way of saving Erg, but my thoughts might as well be shoving their way through wet sand; they go nowhere, mean nothing, scrape along like small dying animals. What plan could I possibly come up with while Sinister has her in that full-body squeeze? And how can I even think about going back for Mr. Night-Doll-Monster while Erg's life would be the price of another attempt, even a hopeless one? I watch the mausoleums on the hill gamboling past, the rooftops, the rotting heads that waft across the clouds behind. Every time I see Joel I feel a fresh twinge of shame and the dull conviction that I've let him down—him and everybody else.

I'll be keeping him company soon. And really, once Chelsea and Stephanie are over the initial shock, what will it matter? If I didn't still have a stubborn speck of hope that I'll somehow rescue Erg, I'd give up caring completely.

I couldn't say how long I go on in this dismal trance, but after a while we stop pitching and start a drowsy plunge. The store must be kneeling, though I didn't notice anyone singing out there. We touch down and the door opens wide, but for a long moment no one comes in. Then I see him: an old man in a tweed jacket, his twisted body propped on a cane. White-haired and scholarly. His smile when he sees me is warm but vacant, and I immediately get the sense that he's not all there.

"Hello," he says. "I seem to have gotten off at the wrong stop."

Picnic and Pangolin exchange glances. Fine. I can't think about them while this old man is here, innocently shambling into danger. Picnic takes Pangolin's paw and they saunter out as if they were going on a nice stroll. I get up and dart over to the old guy, hoping to hustle him out of here before the store rears again. "Let's step out in the parking lot, okay? I'll give you directions. Where are you trying to go?"

He gapes at me as if I were a long-lost friend. "I caught the wrong train, but then I saw the store. It was dancing. Like something in a story I read long ago. The words came back to me, and the melody, as if I had never once stopped singing them since I was a boy. I remembered how wonderful it was then, coming here. The song is inside me, and the dance, even if my legs won't follow my lead. Just as the mistake was no mistake, but a true *directive*. How did I know where to find you, Sabine? I knew I'd see you again one day, my darling girl."

Oh, boy. "That's not my name," I tell him, as gently as I can. "Please, let's go outside." As soon as I've said it I see that it's already too late. We're ten feet off the ground and rapidly ascending. The only encouraging thing is that I don't see Babs anywhere, so maybe I still have time to get him out before she has a chance to intervene.

His expression shifts. He lowers his head and gazes at me from below rambling eyebrows, his smile stealthy and dark. "I understand," he says. "I shouldn't have said it out loud. You had to change your name so that death wouldn't find you. I always said you were too young . . . And your hair. What an odd choice, but a clever one, to blind it with color! And your mouth has changed, too, somehow. I almost didn't know you myself, but then I saw through . . . No, I won't call you that again, dear."

I stamp out the code on the floor. I'll get him out of here if

I have to throw him on his ass in the parking lot. I wait for the telltale sinking feeling, for the buildings gliding up beyond the windows.

Instead the store keeps dancing. I try again, rapping the code emphatically with my heavy boots. My swan foot aches, but other than that nothing happens. And I'm positive I have the rhythm right.

The store is deliberately ignoring me.

It must have its reasons, and that is not an encouraging thought.

The old man softly rests a papery hand on my cheek, still gazing at me, and I step back. "My name is Vassa," I tell him. "We've never met before. I've never known anyone named Sabine. You won't find her here."

Or anywhere, and you used to understand that, didn't you? But then I remember the way I searched the faces of those miniature dancers for some vestige of my mother, and I don't even have senility as an excuse. This poor old man is peering into my eyes as if they were the windows of a dollhouse, hoping that everything he's lost might miraculously be preserved inside. Suddenly disillusioning him seems so cruel that I can barely breathe.

"You're obliged to say that," he tells me tenderly, and I don't have the heart to deny it anymore. "I understand. Death is a crafty old fellow, isn't he? It takes all your wit to slip his clutches, even for a bright girl like you. Shall I call you *Vassa,* then?" He says my name like we're sharing a joke and maybe he's right about that: a joke name for a half girl.

One good thing about Sinister being occupied: it buys us some time. The old guy can probably wallow in his delusions for a little longer without getting offed, at least I hope so. I try stamping the code again, just in case. No response.

"I have a message from *her,*" I try, and he smiles in delight at our complicity. How charming it is, I can see him thinking, that she's pretending not to be Sabine! How witty to refer to herself in the third person! "*She* needs you to wait here by the window, and don't touch anything. Keep your hands tight over your pockets. As soon as the store goes back down to the parking lot, *she'll* have a very important mission for you. There's something you need to bring her from home. Can you do that?" I'm betting that once he leaves he'll forget all about me and never find his way here again.

He nods and covers his right pocket, but he can't cover the left since he needs that hand to clutch his cane. I'm pretty sure Dexter's on my team now, but I still don't like it. "Hang on," I tell him. "Let me get you a chair."

I'm just heading toward the back of the counter to drag that filthy chair out for him when I hear it: the tap of his cane, the scuff of tired feet. I spin around. He's just reaching out toward the nearest shelf for something small and sparkling, something I can tell at a glance doesn't belong here.

"Her ring," he says vaguely, holding it in front of his eyes; golden and gleaming. I see the cherry flash of a ruby. "*Your* ring. It must be here for a reason. . . ."

"Put it back!" I yell at him. "Please put it back!"

He doesn't seem to register my voice. His hand drifts, drowsy as a cloud, toward his pocket. By the time I've run three steps I hear the faint *chink* of the ring hitting loose change.

By the time I've run four steps Babs has him down on the floor. I never saw her coming, but she's kneeling on his chest and looking up at me with a cold, steady smile. He's wheezing loudly, fumbling at her, but she's way too strong for him.

"He's an old man," I say. "He's not right in the head. He didn't know what he was doing!"

Babs doesn't say anything, just keeps on smiling as she reaches to rattle the jar in her pocket. I hear the clack of Erg's wooden shoes on the glass and the muffled thud of Sinister's flesh.

The old man looks at her with a strangely peaceful expression. "You," he says.

Her white eye spins small circles in the air above his face.

I never saw the axe coming, but Babs whips it out from behind her as if it weighs no more than a tuft of grass. I remember how it dragged in my hands and I can't help realizing: Babs isn't just stronger than she looks, she's a whole lot stronger than I am. The blade flashes brightly colored reflections, beaming back images of detergent and the gaudy yellow linoleum. Babs must have known what would happen from the minute he walked in the store; she must have fetched the axe while I was busy talking to him and waited for her chance.

"Babs," I try, though my voice flaps absurdly in my ears. "I think what you're doing is against the rules. Is that ring even yours?"

"Of course it's mine," Babs says softly. "I only set it down for a moment, imp. It was a gift from an old friend of mine, or should I say a friend of *ours*?"

She means Bea. And something about the way she says it makes me understand: she set up this old man as my punishment for violating her space, for freeing her prisoners. He's about to die, but it's got nothing to do with him. It's between her and me.

"Babs, he's innocent! He didn't understand. You know this is wrong!"

She grins at me like I've just given her a million bucks. "Ah," she muses, "you presume to tell me what I *know* of right and wrong, Vassa? And after I warned you not to say such words in my presence."

She hefts the axe over him. I look wildly toward the window hoping that by some miracle dark will be falling early, hoping that I can beg Night for help. But hazy sunlight is whistling off the roofs, battering the parked cars, and Night is still on the far side of the earth where he won't hear me. I'm on my own. And fighting Babs physically means that Erg will almost certainly die—but my muscles are tensing anyway, getting ready to leap at her.

"I understand," the old man wheezes out behind my back. "For Sabine. I'll take her place. Truly, I'm happier than I can say."

It was only an instant, just one razor-fine flash of time, but by the time I turn back to Babs the axe is already falling. Then the head. Blood radiates like the beams of a crimson sun.

Babs hauls up the pale old head by one ear and swings it experimentally. His eyes are white and stunned, his face crimped in fear. No matter what he said, he doesn't look like he was all that thrilled. Against the intolerable yellow of the floor the blood trails gleam scarlet black, writhing across the linoleum like long, emaciated arms. Maybe they're Sabine's arms coming to catch him as he falls.

Maybe.

I feel something hard clap against my knees and then hit my chest. My eyes swarm with yellow, and it dawns on me that I've fallen. The colors are dimming, ocher and violet in long slanting shades.

"Oh, drag her off to bed," Babs orders someone or other. "She'll need all her strength for tonight."

At times I'm aware of the cot underneath me. At times there's a pale and painful intrusion of walls on my retinas. This haze can't really be called sleep, but it goes on and on. "Erg?" I hear my voice calling out. "Doll, they can't take you from me!"

Oh, but they did, Sinister and Babs. They took her and now I can never leave this place unless I can get her back.

Soon enough it will be dark again, and I'll have to confront whatever nasty tricks Babs has planned for me without Erg's help. Night will be back, but after the way I ran out on Mr. Night-Doll-Monster in Babs's apartment I'm ashamed at the thought of facing the darkening sky again. After everything Night and the motorcy-clist did for me I let them both down, I know it.

What was that I saw spinning high up in that vast chamber just before Dex came for me? Two toothed golden disks that gnawed at the darkness. Twin stars. The memory of them keeps eating away at my thoughts, those sharp teeth cycling around and around. I'd seen something like them before somewhere, is the thing, and if I can just remember where—I don't know why, but I feel like that might tell me what I need to know.

Night sees you, Vassa. People like to compare stars to eyes, but if you really think about it what we actually use to see is *darkness*: the dark inside our pupils. Is that how it is for Night, is interstellar space the way it takes us in? Stars in your eyes would be too bright. They would blind you. Is that how it is for Night? I guess I'm drows-ing because the words repeat, a singsong chant in my mind: *You can't see when stars are in your eyes, you can't find your way home. . . .*

I remember Babs flipping up the motorcyclist's visor right in front of me, making sure I saw how he suffered and heard his piti-ful screams. If I hadn't witnessed that, I might have tried to look in his eyes myself; really, Babs did a fabulous job of making sure I'd be too freaked to try it.

And then I sit up so fast the cot squeals. I remember now where I saw those stars before, and I have the barest hint what they could mean.

I'm sick at the thought of how much it will hurt him, but I know all at once that I *have* to lift his visor. No matter how cruel that it is, no matter how he shrieks. Slick and black and opaque as that glass is, a sudden intuition stabs through me all at once: it isn't the motorcyclist's visor that's blinding him. *Please don't believe that the shadow dropped far, or who-oo will you find if you open the stars?*

That's how the song went right after I got back from Babs's apartment. And I'm pretty sure that in all the thousand times I've heard it lilting in the background, it never once had those words in it before.

I wake to a rap on my door. "Rise and shine, Vassa," Babs calls, too cheerfully. "How can you dim down to oblivion if you don't shine first?"

"Good question." I haven't slept without Erg beside me in the last six years. Waking up to the knowledge that Sinister still has her in a strangling grasp leaves me heart-chilled and sickened, and it also leaves me with no choice. For a moment I consider trying to sponge off at the sink, but it doesn't seem to matter anymore how filthy I am. *Just get out there, Vassa. You sure don't stand a chance of getting Erg back while you're hiding in here!*

I eat a few cookies; I know I need to keep myself together, but I'm too queasy to choke down more than that. And I step out into the store's harsh glow and a view of endless evening blue in the window. My heart skips at the sight of the night coming in and my cheeks heat up. Any moment now he'll be here, and the singer's voice is still with me, rippling through my thoughts like slow wind: *who will you find if you open the stars?*

Now that I'm awake it all makes more sense. Maybe there's a reason why I couldn't find him in that vast dark chamber where I chased the sound of his voice. He was there, but maybe not in a form that I could hope to reach.

I've stopped in the middle of the store, caught up in my thoughts, and I jump when I realize how close Babs is standing and how she's staring at me. Her eye is darting so quickly that it looks like a flurry of fireflies. She must know me well enough to realize that Erg and I haven't completely given up yet.

"Did the bits sleep nicely?" she asks. By *the bits* she means me. "The little leftovers?"

"Sure," I say, and then once again I fail to keep a lid on it. I can't resist saying something to unsettle her, knock her awful complacency askew. "It's being awake that's the riddle."

Her eyebrows shoot up. "Ah, but when you prattle in your sleep, you answer every riddle there is, imp." I'm ready to bet that she's lying, just trying to psych me out, so I don't bother responding to that. She's still wearing her gray eyelet dress, blood spatters and all. "Come admire the view."

I follow her to the window. Everything is spotlessly clean again, not the faintest blood fleck anywhere, as if all the horror earlier was only a hallucination. The store turns, gently waltzing now, and the heads flow by like leaves on a river. The old man drifts past, still gazing wistfully at me. With all the blood drained from him he's as pale as a candle. And then Joel, still sad and dreaming. If he'd grown up, I bet he would have gotten away from here, learned to relate better to people, had an amazing life.

Babs watches me greedily, waiting for me to recoil at the sight of her newest trophy, but I'm too chilled inside to throw my hands over my face, cry out, and go staggering back from the window. All the feeling I have left is with Erg and the motorcyclist—and Chelsea, now that I think of her.

"The sky is a beautiful color, isn't it?" I say. Then as we revolve a second time I notice something. "That's interesting. All the stakes are taken now. I thought you liked to keep one free."

The observation annoys her, I notice. "Sinister takes the heads up, and Dexter brings them down. Those are the rules, my imp. It will have to wait 'til Dex is feeling a bit sprightlier." And then she stamps out the code, sharp and staccato. Of course the damn store listens to *her*. As we sink down through the twilight I have time for two thoughts: the first is that I haven't seen Dexter since I left Babs's apartment.

The other is that there was a period sometime today when Sinister was busy—when, if I'd only been paying attention, I might have found an opportunity to save Erg. And I slept through it.

Babs steps out into the parking lot, but pauses long enough to leer at me over her shoulder. She told me about Sinister on purpose, of course—just so I'd understand that I've failed Erg again. I stand in the open door, breeze sighing on my skin.

The motorcyclist is there, perfectly still, waiting for her. I wave to him behind Babs's back even though he can't see me. My breath sharpens with the impulse to run to him, throw my arms around him, and then, as softly as I can, lift his visor. But I can't do that while Babs is out there with Erg still stuffed in Sinister's dead coil—though, now I think of it, I'm not sure Babs's pocket is bulging anymore. Where is Erg now?

I watch while Babs takes the huge helmet between her hands and gives it a little shake. I can make out a trace of her voice on the breeze but I can't hear what she's saying, though I'd guess it's some kind of warning to stay away from me. I hear the rumbling of the engine—and then Babs reaches to turn it on, though the growl of it was already trembling in my ears. She gives him a shove and he starts his interminable circling. It looks to me like he's going more slowly than usual, though.

The violet sky dips to black and the last of the rose fades from the horizon as he drives around. He could be flying through an asphalt sky.

With an airy drumming of wings one of the swans plunges from the roof just above my head—at least my swans haven't abandoned me!—and swoops after him. It flies above his head, a pale shadow on deep gray. It's still wrapped in bandages, though they're starting to unravel like streamers at a birthday party. And it follows him around and around.

"Hello, Night," I whisper. "I know I blew it before. But I'm going to try as hard as I can to make it up to you. Forgive me?"

Night is everywhere, covering every leaf and window across the entire hemisphere. Why, then, can I so clearly feel Night coming close in response to my words? I feel it perch like a moth made of wind on my lashes. I feel it look for me, search for every secret of my deepest identity, inside my eyes.

I feel it kiss me as tenderly as the blood pulsing inside my lips. *Night sees you, Vassa.*

CHAPTER 18

Babs doesn't bother speaking to me when she gets back, just gestures curtly to the chair behind the register. I know it can't be as simple as that—she must have something gruesome planned for me—but I don't say anything, either, just take my seat and chew on a stale pretzel. I check out the shape of her pockets as she stalks off to her apartment; as I suspected, there's no lump that could be Erg's jar. And I don't see either of the hands anywhere.

Once Babs slams the door behind her, I'm more alone in this place than I've ever been before—except that Night is all over the huge picture window, and I know it's watching me. Why did it take me so many years to understand that Night is something you can talk to, something that might even decide to watch over you or kiss you just when you're about to crumple from loneliness?

I wait a while after Babs leaves, listening to the whispering song, the piano notes falling through the air and pooling on the yellow floor. The verse about the stars seems to be gone, so maybe it was just a one-time deal; now the singer is cooing about snakes in the marmalade instead.

Babs will expect the worst from me, of course, but there's no way she can guess everything I've figured out. I'd feel better if

I knew where Dex and Sin are, though. It seems too good to be true that Babs would leave me completely unsupervised.

Whether it's a trick or not, I've got to take advantage while my solitude lasts. Oh, so Babs neglected to assign me one of her psychotic tasks tonight? She doesn't have some impossible mission for me, some job designed to do me in?

That's okay. I can give *myself* a mission. See, Babs? As an employee, I'm learning to be a real self-starter.

I bang out the code on the floor, nails in my palms while I wait to see if the store will obey me this time.

It does. We sink through the ocean-deep sky and land with a delicate shudder. For a few moments I hesitate. As usual the motorcyclist seems completely oblivious, and I have no way to guess if he's aware, on some half-conscious level, of what I'm planning to do. Then, like I'm pulling up something from deep in my own heart, I walk out the door and across the parking lot. There's only one way I can think of to stop his orbit, but without Erg as an intermediary I don't know if he'll realize I'm here before he runs me down. I could get crushed for real this time.

"Hey," I call just in case. "It's me. Vassa. I have an idea about . . . about something that might be causing your problems. About the stars."

He burns around the same circle, not even flinching at the sound of my voice. The whole flock of swans has taken to shadowing him in a cloudy brush and whisper not far above his head, white bandages whipping in all directions and corkscrewing wildly in the wind. Stepping in his path worked in my dream, but the rules were probably different then.

Then something occurs to me. Erg may be gone, but I do still have friends here. "Swans?" I call. "Can you stop him for me?"

Wings pound the air as the flock circles lower, half-loose bandages catching on his handlebars and tangling with the wheels.

Soon his glossy black suit is zebraed in writhing white, the swans towed after him now like so many winged balloons. His engine gives a kind of strangled sound as the bandages drag the swans lower and lower, hiding his head and shoulders in the throb of white wings.

And then he isn't going around and around anymore. His wheels grind at empty space. The swans have hefted him up, bike and all, so that he sways a few inches off the ground. Brilliant, amazing birds that they are, my swans are deliberately flying in different directions from one another to keep him suspended in a more or less stable spot. Their stretched-out necks stripe the dim buildings around us, and I love them so much I want to cry.

"That is *genius*!" I tell them, and I hear a laugh that sounds angelically bright and pure until I realize it's mine, which kind of ruins it. "You guys are absolute visionaries!"

It's got to be hard work, though. That motorcycle can't be any joke to keep dangling in midair. I'm already running over, already bracing myself for the shock of his scream. I stand a bit to one side, feathers sweeping across my body, and his half-hidden face is closer to mine than it's ever been. My hair flies in the pulsing wind of those huge wings.

"I'm sorry to do this to you," I tell him. "Except I think in a way you've been asking me to. Right?" And I reach to lift his visor. It's terribly cold and as slick as ice. By the time I've lifted it half an inch he's moaning like there's a knife in his guts.

It'll be easier on him if I get it over with as quickly as possible. With a sharp flick I send the visor sailing up. His scream slams at my ears and I rest a hand on his cheek, trying to comfort him. His face looks naked in a way no human face ever should. His skin is glossy black from the bottom of his nose up—not black like somebody from Africa, but black like an oil spill—and bloodless silvery white below.

And a pair of gleaming stars is stabbed right into his glossy jet eyelids, pinning them shut. The stars look like they're made of metal except that they're too radiant for that, more like gold glazed with flame. His mouth is open, his scream shaking out of his dark throat, but his eyes are sealed in the most sadistic way imaginable.

Please don't believe that the shadow dropped far . . . Is this what it meant: the shadow fell just as far as this parking lot? *Who will you find if you open the stars?*

I'll find a friend I've known since I was born. Someone who enfolded my mom and me on our walks across the Williamsburg Bridge, who held the moon in place above us; who cared for us then, and who cares more now.

I reach to pull out the star on my right. It will hurt him terribly and he'll probably bleed, but at least he won't be blind anymore.

Before my fingers come within two inches my skin starts to smoke. I yelp and jerk my hand back. The swans are thumping wearily now and I know I can't expect them to keep this up much longer, or I'll be as cruel as Babs.

I hurry to strip off my army jacket and wrap my hand in it. Chelsea would say that the simplest solutions are the best.

I reach again to grasp the right-hand star, its light unbearably rich and deep. Even though it's stabbed into his flesh the points seem to rotate and the color takes on a hypnotic flash, tangerine and blaze and azure . . .

I seize hold of the star with my fabric-swaddled fingers.

And my jacket bursts into swirling fire.

Everything seems to bend, to refract into disjointed images. A sphere of rolling flame is wrapped around my hand and I fling it desperately onto the pavement, but not before sparks leap onto the bandages that tether my swans to the motorcycle. Panicked, they lunge skyward. Then as the bandages yank back at them they go rolling up into the night, wings battering in whirligigs. Snaking ribbons of fire pursue them and then come tumbling in windborne scrolls back to earth. At the same moment the motorcycle crashes down and its still-spinning wheels connect with the pavement. It jolts and takes off on its old course, burning bandages flapping behind it. The streaks of blaze blur from speed, painfully bright against the darkness. And I go stumbling backward, screaming and clutching my ash-smeared hand.

The swans pummel the air, their necks lashing in fear. Higher and then higher still, chasing the darkness—chasing the *anywhere but here* in all directions, out of the parking lot and beyond the ugly buildings, until I can't see them anymore. Only a few charred feathers drift down. The motorcyclist is still shrieking and his voice tears up and down the scale as he circles. Then at last he swerves a little and his visor flops back over his wounded eyes. He falls silent again apart from the engine, which sounds like someone groaning in pain. I used to feel a kind of weird sympathy for Babs—for no good reason, I admit—but now that I understand what she's done to him I'd happily throttle her.

The back of my calves hit the stump and I half-sit and half-fall, gasping for breath.

"Night," I say, since there's no one else to talk to, "Night, what have I done?"

Ah, so now I understand why Babs left me unwatched. She knew I'd try. And fail. How amusing for her. I made it through her tasks, though admittedly with a lot of help—but as soon as I tried giving myself one I was a complete flop. Nice work on the *mission*, Vassa.

My swans are scorched and terrified. I can't imagine that they'll be coming back. And all I did for Mr. Night-Doll-Monster was to torture him. Who am I, to think that I could be the one to help him? If Bea did have something to do with sending me here, then Babs is obviously right: Bea didn't make the savviest choice of pawns. The only upside is that my burns are mostly on the back of my hand and wrist, and they could be a lot worse.

My jacket is still blazing, an amorphous blob of leaping light on the pavement. The arms are loose, though. The loft of the flames carries them upward so that they reach into the air. A fire-girl, drowning in an asphalt sea and waving for help.

"Hey," someone to my left says in annoyed tones. Tomin. What fabulous timing he has.

"This is arguably not the best moment for you to show up," I snap, not even looking at him. "On reflection, maybe *any* moment after you ran away while I got hit by a motorcycle might be less than ideal for trying to talk to me again. How about you go home and wait for *never*?"

"You got *hit* by a motorcycle," Tomin says flatly. He walks around the stump to face me, his dark hair feathering in the wind and his stare confrontational. "When did that happen?"

"When you were here last night. But since you were so busy running like a coward maybe you didn't see it."

I might be willing to concede, if anyone asked, that I'm not in a great mood this evening. Honestly, though, I can't forget the way Tomin reacted when I started talking about Joel's death. He was ashamed, there's no way around that, and the implications of that bother me way more than him disappearing on me—though that wasn't so awesome, either.

I wish he'd take the insults as his cue to leave, but he sits down instead.

"Oh, sorry, I thought you were fine. I usually think that when people are laughing their heads off."

That gives me pause. "Who was *laughing*?"

"You were. I saw the motorcycle coming at you, and then those swans knocked me on my ass. Next thing I knew you were holding onto that creep on the bike like he was your best friend ever and laughing hysterically. You kept riding in circles with him. I tried to talk to you, but you ignored me."

Jealousy leaks out through every syllable he speaks.

"I don't remember any of that," I tell him truthfully. "But I was unconscious for a while, so I guess it's possible."

"Unconscious. But having one hell of a party."

He's not helping his case. "Oh, sorry, do I owe you something? I was unconscious until dawn. I also saw someone get murdered today: this old man who thought I was his dead daughter or girlfriend or maybe his sister, I don't know which. I couldn't do anything to save him. And then you come around with your lame fetish for Extreme Shopping, acting like this is some kind of cute game and I'm the *prize*. . . ."

That's only the tip of the iceberg, of course. But most of what's happened would be too hard to explain. You just had to be there to appreciate it.

"You're not the prize," Tomin snaps. "Though I get why you might think that. You are gorgeous enough that guys probably do totally stupid things to be near you. But, hey, just this once, try to imagine that it *might* not be completely about you? Like I might have reasons of my own for coming here?"

That should not come as a surprise, but it does. "What reasons?"

"But since you started talking about Joel, I kind of thought we might . . . I've been in that thing once by myself and I don't know if I have the balls to face it again. And you're there alone for hours, I know that. So maybe that does give you the right to call me a coward. But that's the *only* reason, and I still think you're a bitch for saying it." He sounds exasperated and his voice buckles like he's fighting back tears. Damned if I know why, though.

"Tomin?" I try. "What are you saying? You thought we might what?"

He stares off at the sky as if he hasn't heard me, arms around his knees and his head thrown back. Yeah, that would be a tear slipping out. In BY's orange shine it gleams like a streak of fire slicing his cheek.

"I'm never going to get anywhere," he murmurs at last. "Going in with Lottery and them."

"Sure," I say, because it's a politer alternative than *duh*. "Seriously, what good did you *think* that would do?"

"You said you *have* to be here. And you said you don't expect to survive."

I wish I hadn't told him that, but there it is. "My odds aren't great," I admit. "So?"

"So are you here on some kind of desperate mission? That's what I've been wondering. Because otherwise I can't understand why you don't just leave already. Do you think I owe *that* to Joel? To just, I don't know, barrel in there and go down fighting? So I'd at least be doing *something*. . . ."

"I guess that depends on whether or not you helped murder him."

For a fraction of a second he looks stunned, then his face goes hard. His gaze swings back at me like a slap. "I had nothing to do with it."

"Oh, of course not. So who did?" It's a relief to hear him deny it, but I still don't sound super friendly.

"Do you really not know? Because I could have sworn . . ."

"I can guess," I tell him. Lottery, Felice, the rest of them. Who else thinks that screwing with BY's is an evening's entertainment? "You *swear* you weren't here when it happened?"

He shakes his head. "After." That doesn't really clarify anything. "Vassa, I joined up with them after it happened. Even though I knew what they'd done. And I know what you think of me for hanging out with them, but I couldn't— If I was going to figure out some way to avenge Joel, I needed help going in there so I wouldn't just get instantly axed. You can see that, right? When I met you I thought, well, maybe you could give me some kind of inside information, and that would at least be a start. Because where *do* you start, fighting something like that? It's been two months and I still have no freaking clue."

It takes me a moment to sort through this. "Wait. You're saying you joined Lottery's crew *so* that you could avenge Joel? *That's* why you've been coming here?" He just stares at me, his eyes raw and wounded. "How did you even know him? You don't go to my school, do you?"

"Our moms are best friends. I don't think I was ever even that nice to him, but then—" He rolls his head like he's trying to escape from the memory. "A week after he died his mom tried to poison herself. She was in the mental ward, and when we went to see her she kept saying that the world hadn't even noticed he was gone. *No more than they care for a rat in a trap,* she said. *What other world is there for me? Because this one is dead. It must be dead, since it feels nothing.* I thought, like, maybe I could prove that wasn't true? Not just to her, but—"

To yourself, I think. God, was I unfair to him. I picture the woman I saw coiled and shaking in the same parking lot where we're sitting now. I imagine her gulping down poison so she could be as dead as the world around her. "I wish somebody would prove that, too. That the world still feels enough to stop this."

"So is that why you're here? To prove it? I kind of can't believe you've made it this long alone."

"I wasn't alone at first," I say. "And that wasn't why I came here. Not as far as I knew, anyway. I came here because I was an idiot." He gazes quizzically. Trying to understand, which I can see might be a challenge. "But . . . it might be why I'm here now. I mean, I didn't have a mission here at first. But now I think I *have* to have one." I feel how utterly true it is when I hear myself say it. I thought my job tonight was just freeing the motorcyclist, and that's still a big part of it. But really, it's a whole lot scarier than that. "And anyway the owner here—Babs—she has like three guns to my head. She's holding my friend hostage, for one thing." My voice chokes up a little, admitting that. It feels like something I shouldn't say, and I'm still leaving out almost everything important. "If I could get my friend back, I'd stand a way better chance of stopping Babs, is all. I'm not doing such a great job on my own."

"But if you're trying," Tomin says softly, and this time I'm the one who can't look at him, "then that's a lot more than anyone else is doing."

"I'm failing catastrophically, though, so it works out about the same. I mean, nothing *changes*. Babsie just got herself a brand-new head today."

"So why don't we work together?" he says so quietly that I barely hear him. "It's not like anyone will ever get the cops to do anything. I tried calling them when Joel died, and the guy laughed and said that BY's was a valuable partner in keeping the thugs and losers under control. Does *that* mean his mom was right?"

"No," I say—and I feel a fresh wave of determination to make sure that's true, even though my failure with the motorcyclist is so recent. Even though trying to help has been such a fiasco. "But Tomin, working with me is *more* dangerous than trying it on your own. Babs—the way she went after that old man today, she did it to hurt me. Because she thinks—" *She thinks I'm a threat, so she's out to break my will once and for all.* It seems too vain to say it, but it might be true. *Shows what she knows.* "If you're with me, that means dying. Almost for certain. I'm here because I got trapped, not because I'm brave, okay? You should run like mad."

"Not your decision," Tomin says. "I'm going to shop till I drop!" He flicks a particularly disturbing smile at me and hauls himself upright, offering me his hand. "It sounds like the first thing we have to do is get your friend back. Where do we start?"

Part of me thinks I should let him know I have a crush on some-one else, but since he just told me this isn't *about* me that seems way too awkward. Besides, the motorcyclist is so utterly not-human that it's probably not going anywhere. Even undead would be an up-grade.

And as for Tomin helping to look for Erg, well, that sounds pretty awkward, too. "She's not human."

He does a double take. "Your friend isn't *human*? Um. Fasci-nating."

Talking about Erg feels wrong, but then if Tomin thinks I'm crazy he might decide not to go through with it. He's really not prepared for what we're up against, I know that, even if he has a better grasp of the situation than most people would.

"A lot of the people here aren't human, actually. I'm not sure where my friend is. And I can't tell you anything about her, or let you see her. You're just going to have to take my word for it that she exists." That should be discouraging, right?

"But you care about her. Whatever she is."

"Yeah," I say. "I do."

"And she can help us win. Against whatever the hell is going on here."

"We'll probably lose, though, even with her. If you want to be realistic about it." I think it over. "Without her, though, I'd guess we'll be toast in no time. As a team we might last like fifteen min-utes." If that doesn't send him scampering to safety, I don't know what will.

"Vassa? Remember how you said that no one sees past the obvi-ous stuff? If I go by what's obvious, then I'd have to assume that you're a raving, pathological liar."

"Fair enough," I tell him. "So go home and save yourself. I'm not kidding."

We've both halted ten feet from BY's, and he steps closer and fixes me with a searching gaze. "Yeah, no. Not doing that." His hand lifts up, drifts toward me. Comes close enough that I feel a tiny stir of warmth, and I almost step back. Then his smile tightens self-consciously and the hand falls again. "Just 'cause it's obvious doesn't mean it's true."

CHAPTER 19

It feels truly strange to be walking back into the acute orange glow of BY's with another human being beside me. I guess I've gotten more used to the company of scaly lawyers and talking dolls. Tomin's presence gives the place a discordant sense of normalcy, even as we lift off the ground and the brightly colored boxes everywhere start pitching gently with the dance.

Once we're already high up it occurs to me to make sure he's observing his *basic shopping precautions,* and in fact he's wearing his jacket with the stitched-shut pockets, bright pink zigzags crudely galloping across gray canvas. The pink is so lurid that it leaves trails of green lightning inside my eyes. Perfect. As far as I know Sinister is busy throttling Erg and Dexter's come around to seeing things more my way, and he's too sick to cause much trouble anyhow. But I can't count on that.

I can't count on anything. Not here.

Tomin's eyes search the store. "So, do you have any ideas at all about where your friend could be?" Something occurs to him. "You said not human. Are we talking humanoid, at least?"

It feels like an intrusion on Erg's privacy to tell him anything at all—but the fact is he won't be much help if he has no clue what to look for.

"She's a lot smaller. Um, the last time I saw her, Babs had her stuffed in a jar. She probably has a guard with her, too. Otherwise I'm pretty sure she could get away by herself. Like, one of my co-workers is watching her? That almost got Lottery?" It's funny, but I feel a kind of inner prohibition, a resistance, to coming out and explaining about the hands; there's a weird sense in my chest that there are things we just don't *talk* about. Is this how it feels for Erg? I consider the problem for another long moment. "The obvious thing would be for Babs to keep my friend somewhere in her apartment. But Babs is not the type to do the obvious thing. She'll want to mess with me more than that. You know, I'd bet Babs hid her somewhere right in the store, like on one of the shelves somewhere."

Tomin kind of drapes back against the display of laundry detergent, arms crossed. He has beautiful fluid posture, but ripples of uncertainty pass over his face as he struggles to take in what must feel like a surfeit of impossibilities. "Your friend. And a guard. Both in a jar."

"See why I'm telling you to leave? Think how much better you'll feel if you decide that I'm just a psycho and get lost. Go play some video games. Doesn't that sound awesome?"

"And then in a few days I'll hear from Lottery that you're dead, and we'll celebrate by ordering pizza?"

"You guys clink slices. A toast to getting rid of me and Joel. Seriously, we'll be honored." I thought I was kidding, but there's an appreciable bite to my tone.

Tomin responds to that by crossing the narrow span of emptiness between us and hugging me. I'm too startled to react at first, and by the time I start considering whether or not I want to hug him back he's already letting go. "I think I'd rather get pizza with you. I'm weird that way."

I pause, wondering how I should respond. Over the wafting piano music I hear a small noise I can't identify, a tiny *pop*. It's very close. "We need to be careful. I just heard something. If we're doing this, we should get started."

I guess that constitutes changing the subject, the way Erg always does, but luckily Tomin accepts it a lot more gracefully than I usually do. He watches me curiously, suppressed questions bubbling just below the surface, then nods.

"Start looking through everything on the shelves? I can do that. It's going to take forever, though. And it's not nearly as intense as what I was expecting. I thought we'd go about this more efficiently, like infiltrate somewhere, or maybe slay some stuff." He smiles archly and swings an imaginary sword at the air. Hopefully he's being ironic.

"I've seen enough slaying to last me a while. But thanks for the suggestion." I think of telling him to search quietly, but the fact is that if Sinister's lurking nearby he must have heard the whole conversation, maybe while tightening his squeeze on Erg's neck. Taking Sinister by surprise is probably out of the question. Even if we find them, what do we do then?

And then on a low shelf under the detergent I notice bottles of Drano next to packages of rubber gloves. I don't imagine Erg will be a big fan of getting doused in some nasty corrosive chemical like that, but that stuff will do way more of a number on skin than it will on wood.

I open a pair of gloves and snap them on, then hoist the Drano. "If you find anything . . . really weird-looking, don't touch it. Just call me right away. Okay?"

Tomin looks shocked. "You're going to use that as a *weapon*?"

"If I have to. Sure. Great for slaying!"

"Oh," Tomin says, a shade too wildly, "so slaying is okay for *you*."

I don't try to answer that, because there's another small popping sound. One rule of thumb I have for BY's: if you don't know what something is, then it's no good. "I think we should move. Tomin, *please* try to be careful." Another tiny snap; if I didn't know that plinking song so well by now, I might think it was part of the music. I grab him by the shoulders and tug him away from the display. "It's time to take your shopping precautions to the next level. Go *advanced*. I'm not kidding."

The store starts dancing more briskly, with simulated cheery enthusiasm, like it wants to keep us distracted and wobbling. Tomin pitches sideways. Under the loud slap of his foot as he catches his balance, I almost think I hear the pop again. A few pops, actually, like the patter of a miniscule machine gun. It makes no sense at all.

"Vassa? I don't know why, but I have this feeling that it has to be tonight. That it's our one chance if we're ever going to stop what's happening here. Is that crazy?"

I don't answer and he sits down to start peering along the lowest shelves, moving jars and boxes around to check the things in back. For another long moment I just watch him, waiting to catch a glimpse of something suspicious, but everything looks fine.

Which just makes me feel worse, but I start searching anyway. I still have that intuition—*Erg is right here*—like a knife piercing tiny slits in my heart. Is it possible that after all our years together I can sense her? I look first at every jar I can find, hoping for that same mostly empty container of strawberry marshmallow butter, but as far as I can tell they're all undisturbed. Babs might have moved her into something else, and I listen as intensely as I can for the faint, muffled cry of a tiny mouth.

Tomin moves into the next aisle where I can't see him. "Hey," I call. "We should really stay together."

"No time for that," Tomin calls back. The store pitches so hard that the shelves creak, then flings itself in a delirious pirouette, gives a rapid shake, and spins again. It appears to be in an exuberant mood this evening, and my head starts to swim a little. Glowing dots and filaments dance across my vision: green lightning, pink snakes. "We have to work fast, I can feel it. Hey, Vassa? It wasn't completely true. I mean that Joel was my only reason for coming here tonight. I didn't want you to be stuck facing this on your own."

I can't focus on that now. My dizziness subsides, but the yellow floor glares so fiercely that looking at it isn't much of an improvement. I feel ill. The colors of the packages must have seared my retinas a little, because I'm still seeing things: floating green dots and what looks like a bright pink squiggle on that immaculate linoleum. The dots drift, but the squiggle stays dead still.

A single loose strand, like a thread.

Then I get it. "Tomin!" I scream. "Tomin, watch your pockets!" And at the same moment I hear him yell. There's a violent slapping sound followed by a rumble of falling objects. I dart around the corner, the store's sway throwing me against the shelves as I reach his aisle, and see Tomin grabbing fistfuls of candy bars, popsicles, toothpaste, yanking them out of his wide-open pockets and flinging them on the floor. The hem of his jacket bulges strangely, and more small objects keep spewing up through his pockets like lava. Foil gleaming and rustling, colored indigo and chartreuse and awful biting-bright scarlet. He's stopped yanking out objects to smack at something, and then I see it: a skittering lump like an obese spider stretches the fabric of his jacket. From the inside.

It must be Sinister. He's wormed his way between the gray canvas and the lining—and the jacket's whole bottom is distended with stolen goods. Popping them out through the pockets is just a tease, because no matter how many Tomin hurls away he'll still be sagging with them.

I shove the Drano onto the nearest shelf and throw myself at him, grabbing his jacket by the collar to drag it off. The whole store leaps and bucks, trying to dislodge me, but after an instant's confusion Tomin understands and starts twisting, too, managing to jerk one arm out. His breath is hot on my ear and his broad chest radiates warmth as I struggle to free him from that fatal gray tangle. I can see Sinister wriggling inside the quilted lining. Panic makes us clumsy, and the store swings violently back and forth so that my shoulders slam into the metal shelves on one side and then on the other. All I can think about is ripping that jacket free, running to the door and dropping it into the parking lot . . . and if Sinister dies from the fall, that would be fine, too.

I'm almost there, still wrestling with the jacket whenever I'm able to stand upright for a moment. It's off now except for the left cuff. I tug but it's caught on his wrist somehow, and he yelps as I yank harder.

Then Babs is five feet away, smiling a horrible pinched smile. "And do you think this is appropriate behavior during working hours, my imp? To be getting yourself in a pleasant tussle with a young man of such dubious character? An unrepentant thief, by the look of things?"

I haul back, irrationally hoping I can save him—though any idiot could see that it's too late—and his jacket rips wide at the bottom. A clutter of nasty junk foods and starry foil-wrapped soaps avalanches down, Sinister flopping on top of it all. He hops on his wrist-stump and jiggles a triumphant forefinger my way: *Got you.*

King of the goddamn mountain.

A grayish-mauve slug, squirming with self-satisfaction.

I will wait for my chance, and I will kill him.

If Sinister is here, then where is Erg? Is she unguarded? Quick and stealthy as she is, can't she get away?

Tomin looks from me, to Babs, to the hand on the floor. "Ugh. Oh, God, is that foul! Look, you can see that I didn't have anything to do with this, right?" He shoots Babs a look of appeal, smiling sweetly at her. She doesn't smile back.

"He thinks I'm a fool for the pretty face, doesn't he, imp?" Babs says, looking fixedly at me. "Poor old woman that I am, with no livelihood but my store, he thinks he can bury me alive in his smiles and I won't lift a hand in my own defense? Ah, wicked boy," she addresses Tomin. "You could at least say you're sorry. A last little glimmer of repentance before you go, wouldn't that make it so much nicer? For you and for me. And for your sweet amour here. She'd have the peace of knowing that you'd made things right before you died."

Tomin's head jerks back. I was so busy looking at Babs that I didn't see Sinister creeping up the shelves behind him, but now those dead fingers are twined in Tomin's tousled dark hair, dragging hard so that his golden brown throat bows forward like the sail of a ship. He still can't believe what's happening, but sparks of terror begin to dart through his green-gray eyes. "*Vassa*," he says, and his voice is soft—though I deserve fury for getting him into this.

"Babs," I say; I won't mention *right* or *wrong* this time, since those clearly aren't details that interest her. "Babs, if you do this, I will take you down." The weird thing is how certain I sound, how utterly confident—though the logic of the situation suggests that if anybody's going down, it will be me. "I used to feel sorry for you, can you believe it? But that won't stop me if you hurt him. I will undo you."

Babs's diseased eye bobs around me as I speak, a startled will-o'-the-wisp. She's too shocked to reply for a moment, her mouth chewing on empty air, but then she manages it. "Why, impling, what a childish declaration it is! And have you forgotten so soon that I have a guarantee of your good behavior?"

"I remember."

She gives me a slow once-over, her eye rolling along the neon green rubber gloves, then taking in my missing jacket. I'm left with just my black hoodie over an olive tank top. "I'm pleased that your recollection is improving. Try to remember how many times you've lost already, my imp. Count those occasions up on your dainty fingers. Perhaps you'll be able to deduce from that how very much loss you have yet to endure."

"I've lost some," I admit, and that uncanny confidence still controls my voice. It's like I'm possessed, but I've got no idea by what. "But I've won some, too, Babs. Maybe I'd rather draw my conclusions from that."

Babs snorts. "Not on your own, you haven't. And your little helper is well and thoroughly neutralized. Dexter!"

"Vassa," Tomin says. "This is not your fault. Always remember that, okay? You warned me over and over. It's not your fault that I did this anyway. I did exactly what I wanted to do."

That's just more kindness than I know how to deal with. I ignore Babs and step over to him, wrap my arms around him, and kiss the throat that they're about to sever. I have a hazy idea that Babs doesn't actually want me dead at the moment—not until she's hurt me more—and I get this delusion that if I just cling tightly enough they won't do it.

"Dexter!" Babs hollers again. I hear a scraping sound and look to see him coming, dragging the axe along the floor. He's not well— his thumb is still inflamed and the bite is still raw-looking and ragged—but he's obviously much, much better.

"He was so sick!" The words slip out.

"Ah," Babs says. "But I took your wise advice, my imp. I soaked him in a medicinal soup, and just see how he's perked up!"

Dexter stops five feet away and raises his nails to gaze at me. His expression is distinctly sheepish. I wrap myself more tightly around Tomin, who's recovered from the shock enough to hug me back. *Not this one*, I try to tell Dexter with my thoughts. *Just this once, disobey, disobey, disobey. You don't want to be Babs's servant, I know it.*

If I say it out loud she'll know Dexter betrayed her, and then who knows what she'll do to him? She's already looking from Dexter to me, monitoring the appeal on my face and the shame in his droop-nailed stance. She grins to herself, a smirk that sits tightly coiled at the bottom of her face. And then she grabs my arms in her claws— and my God, how impossibly, incomprehensibly powerful she is!—and pries me loose. Bony vines seem to wrap my back, my arms, and I thrash with all my strength to get free. I watch To- min's face, still turned to mine, as Sinister drags him away from me and then topples him onto the floor with a thud. Fear glim- mers in his widened eyes, but so do tenderness and concern. Even now he's worrying about *me*.

Dexter heaves up the axe between thumb and forefinger and totters a little with its weight. With a mincing, doubtful creep he approaches Tomin at neck level and looks at me again. Like he's waiting for my damned approval.

"Proceed," Babs says. "I find myself experiencing some impa- tience, Dexter."

I make another effort to break away, yanking at those skeletal arms binding me, bucking to try to lift Babs off her feet. Dexter shifts the axe to get a better grip for chopping and takes a couple of hesitant swipes at the air. Tomin's dismayed eyes reflect in the blade—and then my self-control breaks.

"Dexter!" I hear myself screaming. "Don't do it! I will never forgive you! *Don't!*"

I hear the whistling sweep of the axe in the air before I see it— and by the time I see it blood is already jetting from Tomin's sliced neck. Dexter shudders with bloodlust, and then the axe spins again, chopping off Tomin's left arm. Both hands are hopping delightedly now, drunk on the violence. Sinister grabs the axe from Dexter as if they were fighting over a toy and takes a turn, hacking off the right arm and leg. Dexter perches on the tip of his forefinger like some gory ballerina and twirls in the blood fountaining out of the right shoulder.

Babs lets me crumple to the floor where I throw up, gasping and retching again and again. When I'm able to look up Dex and Sin are doing finger paintings in the blood—hearts and stars—and skating back and forth like kids on an ice slick.

Babs casually picks up the axe where they dropped it against Tomin's rib cage. "Dexter, my dear?" she says coolly.

Dexter's turning a figure eight in the blood, but he pauses to glance up at her. Shy and quizzical. He's slathered in crimson.

And at that Babs slices him right in half: a straight cut between the ring finger and the middle. The pieces crash convulsing onto the floor.

"Sinister, I'm afraid you'll have to do the tidying up by yourself tonight. Don't forget to store the parts for me; they'll be coming in, shall we say, *handy*. You'll have to use these coolers. The ones in back are all full. We don't have a stake free at the moment, so just pop that head in the fridge for now as well. And Vassa, you return to the register. I wouldn't advise leaving your seat again tonight."

I think I might be laughing hysterically and sobbing at the same time. *Erg*, I think, *Erg, you never would have let this happen. If only I hadn't left you behind . . .*

Babs casts a disdainful glance over the scene: me, curled shaking beside a pool of vomit, Dexter in spasms and Sinister suddenly standing rigid and unbelieving. She turns on her heel and stalks off in her scarlet-splashed dress, not even waiting to see if we follow orders.

And for a long time we don't. All the giddiness has gone out of Sinister and he stands glum and shocked, his gaze riveted on his dead partner. I shudder and gasp, tears streaking my face and sick still on my chin. Gusts of icy wind seem to sail through my body. Then, after I don't know how long, Sinister seems to resign himself. He grabs the cuff of Tomin's jeans and starts the laborious process of dragging a chopped-off leg away, one miserable inch at a time.

I suddenly realize that half of Dexter—the chunk with the thumb and forefinger—has moved a little. As I watch he crawls sluggishly toward the edge of the ruby puddle that pulsed from Tomin's heart. Dexter's dying, maybe, but not yet absolutely dead. Like I care.

When he reaches the margin where the yellow floor begins, the Dexter-chunk arches like an inchworm. With his bloody forefinger he reaches out and begins marking the linoleum. *SORRY*, he writes.

"Like that does any good," I tell him.

UNDIE HIM. The words are clearly printed in block letters, but that doesn't mean they're comprehensible.

"There's no such thing as *undying*," I snarl.

PROF PEPP, the thing formerly known as Dexter adds, but the last letter is slurred. Then the half hand slumps and falls still.

"Where's my friend?" I say, too late. And then I think, *Prof Pepp? Do you mean that gray soda Picnic was drinking?* But this time I have the sense not to say it out loud.

No answer. But one idea gradually makes its way through my foggy awareness: with Dexter dead and Sinister with plenty of work to do for the rest of the night, this is the best chance I could hope for to try to find Erg. *Get moving, Vassa.* I drag myself upright and then pause to smear out Dexter's bloody messages with my foot; I'd rather Sinister didn't see them. Peel off those useless gloves, too, and rip open a pack of paper towels so I can clean my face.

I turn and Sinister is right there watching me, his fingers clenched and his knuckles white with rage. He extends one finger and jabs toward Dexter, then waves the finger in a scolding motion. Then he points at me. He performs the sequence a second time, then a third, his movements more vehement with each repetition. I get the meaning, naturally: *This is all your fault. You killed him!*

"Yeah?" I snap. "Have you considered blaming Babs instead? I mean, she was the one with the axe and all."

Sinister hops in a frenzy and I turn my back. My friends are getting trapped and murdered one by one. But Night is still in the window, dark and silent and shining—and maybe it knows more than I do.

I walk up to the clapping door and stretch out my hands. "Night," I whisper, "Night, can you hear me? I've been trying to fight Babs, but it's not going so well. I just got Tomin killed and he was a really sweet guy. And I can't find—my friend." I still can't name Erg in case Sinister is listening, but Night must know who I mean. I pause for a moment and search the sky. There are only two or three stars fighting their way through the orange dust of light pollution, but the crescent moon is strong and clear. "Night, anything you can do to help would *really* mean a lot. If I can just get my friend back we'll have a way better chance of helping you, too. Please."

I take another step forward, but somehow my extended right foot doesn't land on the floor. Something hard is punching my left foot off the linoleum, tipping my whole body forward, and the right foot keeps stretching out into empty space, trying to get some kind of purchase. But it can't, because there isn't any.

I'm in the night, caught between the velvet sky above and the rough asphalt below. And I'm falling. I barely have time to gasp.

CHAPTER 20

"Hi, again," I call to the motorcyclist. I know from the way the buildings look now, like serrated black glass enclosing the parking lot, that he'll be able to hear me. We're back in our shared territory. "You know, if you don't have a name, it's probably about time we made one up. I don't know what to call you."

He's stopped just a few feet away from me. I get up off the pavement—why the hell was I lying there? It's not a bed—and walk unsteadily over to him. "I tried to open the stars for you," I say. "All I did was set my jacket on fire and scare the daylights out of the poor swans. I'm really sorry. I wanted to. If I could pull those stars out, then would you be free?"

There's a long pause, and somehow I can hear his thoughts passing like a whisper on the air. "Then I would return," he says at last. "I, and my brothers. To free one would loose us all."

"You'd return to Night," I say. "That's right, isn't it? You'd be part of *the all above us* again, and that's Night. Right now you're like a doll that Babs tore out of Night, but really you and Night are supposed to be together. Just like she stole Erg from me. She doesn't care who's *bound* to each other."

Somehow he needs a while to think about that. Images of Tomin and Erg rise in my mind, and I'm crying again, though my tears feel strangely hard and cold. I catch one in my palm and it sparkles blood red, a sharply faceted jewel. It reminds me of the ring that doomed the old man who called me *Sabine*.

"I could have a name," the motorcyclist finally offers. "You could call me by a name."

"That sounds like a great idea," I tell him. "But that's beside the point, right? You need to get free. I mean, is that even your *body*? Or is it some kind of weird shell that Babs made? When I fell— inside your brother, I guess, that time when we were traveling together?—my fist hit his throat and it sounded like metal. And there were freaking *rabbits* in there. As his stomach. It definitely wasn't natural. So I started wondering if I was seeing what he's actually built out of, once you rip the illusions away? And then maybe you're like that, too."

I think I'm confusing him. He seems flummoxed. Communication has never been our strong suit. "She made this body," he says at last. "She made a mockery of man. And then she shut the eyes behind me."

"So I'm right! It's not your real body at all."

"It . . . becomes mine. I am becoming . . . more a man. Night seems far away from me now, Vassa."

"Night misses you so much," I tell him. I'm calming down, getting my self-control back. "I don't know how I know that, but I do. Are you saying that you *don't* want to go back? But you're bound to Night. You can't just keep being Babs's slave!" I look around again, and this time the parking lot sparks like a star field. I could be standing on a glass lake cradling the reflections of uncountable galaxies. When I turn my gaze up the sky isn't rusty with ambient light anymore. Its black is lucid, its stars blue-fierce. "It's so beautiful. Don't you want to go home? There has to be a way!"

"I could stay here. In this dream. I could be bound anew. Not to Night anymore. We could close the stars behind you." With that jet visor covering most of his face it's impossible to read his expression. Only his ash-white chin and mouth are visible, and the mouth is set in a flat, cryptic line. But his meaning is about the clearest it's ever been. Maybe he's gradually getting better at talking to me. "Vassa, give me a name."

Something in his tone gives me pause. "Am I making some kind of commitment if I name you? Because I'm seriously too young for that." Maybe *young* isn't a concept he has much grasp of. I remember something he said before, when I was riding on the back of his bike. "Are you talking about going on dreaming forever? Like, as a couple? We'd stay here?"

I gaze around again. It's a gorgeous place, no question, but kind of menacing, with its miniature glossy mountain range and its gleaming emptiness. And I'm honestly not sure it offers much scope for, you know, personal development. What would a life in this place even mean? It definitely qualifies as *anywhere but here,* anywhere but home and Brooklyn, anywhere but any normal human location. And I might even become *anyone but me,* more a dream-ghost than a girl. The idea has its attraction: not-Vassa living in an enchanted nowhere with this not-man. The reality is that I probably have more in common with the motorcyclist than I do with other humans. No one would ever judge me again for not fitting in, or think I was too weird to live, or regard me as a pretty face with no one at home behind it. I would be absolutely free, now and forever.

He leans my way with his arms reaching out to embrace me. To my own surprise, I step back. "We could dream here. We could remake it, and me, dreaming as you will. You can give me a form of your own choice. Whatever you speak you can see here, Vassa."

Worth a try, I guess. "Ocean," I call to the horizon, and suddenly it's there, emerald black with curling waves taller than buildings. Flights of opalescent fish sparkle in the waves' sweep and foam like

fine lace wraps the black. As I give it more thought the sound arrives, slowly rising out of nothing—crash and whisper—and then
the smell, a deep salt pungency.

It's impossibly lovely—and very, very not real. I could make the
motorcyclist dashing and incredibly handsome in the same way,
I guess. But whether he's in a shell sculpted by Babs or by me, it
would still be false and sad. One thing I know from my own experience: beauty doesn't make anybody into a whole person.

"That's okay, actually," I tell the ocean. "You can go now." And
just like that it's gone.

"To go on dreaming together," the motorcyclist says, presumably
doing his best to sound romantic. "Forever, Vassa. To be bound
anew, together."

When I used to say I wanted to be *anywhere but Brooklyn*, I
maybe didn't mean it this literally. And, I suddenly understand,
I *do* want to be Vassa—or technically I want to make *Vassa* into
somebody worth being. The only way to become that somebody is
to live in a real, substantial world: a world that doesn't follow orders,
that's just as willful and independent as I'm going to be. I can only
become a whole girl in a place that offers resistance; a place that
makes me fight for what I want. The idea hits me so hard that for a
moment my mind flares brighter than the stars, and it's all I can
see: who I really, truly am. Who I'm meant to be.

"I really like you," I tell him. "You're an intriguing guy. If I can
never see you again—" I pause, because the idea hurts so much.
"—I know I'll miss you all the time. I get the feeling that you understand me a whole lot better than the humans I know do. But I think
I should go back and find Erg. And you should go home, too. You
belong to Night, even if you've forgotten how that felt." I take a
breath, because I can feel horrible sadness rising up in him, and it's
rising in me, too. "You don't belong with me."

"Vassa!" His voice thickens with reproach and grief. "You can make me become a man. You can give me a name."

"It wouldn't be your real name, though." I'm trying to be gentle, to explain so he'll understand. "It would just be pretend. What you really are is part of Night, and that's a way better name than anything I could come up with." I think about it. "It's really not my choice what you do," I tell him. "If you want to stay in this parking lot forever, then I won't try to stop you, though that does seem unfair to your brothers. But you have to understand, I need to go back. I won't be able to stay with you."

He's still for a few moments, his head hanging. Then he lifts his chin again and raises both hands to his visor. It takes me a moment to recognize that he's going to remove it, but when I do understand I go tense, dreading the impact of his screams. He stays silent, his mouth crumpling with the effort as the visor tips back and exposes his jet black upper face. The two radiant stars seem to spin, their points reaching out like arms. The gold flickers through permutations of color so rich and overwhelming that it hurts to look at them: vermillion slicking into copper, into electric green, into pulsing burgundy . . .

"You mean to *abandon* me here," he says, and now I near deep rattling sorrow in his voice. The sound of it seems subterranean, echoing, like someone howling in a lost cavern. "Then break my eyes open. Let me go!"

"I'll find a way," I promise. As soon as the words are out my insides go cold with fear—that I'll fail again, wound him again. "There has to be a way!"

I hear the beating of wings.

INTERLUDE IN FEATHER

NOW

Wings flash through night, and minds fly through memory.

Each of the swans flew through dreams of the past; to them the past seemed the medium from which the gloaming was made. The dreams came to them in fragments: one remembered the scent of a lawn at twilight as she tripped and her childish body crushed the grass. A sprinkler chugged behind her, and her mother called her name. Was she once called Annabelle?

Another recalled a failing grade and his father's pitiless mockery. A little sister hiding under the guest room bed, her face peering out like a frightened moon.

Another remembered running far ahead of her panting human flock; running until she felt sure she could fly. Now, of course, she understands that flight is another matter entirely, and much sadder than her earthbound exaltation. The strange thing was that she felt heavier in midair than she ever had on the ground.

Each of the swans carried a private and specific childhood, but there came a point where their memories ran together and became one great and common consciousness. They all remembered falling sway to depression and the half-felt lure of death, beckoning them in the form of a luminous orange store that never stopped dancing.

They all remembered a trick that forced them into servitude in one BY's or another; they all remembered waiting for their chance to escape. A dash across a midnight parking lot and the sense of profound release as they passed the ring of rotting heads that marked the cursed border. Without exception, they all carried the stabbing pain of knowing that their triumph in that moment was delusional and desperately foolish. They all recalled, as one, the sensation in their legs as they kept running, giddy with freedom, and then realized that their feet no longer struck the earth. The looming brightness of an amber sphere—was that the sun bobbing just over the nighttime street?

No; a moment's consideration and the sphere resolved into the globe of a streetlamp, already far behind. Dark roofs and blotchy foliage so far beneath that their hearts lurched from vertigo. And, just behind them, a vast stirring in the air, winds pulsing rhythmically. A glance revealed the flock of swans in tight formation just behind.

For a few nights the shock, dread, and denial would be unbearable. The newest swan would lead the others to his or her old home and restlessly circle the sky just above, diving now and then to brush wings against the windows. Family members might appear and laugh in delight, snap photos and call everyone else to come look, but to the new swan's astonishment there was never so much as a glimmer of recognition in their eyes. *Don't you know me, don't you know me?*

The older ones were patient with their companion's grief and circled as well. Offering the newly transformed the comfort of company and voiceless sympathy, they might linger for days, all settling on the roof to sleep. Together they became a cloud of down and feather, white necks snaking tenderly around one another.

Eventually the older swans would become sick of scavenging through garbage and prod the new arrival to fly on. They would find a quiet lake and stay there, skating on their own reflections, until thcy felt themselves called again. They knew by instinct that they had a duty to gather in the one who was about to change. They could feel, too, the unnatural sharpness of every quill embedded in their flesh. Failure would bring immediate punishment.

So they felt her long before they saw her, then: the purple-haired girl who stepped into the BY's parking lot as innocently as all of them had once done. They felt her because of everything she had in common with them, her entrapment and her longing to escape. It was the second time she had walked out of the store, but the night before the swans had known with their shared thought that it wasn't serious; she would never overstep the boundary. But tonight, they felt, she was surely ready to risk it. The surge passed from wing to wing like a wave. Flying through memory, they reached the moment before they knew it: there she was, her violet locks spinning through white strands of snow. She ran as they all had run before. They were ready for her.

Then, to their amazement, she stopped short of the boundary and threw her arms around a taller, dark-skinned girl.

The swans felt the first prickle of warning, their feathers tightening ever so slightly in their skins. If they'd had voices and if anyone had been listening, they would have protested: it wasn't their fault what this strange girl chose to do! They heard the girls' voices tussling; saw the purple-haired one dragged toward the border. She already belonged to them, even if she didn't know it. *Little sister, little sister,* were the words repeated by their wings.

To the swans' confusion, she resisted the dark girl's pull. Suddenly uncertain of the outcome, the swans alighted, slowly and softly so as not to disturb the drama unfolding before them. They followed her. Their needle-sharp quills pierced a shade more deeply with every word their new sister spoke: a pointed reminder of the coming pain if they failed to collect her. How could she fight a destiny they had all accepted?

A struggle broke out: the dark girl yanked their sister forward but she was already twisting away, her body caught in an arc of evasion that seemed to hang suspended in the night. When she fell, every swan felt the change in her right foot as a tingle in their own. They felt their nature passing to her, cradling her—but stopping, as it never had before, at her ankle. They felt the thrust of their own feathers breaking into flesh and could not cry in pain: retribution for their failure to escort her into the sky, though it was no choice of theirs.

After that it seemed unbearable to leave her, this girl who was of their flock but also outside it, her nature permanently unresolved. Such a thing had never happened before; it was beyond their comprehension. And yet through their bewilderment and grief the girl was kind to them, as if she, too, grieved for their sympathy left so strangely incomplete. As she stroked their feathers with a stinging cloth, the sharp points were coaxed from their wings and sides. She soothed them, and her gentleness stopped the steady weeping of their blood.

They stayed nearby, feeling their connection to her through her hidden right foot, brooding over their frustration at her winglessness. They helped her as best they could, even to the point of being chased by ribbons of fire.

And when they saw her lying on the pavement, deathly pale and unmoving, they plunged as one in a flurry of sorrow and indignation. They wrapped her in wings until only her face showed above the massed white feathers; they nuzzled her with their beaks and gently scratched her with their clawed feet until she warmed and stirred slightly. She was alive, but they recognized at once that someone or something had tried to kill her.

The swans had never dreamed of revenge before, but as they huddled over their hurt human flock-mate the idea whirled from mind to mind like a wind coming from a direction previously unimagined.

CHAPTER 21

The crescent moon flutters into view, broken by a dark fringe. After a moment I realize that the fringe is my lashes and that the moon has appeared because my eyes are opening. I'm flat on my back. BY's dances almost directly above me, all tangerine glow the color of molten metal. Right, Sinister tripped me and I fell thirty feet onto solid pavement. If I'm not dead, then at a bare minimum I should be severely injured.

The first thing I do is lift one leg, making sure I'm not paralyzed. Apparently not. I squirm a little, and my whole body aches; I must be a mass of bruises, but I don't feel the jabbing pain that I'd expect from broken bones. There's a huge lump on the back of my head and my thoughts seem to leap uncertainly from place to place, but considering the distance I fell it's pretty miraculous that I'm not in worse shape.

Night sees that I'm awake; its darkness caresses my face. "Night?" I say. "Did you—slow me down? When I was falling?"

No answer, of course. Conversations with Night tend to be one-sided.

Something long and wriggling shifts against my back, squeezing painfully at my bruises. I let out a groan, but I already feel more of those snaking things working their way under me. It seems like

I'm caught in a basket made of living roots, all weaving together. But there are no trees anywhere nearby, which makes that theory even more absurd than it was already.

I lift my head, trying to understand what's happening to me. In place of the parking lot I see glossy pearl-colored arches close around me, forming a kind of nest. Maybe I have a serious concussion after all, because it's hard to believe that what I'm seeing could be real. Especially when my nest starts to move. It shuffles, rustles, stirs like restless water . . .

And bursts into beating wings. I gasp as I feel myself rising in my unearthly cradle. A swan twists its head free and gazes into my face with wise black eyes. It's only now I realize that those snaking roots are actually their necks, crisscrossing my body from below. They carry me up, and the air whooshing from their tightly gathered wings swirls through my hair. Where are they taking me? If they carry me beyond the boundary, I'll change into one of them. The windows of Brooklyn glow gold and the cemetery rises in dark curves. An elevated train rattles across the horizon. My hands shine a feverish orange as we draw closer to BY's, and then I understand that they're not flying away with me at all.

They're taking me back to the same awful place, but it's the place where I need to be. Erg and I came here for a reason and we're not done yet. Or *I'm* not done, and that's even more important.

We burst through the door like a feathered storm and the swans unwind, letting me gently tumble to the linoleum. They look much bigger in the narrow aisles of the store than they did in the cavernous night. One by one they settle in snowy heaps or begin to stalk through the aisles, their feathers ruffling as they turn and examine their surroundings. I'm so sore and dizzy that my first effort at standing only gets me as far as my knees before I lose my balance again. Some of the swans are probing the store's contents with evident curiosity, their long necks coiling between stacks of boxes and sometimes knocking a few random objects from the shelves. I make another effort and this time I manage to get to my feet, though my eyes swarm with green blobs and my head feels like Jell-O on a roller coaster.

Prof Pepp, Dexter wrote. *Undie him.* Chances are excellent that it's meaningless blather, but what if it's not? I stagger to the aisle where Tomin was butchered and find Sinister there with a rag and a small bucket, sullenly smearing Tomin's blood and my vomit across a widening swath of floor. Tomin's dismembered body and the Dexter-chunks are gone. The air reeks of tart iron and acid and some sickening chemical cleanser. Sinister is doing a terrible job on purpose, I'd guess, but if he was in a bad mood before it's nothing to the expression on his chipped lilac nails when he sees me. He rears in fury and then stops, his nails undulating with icy rage.

"Well hi there, Sin," I say. "That's so nice of you to clean up! It'll make things so much easier for your replacement."

He bristles, but there's something unconvincing about it.

"Well, you heard what Babs said, right? Tomin's pieces are going to come in *handy*? You don't really believe she'd want an unmatched pair, do you? That would be aesthetically displeasing."

Aesthetically displeasing was a phrase that Zinaida liked to throw around, usually to describe anyone who wasn't maximally fabulous. When I was first introduced to Iliana I repeated it when my dad asked what I thought of her.

Sinister jabs forward as if he wanted to impale my ankle with his talons, though with my thick boots I'm not too worried. My memory's still shaky, but I think Babs said something about keeping Tomin in the fridge.

I turn the corner and see the long bank of sliding glass doors; behind the nearest one is Tomin's light brown hand and forearm, fingers drooping forward like the fronds of a palm tree. It's standing among bottles of beer and seltzer, lonely and defiant, still in its blood-soaked sleeve. *Tomin? Are you waving or drowning?*

I make myself stop and take in the sight, though I have to clutch the nearest shelf to do it. Near it I see a shoe and ankle poking up above a forest of cans, the foot tipped to pedal away at nothing; I see a thigh laid sideways like a denim-cased sausage in front of the energy drinks. My knees seem to turn into falling water.

"Vassa," I say aloud. "*Deal* with it. You have to!"

I'll have to handle those pieces, press them together, arrange them back into the semblance of a guy who was way too brash and naïve and caring for his own good. But first I have to find a bottle of Professor Pepper's Sippable Shadow. I start in one section of the refrigerator that doesn't have any Tomin in it, putting off touching his dead skin for as long as I can. But after I've rattled though every last bottle of lemonade and tub of greasy-looking pudding I realize I can't escape it any longer. I open the next glass door and force myself to lift his torso out of the way—God, so cold and sticky, his dead flesh compressing under my fingers like mud—so that I can look behind it.

Still no Professor Pepper's. My heart seems to start an icy roll into oblivion at the thought that Picnic could have gulped down the last bottle—and that I was the one who sold it to him.

One of the swans thumps against the back of my knees so that I stagger. He, or she, is rooting through the shelf immediately behind me with a determined clatter, knocking jars against one another. The glass clinks like muffled bells. I wish the swan wouldn't get underfoot when I'm in the middle of something so important. "Do you mind letting me work?" I ask a bit curtly. "This is about as serious as it gets."

The swan kicks me, hard, with a backward swipe of one webbed foot: *No, you let me work!* And it lifts out a sickly pink jar with its bill stretched wide around the lid. A few other jars crash to the floor and shatter, spilling pickled snails and foul-smelling orange syrup. I wait for Sinister to appear and start cleaning, but I guess he's sulking too hard for that. Maybe for the swan the whole point is to make the biggest mess possible, because it arches its long neck back and then whips the jar violently forward.

A thick, gummy glob of strawberry marshmallow butter spurts onto the linoleum in a corona of glass shards. There's something lumpy in the middle of it. I barely notice when the swan wanders off because I can't look away from that lump; I can't let myself hope too much, but I can't believe it's *not* her either.

The something tries to move, though the pink sludge is so stiff and gluey that it barely shifts position. I see what appears to be a tiny arm struggling to break free, gum ropes dragging it back. My heart seizes up and it's all I can do to stop myself from screaming her name. Sinister is still close by, and naturally he'll be listening.

"It's you," I say instead. "Oh thank God, it's you." I've dropped to my knees, and now Erg's goo-encased little figure is in my hands, kicking and squeaking. I manage to sort of peel a mass of it off her face and her azure eyes and black spit curls emerge, still wrapped in rubbery pink threads.

"Gosh," Erg squeals at last. "That was just dreadful, Vassa! I couldn't breathe!"

That makes me smile, though my view of her is blurred by tears. Just hearing her complain seems to heal everything in the world that was ever broken. "Why would you need to breathe, silly? You don't have lungs."

"So just because I don't *need* to breathe, that means I'm not allowed to have any personal preferences? Maybe I like to have the *option*. Ugh, they stuffed me in that goo and I couldn't move at *all*, and no matter how I yelled you couldn't *hear* me. I couldn't even move my jaws enough to *eat* my way out! Oh, Vassa, are you still angry at me? I can't believe you thought I cared more about Bea than about you!"

"All I am is so, so happy to have you back! It was just that—you won't *tell* me anything—and I didn't know you had anything to do with Bea—so when I figured out that you did I got paranoid." Now that she's curled in my palm it really does feel like I was being insanely suspicious and distrustful. I'm still working on pulling pink gunge off her tiny body. The stuff is so viscous that it rips a few traces of azure paint off her dress. Poor Erg!

"Well. I can tell you a teeny bit about that if you want. Don't ask me *questions*, though!" She glares at me sternly for a moment, daring me to say anything; how I missed her impudence! "Bea made me, Vassa. She carved me and painted me and everything. So, I mean, that is a connection. But she made me for you, to be yours forever, and that's what *really* counts!"

It's news to me that Erg was made for me specifically, though I could have figured out that my mom didn't pick her up at Toys "R" Us. "But when you said, like, that we're here on some kind of mission—is that something that Bea told you to do? I know that's what Babs thinks."

Erg pouts. "I've been restored to your company for *two entire minutes*, and already you're failing to respect my wishes regarding not asking me totally stupid questions? Gee, Vassa, I'm just blown away! What a great way to welcome me back!"

I've been so absorbed in cleaning Erg, and listening to her voice, and feeling overwhelmed with happiness that we're together again the way we're supposed to be, that Sinister has completely slipped my mind—until I hear a soft scuffling a yard away. His posture is completely different than it was a few minutes ago; suddenly he's hunched and cringing. He watches us with a single trembling nail. His other fingers are tightly curled into his palm.

"Well?" I ask. "Aren't you going to run and fetch Babs? She'll want to know about this, right?"

Sinister twitches back as if I'd poked him with a burning stick. Really, he's so abject that if it wasn't for Tomin I might start to feel sorry for him.

"The more you put it off, the pissier she's going to be," I say encouragingly. "Seriously, you better get scampering. I'm sure she'll think it's bad enough that you did such a sloppy job of guarding your prisoner. If you try to hide it from her, it will just make your punishment that much worse."

Sinister already knows perfectly well what his punishment will be, and so do I. He flicks a resentful glance toward Tomin's severed hand in the cooler. Ah, rivalry!

"Those new hands are *so* strong and young and handsome, aren't they? Really attractive. Of course, if somebody put that boy back together—if somebody was able to *undie him*—then Babs would be fresh out of luck. She wouldn't be able to use his parts after all. And you'd at least get a reprieve. Maybe then you could think of some way to persuade her that you're not useless and obsolete and revolting after all!"

I've never been so cruel in my life, but it's pretty effective. Sinister's aspect has altered from craven to brooding.

"It's really a shame that I can't find any more Professor Pepper's," I remark dreamily. "I've searched and searched, but it just isn't anywhere! Well, I guess my plan isn't going to work after all."

Sinister probably knows I'm mocking him. I don't get the impression that he's a whole ton of bright, but he's not a complete idiot, either. He scrunches his fingers in irritation as if to say, *All right, already!* Then he crawls toward the door of a nearby cooler—the one displaying Tomin's calf and foot—pries it open, and vanishes behind the sodas. For a while nothing happens, though I can hear some dull clinking noises. Erg's still sticky but she's a lot cleaner than she was and she climbs onto my shoulder to watch, wrapping her little arms around my hair. I can't stop smiling at the feeling of her tiny wooden feet swinging against my collarbone.

Then I see the cuff of Tomin's jeans; the denim is maroon and rigid with dried blood, and it's beginning to distend, bow, and squirm. My stomach curdles at the thought of Sinister's clammy fingers crawling over Tomin's skin. Even if he can't feel anything now, it still strikes me as obscene.

Sinister hooks his pinkie through the loop of Tomin's shoelace, the rest of his fingers still hidden inside the jeans, and gives a particularly foul-looking wriggle. He pops out with a bottle of foaming gray soda clutched in his palm, hoists himself onto the sole of Tomin's upturned sneaker, and wags the bottle at me in triumph. It was actually hidden *inside* Tomin's jeans?

I open the glass door and put out my hand for it. Sinister gives a single twitch of hesitation and surrenders the bottle. He grapples his way back down the leg, disappears, and then comes crawling out of the cooler and inches down the aisle. I'm perfectly willing to see him go.

"Do you already know everything that happened while you were crammed in that jar?" I ask Erg. "I bet you do. Dexter said—maybe Tomin doesn't have to stay dead. I know it sounds like the dumbest wishful thinking ever, but I have to try, right?"

Erg is quiet for a moment. "It's always a good idea to *try*, Vassa," she tells me at last. "I think that sounds just fabulous!"

Knowing Erg that might be her way of telling me this could actually work. I pluck her off my shoulder for a moment to kiss her curls, still crossed by filaments of pink muck, and put her back. I have to take a few deep breaths and straighten my shoulders before I can bring myself to start fetching Tomin's chopped-up segments out of the fridge. I try to tell myself it's not really his dismembered body, that it's just a clever copy made of clay and construction paper, so I won't heave all over again. I try to look at his pieces as something abstract, lumps of a three-dimensional puzzle, and not as slabs of someone who was warm and brave and beautiful, and who definitely deserved a lot more kindness than I ever gave him. I arrange a simulacrum of the boy he used to be, there on the yellow floor, squeezing the cut planes together as closely as I can. It doesn't work that well. The store seems lazier now, but there's still enough swaying to unsettle him. The calves tend to roll outward and the upper arms slide away from the shoulders. I get around that by grabbing piles of sponges and using them to prop everything in place.

The last piece I need is his head. I don't see it at first, and waves of queasy panic shove through me again. But then I catch a glimpse of dark waves toward the back of a high shelf, barely visible behind cartons that purport to contain walrus milk. I have to fetch the chair from behind the register to get up there, but then he's in my hands and I can't pretend it's not really him anymore. His gray-green eyes stare, blank and stunned, filled with dreams that cut off too soon. If I looked close enough I might see the last instant of his thoughts, caught like a film still. His full soft lips are bluish and sagging, his skin as cold and moist as upturned earth in winter.

"Tomin," I whisper. "Hi. I'd give anything for this to work."

No answer. There never is when you really need one. Just for a moment I press my cheek to his. Maybe a trace of my warmth will pass into him, and maybe that will help somehow.

Then I climb down and add his head to the reassembled body on the floor. I can feel Erg's tension where she's perched on my shoulder. "Erg? I guess you're not allowed to tell me the right way to do this, are you? Are those beans you can't spill?"

"I can't tell you," Erg snips, "how very, tremendously relieved I am. That your comprehension of my situation is *finally* improving. I did hope that if I exhibited truly superhuman patience you might get a clue eventually. And, hey! You did! Good *job*, Vassa!"

Oof. Maybe I didn't need to be so happy about getting her back. And I'll have to do my best with absolutely no idea of what I'm doing.

Fine.

I kneel down by his severed neck, gazing into the tubes, which used to vibrate with his voice, the emptiness where his breath once moved, the white-coiled mouse of a vertebra. I nest his head in place, using more sponges to keep it from rolling around, and fit the sliced planes of his neck together as neatly as I can. It seems important to make sure the arteries and the windpipe line up right, so I spend some time making tiny adjustments.

And then I open the Professor Pepper's. Sea-gray foam fizzles into the bottle's neck. I think this is the very last bottle there is, so I really can't afford to screw this up.

Just in case it might help, I kiss his cold blue lips. Just this once. Gee, Vassa, I thought you were too much of a heartless bitch to cry over a boy you barely knew? I lift the bottle, ready to sprinkle him with foam—and stop dead, paralyzed by the thought that I'll do everything wrong. That I'll waste the gray soda like an idiot and Tomin will stay as hopelessly dead as ever, like Joel and my mom and everyone else who I ever let down.

Brace yourself, Vassa. Be strong. There's a tragic shortage of heroes in the vicinity and nobody will do this if you don't.

As an experiment I let a single drop fall on his staring left eye.

He winks.

My hands start shaking so hard I have to put the bottle down to keep from spilling everywhere. Once I get more of a grip I pour a little of it in my palm, still trying not to waste it. A bizarre electric tingling shoots up my arm and I hurry to spatter him with droplets. Opalescent foam froths where the liquid hits his skin and his muscles jump, knocking his pieces askew again. My breath catches in my throat; I picture him getting up with his limbs sloppily aligned to his body, crescents of bloody sliced flesh still exposed to the air, and I rush to straighten him out. Everything has to be in perfect order before he comes back to life.

The spasms become less frequent then die away completely. I stare for a moment, trembling. "Tomin! Please get up."

No such luck. Rainbow-gleaming froth slides off his skin and he's as cold and lifeless as ever. The only difference is that his left eye is closed now while the right still gapes, his iris lacquered with silver light. "Tomin? What do I need to do?"

He's the wrong person to ask, though. "Erg, I know I'm not supposed to ask. But anything you can tell me, please tell me now!"

Erg slides off my shoulder and scrambles down my arm, landing near Tomin's rib cage. She rests both her little hands on his jacket, and from what I can see of her face I know she's suffering just as much as I am. "I . . . really can't, Vassa. Truly really. You need to figure it out yourself."

"But you know how to do it? There's a way?"

She sighs loudly and turns, leaning against him and looking up at me wearily. "I shouldn't even tell you that. But, I mean, I'm not saying there *isn't* a way. I'm not, like, making any major claims that I *don't* know what you should do."

"That's incredibly helpful." She looks so genuinely upset that I can't really be angry with her, though. "Maybe I just didn't use enough of it? Should I try again?"

Erg looks down. "Um, just be sure you save some. In case, I mean."

That's not exactly encouraging, but I don't see what else I can do. I make sure he's in order and trickle the soda slowly through my fingers, shaking them to scatter the gray drops until they look like jeweled rain. This time the opal froth gushes up in tiny fountains and his pieces shake in what looks like an epileptic fit, his right calf drumming violently until it turns ninety degrees out at the knee. From his neck comes a muffled cry and his eyelids bat crazily. "Tomin!" His pupils roll in my direction. I could swear he's looking at me with terrible longing. His lips move, and I know he's struggling to speak.

But only for a moment. His convulsions wind down, and again he's dead, damp, and sticky. "Erg! It was so *close*." The bottle's almost half-gone. "I *need* to use the rest of it. He just needs a little more of a kick, and he'll be fine. Or maybe—do I need to glue him back together first? Will that help?"

Erg's blue eyes are wide and thoughtful. "Um, you should put the soda down for a minute, please, Vassa. Really and for real. Your thinking is going squiggly to a quite appalling degree and that is not going to help you solve anything."

"He was trying to talk! He was almost there!"

Erg bites her wooden lip. "Vassa, can *I* ask *you* something? I mean something that you maybe don't want to think about."

"Sure." All I can focus on, though, is the inescapable dream of dousing Tomin with the rest of that bottle and seeing him join back together, stretch, smile at me . . . "Ask away. I'm not the one with the rules."

"Put the bottle down first. Like, *way* over there." She gestures toward Tomin's foot. I hesitate, but then I obey her. Listening to Erg is usually a good idea.

"Right. So you know how I tell you not to ask me stuff? Because I'm not allowed to give you the answers anyway, and it just makes me feel terrible when you keep bugging me, but you won't ever stop?"

My lips purse. "I know that's what you keep saying."

"So what do you think would happen to me? If I did break the rules. Say, if I broke them too many times, which is not very many times at all, if we get right down to it?"

"How am I supposed to know that?" I sound a little sharper than I mean to, but she's slowing me down. Tomin could be moments away from a brand-new heartbeat, from breathing, from laughing.

"*Vassa*," Erg snaps. "You do know. You just would quite emphatically prefer *not* to know. So you're inventing a whole twisty whirlwind of not-knowing. In your own head. But you're not fooling anybody!"

That gets my attention, I admit, because in an unnerving way it sounds kind of true. An answer drifts into my mind, and she's right, I don't like it at all. I want to say, *Nothing would happen, silly. Words are just words, and you can tell me whatever you want.*

But I can't. Because that's not the case. My heart pounds so fast the beats slur together. "Maybe I know. Oh, Erg. You're my doll and I love you, and I could never imagine . . ."

Erg just looks at me, somehow tender and grim at the same time. *You love me, but you'll still trade part of me to get Tomin's life back. Won't you?* She doesn't say it aloud, but I know we both hear it.

There's a long silence. Erg's gaze falls into me, and mine falls into her, and the echoes become a kind of thrumming music made of both our thoughts.

"So you understand now, Vassa?" Erg says at last. "I can tell you about Tomin. But then it's absolutely and forever the *last* thing I can tell you. Because I already slipped up once, and this will make two. So as-long-as-we-live type forever. Unless you want me to completely . . ."

"I don't," I tell her, fast. "I *never* want that to happen. I couldn't stand it. While Babs had you trapped it felt like I was being ripped apart."

Erg stares a moment longer, making sure I mean it. "Then maybe you need another flavor. Before you use the shadow-flavored soda, you should really try another kind first." Suddenly she looks sick, washed-out, and she grips Tomin's jacket with clenched fists.

What flavor? I think, but I don't say it. *Please, Erg, tell me!*

"Vassa," she says firmly. She's so pale that if she wasn't leaning I'd expect her to fall. "What comes before a shadow?"

I look at her and then up at the cooler—and there in a high corner is a bright gold-white bottle that I never noticed before.

"The sun," I say breathlessly. I can't make out the label from here, but I already know what it says: *Professor Pepper's Sippable Sunlight*.

I'm leaping to my feet when I hear a shuffling step. Babs isn't here yet but her white eye is roaming far from her head, already weaving around me. A pallid sentinel, here to stop me before I go too far.

CHAPTER 22

There's no way Babs won't figure out what that pile of pink goo and glass on the floor means, but still my first thought is that I have to hide Erg. Keep her safe, hold her against my heart where Babs can never touch her again. I double over Tomin's body to cover her and reach my arm down so that Erg can scuttle up my sleeve.

I don't feel her. When I look she's gone. Gone *somewhere*, when she should never leave my side again. But I can't call to her because Babs is standing a yard away from me, examining Tomin where he lies like a broken doll. His head rests inches from her feet. Her gaze rakes back and forth, searching for something.

She wants the Sippable Shadow, waiting where I set it several feet to my right. Grabbing it would be no use when she's so much stronger than I am. She's going to dump it out in front of me, smirk while despair hammers into my chest. Why didn't I think of hiding it while there was still time?

"Impling," Babs says at last. "I thought my instructions were clear enough for even you to understand. Was there some eensy trouble with your attention span? Does your comprehension leave something to be desired?"

What's the point of answering? I stare at her as hard and as coldly as I can, hoping to delay the moment when the last of my hope for

Tomin is gone. Why doesn't she leap over his corpse and seize the bottle? She's probably toying with me, prolonging my suffering— but on the remote chance that she really hasn't spotted it I'm careful to avoid glancing in that direction.

"Not only are you neglecting your duties as an employee," Babs continues, "but you've invited a pack of feathered vermin into my store. Must I really wake up to find those filthy birds heaped like so many old mops all over my register and counter? Sleeping so sweetly and spreading their dander and contagion every which way I look. It isn't sanitary, imp. No amount of scrubbing will ever purge the stench, I fear." Her rolling eye strokes around my bare throat as she speaks. I smack it away, hard enough that I can see her lips pinch.

"The swans are here because they care about me," I say. "We're looking out for each other." I'm surprised to see Babs grimace. I didn't tell her that to hurt her, but of course she couldn't say the same about anyone and maybe that's been true since she and Bea had whatever kind of weird falling-out that happens between witches. "Babs, look, I'm taking care of everything out here. Why don't you just go back to bed?"

Babs responds to that by giving Tomin's head a vicious kick that sends it flying through the air. It smacks into the far wall with a thud, hits the floor, and then rolls to a stop by his leg. Automatically, my gaze turns right to follow it.

And now I understand why Babs hasn't lunged for the bottle of Sippable Shadow. It's gone. I wasn't fast enough to hide it, but it looks like Erg was. I could cry from sheer relief.

"Go back to bed?" Babs asks dryly. "And leave you to play your pretty games with the pork chops and bacon on my floor? Ah, you'll bring down the health department on us, and then where will we be?" She bends down to pick up Tomin's torso, dangling it in one hand while with the other she dabbles at the holes in his neck. "But seeing the meat out here reminds me. I used up my very last heart, making that soup for our poor misguided Dexter. If I'd known what a bad path he was on, I would have saved it for a worthier cause. How lucky that fate has delivered me a fresh one! I'll be ripping it out now, impling, shall I?"

She reaches two fingers into Tomin's jugular, and I know she's about to plunge her hand in, rupturing his throat as she goes, and haul his heart back out through his neck. And then there won't be any magic strong enough to save him. A beating heart is a pretty basic requirement for being alive, right?

If I yell, fight, protest, I'll just hurry the process and enhance her enjoyment while I'm at it. Instead I stare at her like I'm the one who's dead. Like she's already murdered me, but my empty eyes refuse to waver for a moment. She was expecting more of a reaction and my blank look seems to confuse her; maybe not much, but enough that her fingers pause where they are. Moving impossibly slowly, still staring, I take a single step toward her, with absolutely no idea of what I'm going to do. Babs's white floating eye darts back into her face, and for an instant I see a slight, silvery glaze pass over her expression.

Babs is afraid of me. Weak and hopeless and human as I am, she's genuinely scared of what I might try next. How did I fail to understand that before this moment?

And she should be, I realize. Because it's not just me she has to contend with. I've made some friends since I came to this place. I can feel Night watching us through the windows. I can see Babs's hair stirring on her neck with the first breath of a sudden wind.

I can hear their wings.

A throbbing cloud of swans lifts up, obscuring the whole front of the store and half the ceiling. Feathers eddy in time with the raining notes of the piano. In the narrow space of the store huge impulses of wind rebound from wall to wall, and boxes begin to pitch off the shelves. The jars and bottles shimmy until the endless song is confused by a low, relentless tinkling, glass on glass.

Babs looks from that beating mass of wings to me and back again. Her upper lip rises in a snarl, and her hand thrusts deeper into Tomin's gaping neck. I can hear a high-pitched shriek coming from somewhere in midair and my vision blurs white—and then Babs goes staggering backward, slapping wildly at a swan that seems to be landing on her face feetfirst. Its neck coils around her while its clawed toes dig at her eyes. Her upper body disappears behind snowy feathers and two strong wings slap the sides of her head so hard that I'd think her eardrums must burst.

Tomin's chest slips from her grasp. A huge crash resounds from the next aisle, and I turn to see a cluster of swans already at work toppling the next set of shelves. Babs yowls and thrashes with her powerful arms, but she can't seem to drive that swan off her face. I hear shouts of delirious triumph coming from the swan. Aren't they supposed to be voiceless?

It's not the swan shouting. Through the rush of its feathers I see something small, azure, and black clinging to the back of its head.

Erg. She's leading the swans in this assault to buy me some time. Babs is caught between three of the huge birds now, pummeling her from all sides, her scrawny arms waving out of billows of white—but, strong as she is, they probably won't be able to hold her off for long. I leap across Tomin's body and fling open the cooler where that gleaming gold bottle is waiting for me. I have to jump for it and the first time all I do is knock a few bottles of beer off the shelf. The sound of their smashing seems impossibly loud until I see that one of the swans has the axe in its bill, and it's getting to work on the destruction of the refrigerators and everything inside them. Shattering glass sheets down like snow and the axe is getting closer. I jump again, and this time my hand closes on something cold and slippery. The axe misses my fingers by an inch, and a moment later the maddened swan takes out the top whole shelf. I jump back, my skin drooling with soda. Blood beads on my wrist; I must have caught a few flying splinters, but for the moment there's no pain.

All I can feel is what I have to do, now, while there's still a chance. The bottle gives off a soft glow and lights up my flesh. The back of my hand shines dull ruby, striped black by the bones. With my free hand I grab a fistful of Tomin's looping hair and shove his head unceremoniously back into place. There isn't time to fuss with lining everything up just right, so it's going to have to be close enough. I twist off the lid. The soda's gotten a pretty thorough shaking and it froths up the glass neck and spills over: foam the color of candlelight. I swing forward just in time and the first drops splash onto the dark red line where his arm was removed from the shoulder. Frayed gray cloth curls on both sides of the wound.

He doesn't jerk or spasm this time. He doesn't move at all. All the motion is inside me as I stand stock-still above him: blood thumping in my ears and hope jamming where it hits solid despair. Nothing is happening. Did I somehow misunderstand what Erg was trying to tell me? A savage hacking noise bursts out somewhere nearby, and I look away from Tomin for a moment: the swan with the axe is applying it to the door of my room. The other swans have driven Babs almost to the end of the aisle, but she has one of them by the throat now. There's a hideous crunching and the swan collapses to the floor in a twitching heap, its neck lying in broken zigzags on the mounds of glass and crackers. How can I fail when they're ready to die for me?

I look back at Tomin and see new skin spreading as softly as sleep over the gash at his shoulder. For a moment everything freezes inside me and my breath turns to fists in my throat.

I don't feel myself starting to move again, but the next thing I know I'm pouring careful trickles of the shining soda across each of Tomin's cuts in turn: first his severed neck, then the other shoulder, the elbows, hips, knees . . . I lose track of where I am. There are no more screams and wingbeats, no more falling shelves and crackling lights.

There's nothing but the quiet, urgent work of putting back together what never should have been broken. It's a miracle too sweet and rare for me to spare any attention for anything else. It takes most of the bottle, but I can see Tomin fusing back into a whole boy. Still dead, still sad, but at least he looks human again and not like a butchered mess. He's whole and he's beautiful.

And now that I've come this far, there's a hitch. I've got no idea where the bottle of Sippable Shadow has gone. I stare around the chaos that the swans have made of the store. There's not a shelf standing. Ribbons of gashed packaging rustle in flamboyant heaps over the reek of pickle juice and jam and bleach. Crystalline drifts of crushed glass fill the refrigerators, syruped in milk and cola. Night seeps through punctures in the orange walls. I don't see a single intact bottle or jar anywhere. I hear my breath heaving in my throat, but apart from that I can't feel anything. There are no more shelves to block the view. Numbly, I look at a throbbing feathered tangle with a pair of human feet sticking out at the bottom. Almost all the swans seem to be tackling Babs now, and they've shoved her to the brink: black space opens where the picture windows used to be. Glass jags gleam along the top like diamond teeth. All at once I understand. They're going to throw her out into the parking lot— and, since Night isn't especially fond of her, she probably won't be as lucky as I was.

I'm not delusional enough to convince myself that there's any possibility the Sippable Shadow could have survived when everything else has been trashed. I can't save Tomin and I'm going to have to accept that and keep going. I can't save him anymore than I could save Zinaida, so I'd better concentrate on the living.

Because there is one person I can save. She doesn't deserve it, you tell me? She's an evil witch and death is too good for her? Yeah, that's absolutely true. I'm not arguing.

Ask me if I care.

The store has completely stopped dancing, I notice. Like it's waiting to see what will happen.

"Swans!" I yell. I'm running over the rubble, glass crunching under my boots. I'm still holding the Sippable Sunlight, since in this mess there's nowhere good to set it down. They've already hoisted Babs off the floor and they're carrying her toward the darkness— probably to lift her nice and high before they drop her. I see at least three swan corpses scattered around, so the survivors must be raging for revenge. "Stop! Please!"

I can see Erg now. She's perched on the head of the biggest swan and grinning like a maniac. "Um, Vassa? You can tell we're busy here, right? Ooh, we've got some serious splatting to do! I told you we'd show her!"

"Don't kill her," I say.

The swans all pivot their heads to stare at me: dozens of skeptical black eyes riveted on mine. Babs's dangling feet kick below the steady pulse of their wings. She's just outside where the door used to be, space yawning below her.

Erg sighs. "Vassa, you know I don't like arguing with you. But we might just have to agree to disagree on this particular issue. Since you're making about as much sense as a talking sandwich! It's not like Babsie is going to become some delightfully reformed character and dedicate her life to feeding stray elephants. And anyway, you promised! You told her you were going to take her down."

"I told her I was going to *undo* her, dollface. But—is she like you? I mean, the rules that you told me about, about what you're not allowed to say. Do they apply to her, too? So if she says too much . . ."

Erg considers that, her little head tipped and jarring up and down with the rise and fall of her swan. "Sure, that would work. You could knock all the magic out of her that way. But what about my pleasurable anticipation, Vassa? I've been so very much looking forward to killing her as thoroughly as possible! Ever since we got here! You wouldn't want to deprive me of that now, would you?"

I'm not sure why Babs hasn't contributed anything to the discussion. It seems out of character, but maybe she's just too pissed off to speak. "Compromise, doll? Let's try it my way first. If that doesn't work—we can't let her go on the way she has been, I know that. But murder really isn't something that I want to do with my life. Please? And anyway I need information, and you know I can't ask you."

Erg stares. "She won't do it, Vassa. She'd rather be dead than give up her power and just be plain human, and old, and sick. There isn't the slightest doubt in my mind. As to her preferred alternative."

"Babs?" I call. "You're hearing this, right? Would you like to weigh in?"

A muffled snarl comes through the moonish globe of feathers, gleaming pearl bright in the light streaming from the broken windows.

"Um, swans? Do you mind letting her talk? If this doesn't work, I promise you can drop her. From as high up as you want. Okay?"

The swans peel back enough to show me Babs's face, battered and scratched in a halo of flashing white. Her roving eye has swollen shut, but the other glowers at me between puffy lids. Ah, so it's not the swans' fault that Babs can't speak. There's something covering her mouth, though at first I can't make out what on earth it could be. Something pinkish gray, with a pale red round at the end of a fat stalk. It's wriggling.

Sinister. He's clapped himself over her mouth, his nails gouging deep into her cheeks, his thumb shoved between her teeth. What is he thinking? "Sinister? I'd like to ask Babs a few questions. Is that okay?"

With an awful slurping sound, Sinister drags his thumb out of her mouth and peers at me. He's keeping a grip on her by pinching her nose, and with two or three swans holding each of Babs's arms she can't smack him off. After the way they lifted that motorcycle, I should have realized that my swans are just as strong as she is.

"Hi, Babs," I say. "Actually, I still feel sorry for you. Even after everything you've done. I'd like you to get to live, as long as you can do that without hurting anyone else. But I don't get the impression that you have enough self-control to change like that on your own. So I'm—here to help you."

The crazy thing is that I really mean it. I want Babs to live peacefully somewhere, read books and drink mint tea, maybe take up watercolors or something. No matter what Erg thinks, I can't shake the feeling that Babs has the potential to be different—that maybe having too much magic has messed her up, and she'd be a lot nicer without it. If Erg kills her, I know I'll grieve for her. For the person she could have been.

"Ah, but I'll take a whole hatred," Babs snarls, "over the half-pity of a bisected nobody." Her voice is thick and nasal and Sinister sways in front of her lips.

"Too bad that's not an option," I tell her. "I don't know why, but I can't hate you. What I can do is spare your life, though. If you'll just tell me a few things."

Babs glares wordlessly. The biggest swan snaps its bill at me. *Get on with it.*

If I was Babs, I'd try to cheat my way out of this by lying—so I decide to start by asking something I already know as a test. "That guy in the parking lot. Who is he?"

Babs still doesn't answer, and the swans pitch her up a few feet and catch her again. For all her bravado I can see fear wash over her face. "He's nothing, not in himself. But he was part of Night, once. My bitty captive, now."

She gets the same pale, sickly look that Erg did. So far, so good.

"Thanks," I tell her. "For being honest. Okay, so what are you actually selling here? You're not making your money off chewing gum." I'm pretty sure I know the answer to this, too.

Babs is not happy with the question, but she doesn't have to be. The swans start shaking her. "The bits and dabs and glands. The choice cuts below the neck. There are certain rarefied buyers, imp, and money's not their true coin. But you've sussed that out on your own."

Pallor seems to gush through her face and her head sways. Getting there.

"Great job," I tell her. "I'm sorry if this hurts, Babs, really, but we're almost through. Okay, what do I have to do to pull the stars out of the motorcyclist's eyes, so that he can go back to Night?"

Sinister's free nails glance from her to me and back again. Babs groans and tenses—and then I can see her give in. Surrender loosens every line in her face, and she looks like an innocent and very tired old woman: someone's sweet grandma. Maybe even someone who *would* feed stray elephants. Erg is wrong for once, I know it. Babs's pale bobby pins are slipping out of her hair and vaporous wisps hang over her face. I might even visit her sometimes. Make sure she's doing okay.

She opens her mouth to answer.

Sinister dives between her lips fingers first, burrowing viciously. Babs gags and her bruised eyes start to bulge. One of the swans jabs its bill toward Sinister, trying to drag him back out, but he's in too deep now, the stump of his wrist stretching her lips. I can see Babs's throat bloating, the small lumps of fingertips driving up under the skin. Erg is crawling over the top of Babs's head.

"Erg! Help her!"

But it's too late. Another grotesque twist shoves out Babs's throat, and then something ejects from her open mouth.

Her tongue. I can just hear the faint wet slap as it hits the parking lot.

In the darkness beyond the motorcyclist drives around and around, as oblivious as ever. All the store's lights go out at once, and my stomach lurches up into my chest as BY's drops abruptly to its knees. We sway for a moment and then the chicken legs give way completely, the store landing on top of them so that the floor stops at a slant a yard above the pavement.

The swans are far above me now, a jumbled feathery comet soaring up into the sky. By the time they let Babs's body fall it's as small and dark as a knife blade crossing the moon.

CHAPTER 23

Then all that's left in the ruins are three swans with broken necks, a dead boy with gold-brown skin, and me. Hazy light from the moon and the streetlamps fills the store with topaz. There's too much glass everywhere to sit or kneel, so I wander over to the nearest swan and stare down at it for a while. It's beautiful even in its destruction. White feathers reflect distant traffic lights in an iridescent babble of colors. Its black eyes are open and staring at the end of its crumpled neck.

I can't bring it back to life, but at least I can make its corpse intact again in the same way I did for Tomin. The Sippable Sunlight gleams in my hand, and I think there's just enough. I dribble a little over the spots where its vertebrae were snapped, then gently massage the soda through its feathers. The line of the neck is already smoothing and straightening by the time I move on to the second swan, and then the third. It's the only way I have to show them my gratitude and my love: to leave them with the integrity of their perfect forms. As lovely as they were in life.

The trail of swans leads me to Tomin, half-buried in garbage. I start clearing it away. Joel's mom never got to hold his body, she never got to bury him, but I'm going to make sure Tomin goes back to his family in the best shape I can manage. I find some shredded paper towels and wipe him as clean as I can. His wounds are so completely healed that you'd never guess how he died, but his clothes are still hacked apart. Once I'm through in here I'll go search for Erg—though if she was still perched on Babs's head when the swans let the body fall, the search might be futile.

But, as Erg would say, it's time to get started. Futile or not. I stroke Tomin's hair, and he looks about as good as I could hope for. He's too heavy for me to carry on my own, but I don't want to leave him in here. I hesitate for a moment—dragging him through the rubble will mess him up again—but then I grab his shoulders and start the dismal work of hauling him out of this place.

It's not easy with all the heaps of garbage in the way. I keep having to stop and kick them aside. I've gone about a yard when I hear something that sends a flutter through my heart.

The click of tiny wooden feet.

"Hey, Vassa!" Erg says casually, jumping to perch on the top of a nearby squashed can. "The swans gave me a ride back."

"Erg!" I yell, since there's no one left to overhear her name. "Oh, Erg, I was afraid—the last time I saw you, you were on Babs's head, and—"

"And you thought I didn't have the derring-do and presence of mind to ensure my own safety? By, like, hopping back on a swan? Jeez, Vassa." But she's smiling. "And now you're trying to get Tomin out of the store?"

"Yeah," I say. "It seems, like, more respectful? To get him somewhere a little more peaceful than this? But he's pretty heavy."

"Well, have you considered that it'll be a lot more efficient if he walks?"

I stare at her, because the implications are so unbearably sweet that I can't take the risk of believing them. "Erg—look around you. Is there a single bottle that didn't get smashed? Anywhere? In this whole store?"

Erg is grinning so wide that I wonder if her head could come unhinged. "Yup," she says. "There is precisely one."

I follow her over the shredded boxes, the smeared jam, the puddles of stinking detergent up to the splintered door of what was once my room. The swan with the axe did quite a number in there. Even the sink has been reduced to shards of pale porcelain radiating over the floor. Scraps of the electric blanket dangle from the lightbulb, now out. There isn't much light in here, though, so my sense of the destruction is kind of approximate. I bang my shin against the edge of the cot, and puffs of stuffing drift into the air.

There's a very quiet sloshing sound near my foot. Erg giggles. I don't think she's ever been quite so pleased with herself before, and that's saying something.

I kneel down, and as my eyes adjust I can just make out the dim form of a glass bottle wound round with bandages. Erg tied the Sippable Shadow tightly to the inside of the cot's metal leg: probably the one place where it could come through the destruction unscathed.

"Brilliant!" I tell her. "Oh, Erg, you really are amazing. I'm going to start telling you that *way* more often, dollface, okay? From now on, just remind me about this whenever you want to hear how great you are."

Erg turns away in pretend indignation, tipping her tiny nose into the air. "So I trust there will be no further episodes of your shamefully neglecting to save me pancakes?"

We're both giggling now while my nails dig at the knots. "I will make you a *house* out of pancakes if you want. Erg, God, will this really work?"

"Try it and see." She pauses. "But, you know, you might not need to use a whole lot. Less is more and so on. Like, maybe you could remember to save enough for the swans."

The knots pull loose and I stand up, holding the bottle. I can barely believe that it's true, that the cool glass under my fingers is really there. *Undie him.* If I knew what happened to Dexter's chunks maybe I could save him, too. I know I can't ask Erg, but she guesses what I'm thinking and she shakes her head. "Tomin and the swans were alive in, like, the normal way."

And Dexter wasn't; he was only alive by magic. It's not the same. But in a way bringing Tomin back to life is kind of a tribute to Dexter. Giving away the secret was the final act of his tragic little life.

Erg crawls into my pocket and we head back to Tomin, to the unmoving golden length of his body, his head thrown back and his lips parted. My knees shake as I walk. If this doesn't work, the disappointment will crush me and I might never get up again.

"Oh, Vassa," Erg sighs. "You've made it this far, right? For a human you've done really well. Don't start being a total wimp now!"

"Fine." I can't ask her anything, but maybe I understand more than I realize. I just have to calm down, think the problem through. If this is a shadow that can bring somebody back to life, then it's obviously not the type that drags from your heels. It's more the kind of shadow that makes you who you are, the secret you carry at your heart.

A shadow that belongs on the *inside* of your body.

So the soda should go through him, not just get splattered on his corpse. I was doing it all wrong before.

I crouch down in the broken glass and touch his cold lips with the tips of my fingers. Then, very gradually, I pour a thin stream of Professor Pepper's Sippable Shadow into his mouth.

His throat contracts. He's swallowing. And now I know for sure that he's going to be just fine.

"Tomin," I say softly. "Tomin, you can wake up now."

His gray-green eyes turn to meet my face. He looks stunned and sleepy. "Something happened to me?" His voice sounds a little rough. His hand drifts up to his face and he sighs.

"It sure did. You . . . um, you lost a lot of blood. How are you feeling now?"

He stretches a little like he's getting the knack of having a body again. "I've been worse."

No kidding.

"It's good to see you," he adds, still staring at me. "I think I had a dream about you . . . You were riding a swan? Maybe? I'm trying to remember."

I lean down and kiss him on the cheek. "You should rest for a few minutes, okay? Don't try to get up yet. Think about your dream and I'll be right back. There's some work I have to do. Okay?"

"You work too much," Tomin slurs. His eyelids are fluttering closed. "When can you finally stop?"

I smile at him, but I don't think he sees it. "Shh. I'll stop when it's morning."

When it's *really* morning, I mean.

I do my best to be fair with the rest of the Sippable Shadow. There's only maybe two inches left in the bottom of the bottle, so I lever open the dead beaks, one at a time, and pour a third of it down each swan's sinuous neck. In a few moments wings rustle drowsily over their backs and their dark eyes blink in my direction. If nothing else good ever happens in my life again, I think this will be enough to keep me going: that I was finally able to mend a few of the wounds in the world. The trees could all start bleeding, bombs could fall; but Tomin and the swans are healed and there's no gratitude deep enough to take that in.

"Erg," I say. "Can you believe it? I wish—"

My mom was cremated, her ashes scattered over the sea. And when I was ten there was no Sippable Shadow handy.

Erg knows what I wish. I slip my hand in my pocket and she squeezes as much of it as she can manage.

"There's just one thing I still have to do," I tell her. "But I don't know how."

"I know," Erg says. "I know you don't know how. It's going to be basically impossible for you to figure out, really. I was hoping Babs would blab, but Sinister wasn't going to let that happen. He was too mad at both of you."

"That insane dark cavern, in Babs's apartment. That was him, wasn't it? The motorcyclist. I mean that was, like, a form of him. I saw those two golden disk things high up, and now I think I was seeing the stars in his eyes. From the inside. Maybe if I went back . . . Could I throw something at them? Knock them out that way? Sorry for asking, doll. I know you can't tell me."

Erg stays quiet. She can't come out and directly give me information, but if I was on the right track I bet she'd say something vague and encouraging. *Well, gee, it's worth a try, Vassa.* I wait, but she doesn't say a word.

"Is that a completely dumb idea, Erg? Can you just say: dumb or not dumb? I guess that's really just the form he takes in the day, and without Babs to put him back there—"

Day might not come again. If no one can hide the motorcyclist in that secret chamber, then Night will probably hang around indefinitely to be near him. Freeing the night trapped inside that imitation of a man will be the only way to bring day back at all. Why didn't we think of that in time?

Erg squeezes my hand tighter. I can feel her little wooden face pressing hard against my thumb. "Dollface? Are you okay?"

"Not really," Erg says. I can barely hear her. "Vassa, I am really, really sad."

Erg just doesn't say things like that. She doesn't go around announcing her feelings. It's disorienting. "You're sad? What's wrong? We just—I'm finally doing *something* right. I thought you'd be . . ." *Proud of me. Since Zinaida can't be.*

"Can we go out in the parking lot for a minute, Vassa? I want some fresh air."

Breeze is spilling through those shattered windows and raveling in my hair, but this isn't the moment to argue. I jump out of what used to be the door and walk over to the stump, sit down, and then set Erg on my knee. In the darkness beyond, the motorcyclist buzzes around and around just as if this was a perfectly normal night. Erg's azure eyes gaze dolefully into mine. She isn't capable of crying, but this is close enough. "Oh, Erg!"

"Will you tell me a story, Vassa? I mean a true story. You have to promise to be totally honest, though."

I can tell by the look on her face that whatever she wants to know will be exactly what I most want to never say aloud, not as long as I live. But while she's gazing at me in that wrenching way, I know I'll do anything she asks. "Okay."

"I already know what you think. I just need you to say it."

"Erg. What *is* it?" Oh, but I can guess. Can't I?

"Who am I, Vassa? How did I become alive, I mean? Tell me everything. And don't just say magic! Because duh!"

I close my eyes. Somehow I can't stand to see her watching me, not while I say this. "I—well, this is what I *think* happened, okay? Because I don't know for sure, Erg. But my mom found out she was dying, so she went to Bea and had her make you, but you weren't alive then. Not yet. She put you in my hands right before the end, and I couldn't understand why she said you were magic, because you looked so completely ordinary. Just a little wooden doll, right? Or why she made such a big deal about keeping you secret. And when she said I had to feed you it just seemed like some kind of weird joke. I promised anyway, though, because I knew she was dying. I would have promised anything she wanted."

I stop talking, because the next words are already taking shape just under my heart. They hurt so much even in silence that I almost think saying them aloud could choke me.

"Then what?" Erg says. Her voice is gentle. "Because this is the important part."

Right. The important part. The forbidden beans that we don't spill, because the beanstalk that grows from them will skewer our chests, send its tendrils bursting through our arteries, feed on our blood . . . "I saw the line stop. The line for her heartbeat. I saw it while the nurse was dragging me out of the room, and I said I would kill them all if they kept me away from her. And then I stopped screaming, because I felt something kicking inside my pocket. I reached in and you started stroking my hand to calm me down, and I was so surprised that I just shut up."

"So that's what I need to know, Vassa. What brought me to life? I mean, right at that moment?"

I don't answer. If there's one thing I owe Erg, it's the truth, even *this* truth. When I pull in a breath it judders through my lungs. Even with my eyes closed I can feel how intensely Erg is watching me. How she's waiting.

"My mom," I say at last. "I think that's why she had you made. So that the last scrap of her life would have somewhere to go, and it went into you. So that part of her could *stay* with me. I think she made you—so she wouldn't have to leave me completely alone."

Now I know why I didn't want to say this. It's because it sounds so childish.

It's because it sounds like a lie that I've been telling myself for the last six years.

Babs didn't manage to kill me, but maybe this will.

"Vassa," Erg says. "I always knew you thought that. But that's not what happened."

I know that now. I can't say it, but Erg hears it anyway.

"Part of *somebody* went into me. It just wasn't your mom. Your mom died and there wasn't anything left over—except, you know, some memories. And her paintings."

So who went into you, then? Who was it? Stupid question.

"There was part—of somebody—a little girl—and that part hurt so much the girl couldn't carry it inside herself anymore. So it went into a doll. It made the doll alive. And the doll carried it for her. For six years."

I don't want to hear this, Erg.

"But now she's ready to take that part back. I mean, I think she can handle it on her own now. All the doll has to do is tell her one more secret. That's all. And then the Night can be whole again, and *she* can be whole again. And we'll have done what we needed to do."

"And you'll be dead?" I say. My voice cracks with bitterness. I finally open my eyes again. Erg looks at me gravely. She doesn't try to smile, because she knows I couldn't stand it if she did.

"Not exactly," Erg says. "Not dead like a person would be. But I won't be a separate *me* anymore and all the magic will be—used up."

Don't do it, Erg. Please don't do it. I can't lose you.

Now Erg does smile: a wicked, warped, heartbroken grin. "Like you can stop me from talking, Vassa?"

"I've never been able to stop you from doing anything."

"Yup. You sure haven't!"

I almost laugh, except that I can barely breathe.

"Vassa, listen, once I tell you a secret—about the motorcyclist, and the stars—I won't have time to say anything else. So I want you to promise me something first."

If I don't promise, will that stop you from doing this?

"You want to see your mom again, don't you? Even if it's just for a few little moments? That's what I need you to do. You need to go to where she is, and you need to tell her something."

"You just told me she's completely dead. That there's nothing left of her."

"That's not what I said, Vassa."

You said that all that's left of Zinaida are some memories. And her paintings.

"So you need to go back into the painting. Because that's where she is. And because you've been there, too, really. All this time."

I'd like to ask which painting Erg is talking about. I'd like to convince myself that I don't know what she means. But it's too late to pretend.

Erg is climbing up my hoodie now, her tiny hands bunching the fabric and her feet digging into my ribs. I won't help her do this, but I can't stop her, either. Instead I wait, trying to breathe, feeling the cool wind licking at my tears.

When Erg reaches my shoulder she burrows under my hair and hugs the side of my neck. "Do you promise me, Vassa? You'll do what I said?"

I can't, and I have to. Isn't that always the way? "I promise you—everything, Erg." *If you're coming back into me, then I promise I'll do whatever it takes to deserve you.* I curl my hand around her to feel her little wooden body moving for as long as I can.

"Vassa? One more thing?"

I squeeze her.

"I didn't do any of this for Bea, Vassa. Truly not, even though I . . . remember her. I never forgot how much Babs hurt her, and I guess that gave me the idea. But it was *really* for you. And I think you know why, now, don't you?"

Then for a while she's talking not to me, but to Night, in a strange trilling tone that I can't make out—though it sounds like words. It *feels* like words. And then Erg whispers something into my ear. A set of instructions. I listen hard. If Erg is giving up her life for this, then I'm sure as hell going to get it right.

The tiny joints in her knees and waist go lax in my hand. When I lift her out her painted face has frozen into a secretive, faraway smile.

CHAPTER 24

She's right; I never would have figured it out on my own. It's not the kind of thing a human girl can pull off without help. But to be fair Night couldn't do it without help, either. It doesn't matter if I want to curl up on the floor of a closet for a month, repeating every word Erg ever said to me again and again and holding her lifeless body to my cheek. I need to get up and do this, and I need to do it for her. I give her head one quick kiss—those black lacquered curls with no one behind them now—and then tuck her away in my pocket.

Once this is done I'll never see the motorcyclist again, either, I know that. Just like Erg, he won't exist as a distinct being anymore; he'll dissolve back into the dark consciousness of the midnight sky. I don't know if he'll even be capable of remembering me. To free him is to destroy him as he is now, as something that could almost seem to be a man.

Almost, but not quite. Not ever. Because being human is a hard lesson to learn and you really have to start young, and practice constantly, if you're going to stand a chance of getting good at it.

My swans are dispersed and they've done more than their share of the work already anyway, so it's up to me to stop the motorcycle without them. I have to remind myself that the form on the motorcycle isn't a body in the usual sense; it's more a husk, an artificial shell. As I stand up my legs waver, but I could swear Night steadies me.

I go back into the store, clambering up to the sill where it leans three feet off the ground with sad-looking chicken toes poking out beneath. I get that rolling chair that used to sit behind the counter, both counter and chair now crushed beyond all recognition. The chair is still a heavy lump, though, no matter how mashed its frame is. The grubby mustard upholstery has been ripped into a dusty stew.

I pause to check on Tomin, sleeping peacefully on the floor. His chest swells in a tidal rhythm and the last three swans have come to cuddle near him, their necks draped across his shoulders and his arms around their silky backs.

Then I pick up that hulk that was once Babs's chair and drag it back outside. A blind watchman doesn't have much chance of avoiding stationary objects that might happen to wind up in his path. He goes around and around, his helmet gleaming and his engine whirring piteously. A slave who can't get free even now that his captor is dead. The idea is so sad that I have to shake my head to clear it so that I can keep going.

I watch him circle a few times, just to make sure I know his course. And then I shove the chair right in his path and step way back. It's only a matter of moments before the black bulk whips along its familiar orbit, the front wheel spitting up with the collision. The shining black rider leaps into the air, glimmers spinning on his visor. The bike twists against the glow of distant windows and then crashes down on its side. Metal screams on pavement, sparks fan out. If it were a regular motorcycle, I'd worry about the gas tank exploding—but like Erg said, that's not really a motorcycle. It's a doll, a mess of death and steel wrapped in an illusion; one thing I'll say for Babs, she did some impressive work. There has never been a drop of gasoline inside it.

I know that now. Since when did I get in the habit of knowing these things?

The motorcyclist doesn't fly off his bike. Instead they skid along together, a single dark tangle. A horse that is also its own rider. Babs made him that way, fused him with his machine. She made the motorcycle as an extension of his body. Why not? After all, she never intended him to have any life beyond driving in circles in her parking lot. Forever asleep and helpless, his presence taunting Night and drawing it close. By day—because it has to be day *sometimes*— she could store him in her apartment. Then Night would give up hanging around until it saw him again. She had a really neat system going while it lasted.

The bike grinds to a stop twenty feet from me, night within Night. A human would be screaming, but he's perfectly silent. Pain, for him, is not located in his body. His wheels are still whirring frantically and he makes an awkward effort to get up. When I reach him and rest my hands on his shoulders he stops struggling. I'm surprised he can feel me, but I guess we know each other now. "It's me," I tell him. "It's Vassa. I'm here to send you home."

Night sees me, Night holds me, and Night knows what the messenger told it to do.

When I lift the glossy black visor the motorcyclist lets out a thin whine of repressed pain, but he doesn't scream this time. I'd like to think it's because he understands: he only has to endure this suffering for a few more moments, and he'll be free. The stars stabbed into his eyelids wheel savagely golden against his black skin.

I raise my hands—hands that are burned and bruised and streaked with cuts—up into the darkness, and I call to Night the way Erg taught me to call.

Night lands like a pair of star-flecked falcons and enfolds both hands up to the wrists. When I lower them I can just make out the pale lines of my fingers through an inch of gray-black so dense it looks almost gelatinous, shot through by meteors and buzzing with the voices of far-off frogs. Night gloves me in the hush of dark creatures and moonlight scripted on puddles in the gutter. Its touch is cold, moist, and so smooth I almost think my skin might liquefy inside it.

Together Night and I reach forward. The stars rotate faster in protest, spitting golden fury, flashing scarlet. I can't feel their heat at all through the Night covering my skin. There's a sensation of pressure in my fingertips as we seize both the stars at once, one in each hand. I can feel their edges slicing the eyelids more deeply as they resist us, and I brace my knee against the motorcyclist's chest. On its own Night could dabble with breezes, catch flying dollar bills in light spirals, lift blood cells one by one from the snow. It has airy precision and sensitivity far beyond mine. What it doesn't have is the focused strength of human arms.

With all the force and control I can muster I lean back. My muscles tense: slow, taut, and aching. Those stars are sharper than anything on earth and their points draw from his flesh with brutal delicacy, fighting all the while. He trembles under my knee and a scream lifts from his throat like something taking wing.

When his eyelids finally fly open there is nothing behind them but torrential dark. I hear a terrible airy *whoop*, a vast suction, and my vision streaks with hurtling stars. Night gushes out between wide lids. Night deep enough to drown me, and with it comes sleep in heavy whorls. Sleep is larger than any night, so even the night can be lost inside it.

Have I ever been so tired?

"Baby," Zinaida says, "can't you stay still? Give me just a little longer. We're almost through."

I can smell her oil paints and see the ruby glow of lamps staining my closed lids. But with the gun in my mouth I can't answer. The bitter tang of the steel melts in my saliva and floods my throat. I swallow, choke, swallow again. My hand is made of paint: a thick, greasy impasto. But the gun I'm holding is very solid and terribly heavy, weighing on my jaw and my curled paint fingers. I remember believing, once, that the gun was just a toy, but that's not true now, and probably it never was. Not in the ways that matter. It's real and it's loaded, the trigger cold against my fingertip. I don't have to open my eyes to know that the roses behind me are white, waiting to be stained crimson with flying blood.

That's the last touch. Once I blow my brains out the painting will finally be complete. A real masterpiece.

"Vassa, sweetie, don't fidget, okay? You're messing up my shadows." Zinaida's voice is warm and playful, and she laughs. Precarious turrets of curled hair wobble on my head, all of them made of violet paint. Stiff ruffs of painted lace bristle at my throat. "It's bad enough that you keep getting *older*. I started this picture when you were what, eight? And now you've grown up so much that I keep having to redo everything."

She's right, I realize. I'm not the little paint girl who sat down on this brocade sofa all those years ago. I've grown up inside the painting and now I'm almost seventeen, still squashed into the same frilly dress and balancing the old absurd curls. And still composed of pigment and linseed and turpentine, no more substantial than I ever was.

My jaw aches from being held in the same pose for so long. It occurs to me that I'll have to kill myself soon, and I'll never get a chance to take the gun out of my mouth first. I'll never get to tell her goodbye. I won't even get to look at her. I can feel my hand starting to quiver. That's what she's been waiting for all these years, even if she won't admit it.

"Oh, Vassa! If you keep moving I'll never be able to finish. We'll both get old and the picture still won't be done. If you could just hang in there and be *patient* . . ."

Like a breath, like someone whispering in my ear, it occurs to me that there might be an alternative. Very gradually I draw back the gun. The barrel leaves my mouth with a somnolent glide like a dream slipping out of mind. I open my eyes, gazing into Zinaida's startled face for the first time in so very long. She's gotten older, too, and her illness has shriveled her cheeks. Her black hair is tied in a ponytail to keep it from dragging across the pallet. Her hazel eyes look huge, her lids worn.

I lower the gun and set it on an end table. She bites her lip. "Well, maybe it *is* about time for a break! I'll order up something to eat, and you can go back to the pose after lunch. Okay, baby?"

"No," I say. The first flush of real human warmth suffuses my lips as I say it. "No, Mom. The painting is finished."

"It's not finished! It's getting so close, but we're not there yet! Baby, if you would just cooperate a little *longer* . . . I know it's going to be my greatest work. People will remember me in a hundred years because of this! But I can't do it without your help."

I stretch myself and stand up. Those roses will just have to stay white, even if that messes up the composition Zinaida had in mind. With every move I make more of me becomes skin. I can feel muscles gathering, bones extending; I can feel the rumor of a heartbeat under my ribs. My body is stiff, bruised, battered, but I can't remember why.

"The painting is finished," I tell her. "You can't keep working on it. *I'm* finished." She's standing very close to me with her brush in hand. Her loose blue shirt grazes my arm. Impulsively I lean my head against her shoulder. "I'm sorry, Mom. But it *has* to be done now. It has to end."

She doesn't answer at first. Her breath scrapes from her lungs, dry and labored. Then she raises her hand and starts running her fingers through my psychotic purple-paint curls. They loosen at her touch, unwinding into silky human hair. Long locks drop around my neck and I wrap my arms around her, feeling the skeleton that is much too close to her skin. She's dying all over again and there's nothing I can do to stop it.

"You know what, baby?" Zinaida whispers at last. "I think you might be right. I think maybe the painting *is* finished. I was just too wrapped up in it to realize! Any more work now would spoil it, don't you agree?"

I don't answer. Why don't we ever get to hold on to what we love?

She gently unwinds me. Clasps both my shoulders and leans back to look at me. I make myself raise my head and meet her gaze.

"So, darling, what do you think of it? Isn't it my greatest work? Do you like the way it came out?"

That makes me laugh a little. How can I look at the painting, when the painting is me? "Mom, you know I can't see it."

"Well, I can see it," Zinaida says. She strokes the jumbled hair back from my cheek. "I can see it. And it's beautiful."

CHAPTER 25

"Vassa?" somebody says. A hand squeezes my arm. "Vassa!"

"Can't you let me sleep?" But now I'm half-awake I notice that there's something extremely hard under my side, that dull pain surges through my back with every breath, and that harsh sun glares into my face. Why am I not in bed? I reach into my pocket to hold Erg. She's right where she's supposed to be, her little wooden body stiff against my fingers. Is she asleep, too?

"I think you're off work now," the someone says in a voice sagging with irony. "So you might want to sleep somewhere more comfortable."

I open my eyes to see bare brown legs sticking out of cut-off shorts—but the cut edge of the fabric looks stiff and reddish black. The sun stabs at my vision and I shut my eyes again.

"Vassa?" a second voice says. "Please wake up. I'm here to take you home."

"Chelsea?" I say. I try to sit up, and arms catch me and cradle my aching shoulders. "Chelsea? It's really you?"

"It's me, li'l sis. And boy do you need a bath! And an epic breakfast, and maybe a choir of trained psychologists to sing you lullabies afterward. Anyway, I am definitely staying home from school today to look after you."

I manage to keep my eyes open now. Chelsea and Tomin are both holding me, their concerned faces gleaming in the brightest morning light I've ever seen. I'm not feeling too good, so Chelsea's plan sounds pretty appealing.

"Hey," Tomin says. The sleeves of his canvas jacket are missing, too, the collar and shoulders dark and brittle. Right: that's his blood, and I must be one impressive mess myself. "I remember what happened now. Everything. You saved my life." He says it kind of aggressively, like he's accusing me of something.

"Well, I also got you murdered, so that all works out. Right?"

Chelsea's face is, as they say, a study.

"You may notice," Chelsea says, "what remarkable restraint I'm showing in not asking you—*yet*—what you're talking about. Or about what happened here." Her head tips to indicate the shattered orange block that was BY's, detritus spilling out of its wounded windows and onto the pavement, its chicken feet withering in the sun. "But it's hard not to think that you might have had something to do with all this?"

I gape at the mess, remembering. We're getting back to issues that are awfully hard to explain. "I—didn't have *nothing* to do with it. I mean—a lot happened, Chels." I stroke Erg's back, wondering what she's thinking about all this. I can't understand why she won't wake up. "Oh—and the nights should go back to normal now. I'm pretty sure that's fixed."

"I see. And I suppose you also had not-nothing to do with fixing the nights?"

Chelsea's voice is so laboriously calm and reasonable that it makes me crack up in a sputtering laugh. Total insanity is not her natural milieu. I pull myself to my feet and she clutches my arm, obviously afraid I'll fall; it's sensible of her, really. "I helped with that part, yeah. I really did." *You did it, Vassa.* I'm conscious enough now that I look around for the motorcyclist. If there was a corpse nearby wouldn't Chelsea say something? Just a few feet away there's a pile of strange garbage that looks like an explosion at a rummage sale, but it's not remotely humanoid and I turn my head, still trying to find him.

Then realization jolts through me, and I look back at the pile. There's an old-fashioned cookie tin decorated with a scene of ice skaters on a pond. There are two taxidermy ferrets, a carved wooden duck, a tape deck and a few volumes from an encyclopedia, teapots and music boxes, steel pipes, a needlepoint footstool. Curved slabs of painted metal. Large bones, quite possibly of human origin. Control panels from obsolete electronics. Black leather scraps—lots of those.

Two motorcycle tires. And a black globe printed with the constellations.

Perched on top of it all is a jet black silk lampshade with a silvery fringe.

Can that be called a man, Vassa?

The amazing thing, really, was that it almost could. I mean, Erg is just a chunk of wood and she is emphatically *somebody*. She's one of the strongest personalities I've ever known. If Chelsea and Tomin weren't right here I'd pull her out to look at the mess. I'd say, *Wow, doll, you knew this all along?*

Then I remember. My knees pleat under me and both Chelsea and Tomin grab me hard.

I want to scream out for Erg, shake her, tell her she has to come back to life. Tell her how utterly I need her and that she's not allowed to die on me.

Begging people not to die has never really worked out for me, though. I squeeze her empty body as tight as my hand will go and darkness seethes in my head.

"Can I help you get her home?" Tomin asks Chelsea. In the corner of my eye I see her dark curls bobbing affirmatively. We're walking across the parking lot, and I know that I can step beyond its borders without anything happening to me. The severed heads stand watchful and silent on their stakes, and there will never be any more of them. I've served my time here. Three nights, just like Babs said. I've succeeded in my last task, too: the one I finally gave myself. Erg and I, we did what we had to do, even if the cost of doing it was almost more than I can contemplate.

"One moment!" a voice yells. "Please, if you please, one moment! We have certain official notifications to impart before Miss Lowenstein goes on her way." There's the rapid scratch of conical claws on asphalt, the pad of shoes on not entirely human feet. Chelsea's mouth goes wide with shock, and I turn to see Picnic and Pangolin scampering toward us, brass plaques flashing in the sun.

"Listen." Chelsea's mastering herself. "Vassa has been through I don't know what, and she is in *no* condition to—"

"I'm better, Chels," I say. It's true. I'm holding myself straight, not sagging against her arm anymore. "And these are—my good friends. Picnic, Pangolin, thank you for coming to see me off."

Picnic grins and bobs in silence and Pangolin flusters. "We wished to inform you that our case against BY's has been unambiguously won. In the court of possibilities. There will be no more of their circadian trickeries, and no more unfortunate, shall we say, sapiens terminations. And not only at this *particular* establishment, my dear. The entire organization has conceded and all the franchises ceased operations last night. A splendid victory!"

"That's awesome," I tell him. I could have figured that out on my own, though. "Congratulations. Really."

Pangolin has a new file folder with him and he shuffles through the pages inside with a look of perplexity. Shiny new glasses glint on his snout. "And as for you, Miss Lowenstein—your formal obligations to—to certain other-than-quotidian forces—are now entirely discharged. You are quite free. And our congratulations are owed to *you*."

Is this supposed to make me happy? Maybe it should, but depression wells up in me again. Of course, with Erg dead, what connection could I still have to their world? "Thanks," I say dully. "Good to know."

"However, in appreciation for your remarkable contributions you will retain an honorary status as—shall we say—something of an auxiliary member of our society. That is, you would be welcomed at parties, events of that nature. You can expect to be acknowledged by sub-visible persons. And Picnic and I had a passing thought." They exchange freighted glances.

"Vassa?" Chelsea says. She sounds worried. "Seriously?"

"With your employer so abruptly deceased, well, Picnic and I wondered if you might require a new position. Perhaps as an assistant in our firm. No need to give us your answer at this moment, of course. And Miss Bea Yaggen asked us to mention that she would be honored if you would join her for tea one day soon." He sheds papers and gawks at me intently for a moment. "Miss Yaggen tells me that your mother was none other than Zinaida Annikova? A charming woman. We were very pleased to claim her as an acquaintance."

"Oh," Tomin tells Chelsea behind my back. "This is *beyond* serious. I don't exactly know what Vassa did, but I know she changed everything here. And not just for—for regular people."

Chelsea shoots him a look, but I'm too busy puzzling through Pangolin's message to deal with them. Later I'll try to figure out how to explain.

"I don't know where to find you," I finally tell Pangolin. "Or Bea." I'm having trouble taking everything in, but it sounds encouraging.

Pangolin wallops me on the head with a patronizing claw, smiling broadly. "Float first," Picnic explains. "Find later."

Well, okay then. Chelsea's arm tightens around my shoulders as they turn and shuffle away. "I'm not sure I even *want* to know," Chelsea sighs. "Okay, so now are you all through here? That's it?"

"You heard him," I tell her. "I'm free."

"Stephanie feels terrible about what she did, Vassa. You'll see. Though . . . she still kind of believes you stole her locket, honestly."

Right. Stephanie. I understand now: Erg never would have stolen that stuff if there weren't part of me that really, really wanted to. Chelsea's psychoanalyzing was pretty much on target, embarrassing as it is to admit that. "Chelsea? I wasn't lying to you before. Not on purpose. But the thing is . . . *part* of me stole it. That's the truth."

Chelsea stares. "So how is that part of you feeling now?"

"It's a lot calmer now," I tell her. I think about what Erg said and I know that she was absolutely right, as usual. "I mean, I can *handle* it now."

Chelsea kisses me on the cheek. "That's great news, li'l sis. I'm proud of you. Are you ready to come home? And, you know, actually stick around for a while?"

"Yes," I say, and then I realize it's the first time since my mom died that the word *home* has sounded meaningful to me, and not like some squeaky little lie. No matter how Chelsea and I are or aren't related, she's as much my family as anybody ever was. She's my family because she cares enough to make the effort. No matter who I've lost in my life, Chelsea is here now and I'm grateful to have her. "Yes, Chelsea, I'm ready to go home."

Tor Teen Reading and Activity Guide to

VASSA IN THE NIGHT
BY SARAH PORTER

Ages 13–17; Grades 8–12

ABOUT THIS GUIDE

The questions and activities that follow are intended to enhance your reading of *Vassa in the Night,* a reinterpretation of the Russian folktale "Vassilissa the Beautiful" wherein the story is moved to a fantastical Brooklyn and enriched with additional elements from Russian history and folklore. Please feel free to adapt this content to suit the needs and interests of your students or reading group participants.

Vassa in the Night is an excellent text for developing skills outlined in the following Common Core State Standards (www.corestandards .org) areas: RL.8.9 (analyze how a modern work of fiction draws on themes, patterns of events, or character types from myths or traditional stories . . . including describing how the material is rendered new); RL.9-10.9 (analyze how an author draws on and transforms source material in a specific work); and RL.11-12.7 (analyze multiple interpretations of a story, drama, or poem . . . evaluating how each version interprets the source text). The activities in this guide correlate to these additional Common Core State Standards: RL.8.1-6, RL.9-10.1-6, RL.11-12.1-6; W.8.1-7, W.9-10.1-7, W.11-12.1-7; WHST.8.7, WHST.9-10.7, WHST.11-12.7; SL.8.1-2, SL.8.4-5, SL.9-10.1-2, SL11-12.1-2, SL.11-12.4-5.

BEFORE READING THE BOOK

1. As indicated by the title, the action of the novel takes place almost entirely at night. Consider how you would define the word

"night." What notions do you have about night in terms of nocturnal creatures, the Earth's rotation around the sun, and even
dream theories? What books, movies, television programs, types
of music, or visual artworks do you associate with night? Given
your sense of the word "night," and the way it is used in the title,
what assumptions might you make about the novel you are about
to read?

2. In his 1949 book, *The Hero with a Thousand Faces*, writer and
    mythologist Joseph Campbell presented the notion of the "Hero's
    Journey" or "Monomyth"—a storytelling pattern that can be
    identified in many folktales, as well as works of science fiction
    and beyond. Go to the library or online to learn about Camp-
    bell's stages of the "Hero's Journey." (Hint: A handy resource
    can be located at www.wiu.edu/users/mudjs1/monomyth.htm.)
    Consider whether a favorite fairy tale, modern-day novel, or re-
    cently viewed film fits into Campbell's pattern.

3. Read a traditional version of the Vassilissa folktale, such as *Vasi-
    lisa the Beautiful and Baba Yaga* by Alexander Afanasyev or *Baba
    Yaga and Vasilisa the Brave* by Marianna Mayer.

After Reading the Book

Discussion Questions

1. The novel begins with a "Prelude in Night." What is the purpose
    of this prologue? What is significant about the absence of "the"
    in the chapter title—why is the chapter not titled "Prelude in *the*
    Night" in the way the novel is called *Vassa in* the *Night*?

2. As Chapter 1 opens, Vassa tells readers that "People live here on
    purpose." What sense of attitude and mood does this opening
    give to readers? How is the situation with night introduced in
    this chapter, and how is it connected to BY's both through imag-
    ery and dialogue?

3. *Vassa in the Night* is set in Brooklyn. Classic Vassilissa folktales
    are set in a forest. What qualities make these settings similar?

What language does author Sarah Porter use to create a forest-like vibe for an urban setting? (Note: This question is best discussed after completing "Before Reading" activity #3.)

4. Can a "time" (such as "Night") be a setting in a novel? Can it be a character? Explain your answer using quotes from the text.

5. What four key words would you choose to describe the character of Vassa? How do these attributes relate to her decision to stay at BY's?

6. Vassa says of her mother, "Once I got wise to Zinaida—or, at least, *wiser*—then I didn't want to be like her anymore. Then there was no one left for me to want to be," (Chapter 14). To what does Vassa "get wise"? Is it important to want to be someone? How might you understand Vassa's reference to "no one left" in terms of her larger journey in the story?

7. Throughout the novel, there are chapters titled "Interlude in Fur," "Interlude in Feathers," etc. How do these "interlude" chapters relate to the larger story? Why you think the author chose to create these special chapters? Why do you think she chose to use the terms "Prelude" and "Interlude" to create offset chapters in the story?

8. List the tasks Babs assigns to Vassa on each of the three nights of her stay at BY's. What relationships or progressions do you see in the list? What discoveries docs Vassa make after engaging in each task?

9. What do the swans represent? How are they connected to Vassa's father's ambition to be transformed into a dog? How does the novel blur the lines between human and nonhuman, magical and nonmagical?

10. Who and/or what are Dexter and Sinister? What is their role in the story?

11. Do you think Erg is "real"? Is she always hungry? Does she steal? What has really happened to her at the end of the story?

12. In Chapter 18, Tomin tells Vassa, "Just 'cause it's obvious doesn't mean it's true." How might this statement be understood in

terms of Vassa's experiences at BY's? Can you apply Tomin's insight to an experience in your own life?

13. In Chapter 20, Vassa considers staying in the Night with the motorcycle man: "What would a life in this place even mean? It definitely qualifies as *anywhere but here,* anywhere but home and Brooklyn, anywhere but any normal human location. And I might become *anyone but me,* more a dream-ghost than a girl." Answer her question.

14. Is Vassa wrestling with sanity, with grief, or perhaps with both? How might these struggles be regarded as the central motif of the novel, especially in terms of her relationship with Erg?

15. What are the most important relationships Vassa forms in the course of the story? Are her most powerful relationships with humans, with places, or with other sorts of creatures?

16. Compare and contrast the ways in which Vassa's relationships with the motorcycle man and with Tomin change over the course of the story.

17. In Chapter 3, Vassa asks Babs, "What do you think I owe you?" Later, in Chapter 13, Vassa wonders, "What *do* I owe myself . . . What did I borrow from myself, and how on earth will I ever give it back?" How are these two questions related? What is important about the person of whom they are being asked? What does Vassa owe to Babs? To herself? Do you feel a sense of obligation to yourself, or to others, in your own life? How might you understand Vassa in the context of your own experiences of obligations?

18. In Chapter 23, Erg forces Vassa to to spill the "forbidden beans that we don't spill, because the beanstalk that grows from them will skewer our chests." What does Erg tell Vassa (and how is this simply Vassa admitting to herself) the truth about the kind of "magic" that went into Erg's wooden form the moment Zinaida died?

19. At the story's start, Vassa tells readers, "My sisters think I'm the greedy one, always stashing cookies in my pockets for later. They

think I suffer from strange compulsions," (Chapter 1). After finishing the book, do you think this is true or not? In what ways might you answer this question "yes" and/or "no"?

20. At the end of Chapter 23, Erg asks Vassa to "go back into the painting. Because that's where she is. And because you've been there, too, really. All this time." How does Vassa re-enter the paining? What is the "all this time" to which Erg refers, and in what way has Vassa remained in the painting for this duration? How is Vassa's re-entry into the painting related to the silencing of Erg? To Vassa's return to Chelsea and her ordinary world?

21. In *The Hero with a Thousand Faces,* author Joseph Campbell writes:

> The hero's journey always begins with the call. One way or another, a guide must come to say, "Look, you're in Sleepy Land. Wake. Come on a trip. There is a whole aspect of your consciousness, your being, that's not been touched. So you're at home here? Well, there's not enough of you there." And so it starts.

How can Campbell's statement be applied to *Vassa in the Night*? Who do you see as Vassa's guide: Babs, Erg, or someone else? Can you define her "Sleepy Land" in three different ways? To what "aspect of [her] consciousness" do you think Campbell refers? How can *Vassa in the Night* be read as a story of the main character's conscious and subconscious journey of self-discovery? Of liberation from grief? Cite quotations from the story to support your answer.

Research and Writing Activities

WRITE: Vassa's journey begins when leaves home to buy lightbulbs at BY's. In the character of Chelsea or Stephanie, write a journal entry describing your feelings immediately after Vassa has left the house, noting whether you think Vassa is acting naïvely or intelligently and if/how you feel a sense of responsibility for her departure.

DIAGRAM: The author creates an almost telescopic setting for her novel, beginning with Night, narrowing to Brooklyn, then closer in to a neighborhood, and ultimately into dreams and memories. Create a diagram of the most important settings in the story and annotate each point with key events that take place in that setting. What was the most surprising or revealing discovery you made as you completed your diagram?

MIXED MEDIA: Vassa's half- and stepsister are distracted by a BY's television advertisement. Using clues from the story, and your imagination, make a video recreation of the advertisement to share with friends or classmates.

RESEARCH AND CREATE: Who is Baba Yaga? Is she kind or cruel? Is she one person or three? Why does she live in such a strange house? Go to the library or online to research answers to the questions. In the character of Baba Yaga (in first person), write a poem, song lyrics, dramatic monologue or other theatrical piece beginning with the words, "I am."

WRITE: Has reading *Vassa in the Night* changed your perspective on how your family's past impacts your sense of self? Write an opinion piece, using an interpretation of the novel as your basis for exploring the reasons it is good to know your family history and ways to keep this knowledge in perspective as you develop your own personal identity.

LIST: List at least eight events, characters, or images found in both the traditional Vassilissa tale and the novel. (If desired, also read other Russian folktales, particularly "The Firebird," to find other shared matter.) For each list entry, note how the author reinterprets the notion for a contemporary reader and setting. (Note: This exercise is best done after completing "Before Reading" activity #3.)

MIXED MEDIA: In "Interlude in Scales," Pangolin observes that "Harmony has no better preservative than obliviousness." Is this an observation, or a warning? How might those words be understood in terms of contemporary geopolitical and environmental issues? Create a visual answer to these questions by writing the quote on a large piece of poster board, then surrounding it with newspaper clippings, drawings, photographs, and your own interpretive words and phrases.

ROLEPLAY: With friends or classmates, discuss what has truly happened to Vassa over the three nights of the story. Were there really three nights at all? Why does Vassa remain secretive about Erg when she interacts with others? Roleplay a conversation between Vassa and Chelsea, or between Vassa and Tomin, in which they both share their own truths about what happened.

DEBATE: Babs tells Vassa, "It's unwise to bring up terms like *good* or *bad, right* or *wrong,* in my store. As long as you're here the meaning of such words is entirely mine to determine," (Chapter 5). Divide into two groups to debate whether there is such a thing as "absolute good/right" and "absolute bad/wrong" or whether such values are only ever relative.

READ AND DISCUSS: Fairy tales and Bible stories have inspired works by many contemporary authors. Go to the library or online to find and read *Enchantment* by Orson Scott Card, *Briar Rose* by Jane Yolen, *Riders* by Veronica Rossi, or another novel inspired by an old or ancient narrative. Discuss how modern authors connect classic tales to contemporary teen experiences.

RESEARCH AND WRITE: Write your own modern fairy tale interpretation. Select a folktale for your adaptation and research its history. Brainstorm ways to connect the story and your research to modern characters and settings. List at least five characters you will include in your rendition of the story. Write a synopsis of your plot idea. If desired, outline your idea based on the steps of the "Hero's Journey" as described by Joseph Campbell.

ABOUT THE AUTHOR

SARAH PORTER is a writer, an artist, and a freelance public school teacher. She is the author of the Lost Voices Trilogy: *Lost Voices, Waking Storms,* and *The Twice Lost.* Sarah and her husband live in Brooklyn, New York.